# NIGHT HAWK

NIGHTHAWK SECURITY - BOOK THREE

SUSAN SLEEMAN

Published by Edge of Your Seat Books, Inc.

Contact the publisher at contact@edgeofyourseatbooks.com



Cover design by Kelly A. Martin of KAM Design

# 1

They killed Toni's father. She wouldn't let them kill her too.

She lifted her gun and eased into the musty-smelling abandoned high school in Rugged Point, Oregon. Sweat beading up on her lip despite the frigid January night, she crept down the inky dark hallway.

One foot in front of the other. Inch by inch. The darkness like a cloak around her. Her fingers itched to flick on her phone's flashlight. She couldn't. Not without alerting anyone in the building to her arrival.

Besides, she was an experienced FBI agent. She could handle a little darkness, right?

She continued forward, her ears tuned for any sound, even as tiny as a mouse scurrying across the floor. A nearby broken window let in the sharp cry of a hawk soaring overhead. Almost as if the bird was warning her to take care.

But it was as clueless as she was as to why the note she'd found lodged under her vehicle's wiper summoned her to this school and told her to arrive at exactly five p.m. The note claimed it had to do with her father's murder a year before, but what did he have to do with an old rural schoolhouse halfway across the country? He'd recently lived in

Virginia. This place was on the southern Oregon coast. No connection that she knew of.

A pinpoint of setting sun razored through a hole in the wall and spotlighted the crumbling tile floor beneath her feet. She was probably being exposed to all kinds of environmental hazards in the 1940's building. Asbestos being the number one concern. But she'd risk just about anything to find the person who killed her dad.

At the end of the hallway she turned left, following the instructions she'd received. She paused to assess the new space. The directions told her to go to the basement to a janitor's closet at the bottom of the stairs. There she would find the information she needed to arrest the killer she'd been seeking since the day her dad died.

She inched down, a step at a time and paused on the first landing located above ground. She glanced out a wide window that was so covered with dirt she could barely make out the miles of abandoned land surrounding the property. Giant cobwebs clung to the corners of the window, and her imagination soared. She pondered the immense size of spiders needed to create those webs.

She shuddered, wanting to call it quits. She wasn't much for the outdoors and the creatures it entailed. Not like the native Oregonians she worked with every day.

A bat launched itself from above. She ducked and cringed as it cried out, winging its way across the space. The creature lit on the top of a doorjamb below. *Yuk*. The spiders were bad enough, but this?

Could she keep descending the stairs with the bat above? She could face down killers, but a bat?

*Remember Dad. Gunned down in front of you. Deep breaths. Keep going. You can do this.*

She inhaled the air with dust particles dancing in the

last of the sunlight. Blew it out. Drew more in. And started down the last flight of stairs. One, two...pause. Listen.

Three, four, five...pause. She swiped sweaty palms against her pant leg and gripped her gun again.

What she wouldn't give for this place to have electricity so she could turn on one of the white schoolhouse globes above.

She took another step. Only one more to go.

A car engine rumbled in the distance growing closer. Likely not a concern. Not with the highway running nearby.

She took the last step, sliding her feet over the tiles and letting out a breath. The pale light shone above the door, where the bat watched her with beady little eyes.

She drew in another long breath. Stepped forward into a hallway. Looked both ways. Shadows clung to the area. She squinted, but murky blackness greeted her. She couldn't see a thing beyond six feet. Nothing for it but to move ahead and open the door. A wide bar lifted perpendicular to the door could drop down and hold it in place. A padlock hung from the end. Overkill for few chemicals and a mop bucket, but maybe the room hadn't always been for the janitor.

Shaking her head, she stepped slowly forward. Grabbed the old knob. Opened the door. Entered.

She would need light to see this supposed lead. She reached for her phone to use the light, noticing she had no cell service in the basement. Hopefully she wouldn't need to call for help.

A telltale rattle sounded from the floor near the back of the room.

Her heart lurched, the high-pitched sound like a baby rattle shaken at supersonic speed paralyzing her. A rattlesnake. No doubt.

*Move, for goodness sake! Move! Get your gun. Shoot it.*

She couldn't. Not when her worst nightmare was unfolding in front of her.

She tried to lift an arm. Her muscles wouldn't move. Not even in a finger. Or her feet. She opened her mouth and screamed like there was no tomorrow. If she didn't get her feet going, there might not be one.

The door slammed shut behind her, sealing her in the tiny space with the snake slithering even closer, and she prepared her mind for the fangs to puncture her skin.

~

Clay stood in the lobby of the yellowed brick school building. A bloodcurdling scream shattered the eerie silence.

His pulse kicked up.

A woman. Obviously in danger. Not at all what he'd expected to find here, but he'd seen a car in the parking lot. Maybe this mystery woman was the reason he'd been sent the note to show up here at precisely five-fifteen p.m. As usual, he was five minutes early. It sounded like it was a good thing he was.

He drew his gun and moved toward the stairwell. The sun had made its last gasp for the day, leaving the space in heavy shadows. Pale moonlight streamed through a broken window. Not enough light to see much, just old bulletin boards on the walls and an empty trophy case with shattered glass.

An ominous feeling permeated the air, and he swallowed hard.

He might've once been an ICE agent and was now a partner in the Nighthawk Security agency, but his heart thudded in his chest. People thought law enforcement officers didn't get scared, but the reality was, they just knew how to deal with the fear and still act.

Following the note's instructions, he moved as fast as he dared without putting himself in danger. He wanted to help the woman, but he couldn't if he sustained a serious injury.

He paused at the stairwell to listen. Nothing. Only the beat of a clock ticking down in his head. He started down the stairs where he was sure the scream originated, counting as he moved. Seven stairs to the landing. He stopped and waited. No sounds. Not even a rodent scurrying around.

He continued on to an unfinished dungeon-like basement that smelled like years of mold buildup. He listened. Heard a faint rattle.

Rattlesnake? Seriously? As a Boy Scout, he'd learned that rattlesnakes lived in the area, but he'd never seen one.

He stepped to the closet door, marked Janitor. The note told him to go into this room, but the windowless door was closed, and he couldn't see inside.

A faint sound reached him.

What was that? The whimper of a woman from the other side?

Was the woman in there? She must've screamed before the door closed or he wouldn't have heard her.

He twisted the knob. It turned under his hand, and he opened the door. Made out a silhouette of a person standing just inside the small room. Heard the unmistakable rattle of a snake.

A snake? What in the world?

He had to know what was going on or he couldn't fix it. Even if this person meant to harm him. He flipped on his flashlight. A woman stood terrified as a brown snake with cream and black stripes slithered their direction in the long narrow room, its tongue sliding in and out.

Clay aimed his gun at the reptile.

The door slammed behind him. The lock bar dropped and slid into place with a solid thunk.

He stifled a curse, his brain racing for a plan of action. No time to check the woman's identity. Clay had a snake eyeing him up, and he couldn't predict the snake's actions.

He ran the light over the room and spotted a long mop handle. It had a metal bar on the end, the mophead missing. *Perfect.*

He propped his flashlight on the shelf to keep the beam on the snake and grabbed the pole. He angled it toward the slithering creature now focused on the mop, its rear section pulling up into an accordion coil.

The head raised. Arched in a death pose and struck the metal. Good. It was no longer going for the woman or him.

Clay moved quickly. Jabbed the metal end under the middle of the long body and lifted. The snake dangled in the air, perfectly balanced, but the reptile wiggled to regain control. He pushed the woman aside, and she wobbled.

"Sorry," he said. "I'll fix this in a flash." He stepped toward an empty five-gallon bucket, the lid propped against the side.

Now came the tricky part. He maneuvered around, requiring him to point the snake at the woman.

She screamed again, the sound curling his toes. He hated seeing her pain but had to let the sound roll off him if he was going to keep them alive. He picked up the lid then lowered the snake into the bucket and held it down with the handle. He shoved the lid over the top, jerking out the pole as he moved and making sure the lid latched. He dropped down on top of the bucket, his muscles shaking. The snake continued to hiss below him, but they were safe for now.

*They. The woman.* Who was she? He looked at her in the pale glow reflected from his flashlight. She was tall and lean, wearing dark blue jeans and a mint colored sweater under a waterproof jacket in a deep burgundy. He let his gaze fall on her face, framed with black hair in a feathery cut, and his mouth dropped open.

"Toni," he said. "Is that you? What are you doing here?"

She didn't respond. Her eyes were wide, her mouth open as if she'd frozen in place. Apparently, the snake still terrified her even though it was contained in the bucket. He spotted a rusted but heavy vise sitting on a small workbench, he stood, picked it up, and set it on top the bucket for extra measure.

Toni let out a cry of distress.

"It's all right." He walked toward her. "The bucket is latched, and the vise will ensure it stays closed."

She whimpered.

He'd seen people afraid, but this went beyond normal fear. Had she experienced a rattlesnake in her past? An experience that caused such an overwhelming phobia? If so, nothing could be worse for her than being stuck in the room with the snake.

But maybe he was wrong. Maybe the door wasn't locked. He grabbed the knob. Shook the handle. The old wood held fast. He put his shoulder to it and shoved against it. Tried it a few times. Nothing. Not even a fraction of an inch in movement.

They were stuck for sure. But who'd lowered the bar on the door?

He looked at Toni. "Did you see who locked the door?"

She shook her head.

"Someone dropped the bar lock into place. Probably took off thinking we'd die in here."

Her only response was a sharp intake of air.

"Does anyone know you're here and will come looking for you if you don't come home?"

She gave a single shake of her head. He grabbed the flashlight to do a thorough search.

"No!" Toni shouted, her breathing quickening. "The light. Please. Oh. Please. Keep the light on the bucket. I have to see."

She'd totally lost it. He had to get her out of there, but how? He could call the police, but it would be humiliating to be found locked in a closet. It would be embarrassing if he had to call in his family too—maybe more so—but at least he wouldn't be the latest gossip in law enforcement circles that could spill over into their agency's reputation when they were getting the business going.

Didn't matter. He had to call someone. Thankfully, he'd brought one of the agency's SAT phones and could access signals most everywhere. His brothers would take hours to get there, but Blackwell Tactical's facility was just a few miles away. The fastest response without all the danger to their agency's reputation.

In addition to clearing the building of any danger, he'd want the room dusted for prints, so he'd start with Samantha. She was a former criminalist with PPB—the Portland Police Bureau. As such, she'd been required to serve five years as a patrol officer and could not only clear the building, but could also get them out of this place, and then process the evidence.

He tapped her icon and turned to face the wall.

"Samantha Griffin," she answered cheerfully.

"Sam, it's Clay Byrd." He explained his predicament and the need for forensics.

He had to give her credit. She didn't laugh. At least not aloud. "I'll head out right away. Griff can come with me. Or do you need a tactical response?"

"I doubt the person who locked us in is hanging around," he said, but was glad to have her husband along to help. "But if you'd feel better with backup, bring someone else."

"Better to be safe than sorry, right?"

"Right."

"Riley's on call, so he'll be with us."

"If you don't mind, could we keep this between us and Riley?"

"Sure thing."

Getting her agreement was far easier than he'd expected, but his brother would be a different story. Clay wouldn't call Drake, but Clay was supposed to work out with him later that night.

"Yo, man," Drake answered. "Where'd you disappear to?"

Clay told him, describing the snake and locked door. Drake started laughing.

"Not funny, bro," Clay snapped. "This is serious. Toni Long's here. The note we both got said this is somehow related to her father's death. She's in shock."

"Toni," Drake said. "Aw, man. After her dad died, I bet you never thought you'd see her again."

Drake was right, but Clay would never discuss it in front of Toni. "I can do without the commentary."

"Seems like you might need help. Erik's here with me. I'll bring him along too."

"No need. Sam will get us out."

"Are you kidding," Drake said. "I wouldn't miss this for the world."

Before Clay could respond, Drake ended the call. Fine. They were coming from Portland and if Erik was driving, this school was a good five-hours from their office and condos at the Veritas Center. If Drake was behind the wheel, it would take more like four. At least by the time they got there, Clay would be out of the room. And it would help to have his brothers give the school a good once-over for leads.

Clay turned to observe Toni. She wasn't in medical shock. Her breathing was normal but shallow, and her skin didn't appear to be clammy or pale. He'd seen people react the same way after a car accident. The shock caused adrenaline to flood the body, but a healthy person's body regulated itself as hers seemed to have done. Still, he would watch for symptoms declaring her situation had become a medical emergency.

"Sam from Blackwell and Drake and Erik are on the way," he said. "You remember my brothers, right?"

She didn't speak.

He feared she might hyperventilate. "Just breathe, Toni. Deep breath in. Then out."

He mimicked the actions, drawing in the musty air, making sure to fully expand his chest, and letting the air slowly out. She followed suit.

Just when she seemed to be gaining control, the snake rattled in the bucket.

She jerked back and flailed out. She grabbed onto an old porcelain mop sink stained a rusty-yellow and climbed into the sink. She crouched down to wrap her arms around her shaking knees.

Man, he hated seeing her like this. Scared to death. When they'd worked together on the Child Exploitation Task Force, he'd gotten to know her quite well. She was as tough as any of the agents on the team. Maybe not physically, but mentally she'd endured everything with valor. Now this. Looked like whoever locked them in here knew she was terrified of snakes and was taking advantage of her fear.

He tried to make eye contact, but she fixated on the bucket. "You want to talk about what's going on?"

She gave a quick but fierce shake of her head.

Since she didn't seem to notice him looking at her, he didn't bother to look away. He loved seeing her again, but the joy of the moment was tempered by the pain in his heart. Not just from her terror right now, either. He took her father's death personally. Clay had been in charge of the op where Grayson Long had been gunned down. Clay still had no idea what her dad had been doing there. He'd retired from the DEA many years prior and had zero connection to the op. He shouldn't even have been in the area, much less knocking on their suspect's door.

Clay had held Toni that day and played the op over and over in his head. He'd felt like a total fraud. Comforting her when he believed he was responsible. He didn't know what he could've done differently, but no one should die on an op. No one. Especially not an innocent member of the public.

Now, her electric blue eyes were wide and unblinking. He'd never seen her so terrified. He had to do something to help. There was no getting out of the room. Maybe he could block her view. He stepped between her and the snake. "What can I do for you?"

Her hands clamped on his shoulders, and she pushed him out of the way. He didn't fight her, but even if he had, she was strong enough to move him. When they'd partnered on the task force, they'd often worked out together, and he'd seen her toned arms firsthand.

"I'm worried about your stress level. Can you try to focus on something else while we wait for help to arrive?"

She didn't respond.

He took her hand. The skin was soft but icy cold. She glanced at their intertwined fingers for a beat of a moment before she locked on the bucket with the snake in it again.

"Come on, Toni. Take some breaths. You can do it. The snake can't get out."

"I...I..." She shook her head.

His heart cracked under her fear. "Do you want me to sit on the bucket again?"

"Yes, please." She sounded like a child terrified of the boogeyman.

He wanted to lift her out of the sink and hold her until her fear evaporated. Instead, he took the vise's place. If she were in her right mind, she wouldn't appreciate the hug. She was too independent to need a man. She'd told him that. Three times to be specific. Her mother died when she was a kid, and her dad had brought her up to be tough. She'd even been stoic when the gunman took her dad down right before her eyes.

Clay shuddered at the memory and shoved it into the back of his mind to focus on their current situation. He looked around the room, wishing he'd brought someone with him. All four of his brothers would've warned him not to go alone if he'd told them. Even his sister, Sierra, a forensic expert at the Veritas Center, would've said something. So would his former deputy dad.

His mom—well, she would just as likely choose to keep him home and out of danger no matter what. But once Drake told them all about the night—and he would for sure—they wouldn't let it go, and Clay would never live it down. Searching for whatever lead they were supposed to discover. Nothing in the space spoke to the investigation or provided the lead they were promised. He just spotted old janitorial supplies.

Clay took a deep breath to clear his brain, and a hint of smoke slithered through the air.

*Smoke?*

Smoke from a nearby campfire wouldn't settle into this basement room. And it wasn't camping season. He flashed his light at the door. Toni cried out, but he couldn't deal with her fear now.

Smoke seeped under the wood, curling up and into their small room.

"Fire." He jumped up and put the vise back on the bucket.

Toni remained frozen as if she didn't hear him.

He raced across the room. Got in her face. "There's a fire in the building. We have to get out of here, and we have to do it now!"

# 2

The room filled with smoke at a faster rate than Clay could've imagined, and Toni wasn't responding. He ripped off his shirt, tore it in half, and handed it to her. "Tie this over your mouth."

She complied, her eyes widening even more with terror. "I…I…"

He couldn't waste time trying to break through her stupor. He tied his half of the shirt around his head and searched the room for anything he could use to get them out. He couldn't possibly bust through the cinderblock walls before he and Toni succumbed to the smoke.

He could call 911, but Sam and the guys would be here sooner than a patrol deputy. For now, the door was his only option. He started kicking the wood. No movement. None. He turned and back-kicked. The doorjamb and lock held.

*No. No. No.* He couldn't fail. Somehow he had to make an opening big enough to crawl through.

He shone the light over the space. A gasp came from Toni, but he needed the light. Junk was heaped up in the corner, and he hurried over to tear through it. He discarded worn boards and trim pieces. Empty paint cans. An old oil can. Rags. There on the floor. A small hatchet. The wooden handle was broken. He had little to hold onto. He'd make do. He raced back to the door. Ran his fingers over the wood. Not hot. At least the fire wasn't raging in the hallway outside.

Wouldn't do to slice his hand open on the splintered handle. He tore the shirt from his head. Wrapped the fabric around the broken handle. He hauled back and slammed it into the door. Small wood chips flew. Not many, but it was working.

He slammed the hatchet again. Once more. Over and over. A small hole appeared. Heavier smoke poured through it. He tried not to breathe, but how could he not under the exertion? He coughed. Hard. His eyes stung, tears pouring down his cheeks. No matter. Toni needed him.

He swung the ax, putting his weight into it. At last the head went through the wood. Had he weakened the wood enough to break through? If not, they would suffocate. Soon.

A swift kick of his boot into the hole, and a satisfying crack sounded in the tiny space. He grabbed the wood morticed into the thicker frame and pulled it free to enlarge the hole. He would help Toni through the opening first, but she was too dazed to move fast. Better to unlock the door and then assist her.

Breathing hard now, he dropped down to the hole. His chest convulsed with a deep cough. He placed his shirt over his mouth again and shimmied out. The thick gray smoke obscured his vision, but he felt for the bar and lifted it.

He jerked open the door and rushed to Toni. "We're leaving now."

He didn't wait to see if she would move but lifted her out of the sink and took her by the hand. They stayed low and started forward. To his right, flames burned in a large barrel someone had slid in front of the stairs, blocking the exit.

His heart fell. They couldn't get out unless he could move it. But the glowing metal told him it was way too hot to touch.

"Clay!" Sam's voice came from above.

"Down here!" Clay called back. "Fire in a barrel at the bottom of the steps blocking our exit."

"Griff's got an extinguisher."

Boots pounded down the stairs.

*Yes.* The best sound Clay had heard all day. He tugged Toni back from the flames and buried her face in his chest to protect her from extinguisher fumes.

Griff, wearing a fireproof hood and gloves, aimed the extinguisher at the barrel. The flames died a quick death, but heavy smoke poured out at an alarming rate.

"Come on." Griff curled his hand in the air. "Let's get you out of here."

Clay led Toni to the stairwell, but her steps were hesitant. He had to get her moving faster. Nothing for it but to lift her over his shoulder and carry her. She didn't protest, telling him how dire her state of mind was.

Sam stood at the landing, a mask over her mouth. "You okay?"

He nodded but raced past her to charge outside and gulp the clean night air into his burning lungs. Riley stood guard at the door, but Clay kept going, moving across the crumbling driveway. He kept his head on a swivel as he ran, searching the area for danger. Spotted only grass blowing in the gentle breeze.

His body wanted to collapse under his strained lungs. No, he couldn't. Not yet. Not until he reached a soft grassy area and gently set Toni down. Racking coughs caught both of them. She got to her knees and nearly heaved trying to clear her lungs. His already protesting lungs argued even more and a misty rain wet his face.

She dragged in deep breaths. Coughing. Gagging. So did he. Until his lungs seemed like only a hundred razor blades occupied them instead of a thousand.

She looked at him. He searched her face. She seemed to be semi-alert. Maybe she'd broken free of her paralysis and was trying to process what was happening.

Griff stopped to talk to Riley, who after a brief conversation, started around the building perimeter. Still gasping for air, Clay was grateful Sam thought to bring Riley along for extra security.

Griff and Sam joined them. She pulled the mask off and brushed long blond hair from her face. She was tall and trim, but not as tall as Griff, who was built like a linebacker and had reddish-blond hair in a fashionable cut.

"Toni, this is Sam with Blackwell Tactical and her husband, Griff, who's a firefighter in this county."

Toni looked confused. He thought she'd heard of Blackwell, but maybe not. He explained and she nodded.

"Nice to meet you," Griff said. "I'll call medics."

"I'm good," Clay said and looked at Toni.

She waved a hand. "Not for me. I'll be fine."

"I still think it would be a good idea if—"

"We're fine," Clay interrupted. "If that changes, I'll let you know." Clay would keep an eye on Toni to be sure she didn't seem to be suffering any ill-effects from the smoke.

Griff clamped his hands on his hips. "I'm going on record as saying being checked out would be the wise thing to do."

"And when he goes on record..." Sam wiggled her eyebrows.

"I'm serious."

"I know," Sam said, "but you can keep an eye on them. If they look like they're in distress, you can call."

"Fair enough." He smiled at his wife. "Fire was contained in the barrel. Built to distribute maximum smoke with minimum damage. I assume your suspect has taken off, but once the smoke dissipates, we can clear the building to be sure."

Clay took in that information. "So whoever set the fire wanted us to suffocate, not burn."

"Looks like it."

"They must've known we couldn't get a phone signal in the basement," Toni got out between coughs.

Clay nodded. "Good thing I brought a SAT phone."

"Odd that they just didn't take you out with a bullet," Sam said.

"I was thinking the same thing." Toni frowned. "It's like whoever set this up wanted us to suffer before dying. Maybe as payback."

"Or they're just fond of fire," Griff said. "Some people are like that and will take any reason to start one."

Clay thought about the snake but wouldn't mention it unless he had to.

Sam ran a hand over her hair. "I should call Trent Winfield. He's our county sheriff. He replaced Blake."

"Blake?" Toni asked between breaths.

"He was the sheriff here," Clay said, "but now he works at the Veritas Center where my sister Sierra is the forensic expert." He didn't bother telling her about Nighthawk's office at Veritas. That could come later. He cleared his lungs with a deep cough and turned his attention back to Sam. "I don't want to call Trent before we have a chance to scope this place out."

"Without fans, the smoke'll take a while to clear enough to go back inside and not annihilate your lungs," Griff said.

"I can wait." Clay looked at Toni. "What about you?"

She nodded, but she looked exhausted. He wasn't sure if it was due to the snake or the smoke inhalation. They'd both had a jolt of adrenaline, but her body had been raging with it for some time.

Clay looked at Griff. "Glad you arrived when you did."

"I often put him to work as my assistant." Sam circled her arm in his and smiled up at him.

"Can't think of a better boss." Griff grinned at her.

The two were obviously very happy together. Clay had seen their happiness firsthand when he'd trained at Blackwell. Not only her relationship with Griff, but every member of the Blackwell team had gotten married in the last few years, and Clay had to admit they were poster children for wedded bliss.

Sierra was also happily married, and Clay's older brothers, Aiden and Brendan, had recently gotten engaged. Clay had thought maybe he'd be getting on the happily-married train, but not so long ago, a woman he'd cared for had cheated on him. So, despite the happiness surrounding him, he wasn't about to get involved again. Been there, done that, had the cracks in his heart to prove it.

On the other hand, if he were willing to take another shot at that whole relationship thing, Toni would be tops on his list. If he could let go of what had happened to her father on his watch, that was.

She stared at him, the pale moonlight fighting through the drizzle and highlighting her furrowed forehead. She was clearly still troubled.

He looked up to ask Sam if he and Toni could have a moment alone.

"Griff and I'll wait in his truck," she said, her gaze going between Clay and Toni.

Griff took a step closer to Sam. "But I—"

"He'll tell you when it's safe to go in." She tugged on Griff's arm.

"I'll also notify my department of the fire in case someone reports the smoke," he called out as Sam dragged him off.

When they were out of earshot, Clay turned his attention to Toni. "You really doing okay, or was that just for everyone else's benefit?"

"A little more fresh air, and I'll be fine, but I'm totally embarrassed." She kept her gaze downward.

"Because of the snake?"

She nodded and looked at him, her eyes tortured.

"I'm guessing you had a bad experience with a rattler once."

"I...when I was a kid. I almost died." Her tone was low and raspy from the fire. Sexy as could be.

Gave Clay far too many things to imagine when he needed to remain focused.

*Concentrate, man.* "From a snake bite?"

"A rattler spooked my mom's horse. He threw her." Toni clutched her hands together. "She landed right next to me at the corral fence. Broke her neck and died."

Not only had she seen her father die in front of her, but her mother too. How horrible was that?

He reached for her hand. Stopped. He didn't know if she would like it if he touched her. "I'm so sorry."

She took a deep breath, her chin trembling. "I was paying attention to my mom. Didn't even notice the snake. It struck me too. And if that wasn't enough, her horse ran off. Crashed into a fence. Broke his leg. Had to be put down. So I lost my mom and our horse the same day. And if my dad hadn't found me when he did and got me to the hospital, I would've died." Tears formed in her eyes, but she swiped them away. "I was only ten, and I've probably never dealt with that day the way I should've."

"No wonder the snake threw you for a loop."

She sucked in another breath. "Yeah. Sorry."

"No need to apologize. You can't stop how your body reacts to something like that."

A wavering smile crossed her mouth. "I see you're still Mr. Diplomacy."

"I mean it, Toni," he said emphatically. "It's not your fault."

"I haven't been near a snake since then." She shuddered, and a coughing fit hit her as she stared at the building. "I never imagined I'd experience that kind of paralyzing response. I mean, I've seen some horrific things on the job without losing it. I never imagined a snake could freeze me in place."

"Did you get counseling after that day?"

"They didn't really do things like that back then. Or maybe my dad thought I should tough it out."

"I can relate." As a former deputy, his father could be a taskmaster at times. "Law enforcement dads can be tough."

She arched a brow and tucked her hair behind her ears. It was a deep rich brunette with feathery edges that barely touched her shoulders. She usually wore it up in a clip when working and left tendrils on the side free. He'd always wanted to tuck it behind her ear as she'd just done. He hadn't seen her with it down very often, but the style softened her face and made her seem much more approachable than the straight-laced FBI agent normally appeared.

She took another long breath, and the terror in her eyes seemed to lessen. "What are you doing here?"

"Someone left a note on my Jeep saying to show up at that janitor's closet at five-fifteen if I wanted to find

Hibbard." The prime suspect, Rich Hibbard, had remained elusive and the task force had never been able to arrest him.

"Yeah, me too. Except my time was five." She bit her lip. "I should've figured it was a trap and brought someone with me."

"You've been accused of being a lone wolf."

"Where you're Mister Personality, making friends left and right."

She was right, and he didn't argue. She'd told him she was an only child and that her dad had kept her busy most of her free time. Where he had an older sister and was the middle child of five boys and had to learn to get along with people. He'd often taken heat from the older pair of brothers and the younger pair, which meant he looked for friends outside the family. He'd frequently ended up being the peacemaker between his brothers.

His birth order also made him more independent. Which was why he would've been okay to come here alone even if his brothers hadn't been on a job when he'd had to leave Portland to get here on time.

"The note said this was about my dad, so I get why someone tried to lure me here," she said. "But why do you think they targeted you too?"

"I've continued to investigate Hibbard. Seems like they wanted to stop us both from looking into him."

She arched an eyebrow above those amazing eyes he always had trouble looking away from. "Did you find anything?"

"Nothing that panned out. I'm assuming you've kept working the case too."

She nodded. "But like you, I struck out."

"With this attempt on our lives, I figure at least one of us is getting close."

"Makes sense." She looked back at the school. "We

might be able to persuade our agencies to reopen the investigation."

Her comment stopped his thoughts. "You wouldn't have heard. I'm no longer an ICE agent."

"What?" She locked onto his face. "You bled ICE from your veins. I figured you'd die before leaving the agency."

"Things change."

"What happened?"

He didn't like talking about the change. Too personal, and he had to be careful with her or it could lead somewhere he didn't want to go. But they'd shared enough about their past when working together that she knew his family and deserved a response. "My dad needed a kidney transplant. My—"

"Is he okay?" She gripped his arm, her concern evident in her tone.

"Yes, thank God. My oldest brother, Aiden, donated one of his. But that put Aiden at risk in his ATF job. Too many dangerous weapons raids that could take out his remaining kidney. So we all quit our jobs and formed an investigation and protection agency."

"Oh, wow." She pulled her hand back and ran it over her hair, releasing flecks of ash residue. "I'm glad everything turned out okay, but what a change for you. When did this happen?"

"About six months ago."

"I still can't believe you're not an agent anymore." She shook her head. "It's hard to wrap my mind around."

She didn't know the half of it. "Me too, some days. But it's good. I'm surprised by how much I like working with my brothers. It can be frustrating not to have access to official reports, but it's freeing not to have all the rules and regulations of law enforcement."

She tilted her head, her feathery hair crossing her face,

and she pushed it aside. “The rules are there to keep us safe and to bring people to justice.”

“Yeah, I know. Still easier to work without them.” He grinned at her.

Her full lips quirked up in a smile, taking him back a year to a time when he’d wondered if she could be *the one*. They hadn’t even dated, but he’d just felt complete when he was in her company. Like a peace descended over him that he’d never experienced with another woman.

Especially not during his latest dating fiasco with Grace. With her, he’d been trying to find that feeling again and failed. Foolishly, he’d continued to date her. He should’ve asked Toni out when they were on the task force, but he didn’t mix work and his personal life. So he’d decided to wait until they’d brought Hibbard to justice and the task force disbanded, at which point they would no longer work together. But it didn’t happen that way. Her father was murdered and Hibbard skated. Then the investigation they’d named Operation Safe Harbor went cold, and the case was closed. Not like Clay would’ve asked her out when she was grieving, and he blamed himself for letting her dad die on his watch.

“Clay,” she said. “What’s wrong? You’re a million miles away.”

“It’s nothing.” He swallowed and forced his attention back to their current situation.

“So, what do you want to do here?” she asked. “Call in the locals?”

“No!”

She eyed him. “Why not?”

“This is *our* investigation. I’m not handing it over to anyone else. Besides, the locals can’t do anything we can’t do except make an arrest, and we can arrange that when we find our guy.”

"Still, we need to process this place for evidence."

Clay noticed Riley still walking the perimeter. Once Clay recovered from the smoke, he needed to thank the guy. "Sam can do that. Plus, Nighthawk just finished an investigation. We're free to work this one."

She held his gaze. "Not without me."

"I'm glad to keep you updated, but you're not here in any official capacity, right? And even if you were, your supervisor will likely refuse to partner with a private agency."

She sat up straighter, her back stiff. "I work it *with* you. No matter how we have to do it. If Adair doesn't approve, I'll take leave."

"I don't know." Clay watched the face he'd dreamed about for the past year. The woman who'd just been stuck in a room filling with smoke. Could've died.

The thought stilled his heart. She needed protection. Sure it wasn't a good idea to work together again. Not good at all. But if they did, he could keep an eye on her. After all, the person who put the snake in the closet could pull the same trick again. Or do something worse. Then where would she be? Helpless and ripe for a lethal attack.

"I know that look," she said. "You're plotting something and not planning to share it with me."

"I was thinking that it might be a good idea if we did pair up on the investigation. Since someone just tried to take both of us out, my team can provide protection."

She crossed her arms, her pit-bull look darkening. "I don't need protecting."

"You do if someone tosses another snake in your path." Maybe a low blow to mention her phobia, but he told the truth, and she had to recognize it.

She tightened her arms. "Please don't tell me my fear of snakes is going to make the rounds in law enforcement circles."

Not the response he'd expected at all. He mimicked zipping his lips. "Won't get beyond me and my brothers."

"Your brothers? Why do they need to know?"

"If they're going to provide a protection detail, they need to know the areas of vulnerability."

She sighed. "Just make sure it doesn't get beyond them, or I'll be a laughingstock. And you know how hard it is for a woman in law enforcement without added baggage like this."

She spoke the truth. He'd seen enough proof of that on the job.

Sam and Griff got out of his truck and started across the lot.

Clay owed Sam a lot. Likely his life. Toni's life. He would hate to put Sam in a difficult situation, and maybe he'd been too hasty in calling her and shouldn't involve her in this investigation.

Griff kept going, and she stopped by Clay. "Griff'll check the place out."

Clay thanked her for her help. "But I've been thinking. Having you do the forensics could be a problem for you with the sheriff."

"How's that?" Sam asked.

"A crime was committed here, and we should report it to him, but we're not going to. If you do the forensics and he finds out, he might not use your agency in the future."

"True, but—"

"I don't want to do that to you or Gage. Not when my sister will be glad to do it and not worry about offending the sheriff."

She looked disappointed. "If you didn't have anyone else, I'd do it no questions asked, but I don't want to cause an issue between Gage and Trent. So it's probably the right thing to do. Thanks for thinking of that."

"Besides," he said. "You can go home and have a nice night with Griff instead of digging around in a dirty closet."

"Don't tell him this, but I live for dirty closets." She laughed. "I'll go tell him we'll be going home earlier than we'd planned."

She strode off, her long legs carrying her quickly across the parking lot.

Clay looked at Toni. "I'll call Sierra. She'll head right out, as will my other brothers. My family has a beach house in the area, and we can stay there and set up our command center."

He waited for her to argue about staying under the same roof with him, but she gave a firm nod.

Maybe being with him wasn't an issue for her. Maybe she'd forgotten all about her interest in him that had been obvious from the first day they'd met.

Good. It would make things easier.

Right, like he believed that.

# 3

Toni held a notepad and sketched the school layout as she circled the exterior with Clay, looking into windows to get a feel for the place. They would divide up the structure into quadrants so that, after his family arrived in a few minutes and Sierra took interior photos, they could thoroughly search the building.

Toni was already cold and damp and a bit cranky from waiting the past few hours for the Byrd family, but even if they didn't involve law enforcement in their incident, a crime had occurred here, and they needed to treat this place as a crime scene.

Lights from oncoming vehicles flashed down the driveway. Clay took her arm and pulled in behind a stand of maple trees.

She glanced at him.

"Can't be too careful," he said, but his attention was on the drive.

Two SUVs, and a van entered the lot and parked near her car.

"It's them." Clay sounded proud even though they hadn't done anything yet but get there. "Let's go."

Toni had heard a lot about his family, but she'd never expected to meet them. Especially in a situation like this. Clay had told them that she'd frozen in the closet. What would they think about an FBI agent who should be strong and resilient, freezing like a little girl at the sight of a snake?

The guys got out and stretched. All of them were dressed like Clay in tactical pants and polo shirts covered with dark windbreakers. The only woman had to be Sierra. Wearing jeans and a green turtleneck, she moved to the back of her van and slipped into a white Tyvek suit.

Toni blinked a few times then strained to get a better look at Sierra. A baby bump. She had a baby bump. A small one, but it was obvious. Her husband, Reed Rice, was an agent in Toni's office, and he worked in violent crimes just like she did. She hadn't heard him mention the pregnancy, but he was a very private guy.

"Sierra's expecting," she said to Clay as they strode across the lot.

"Due in June. It's a boy. I'm gonna be an uncle. I can't wait to teach him all kinds of things Sierra won't be happy he learned." He grinned.

Toni caught his mood and wondered what it would be like to be part of a big family like the Byrds. As an only child and having just her dad after her mom died, she had no idea, but Clay had spoken fondly of his siblings. She just figured having them all together would be loud and messy and likely overwhelming for her.

"I hate to call her out at night when she needs extra rest," Clay continued. "But she keeps telling us not to let the pregnancy affect how we depend on her, so we all try not to."

"I get that," Toni said. "I'd be the same way. If I ever got pregnant, that is."

He fired her a questioning look. "You don't want kids?"

"It's not that I don't want them. I just never thought much about having any. Guess I need to find the right guy first." She chuckled, but for some reason her words made Clay frown.

Sierra hung a camera around her neck and stepped out to peer at her brothers. "Can I get some help with lights and a generator?"

The guys started lifting bins and a small generator from the van. At the building, they put on booties, and one of them fired up a generator. Another carried in big Klieg lights. The others stacked bins by the door. While they worked, Sierra joined Toni and Clay.

"You must be Toni," she said loudly, her voice carrying above the generator. "Reed says you're a great agent."

Just what Toni didn't need. "Checking up on me?"

"I just mentioned you to him when I was heading out. But don't worry." Sierra waved a hand. "I didn't tell him anything about this scene or your involvement."

"Thanks for that." *And for not mentioning my behavior with the snake.*

Sierra slipped her fingers into disposable gloves with the ease that only someone who wore them frequently could manage. "Clay told us a lot about you when you worked Safe Harbor together."

Toni shifted to face Clay.

A sheepish look flashed on his face. "I might've mentioned that you were a great agent."

"It was a *lot* more than that." Sierra wrinkled her nose at him.

Toni thought she saw Clay's face color, though it was too dark to be sure.

Sierra looked at Toni. "I need to get to work to please my taskmaster here, but we should get together for lunch or coffee sometime."

"Sierra," Clay warned.

"What? Can't two women have lunch together?" Sierra sounded innocent, but her eyes held a playful gleam. "Okay, gotta get the photos taken. Let me know if you want me to process any other rooms after your building search."

Toni doubted his sister would need further directions. He'd already given her detailed instructions on the phone, and as a competent professional, she could handle this scene. Clay's brothers flooded out of the building, and the only guy with light hair in the group trailed an extension cord, which he plugged into the generator.

"There," he said. "Sierra's up and running."

Toni had never met the brothers either, but she knew their names. Aiden, Brendan, Drake, and Erik. Clay mentioned that his parents had named them in alphabetical order by birthdate. He said it got tiring when they were growing up, but she appreciated it. Would make it easier to remember their names. She just didn't know who was who yet.

All but one had dark hair and resembled each other. The odd guy out's hair was dishwater blond, very much like Sierra's. They all clearly worked out and exuded confidence.

Toni stepped closer, and they cast a judging look her way as they fired off their names. As expected. An agent couldn't freeze like she'd done and still be effective. None of them would want to rely on her to have their backs. She didn't think they meant anything personal by their looks, but the judgment was there just the same.

In the tightening of Aiden's deep blue eyes. Brendan's similar eyes, inquisitive yet assessing. Drake, who seemed totally intense, watching her with a dark gaze. And Erik, a tilt of his head as if the verdict might still be out on his opinion.

"Knock it off, guys." Clay ran his gaze over his brothers and shared her childhood trauma.

He looked uncomfortable. Like he didn't want to rock the boat, and he kept glancing at Aiden as if checking his reaction. Basically he was the middle child of the boys, and her psychology training at Quantico told her that middle kids often acted as peacemakers in adult life, both at work and at home. She could see that behavior in Clay. When a dispute arose on the task force, he'd mediated and kept them moving forward.

But his demand and explanation for his brothers didn't sway them at all, or at least didn't change their appraising looks.

"I get it," she said, looking from one solid guy to the next. Many women would be intimidated by them. Shoot, a lot of guys would be, but she was used to working in a man's world where testosterone flowed as fast as the Willamette River through Portland, and she wasn't in the least bit afraid. Concerned they'd let her secret slip, yes. Afraid, no.

"I'd be looking at me the same way," she continued. "A law enforcement officer who freezes for any reason is a liability. You can't count on me having your back. But trust me when I say I had no idea I'd react that way. I haven't seen a snake since the terrifying incident. And after today, I'll see someone about it so it doesn't happen again."

"You don't have to justify yourself to us." Clay curled his hands into fists at his sides as he watched his brothers. "It's not like we're perfect or anything. I could start airing our dirty laundry. Who should I start with?"

He eyed his brothers, and they relaxed a bit. All except Drake. She figured him for the family bad boy, bucking rules and tending toward the wild side.

"Just like I thought," Clay said. "Let's move on."

She smiled her thanks at Clay. He'd always been so

supportive when they'd worked together. He was a total charmer, but underlying it all was a sincere heart, and she'd had a hard time resisting him. If her father hadn't died, would they have gotten together?

Didn't matter. Her dad *had* died. When he'd appeared unexpectedly on their op, she was ogling Clay instead of putting her focus where it should've been. She'd only looked away for a few seconds, but that was all it had taken.

Clay sucked in a sharp breath and turned back to his brothers. "Okay. We'll get started once Sierra has finished all the photos. We've divided the building into quadrants. We'll team up and search every inch of this place." Clay shared their assignments.

"Let me guess," Drake said dryly. "You're partnering with Toni."

One of the brothers snickered, but she didn't see which one.

"Let's get some gloves on so we're ready to act when Sierra is done," Clay said.

"A word alone before we do," Aiden said.

Aiden was the eldest, and she expected Clay would readily follow him, but Clay glanced at his watch instead. "I know what you're planning to say, and you can warn me anytime to not make this personal. I'd like to get this place processed, so let's move."

Clay jerked his head at Toni, telling her to follow him. She forced out a smile for the others and trailed Clay toward the building. Should she mention what had just happened with his brothers, or was it better to keep quiet? Quiet. She would let him take lead in any conversation.

They passed the roaring generator powering the lights and creating a sharp glow from the basement stairwell.

"We'll hold here until Sierra returns." Clay stopped at the head of the stairwell.

Of course, he'd taken the quadrant with the storage room. Under normal conditions, she would be glad he'd chosen the place that should have the strongest lead. But, man, she didn't want to go back down there. Not even if Clay had already hauled the pail out to his Jeep and locked the snake in. Snake or no snake, she couldn't predict her reaction when they reached the janitor's closet.

It took every ounce of her willpower to stand there and wait for Sierra. But Toni was a professional. She wouldn't bail. At least not yet.

Sierra soon climbed the stairs and lifted her camera strap from around her neck. "I'll grab my field kit and get to work in the closet first. You're clear to move around the building."

Clay led her down the stairs, the smoke barely lingering after Griff sucked it out with a big fan. The light revealed faded blue walls with flakes of paint waiting for any movement to go flying into the air. They hit the basement's concrete floor painted a dark gray and worn in the middle. She forced her feet forward. Step by step. Closer. Closer. Her heart rate kicked up. *Thump. Thump. Thump*. Pounding like a drum. Her breathing grew shallow in already irritated lungs. Labored.

A cold chill swept over her. Her hands got clammy.

*Stop it. The snake isn't even in there. Keep moving. You can do it.*

Her feet didn't listen, and her footsteps faltered.

*Please. I don't like this. You know I like to be in control. In charge. Not needing anyone.*

The only person in her adult life she'd been indebted to was her father, who'd taught her to be self-sufficient. To live her faith by helping others for sure. But asking for help? Never. And now she was beholden to Clay for his rescue from the snake and fire, and she didn't like it. Not one bit.

He turned, his gaze landing on her face and holding, his eyes filling with compassion.

And that look. He thought she was weak. Needed help. And she did.

*Oh, God, why? What's going on? Why are You letting this happen?*

"Let's split up. I'll talk to Sierra, and you head toward the back to search for leads." He offered her a flashlight.

She grabbed it like a lifeline, clutching the cool metal and letting the raised switch press into the tender flesh of her palm to distract her from the open closet door, where big Klieg lights illuminated the room.

She got her feet moving, hurried past the closet and around a corner to an area shrouded in darkness. Flicking on the flashlight, she took several cleansing breaths and let the stress evaporate with each exhale of air. She concentrated on the area where the hallway opened into a small room with an arched doorway.

She flashed the light beam over the space, finding the same painted floor, but the walls were made of rust-red bricks. Shelves lined three of the walls, holding various sized paint cans, but the brick on the walls had crumbled to the floor, a mound of bricks and dust at the base of the studs.

She stepped closer and shone her light into the void. She took a good look, gasped, and stepped back. Her heart galloped into top speed.

"Clay!" she yelled. "Come here. You have to see this."

~

*Toni.* Clay spun at her call.

She was panicked again and needed him.

He clicked on the headlamp he'd gotten from Sierra

and charged down the hall. Toni stood in a small room staring into the open void in a wall. The back side of the wall was intact, but the brick wall in front had tumbled to the floor.

"What is it?" he asked.

She pointed at the mound of bricks.

He took a long look and blinked a few times. He had to be certain of what he was seeing.

"Man. Never expected this." He shook his head but kept his gaze glued to the human skeleton. Mostly bones but with patches of flesh and clothing clinging to them. He couldn't tell the person's gender, but the frame was small, the shirt feminine. So likely a woman, but they needed a forensic anthropologist like Dr. Kelsey Dunbar at the Veritas Center to verify.

"You think this is what we were supposed to discover when we came here?" This was a strong lead, but Toni's tone was wooden, her expression tight.

"Maybe." He gave it some thought. "But why start the fire or put the snake in the closet? Or for that matter, why send us to the closet at all and not direct us here instead?"

"Maybe it wasn't about telling us anything." She considered the options. "Maybe the killer was worried we'd find this place and the body in our search, so he wanted to take us out before we did."

"Could be."

"We're looking at murder here. Guess we'll have to call in the local authorities after all."

"I'll take care of that." Clay dug out his phone. "Blake knows Trent and should be able to persuade him to let the forensic anthropologist from the Veritas Center handle the recovery."

"You think he'll be able to do that?"

"Blake's a pretty hard guy to say no to, so yeah. He'll get

it done." Clay forced out a smile. "In the meantime, can you cordon off the area? I can grab a roll of tape from Sierra."

"No," she said firmly. "I can get it."

"You sure?" He tried not to sound skeptical, but she'd looked terrified when they'd passed the closet, which was why he'd sent her to the room in the first place.

Her irritated expression told him she wanted to snap at him, but she took several slow breaths. "Please don't baby me."

"Not babying, just concerned for you is all."

She sighed. "Don't be."

"I get it. You like to be in control. Goes against your personality when you aren't."

She shook her head, lips pursed.

"What?"

"You have me pegged, don't you?"

"Not any more than you do me."

She tilted her head and watched him for a long moment. "Do you think we might've gotten together if my dad hadn't died?"

*Right.* She'd said exactly what he'd been thinking for a year but was too chicken to ask. "I would've asked you out, that's for sure. What would've happened after that..." He shrugged. "I don't know."

"Clay," Drake's voice traveled down the hallway. "You back there?"

"Better see what he wants." Clay spun and heard Toni following as he headed back down the hallway.

Drake stood on this side of the closet, the light spilling out behind his body and making him look other-worldly.

"You gotta see what Erik and I found." Drake's tone was filled with more excitement than was normal for the guy.

Clay didn't want to leave this area if it was some lame lead. "Can't you just tell me about it?"

"Better you see it."

"Does it trump human remains? Because Toni just found them down the hall." He jerked a thumb over his shoulder.

He looked over Clay's shoulder. "Seriously?"

"Seriously," Toni said. "In the wall. Skeletonized, so the body's been there for a while."

"Man." Drake shoved his hand into his hair and met Clay's gaze. "That's rough, but before you call in law enforcement, you really need to come with me."

Clay peered back at Toni. "I know you'll want to join us. I'll get Sierra to cordon off the area."

Toni nodded, and he stepped into the janitor's closet. "I need you to tape off the area down the hall to our left. We found human remains."

She gave a sharp nod and clamped her hands on her hips, her gloved fingers wrinkling her white Tyvek suit. Her stoic response came from frequently working crime scenes where she'd seen things turn dark and difficult in mere moments.

"We're heading upstairs with Drake," Clay continued. "He found something but won't tell us what. Wants us to see it."

"You're calling in the locals on the body, right?" She dug in her field kit for a roll of yellow crime scene tape.

"I'll call Blake after I see what Drake found. Figure he can convince the local sheriff to let Kelsey recover the remains."

"Good thinking." Sierra picked at the end of the tape to release it. "I'll get the area secured and take photos. Then get back in here to see what I can find before we have to turn things over to the authorities."

"I'll ask Blake to put in a good word for you too. Hopefully, all the evidence can be processed at Veritas."

"Or not. The sheriff has used Sam at Blackwell in the past. He'll probably call her. Gives him greater control over the forensics."

"Either way," Clay said. "I hope to have access to reports."

Sierra eyed him. "You know once this is an official crime scene, I can't share details unless we have the sheriff's permission."

"Then I'll work on that too."

Drake poked his head in the room. "You coming or what?"

"Just a sec." Clay turned back to his sister. "I'll let you know what Blake has to say and what Drake is jonesing to show us."

Sierra gave a firm nod, and he followed Drake and Toni down the hall. She was immediately in front of him, illuminated by the headlamp. He had to work hard to keep his gaze from her hips. Her very feminine walk was in total odds with her tough demeanor and sturdy build. Still, she had plenty of curves to turn heads, something he'd noticed far too many times on the task force.

Drake led them over worn concrete, through thick cobwebs, and up two flights of stairs. On the second floor, he stood back by the first room. "Have a look."

Clay followed Toni inside. As he entered, he noted a heavy-duty hasp and dangling padlock on the exterior. Someone definitely wanted to keep people out of or even in this room. He took a quick look at the space, and his feet came to a stop just inside the doorway.

Four sets of bunk beds with ratty mattresses and rumpled bed linens filled the room, but otherwise the space was spotless, suggesting the room wasn't occupied by squatters or homeless people. And no drug paraphernalia, so not likely addicts. Plus, the windows were covered with blackout drapes. Not something these groups might do.

So who?

Was this related to the notes they'd received? Was Hibbard using this building?

He shot Toni a look. "Seems like a perfect set up for human trafficking."

"Agreed." She held his gaze, her eyes dark with concern. "But we're a long way from the I-5 corridor."

She was right. Most trafficked victims were transported up and down the corridor, many of them participating in the West Coast Circuit, where there was a ton of money to be made. Originating in Canada, the highway ran through the state and all the way to Mexico. It was one of the reasons Portland was often named number one in the country for juvenile trafficking and why Hibbard worked out of there. The task force had never found any leads to indicate a significant problem in this area.

So, could this be a case of trafficking? Or was it more about prostitution?

"The coast is nearby," he said as he continued to think this through. "Maybe we couldn't pin anything on Hibbard because he set up shop here instead. Maybe he's no longer running vehicles on I-5 but boats along the coast."

"Maybe you should hold off discussing this until you see the other rooms," Drake said from the doorway.

Rooms? Plural? Clay's gut clenched. "There's more?"

Drake gave a solemn nod.

"Lead the way." His stomach churning, Clay followed Drake down the hallway and into another room. Toni's footsteps sounded behind them. A four-poster queen-size bed with a gauzy lilac canopy and a shiny purple comforter and matching sheets took up half the room. Blackout drapes covered these windows too, but this room also held a sitting area, rug, and mirror tiles on the ceiling.

Clay's heart sank. "Are there more of these rooms?"

Drake nodded. "Every classroom on this floor has a similar set up or is like the bunk bed sleeping quarters. One person per bunk bed means the place could house at least thirty-two people, and four rooms are tricked out like this one."

This was just sick. Awful. Clay didn't even want to think about it. His stomach churned until he feared he might hurl.

Toni didn't seem to be faring any better. Her hands were fisted tightly by her side, her posture rigid.

She inhaled a long breath. "This investigation goes way beyond the local sheriff's ability. Even if he *is* topnotch, he doesn't have the staff to run an investigation of this magnitude."

"Agreed," Clay said. "He'd have to call in the state or Feds. Your squad would be the ones to work this. Call it in to them."

She bit her lip.

He was confused. "You're not glad to get your agency involved?"

"They're the right people to handle the investigation, but with my father's connection, my supervisor will ban me."

Clay understood her hesitancy. When he was an agent, he would've wanted to keep charge of this investigation, but they had no choice.

He locked gazes with her. "No matter our personal preferences, there are thirty-two young girls who could be counting on us, and we have to do the right thing to save them."

# 4

While Toni waited for her co-workers to arrive, she and Clay walked through the building to snap pictures and gather any information they could before they were both persona non grata. Her supervisor would send her packing. And quickly. Toni didn't like it. Not one bit. But even worse, she feared when they interviewed the Byrd brothers, one of them would forget and spill her reaction to the rattlesnake. And they *would* be interviewed. Each and every one of them. Her as well. Something she wasn't looking forward to. Especially when she had to admit to her supervisor she'd continued touring the building after finding the body and discovering the bedrooms.

Clay turned to look at her on the stairwell landing at the second floor. "What put that look on your face?"

She shared her concerns. "I wonder who'll interview me and what'll happen when I admit I lingered here even after I knew it was a crime scene."

"You think there'll be backlash?" He leaned against the peeling wall. "Other than keeping you off the investigation."

"My supervisor is pretty tough. So yeah, there could be a problem."

"I'll pray there isn't."

"Thank you." She'd prayed with him a few times on the task force, and he obviously lived his faith and shared about it, but they'd never really discussed their beliefs.

She heard cars arriving and stepped to the window to look out. "They're here."

Clay joined her, and she caught a hint of his musky scent momentarily covering the building's mildewy smell.

The FBI arrived in full force, cars, SUVs, and trucks crunching over the gravel lot. Agents. Evidence recovery squad. Supervisors all the way from supervisory special agents up to the big boss, the Special Agent in Charge of the Portland office.

"We should go meet them." She turned to leave.

Clay grabbed her hand and squeezed. "It'll be okay."

His hands were that of a hard-working man. Callused and firm. And still, his touch was gentle.

"I could lose my job."

"Even if you do, God will work it out for good."

"I get that. Even believe it. Most of the time anyway. But I struggle when the outcome could be something so serious. Something like this. Or like when my dad died." She shook her head. "I'm still struggling to see any good there."

"Maybe the good is in the fact that we've continued to work this investigation. If he hadn't died, I don't think we would've found this school."

"Yeah, maybe." She started down the rest of the steps. This might be for someone's good, but not hers as far as she could see.

At the door, she looked at Clay. "I need to talk to my supervisor alone."

He opened his mouth as if to say something, but snapped it closed and marched outside. "I'll be with my brothers if you need me."

"Thanks." She continued on into the moonlit night, the soft rays illuminating the agents bustling around. Clay joined his brothers, and she felt alone. Abandoned, even when she was the one who asked him to go. Maybe she'd hoped he would object and demand to speak to Adair. She had no idea what she hoped right now. Her emotions were in too much of a turmoil to know anything for sure.

She planted her feet in a stance she hoped displayed a confidence she didn't feel and waited for Assistant Special Agent in Charge Nathan Adair to stop talking to the special agent in charge of their office. The earlier misty rain had disappeared. For now, anyway. At this time of year it would be back in short order.

Adair spun and marched straight over to her. Gut churning, she watched his confident walk. He was fit from hours at the gym and was dressed in deep gray suit pants and a white shirt with a gray-and-blue striped tie. But instead of his usual perfectly tailored suit coat, he wore a blue windbreaker with FBI emblazoned in yellow on the chest and back. His hair was short, inky black, and laced with fine threads of silver. His emerald green eyes pierced Toni. She'd never seen him quite this upset, and she'd seen him angry in the past.

He took a wide stance in front of her and locked onto her face. "Update me in a minute or less."

*Good.* A minute or less meant she didn't have time to tell him about her reaction to the snake. She formed her words carefully and shared the highlights of the night, feeling like a liar when she left out snake details.

She must have pulled it off, though, as he looked across the lot to where the Byrd family lingered by their vehicles. "You know these guys before tonight?"

"Clay, but not the others. And Sierra—"

"Is married to Rice. I better not find out he knew about this too."

"I didn't tell him."

"It goes without saying that you won't be involved in this investigation."

"Got it."

He lifted a dark eyebrow. "What, no fight?"

"I knew it was coming."

"Still, you're not one to back down." Those green eyes dug deeper. "You're not planning on investigating on your own, are you?"

*Planning on it?* She glanced at Clay, who was now being interviewed by the big boss. He was curling his hands into fists. Not a good sign. He caught her eye and transmitted his frustration, and in that instant, she knew they would definitely work this together.

"No plans, sir," she said as they hadn't made plans. Just a commitment.

"See that you don't make any." He turned to look at the building. "I'll walk the scene, and I'm sure I'll have additional questions for you."

"Would you like me to join you?"

He gritted his teeth. "I don't want you anywhere near the place. In fact, go wait in my vehicle."

"Yes, sir."

He marched back to the special agent in charge, and together they stopped at the door to don booties before entering the abandoned school.

Finished with his interview, Clay headed over to her.

"Guess you didn't have a friendly conversation either," she said.

"He reminded me why *civilians* like me and my brothers aren't supposed to investigate crimes."

"What did you say to that?"

"If it wasn't for me and my brothers, he wouldn't have a crime to investigate." He brushed his jacket out of the way and shoved his hands into the pockets of his tactical pants.

*Interesting.* "What happened to Mr. Diplomacy?"

"Your boss was condescending to the max, and a guy can only take so much arrogance." He grinned, a cute smile reminding her of the nights they'd worked late and had gotten slap-happy. "And what about you? Adair didn't look pleased."

"He warned me not to plan to investigate this on my own."

Clay didn't respond for a moment but held onto her gaze as if mining for information. "But you aren't going to listen to him, are you?"

Not ready to admit aloud that she intended to go against her supervisor's wishes, she shook her head. "I feel the need to take some leave."

"Will Adair go for it?"

"He'll probably see right through it, and I can't lie to him, so don't talk about working this investigation together right now or I'll have to tell him."

"How do you plan to get the leave approved?"

"I'll tell him if he lets me take time off, I won't be in the office bugging everyone for information. Which is the truth. I might need to call in to ask some favors, but..." She shrugged. "Anyway. He should go for it."

"And if he doesn't?"

She looked at the door where the FBI forensic staff were marching past Sierra and giving her the stink eye. "Then I might have to become a private investigator like you."

~

An hour later, Clay looked at Adair's SUV where Toni sat in the backseat with him. Clay's family had already departed for home. Clay would meet with them to form an action plan and return tomorrow with items needed to work this investigation. Return with Toni. And spend time together again. Oddly enough, he was more drawn to her now than he'd been when they were on the task force. Maybe because she was so emotionally vulnerable tonight.

Even from a distance, he could see the frustration in the rigid set of her shoulders. And the tight expression on her face said she was working hard to control her temper. Something else he loved about her. She had a fierce temper and let it explode occasionally. Having gotten it out of her system, she generally sat back all relaxed and moved on.

Not him. He stewed over things. Let them simmer and fester. Probably from being the middle boy. He didn't mean to sound pitiful. He'd had a great life growing up. Two wonderful parents who loved him unconditionally no matter which birth order he fell in. Not a one of his siblings was lacking for love, support, and encouragement from their parents to become the best person they could be.

He had that in common with Toni, but he'd felt competitive toward his brothers growing up, and because they linked up in pairs, he found his place in the group by trying to break up their disagreements. And man, in a family of so many guys, there were plenty of them.

On the bright side, he was the closest of all the guys to Sierra. He didn't know if she paid more attention to him because she pitied him or because she needed an ally in the family too. Either way, as the eldest in the family, she looked out for him.

Adair's car door opened, and Toni jumped out, marching across the lot and heading for the remote corner of the building cloaked with dark shadows. She must really be upset if she needed to isolate herself.

Clay wouldn't let her suffer alone. He went after her and found her bent over, hands planted on her thighs and taking deep breaths. He made sure to make noise on his approach so she'd know someone was coming. She looked up at him, her eyes awash with tears.

His heart tore, and he went straight to her. He rested his hands on her shoulders. "I take it your talk didn't go so well with Adair."

"No, but that was expected."

"Still, you're upset."

She shook her head. "Sure, I didn't want to be thrown off the investigation for personal reasons, but it's more than that. The girls. There could be over thirty of them in Hibbard's clutches. Suffering. Scared. Traumatized. This investigation has become even more personal to me, and I need to find them as well as find my dad's killer. Adair taking me off the case doesn't help."

Clay loved her heart for others, and it was just like her to put the girls first and be more upset about not being able to help them than her career setback.

She spun and faced the school. "Hibbard dodged us at every turn in Safe Harbor. He's done the same thing here. We can't let it happen again."

Hands free now, Clay shoved them in his pockets. "We have my whole family behind us, and I'm not bragging when I say they're good at what they do. We'll find Hibbard."

She looked at him, the tears still in her eyes.

She gave them an angry swipe. "Let's get moving. I want to head back to Portland to pick up the records about this guy's operation from Safe Harbor. See if we can find any mention of this place in them."

Clay didn't relish the long drive tonight, but he would make it for her. "We'll leave your car, and I'll drive you to Portland."

She glanced back at her vehicle. "It would be better if Adair didn't see us leave together."

"Let me get on the road first, and we can meet up as soon as we're out of his eyesight."

She gave a sharp nod and charged across the lot to talk to one of the agents. Clay went to his Jeep, glad he'd already turned the snake over to the Feds. Not only because he didn't want to deal with it, but it was evidence. Plus, he wanted the rattler as far away from Toni as possible.

He got his Jeep running and on the road, checking the mirror every few seconds to watch for her vehicle. Someone had tried to kill her, and he wanted her in his car and by his side. From that point on, he wouldn't leave her out of his sight for very long. No matter what he had to do, he would keep her at his side until they found the creep who put the snake in the closet.

Clay pulled into the Veritas parking structure, glad to be safely behind secured gates. And soon to be out of the Jeep and away from the discomfort between him and Toni. Whatever topic he'd broached on the drive to her apartment, and again on the way here, she'd given short answers. She'd even quickly agreed to spend the night at Veritas. No objection. No question. He'd just said she would be safer there, and she'd acquiesced. So unlike her. Her dejection over being booted off the case seemed to be festering. Why didn't she blow up and let it go like she used to do? Maybe she'd changed in the last year. Maybe she no longer exploded with anger. He'd changed, so why wouldn't she have as she'd come to grips with her father's death?

Still, he didn't like seeing her so miserable. He had liked getting to see her home. The recently renovated warehouse apartment with a contemporary flair in the trendy neighborhood. The style fit her somehow. They'd made quick work of gathering her boxes, taking pictures of the murder board on her wall, and then dismantling it to take the items with them. They'd also brought along a box of her father's belongings from his office in Virginia, where he'd retired and worked as a private investigator at a friend's agency. She hadn't found anything helpful in it, but he agreed to look through it just in case.

He ramped up in the parking garage to the top floor, and she faced him. "You actually think we'll catch Hibbard this time? In the past, he thoroughly cleaned the places he abandoned but left his prints. It's like he wanted us to know he was there, but not leave enough for us to find him."

"He could be taunting us to stroke his massive ego." Clay glanced at her. "But this time was different. He bolted and left plenty of items behind."

"And yet, we don't have access to them."

"That's true, but we'll figure this out. I know we will."

She shook her head. "I forgot how positive you always are. It's great, but honestly, it can be irritating. You make it hard to be in a bad mood when I want to let my anger fuel my passion."

He didn't know how to respond to that so he didn't. "You okay with leaving your files in my Jeep tonight?"

"Yeah. I'm way too tired to haul it all in."

"I probably have all the same files. I made a copy of everything when we closed down Safe Harbor."

She studied him. "I'm surprised we didn't cross paths at the copier."

Another thing he wouldn't respond to. When they'd disbanded the task force, he'd tried to make himself scarce whenever she was around. He wasn't proud of not being there for her. Not proud at all. Sure, he'd offered his condolences, but that was all. He would've—should've—done more. But the minute he started blaming himself for her dad's death, he'd hardly been able to look her in the eye.

It took a lot of prayer and introspection to finally realize her father dying wasn't his fault. Sure, Clay might've been in charge of the op, but how could he have predicted her dad would show up? He couldn't have. Not when the guy wasn't on anyone's radar as related to the case. Even now, they couldn't find a connection. So Clay might still feel some guilt, but he knew for certain that he wasn't to blame.

He pulled into his parking spot, and his phone dinged. After shifting into park, he looked at it. "A text from Blake. He said Hibbard's name never came up when he was sheriff, but he'll give Sheriff Winfield a call first thing in the morning for us."

"Perfect."

They got out into the blustery wind howling through the parking structure, and he grabbed her overnight bag.

"You don't have to carry that," she said.

He slammed the hatch. "No worries. Always aim to please."

She arched a brow like she had him pegged—knew that he really did have a thing about pleasing people if he could. Don't rock the boat. That was him. Except when it came to suspects. They deserved as much rocking as he could offer.

He got the door open using his fingers on the print reader. "We'll have to get a security badge for you at the front desk. Keep it on you at all times, and you can't go unescorted anywhere in the building."

She gave the easy smile of acquiescence again, and they

boarded the elevator. He punched the lobby button and a yawn caught him off guard.

"Late night," she said.

"They all are these days. After we formed the agency, I foolishly hoped we'd be working fewer hours, but I underestimated the work it would take to get a business off the ground. There's so much more than doing the job. Payroll. Taxes. Reports. Record keeping. Planning. Budgets. I could go on for hours. Still, I think it'll slow down once we're established, and I might be able to think about a normal life."

"I totally get that. I want to get a dog someday, but I'm not home long enough even to feed a goldfish."

"Erik got a dog," he said as if his brother's actions proved anything. "Erik's really into vintage video games, so he named the dog Pong. He's trained as a sniffer dog for electronics."

She leaned back and tipped her head, looking casual. "Sniffer for electronics? Never heard of such a thing."

"Not a lot of these dogs in the service." He rested against the wall. "You remember when that spokesman for the fast food place was found guilty of possessing child-porn and having sex with underage girls?"

"Yeah, sure."

"Over a dozen federal agents missed a key piece of evidence at Fogel's place that a trained K-9 found. The flash drive containing child-porn images would never have been located without a sniffer dog. We haven't used Pong on the job yet, but who knows? He might come in handy someday."

The doors opened, and they stepped into the hallway.

She turned to look at him. "Be honest with me. Do you think whoever put the snake in the closet and started the fire really wanted to kill us?"

He glanced at her. "I'd rather not think we have a target on our backs, but there's no other good explanation."

"But they couldn't know we'd come alone."

"True, except the note told us to do so if we wanted to get the information." He opened the lobby door. "Is your note in the boxes?"

"Yeah, why?"

"I'd like to give them to Sierra to analyze. Maybe she can find the lead we need to really move this investigation forward."

# 5

Being in law enforcement, Toni had heard great things about the Veritas Center and always wanted to tour the place. But, man, the building was even more impressive than she'd imagined. She hadn't even been able to find the words to say how great the glass-enclosed skybridge was that connected two six-story towers at the top, and the warm feeling of the lobby that sat between them on the ground floor. It was all so unexpected for a place that processed crime forensics.

But the lab vibe came through loud and clear as they walked down the hallway in the lab tower, planning to leave their letters for Sierra to process in the morning. Clay pressed his fingers against print readers to get the door unlocked and opened it. She heard fans humming in the background, but still, a hint of caustic chemical smell rose up to meet her. The place held more high quality machines than most local police labs. It seemed to be on par with the FBI's national lab in Quantico, Virginia, although much smaller.

"What are you still doing up?" Clay marched straight

over to Sierra, who was sitting at a table in the middle of the room.

Dark circles hung under her eyes, and strands of hair had escaped her ponytail.

Clay lifted her from her stool by the elbow. "Come on. You look awful, and you're going to bed."

"Gee, thanks." She eyed her brother. "I wanted to get through my photos from the high school."

"I thought you turned everything over to the Bureau forensic team," Toni said.

"I made a copy of the pictures before I gave them the memory card." Sierra grinned, and Toni looked for a resemblance to Clay's bright smile but didn't see any at all.

Clay crossed his arms. "Resting for the baby is more important than reviewing the pictures."

Sierra opened her mouth, looking like she planned to argue.

Clay moved closer. "Don't make me wake Reed up. You know I will."

"Fine. I'll leave right after I lock up this evidence." She grabbed three bags lying on a table covered in white paper. "You go ahead and get Toni settled for the night. I can find my own condo."

"And have you go back to work the minute we leave?" He eyed his sister. "Not happening."

"I wasn't going to."

"Not purposefully, but I can just see it. You discover or think of something on the way to the evidence lockers and forget you were on your way out."

"Fine, then. Hold on." She took the bags across the room to the lockers.

Clay followed her with their letters. "Work on them tomorrow only."

"Yes, sir." She saluted and tucked them in another locker.

"Do you know if the FBI called Kelsey to recover the remains?" he asked.

"If they did, she hasn't told me." Sierra deposited the items in a locker and closed it. "Wouldn't be great if she got called out tonight though. She needs her sleep even more than I do."

Clay looked at Toni. "Kelsey is expecting too. Not sure when."

"She's only said she's due in April a million times." Sierra wrinkled her nose at her brother. "But just like a guy not to remember the details."

"She's having a girl," he said and raised his chin. "See, I remember details."

Sierra swatted a hand at him, and he circled an arm around her back then gently knuckled her head. She looked up at him with a fond smile and they started for the exit. This was exactly the way Toni had imagined having a sibling would be like, and seeing them together left her feeling sad that she was an only child.

In the hallway, they boarded the elevator and took it to the sixth floor. Clay kept his arm around his sister. She rested against him and yawned, covering her mouth.

"See," he said. "You really are tired."

"Never said I wasn't, but I know how important this investigation is to you both."

"We've waited a year to find Hibbard," Toni said. "One more night shouldn't make a difference."

"But I—"

"But nothing," Clay protested. "Your health comes first."

Sierra looked at Toni. "Do you have any brothers or sisters?"

She shook her head. "But I always wanted a sibling."

Sierra fixed her focus on Clay. "Where I often wished I was an only child."

"Hey." He removed his arm and mocked upset.

Sierra chuckled. "Seriously, these guys can be a real pain at times, and then they do something like this to show they care, and it's all forgotten. I'm really blessed."

Clay's feigned bad mood disappeared, and he grinned at his sister. "I'm only looking out for the future flock of Byrds."

Sierra groaned. "And then there's the lame humor."

"Saddle me with a name like Byrd, and I got teased enough as a kid that I figure I can use the lame jokes as an adult." He met Toni's gaze and laughed.

His laughter was contagious, and she joined in. She loved this insight into his family life. His tender care of his sister endeared him to her, and she could imagine he would be even more protective and tender with his wife. Especially so if she was pregnant with his child.

The doors slid open. A good thing as she was starting to imagine what his child might look like. What *their* child might look like.

He held out his hand, gesturing toward the end of the hallway. "We have to cross the skybridge to get to the condo towers."

"The view of the city from there is amazing." Sierra took off down the hallway, but her feet were dragging. At the skybridge she paused. "See what I mean?"

Toni looked through the floor-to-ceiling glass toward the city skyline, lights twinkling in the clear night. The moon shone on the glass above, and a soft glow brightened the area.

"It's beautiful." Toni glanced at Sierra then looked at Clay, who was intently watching her. His focus had been on

Sierra, and Toni had honestly missed having his sincere concern focused her way.

"You two could stay here and look at the view," Sierra suggested.

"I think we're better off getting a good night's sleep." Clay gave his sister a pointed look.

She held up her hands, but an impish expression had claimed her face. "I'll let it go. For now." She spun and marched across the bridge, a renewed purpose in her steps.

Not having a clue what had just transpired between the pair, Toni followed, feeling the floor sway beneath her feet. They boarded another elevator, and Clay tapped buttons for floors three and five.

"Sierra's on five," he said.

Toni leaned over to look at Sierra. "One thing before you go. I'm on leave, and Adair forbid me from working on the investigation."

"So don't say anything to Reed," Clay added.

"What investigation?" Sierra wrinkled her nose. As the doors opened on five, she turned back to look at Toni. "It was good to meet you tonight, and I look forward to getting to know you better."

"Nice to meet you too." Toni smiled but didn't add the *getting to know you* part. They were headed back to the coast in the morning, and Toni doubted she would see Sierra again.

The doors closed, and an unusual sense of peace and stillness from the easiness of the siblings' banter filled Toni. She never had that sense of lightness with her dad. An excellent taskmaster, he always kept her busy and working hard. He'd rarely been satisfied with her results, so she had to try harder. Work faster. Be better.

That didn't give her much downtime growing up. She'd once thought her dad acted this way because he missed her mother so much, that if he took time to breathe, he would fall apart. But then, she remembered he'd been that way before her mom died, so maybe it was just his nature. In any event, it became a habit for her, and now she rarely relaxed.

They hit the third floor and stepped into a long hallway with only two doors.

Clay went to the closest one. "Brendan's just next door and I'll be staying with him if you need me. I'll just grab a few things for the night and let you get some sleep."

She nodded, but she really wanted him to stay for a bit. Not the night, of course, but just until her eyes started drooping.

He unlocked the door and held it open. She'd only gotten a quick look at his place when they'd dropped off her suitcase, and she looked forward to taking the place in now. She entered the family room, and her mouth fell open. She didn't expect this. Not in a million years.

A tall and trim older woman with spiky blond hair hopped up from a huge sectional and rushed toward them. A man looking like an older version of Clay with salt-and-pepper hair, more salt than pepper, remained seated but peered over the sofa at her.

"Mom. Dad," Clay said, sounding as surprised as she was. "What are you doing here?"

His mother rushed to him and clasped his arms. "You're okay?"

"Fine. Why?"

Her honey-brown eyes narrowed. "I was talking to Erik and wormed out of him that you had a major scare today."

Clay slipped out of her hold. "It was nothing."

She clasped the sides of his face and stared him in the eye, a fierce mother-bear expression in place. "You're sure you're fine."

"Positive."

She lowered her hands to his shoulders and turned him in a circle, running her gaze over every inch.

"Mom," he said. "This is embarrassing. I'm not a little kid anymore."

"Peg, give the guy a break," his dad said.

A quick nod, and his mother turned her attention to Toni. "Peggy Byrd, and you must be Toni." She stepped over to Toni and slid an arm around her shoulders. "Come on, sweetheart, let's get you settled in."

"My mother is everyone's mother." A hint of humor lingered in Clay's voice. "And this is my dad, Russ."

Toni glanced at him as Peggy led her to the other part of the sectional. His grin reminded her of Clay. Clearly, most of the boys took after the dad, but Erik and Sierra resembled their mother.

"Nice to meet you, Toni." Russ smiled, then shared a what-are-you-gonna-do look with Clay, who remained standing.

"Now, Toni." His mother removed her arm. "I just made a pot of chamomile tea. Would you like a cup?"

"Not everyone likes tea," Russ said. "At least me and the guys don't."

Peggy ran her gaze over Toni. "Toni is obviously not one of the guys."

"Tea would be nice." Toni settled onto the soft cushion. She'd never had chamomile tea in her life but had heard it helped with sleep, and she could use help to still her mind tonight.

"Get her a cup, would you, son?" Peggy flicked her hand in the air as if swatting at a mosquito but didn't take her gaze off Toni. "We heard a lot about you and your father from Clay. I'm so sorry for your loss."

"Thank you," Toni said, realizing this was the second time someone had mentioned Clay talking about her.

She watched him go to his very contemporary kitchen and lift down a mug for her tea. How much had he told his family about her? And why had he even mentioned her? Did he share all of his investigations, or was she an exception?

Interestingly, she wanted to be the exception. To be important enough to him to share with the people closest to him.

"He was torn up for months." Peggy dropped onto the plush sofa next to Toni. "Never seen him so upset."

"Mom." Clay poured tea from a contemporary gray teapot into the mug.

Why did he even have a teapot when his dad claimed they didn't like it? Perhaps his mother brought it with her, or maybe he kept one just for her. From what Toni was learning about his love for his family, she could see him going out of his way to have a pot for his mother to use when she visited.

"Erik mentioned you ran into a snake," Peggy said. "And that you had a bad experience with one as a child."

"That's personal, Mom." Clay handed Toni a mug of steaming tea and eyed his mother as he rested on the arm of a leather chair.

Toni cupped the hot mug in her chilled hands and smiled at the older woman who Toni already liked. Sure she was a bit nosey, but she seemed free to express her emotions, and Toni could feel the woman's legitimate concern. "It's okay. It was a long time ago, and I didn't know until tonight that it still had a hold on me."

She recounted the incident, not surprised when her voice started to waver. She took a sip of the tea, liking the apple flavor with a hint of honey sweetness. "This is good."

A wide smile danced across Peggy's face, and Toni saw Sierra in the smile.

"A girl after my own heart." Peggy leaned closer. "You can't imagine what it's like to be surrounded by so many guys for your entire life. Poor Sierra has taken the brunt of my need for girl talk. But now I have Harper and Jenna. True, they're not yet officially members of the family yet, but Aiden and Harper have finally set the date. May fifteenth. She's an Olympic skier, so they have to work around her competition and training schedule."

"Congratulations. That must be so exciting for you." Toni tried to sound cheerful when she'd never been one to get excited about weddings. Could be because she never had a mother to talk to about them and didn't have many girlfriends. And no way her dad would have a conversation about such a girly thing, plus her grandmothers were both gone, as was her one aunt.

Peggy nodded enthusiastically. "Brendan and Jenna are getting married in March, and Brendan has already petitioned to adopt Karlie. She's Jenna's four-year-old daughter. Jenna's husband died."

"Now, Peg," Russ said. "Toni doesn't need to hear the entire family genealogy in one sitting. She's had a long day."

"And here I was planning to talk about Sierra's baby next." Peggy grinned at her husband.

Toni honestly liked hearing about the family. It took her mind off her own situation. Plus, she loved learning more about Clay and how he'd grown up. From seeing his parents, she understood why he was such a well-adjusted guy.

"In fact." Russ stood. "Now that you know Clay is fine, we should be getting out of their hair."

She looked up at her husband. "But I've barely had a chance to talk to Toni."

"I'm sure you'll see her again." He took Peggy's hand and lifted her to her feet.

She glanced between Clay and Toni, mining for information, but Toni had no idea what she was searching for. Her gaze fixed on Clay. "Don't miss Sunday dinner, and please bring Toni."

"We'll be staying at the beach house. It's closer to tonight's crime scene. And before you say anything, all the guys will be staying with us. That is, if it's okay with you that we use the place."

"Of course it is," Russ said. "I always love being there in the winter. Like the beach a whole lot more when it's raining and the wind is blowing the waves in."

"But you'll all come back for dinner." Peggy issued the statement in a tone Toni wouldn't dare to argue with. Peggy kissed him on the cheek and drew him close for a hug. "Be careful. And keep Toni safe."

"Always." He pulled back.

Peggy came over to Toni and squeezed her shoulder. Oddly, Toni wished for a hug of her own, even though she wasn't much of a hugger.

"I'm so glad to have met you." Peggy gave Toni another one of what seemed to be her very frequent smiles. "Please let me know if there's anything you might want for dinner on Sunday, and I'll be glad to make it for you."

"I don't know—"

"Of course you'll be there." Peggy smiled again.

Russ handed Peggy a bright red coat from the end of the couch. With a flick of her wrists, she tossed it over her shoulders and headed for the door.

"Night," Russ said, following her.

Toni watched them leave.

When the door closed, Clay turned to Toni. "Sorry about that. I had no idea they'd be here."

"It was fun to meet them, and now I understand a bit more about you."

"You mean why I'm a lunatic?" He laughed.

*No. why you're the special person you are.*

And why working together to find Hibbard was going to be so very difficult if she didn't find a way to gain control of her growing feelings.

~

Clay packed a bag for the night and decided he might as well prepare for the next few days too. He didn't like the reason for their trip, but they would be headed to one of his favorite places—the beach house handed down from his grandparents. He had no idea how many days to pack for, but the house had a washer and dryer, so he could do laundry if needed.

He closed the duffle and changed the sheets on his bed for Toni. Warmth curled in his heart just thinking about her sleeping in his bed. It was almost like an unspoken connection between them.

He shook his head. He'd been taking hints from his mother for too many years to find a wife, and he needed to forget about anything developing between him and Toni. They would always have the memory of losing her father to overcome to be together, and he doubted she'd dealt with it. After all, it was clear tonight that she hadn't gotten over losing her mother, and how many years had passed?

He shoved the dirty sheets into the hamper in the bathroom. Put out fresh towels and took a minute to clean the sink with a disinfecting wipe. He wasn't the neatest of guys, not like his brother Brendan, but he wasn't a slob either. None of them would disappoint their mother that way.

He chuckled. To anyone watching the family from a distance, they might think the guys were all henpecked. Truth was, they often did things out of respect for their parents. Their mom and dad raised them with the utmost care and compassion, and each of the kids wanted to make them proud and repay them by becoming the adults their parents had hoped they would be.

His phone rang, and he dug it from his pocket to see Kelsey's name on his screen.

"Hey, Kelsey. What's up?" he asked, assuming her late-night call would be related to the body they'd found.

"Just a heads up." She sounded very alert despite the time of night. "The FBI called me in to recover the body at the high school, and I've done a preliminary assessment."

"Glad to hear they chose the most qualified person in the area for the recovery."

"Thanks to Hunter," she said, referring to Hunter Lane, an FBI agent who'd married Maya, the Veritas Center's toxicology and controlled substances expert last year. "He caught the investigation and persuaded Adair, who's heading it up, to go outside of their agency and call me so they could get things moving forward."

*Perfect.* Hunter might be a good source for them. "I'll be sure to thank him, but that's not why you're calling, is it?"

"No, it's not. Adair told me of your involvement, along with his agent, Toni Long. And he made it clear that neither of you are a part of the official investigation. Which means I won't be able to share any information with you. I wanted to let you know right up front so there won't be any hard feelings when I refuse."

Clay fisted his free hand. "I understand."

"Sorry, I wish we weren't bound by the rules of engagement, but we are."

"Hey, don't worry about it. I get it. I'm just glad you're the one doing the recovery. Means it'll be done right and the girl will have the best chance at finding justice."

"Girl?" Her voice went up. "Someone told you it was a girl?"

"Nah, I'm assuming it is. The remains were small, the shirt feminine, and with girls being trafficked at the school, it seemed to make sense."

"I can't confirm that, of course." She paused for a moment. "But you *do* make a lot of sense."

He couldn't tell if she was indeed confirming the body belonged to a girl or simply saying his logic wasn't faulty. If he asked, she wouldn't confirm it either way. "Thanks for the head's up."

"Sure thing. And good luck with your investigation."

He didn't correct her assumption, just said good-bye and took his bag into the family room. Toni was sitting on the couch looking at her phone. He was still uncomfortable about his mother's forward behavior. He'd seen it directed at Harper and Jenna, so he should've expected it. She instantly mothered every person any one of them brought home. It'd been far more embarrassing in high school, though. Even if their mom had been their teacher, they still participated in homeschooling groups.

Toni looked up, her eyes troubled.

Clay set his suitcase near the exit. "Everything okay?"

"Just trying to find out who's working the investigation." She shoved her phone into her pocket. "I've been getting the runaround."

"Adair's lead and Hunter's his wingman."

She blinked a few times. "And how do you know that?"

"Got a call from the forensic anthropologist at Veritas." He shared the gist of Kelsey's call.

She frowned. "So we've got a challenge before we even begin."

"Hey." He dropped onto the couch next to her. "You've

got five former law enforcement officers working with you. We'll figure this out."

"Still, it would help if I could get someone on the inside of the investigation to help with official records or documents if we need them." She clasped her hands together.

"We've solved two big cases recently without an inside source. We can do this one, too." He made sure he sounded positive, though he had his doubts.

She took a long breath and pinned her focus to him. "How can you sound so confident? Especially on an investigation we couldn't close when we *did* have access to all the databases and files?"

He returned the same focus her way. "Because we have to figure it out. Your life could depend on it."

# 6

After a sleepless night, Toni stepped off the elevator with Clay and entered the Nighthawk Security office. A wall just inside cordoned off a small reception area where a perky redhead Toni put in her early thirties with big green eyes and a ready smile sat behind an aged wood desk.

Clay stopped by the desk. "Toni Long. Meet our receptionist, Stella Carpenter."

Stella held out a freckled hand. "Nice to meet you, Agent Long. I heard we're working with you on an investigation."

"Please call me Toni," she said.

Stella smiled. "They're all inside waiting for you. Aiden's chomping at the bit to get going."

"We best get in there. Hold all calls, please." Clay opened the door and stood back.

Toni stepped into the wide-open space and found the brothers sitting at a long live-edge table with eight chairs and black steel legs. Three flat-screen TVs were mounted on the wall behind the table. Industrial in design, the space had exposed metal ducts and beams. A small office took up one wall, and cubicles lined the back of the room.

No longer in shock from a snake, she took a good look at

Clay's brothers. Thankfully, their expressions were more relaxed today. Still, she had to dig up confidence to walk into this fierce group of men.

"Glad you could make it. When you were late, we all figured you might've gotten locked in a closet again." Aiden grinned, and his brothers chuckled.

Clay fired a testy look their way, silencing them all.

Toni wished the brothers weren't teasing Clay, but she couldn't do anything about it except change the subject. Her attention went to a golden lab sitting on the floor by Erik. Interesting to see Erik had chosen a dog with his same light coloring.

She went over to the dog. "And you must be Pong."

He looked up at Erik, his eyes big.

"It's okay, boy," Erik said. "You can say hi."

Pong shoved his snout under her hand, and she dropped to the floor to pet him. "Aren't you a pretty boy."

"Takes after his owner." Erik laughed.

She smiled up at him for only a flash before she returned her attention to the dog. She'd loved dogs since she played with the neighbor's poodle, named Sprinkles, and she wasn't kidding when she'd told Clay she wanted one someday. She would have to change jobs for that to happen, and she wasn't ready to make a change. Maybe wouldn't ever be ready. She loved being an agent.

She kept petting Pong's soft fur but looked at Erik. "Why a Lab?"

"Temperament. Sniffer dogs need to be methodical in their searches. Be calm, handle confined spaces, and be around a lot of people and not get easily excited. Labs fit that profile."

"Our family gives him a lot of practice with the last one." Clay grinned.

"That we do." Erik laughed.

"We should get started," Aiden said.

She reluctantly got up and wondered if Clay would ever want a dog. Or children, which would mean an even bigger commitment to time off. She might love dogs, but children were foreign to her, and she didn't know if she ever wanted to be a mother.

Embarrassed at the route her thoughts were taking in front of his siblings, she slipped into the nearest chair and took her time getting her phone out of her purse and setting it on the table.

Clay went to the whiteboard, but the door opened, and Sierra stepped in. The dark circles were gone from under her eyes, and she had a spring in her step. "Don't mean to intrude, but I have a couple of things for you."

She handed a flash drive to Erik. "Will you put the slideshow up on the TV?"

Erik inserted the drive in his computer. A photo of one of the high school bedrooms filled a screen. Toni's stomach churned at the sight.

"We all saw this last night," Clay said. "What are you seeing that we aren't?"

"Next picture, please, Erik." Sierra took a seat at the table as he advanced the slide. "This image is the same as the first one, but Nick cropped and enhanced it for me. You can clearly make out the carving on the inside of the bedpost."

Sierra looked at Toni. "Nick's our cyber expert and handles everything computer related for us and, Erik takes care of computer needs for this team."

Erik frowned. "I could've enhanced this for you."

"Nick pulled an all-nighter and was in his lab. You were still sleeping."

Erik clicked the arrow, and it advanced to a close-up of a

bedpost. Engraved into the wood was a tiny crown above back-to-back Rs.

"It's him." Toni fired an excited look at Clay. "It really is Hibbard. He's involved. It's the same bed as the video we have from Safe Harbor."

"How can you be sure?" Drake leaned forward.

"Hibbard's first name is Rich, and he goes by Richey Rich from the cartoon." Clay sounded excited about the lead too. "He uses their family logo—the double Rs you see on the screen—which proves his involvement."

Sierra gave them all a satisfied smile. "I also analyzed the notes you both received. The paper matches and both were printed on the same printer."

"How can you tell?" Clay asked.

"Erik." She wiggled her finger, and he advanced the slides again.

She stood and stepped over to the screen where the corner of the note had been magnified. She pointed at the edge. "An old dot matrix printer was used to create the notes. You can see the perforations on the side of the page where they've removed the tab that feeds the paper into the printer."

"We had one of those when we were kids," Erik said. "I remember the fanfold paper and how the pins on the side grabbed it and pulled it through."

"Exactly," Sierra said. "And the next slide will tell you how I know they were the same printer."

Erik tapped a key on his laptop, and the slide advanced to a close-up of the words *high school*.

"As you can see, a dot matrix printer creates letters by connecting dots together. In this example, the g in high is missing the dot in the right corner. It's the same everywhere the letter appears in the document."

She looked at Erik. "Last slide, please."

He advanced to a slide that looked exactly like the prior one.

"The first g I showed you was on Clay's note. This is a close-up of Toni's note."

"They're the same," Clay said.

Sierra nodded. "The specified arrival time is different in the notes, but the same printer generated them."

"I still don't get why we were sent to the closet," Clay said. "Was it just to kill us?"

Brendan leaned back. "What if one person sent the note and another person tried to kill you? The first person wanted you to find the body and the rooms. They knew you'd search the whole building, but the closet is easier to describe than an unidentified room. The second person found out about the note bringing you there and decided to kill you before you could report it to anyone."

"That makes sense," Clay said. "But something that doesn't make sense is why Hibbard would leave the beds and other items behind."

"Maybe he didn't have time to move things," Drake suggested. "All he had time for was to get the girls out of there."

"Could be," Clay said.

Sierra looked at Clay. "You might want to give Malone a call. She works with runaways. Maybe she'd heard something about this."

"Sounds like a good idea." Clay shifted to face Toni. "Malone is Reed's sister, and a defense attorney."

"If you don't have any questions for me," Sierra said, "I have other photos to review."

"Can you send them to me?" Toni asked. "If Hibbard really did leave in a hurry, Clay and I might recognize something from Safe Harbor."

"I knew one of you would ask." Sierra held out the flash drive. "They're all on here."

"Thank you." Toni loved Sierra's proactive attitude. If only she'd been allowed to keep the forensic samples she collected instead of turning everything over to the FBI.

"Okay, gotta get back to the lab." Sierra's eyes tightened, and her focus traveled around the table. "You guys be careful out there. Someone who would traffic young girls like this won't hesitate to take you out without a second thought."

After Sierra closed the door behind her, Clay knew he had to tell the story of Safe Harbor. He didn't want to share the information on such a gruesome investigation, but his brothers needed to hear about Hibbard's deviant ways. And they needed all the facts to remain safe.

He took a wide stance and resisted crossing his arms. "Hibbard was on ICE's radar for six months before the task force launched Operation Safe Harbor. We had very little information on him at that time, but an informant who escaped from him told us how he worked. He and his men would befriend or romance uneducated teens in Mexico, then promise a new life in Oregon and smuggled them into the United States. Instead, they put the girls to work as prostitutes. From there, Hibbard started grooming homeless teens in Portland and adding them to his stable."

"The informant was one of his original girls," Toni took over. "Heidi said his guys would take every penny the girls earned, giving them only a small allowance to buy things from the store he set up for them. Things like shampoo, soap, toothpaste. Nothing extra. Just the basics. He kept them in line through physical and sexual abuse and by threatening their families."

"Even worse," Clay said, so Toni didn't have to, "she told us that several of the girls had children with the Hibbard men. The men didn't care about the kids. Not at all. In fact, they threatened to take the children if the girls didn't cooperate."

Aiden gritted his teeth. "That's disgusting."

Clay couldn't find his voice to agree, so he nodded.

"Heidi also told us Hibbard appointed certain girls as group leaders," Toni said. "He gave them extra perks to do things like post commercial sex ads online and book cross-country travel for men to engage in sex with the girls. He even tattooed the crown logo on their bodies to show they belonged to him. And they were trained to lie about everything. His motto is, you snitch, you die."

Aiden shook his head. "Sounds like a real piece of work. So why couldn't you bring him in?"

Toni sighed. "Trust me, we tried. How we tried. Heidi even led us to one of the houses he used, but he'd moved on. Likely because she'd escaped, and he feared she would turn on him."

"Over the course of our six-month investigation, we'd get hints of him in the area," Clay said. "Photos of him and three of his victims appeared on the dark web, which is where we got the picture of the bedpost. We believed other photos were of his victims and johns, but could never prove it. The guy's smart. Real smart."

Brendan clenched his hands on the table. "What's the creep's background?"

Clay took a long breath. "He came from money. His dad, Rich Hibbard Sr., made a fortune in day trading. Rich Jr. worked with his dad for a few years but then did something to cause his dad to cut him off. We've never found out the reason, since the dad died ten years ago, and Junior isn't talking. When the dad died, he gave all his money to charity. Junior contested the will and lost. That's when he basically disappeared, and we assume he started his own business."

Drake shook his head. "Guess he got his entrepreneurial spirit from the dad, but man, what a business to choose."

"Maybe he chose it because there aren't any startup costs other than the incidental money needed to woo the first woman," Aiden suggested.

"It's often said that trafficking women is easier than the drug trade," Toni said. "You have to replace drugs, but you can sell girls over and over."

Clay gritted his teeth. "One thing I know for sure. Finding a sign of him out in Rugged Point is a strong lead. Maybe we couldn't catch him because he was working a totally new market. If so, we need to investigate human trafficking along the coast."

Clay looked at Drake. "Sierra's right. Malone might be able to help. Since you've worked with her on prior abuse situations, can you call her? See if she knows anything about this, and if not, ask her to keep her ears out?"

"Sure thing," Drake said.

The door opened, and Stella poked her head in. "I'm sorry. I know you didn't want any interruptions, but Blake Jenkins says he needs to talk to Clay right away, and he's kind of insistent."

"Send him in," Clay said and looked at his brothers. "He was calling Sheriff Winfield to see if he'll talk to us."

Blake marched into the room looking very much like the former sheriff he was. He was over six-feet tall with dark hair and a muscular build. He wore the same black tactical pants all the guys liked to wear and a fleece jacket with the Veritas Center's logo embroidered on the chest.

"Sorry to interrupt." He stepped to the end of the table and held out his hand to Toni. "You must be Toni."

She shook hands. "Nice to meet you, and thank you for your help."

He gave her a tight smile. "No problem."

"What's so urgent?" Clay asked.

"Hunter's already called Trent and has an appointment at one. But Trent will see you this morning—if you can get there before Hunter."

Clay looked at his watch. "You know we can't do that. The drive alone would make us late."

"No worries," Blake said. "I called Gage, and you're in luck. He's in town for a doctor's appointment with Hannah. You can catch a ride in their helo if you book it to the helipad."

Clay jumped to his feet, dropped his car keys on the table, and looked at his brothers. "My car's filled with boxes of records we'll need in Rugged Point. There's another stack in the closet in my spare room. Make sure you bring them and our usual equipment."

He locked gazes with Toni, whose eyes flashed with excitement. "C'mon. We have a helo to catch."

# 7

Clay found the county sheriff's office to be small but organized with a security window in the lobby manned by an officer who called the sheriff. Trent marched out of a doorway next to the window. He had a definite swagger and perfect posture, exuding confidence that Clay respected.

"Sheriff Winfield," he said, holding out his hand to Toni first. "Call me Trent."

"Special Agent Toni Long with the FBI." She gave Trent a wide smile.

Clay almost snorted, considering they weren't meeting with Trent in any official capacity. Mentioning her FBI role could be misleading. Maybe she wanted that.

He jutted his hand out to Clay. "Blake tells me you're former ICE."

Clay nodded and waited for a negative comment about Clay having left law enforcement.

"Seems like a lot of the good ones are leaving for private employment." Trent shook his head, his blond hair moving with the motion. "I never thought I'd see the day Blake would jump ship, but the guy's happier, that's for sure."

Clay was uncertain how to respond. "Stresses are different, but the stakes are still high. Like in this investigation. I'd like to bring you up to speed and pick your brain."

"We can meet in our situation room. Follow me." He tapped a code into a keypad by the door and held the door for Toni. Once in the hallway, Trent eased past her and took them to a small conference room.

One wall held a large flat-screen TV, and above it three smaller TVs were tuned to news programs. Computer stations ringed the walls below, and a long table took up the middle of the room. The remaining walls were covered by a map of the county and whiteboards.

"Nice set up." Clay pulled out a chair for Toni.

She eyed him and chose a different chair. He almost laughed. She was so independent and out to prove she was one of the guys. She saw him helping with her chair—something his mother insisted all of her sons did—as a negative. He dropped into the one he'd pulled out.

Trent sat across from them. "Tell me how I can help."

Clay met the man's intense gaze. "You must know what went down at the high school last night."

"I do, but no thanks to you calling in the feds before me."

"Sorry. It's my fault." Toni smiled at Trent, and the sheriff's tight expression relaxed a notch. "I work violent crimes for the Bureau, and I thought they were best able to handle the investigation."

"It's done." He clenched his jaw and released it. "We reached a compromise. I'm taking lead on the murder, and your team is working the trafficking angle."

Clay hadn't heard this, but it made sense as the high school was in Trent's jurisdiction. As such, the entire investigation fell under his command, but the FBI didn't usually handle murders unless it was a serial killer. "You're still using Dr. Dunbar at Veritas for that, right?"

"She's finished recovering the body, so it only makes sense to have her analyze the bones." He locked onto Clay's gaze. "But I've reminded her of her contractual terms with the county not to disclose information to anyone but me."

Clay clasped his hands under the table. "She reminded me of that as well."

"Good. Then we're all on the same page."

"Has anything happened at the high school prior to this?"

"The usual issues with kids partying in the summer, but nothing in the last few months."

"Because we were both summoned to the school," Clay said, "we believe this is related to a human trafficking investigation we worked as a task force."

"Tell me about that."

Clay gave Trent the details on Hibbard. "Toni's father was killed in an op that went sideways. We were trying to bring in Olin Kraus, Hibbard's lieutenant, when Mr. Long arrived and inserted himself in the op by knocking on the suspect's door. An unknown subject opened fire from a hidden location. Took Mr. Long and Kraus out. Long was a retired DEA agent, turned PI, and was in town visiting Toni."

Trent raised an eyebrow and looked at Toni.

She shifted under the study. "I have no idea why he showed up or how he even knew where I was. Or maybe it was just a weird coincidence. One thing I do know is that my dad didn't usually take vacations. Even when he retired from the DEA and went to work for his friend, Dad gave a new meaning to the word workaholic. I was typically the one who went to see him, so it looks like he had another reason to be in town."

"Could it be work related, but he didn't let his supervisor in on it?" Trent asked.

"I don't think so," Toni said. "I went to see Vance Danby after Dad died. Vance owns Danby Investigations in Virginia, where my dad worked after he retired. Vance said Dad's caseload included three pending divorces and one cheating husband. Nothing like this and no connection to Kraus. I boxed up my dad's personal things from his office, and I've been through it all a million times. Found nothing to help."

Clay didn't know how she could talk so matter-of-factly about her father's death, but she was the ultimate professional, and she'd probably compartmentalized the loss like she'd done with her mother's accident.

"Did your father know about your investigation?" Trent asked.

"I'd said I was part of a task force focused on human trafficking but never gave him details."

Trent rested his hands on the table. "Not knowing what he was up to must be driving you crazy."

"You have no idea," she said, and for the first time in this interview, her tone confirmed that she was troubled. "It's like one of those cases that you can't close, only worse. Much worse."

Trent shifted his focus to Clay. "And how does my agency fit in with this investigation?"

"We believed Hibbard was solely working out of Portland, but evidence from the school suggests we might be wrong," Clay said. "We hope you can tell us if you have issues in the area with human trafficking."

Trent pressed his hands flat on the table. "We have a problem, that's for sure. Nothing like Portland, but it goes on. In fact, a tri-county task force made a bust a few days ago. Guy named Jason Rader was using social media to groom underage girls. He pretended to be a tech millionaire. Promised the girls a great lifestyle with him at the beach."

Trent paused for a moment. "He's the typical offender. White male, in the twenty-five to forty-five age range. Has strong computer skills. Good looking guy, and even in his thirties, he managed to suck the girls in. Two older men working with him pimped the girls out, insulating him from arrest until one of his girls came forward to report him. Social media evidence corroborates her story, so the DA is willing to roll the dice in court to take that scumbag off the streets."

Clay glanced at Toni. "Sounds like Hibbard. Except he has more than two people working with him."

"Did you learn anything else about Rader?" Toni asked.

"He had a boatload of cash at the beach house he was renting and no legal employment." Trent leaned back. "I have to say, it's very satisfying to rid the streets of a guy like him. Now we need to be sure he pays for each girl he conned and goes away for a long time. Problem is, he retained a high-powered attorney. Could make things more difficult."

"Any way we can talk to him?" Toni asked.

Trent frowned, and Clay waited for him to say no. "Visiting hours are open to anyone."

"Sure," Clay said. "But he has to put us on his visitor list, and we need to be approved. That takes time. Time we don't have. And even if we did get approved, he isn't likely to agree to a visit from us."

"He's still in county lockup. Let me see what I can arrange." Trent stood. "But don't hold your breath. His lawyer might stand in your way."

"We'd appreciate any help you can give," Toni said.

"I'll be right back." Trent strode out of the room, his black boots squeaking on the tile floor.

"He seems like a stand-up guy." Toni's focus still lingered on the door where Trent had exited.

"That's what Blake says, and if Blake approves, you know he's topnotch."

An older woman with silvery blond hair poked her head into the room. "I'm Lorraine, Sheriff Winfield's assistant. Can I get you some coffee or something else to drink while you wait for him?"

"Not for me, but thanks," Clay said.

Toni gave her a practiced smile. "I'm good too."

Lorraine nodded. "Clay, since you work in the same building as Blake, could you tell him we miss him and say hi."

"Will do."

"Oh, and make sure to tell him Trent is doing a fine job. Blake should be proud of the way he brought him up through the ranks."

"He'll be glad to hear that," Clay said, getting the idea that this woman might be a gossiper, which he could use to his advantage. "Say, you don't know anything about Jason Rader, do you?"

"The guy they locked up for trafficking those poor girls?" She tsked. "I saw his name often enough when he was a teenager. He was in and out of juvie for all kinds of offenses. His mother split when he turned sixteen, and his daddy, Fritz, didn't give a hoot about what the kid got up to. Fritz was too busy drinking his life away over losing Ursula. Not that she was such a catch. Beautiful woman, but she liked to party and had a reputation with men in the area."

Lorraine had just saved Clay hours of research. "Fritz still live around here?"

"Sure thing. Right out on the highway heading back to Portland. East side of the road. Can't miss his house. Back when Prince was a superstar, Fritz painted it purple and hasn't ever changed it. House sits back from the road, but not far enough to hide *that* color." She looked like she wanted to tsk again but held back.

"Was the mother ever seen again?" Clay asked.

"Nope. Fritz said she left him and they never reported her missing. She didn't have any relatives that anyone knew of, so there was nobody else to request we look into it. Still, if you ask me, there was something fishy going on there."

"Like what?" Toni asked. "You think Fritz might've killed her?"

Lorraine shrugged. "He has a mean streak. Wouldn't surprise me at all."

"Who was sheriff when she left?" Clay asked.

"Raintree was in office."

"Is he still living?"

She shook her head. "Passed away nearly ten years ago, but Sheriff Ziegler's still going strong, and he was a detective at that time so he might know more."

"You telling tales again, Lorraine?" Trent's deep voice boomed behind her.

She spun. "Nothing I wouldn't say in front of your face, you know that."

"I do indeed, but it doesn't mean it's something I'd want you to tell people."

She waved a hand. "Best get back to my desk."

She disappeared, but the sound of her heels clicking on the tile rang in the air.

"She's been the admin here for so many years that she sometimes thinks she runs the place. Who knows. Maybe she does." Trent chuckled, and it was clear he was fond of her. "Wish I had good news on Rader, but as suspected, the lawyer's controlling his visits."

"Thanks for trying," Clay said, trying to hide his disappointment. "Would you keep your ears to the ground on Hibbard?"

"I can do you one better," Trent said. "I'll check in with the nearby counties to see if he's on anyone's radar. And ask about the high school. It sits right on the county border, so seems like one of us should've seen something going on there."

"But it's way back from the road," Toni said. "And Hibbard had blackout drapes on all the windows."

"Yeah, but still." He planted his hands on his hips. "Grinds me that we missed something like that going on right under our noses. And now we'll have the feds breathing down our necks. Nobody wants that." He cast a wary glance at Toni. "Sorry, I know you're one of them, but we don't like anyone coming in and pointing fingers at us."

"I wish I could say that won't happen, but I can't." Toni came to her feet, keeping her focus pinned to Trent. "I'd appreciate it if you didn't tell anyone we were here."

"I won't volunteer the information, but if Agent Lane asks, I won't lie."

Clay walked beside Toni to the exit. "Since we can't visit the son, let's go talk to the dad."

"My thoughts exactly." She smiled at him, a glorious happy smile he'd seen often before her dad was killed, and his heart went *twang*.

He started to lift his hand to squeeze her arm, but lowered it before he took them into the personal realm. They stepped outside and he got them heading in the right direction.

Within thirty minutes, he was turning into a long driveway, a small purple farmhouse sitting at the end. The paint color was an even brighter purple than Clay expected, though much of the paint had weathered and flaked away.

He killed the engine and leaned forward, letting his gaze wander the property, studying every detail.

Home visits could be dangerous. An officer never knew

who was behind the front door. The occupant could be afraid. Mad. Combative. Armed. The condition of a house and property could tell an officer a lot about the people inside. Like the abandoned tractor near the house. The lopsided chicken coop on the side. Cars on blocks and two rusty old motorcycles.

And the house itself.

This one was sad and neglected. Maybe Rader was lazy. Maybe he didn't have enough money to fix the place up. Maybe he just didn't care. In any event, he could be defensive from the moment they knocked on the door.

"Looks safe to proceed." Clay got out and Toni joined him.

A hawk soared overhead, swooped down in the side yard, and came up with a rat dangling from its beak.

Toni shuddered. "In my opinion, rats are second to snakes in things God should never have created."

"I don't know," Clay said, marching up to the door. "It's obviously not a nighthawk, but we named our agency after hawks, so if I believed in signs, this bird could be a good one."

He knocked on the worn wooden door and listened for approaching footsteps. Nothing. Listened for a television or radio. Nothing. Listened for any sound. Nothing.

"Looks like he's not home," Toni said.

"Truck's in the driveway."

"He could've gotten a ride with someone."

Clay pounded harder. The catch released, and the door swung in revealing pry marks on the jamb where the door had been forced.

Death's rancid odor oozed out of the house, and Clay lurched back.

Toni cupped a hand over her mouth and nose. "Guess he's home after all, but I doubt he'll be talking."

# 8

There was no question. A person had died, and Clay mentally prepared himself for what awaited them in the house. Nothing compared to the almost caustic odor of decomp. Based on the intensity, Fritz Rader had been gone for days.

"We probably should call Trent." He leaned against the wall and put a bootie on that they'd retrieved from the SUV. "But he won't likely share details on a new murder investigation."

"We need to get a firsthand look before you make that call." Toni dug out her phone. "Might not be Fritz in there, so I'm going to find a picture of him for comparison."

"Good thinking." He put on his other bootie, keeping his eyes alert for any danger.

"Got it." She showed him the photo of a guy who looked like his son and slid the phone back into her pocket.

"The mole by his nose should make him easy to ID," Clay said.

She nodded and put booties over leather loafers the same color as the black suit she'd chosen to wear again today. She continued to dress in work attire, but he'd seen her lock her agency-issued gun in the safe at her apartment and withdraw a different weapon last night.

He drew his gun. "If you'll wait here, I'll clear the place."

She planted her hands on her hips. "I can do it."

"I know, but would you mind if I do?" He did his best to ask and not demand, but the last thing he wanted right now was to send her into this place before someone cleared it.

She stared at him for a long moment. "I guess not."

He didn't wait for her to change her mind but pushed the door all the way open. He hated that she even had to be a part of this horrific scene. He wouldn't want any person he cared about to view this body, but if he asked her to sit it out, she might think he was treating her differently because she was a woman. Then to prove he wasn't discriminating against her because of her gender, he'd have to admit the depth of his feelings for her. Neither of them needed to talk about his feelings. Especially since he didn't actually know what they were.

He stepped inside to find a man lying on his back on the worn linoleum floor near a sagging recliner, flies swarming his body. No pool of blood, but plenty of other body fluids. His face was bloated and discolored, but Clay could still confirm a match to the photo Toni had showed him. The guy was thin with blond hair like his son and had a large mole by his nose.

Clay moved on, clearing a small kitchen and three bedrooms. One held a large birdcage but no bird. Clay didn't waste any time moving back to the front door. "We're clear."

He holstered his weapon, put on his gloves, and took a few pictures in the family room before forcing himself to move closer to the body when everything in him screamed to run the other way. He squatted and got a close-up look at bruises circling Fritz's neck. "Looks like he was strangled."

Toni squatted on the other side. "Face is distorted but not too terrible. It's Fritz Rader all right."

"Based on the blowflies, it looks like he's been here a few days." Clay stood.

"Jason was arrested a few days ago. You think Rader was part of his son's group? Or the kid killed him?"

"Trent didn't mention any connection to the trafficking, but if so, someone might have wanted to shut him up. Maybe the two guys working with Jason."

She tilted her head. "We need to start referring to the son as Jason and to the dad as Rader, or it'll get confusing."

Clay nodded. "Wish we could check his pockets for a phone and ID, but I wouldn't want to have to tell Trent we touched the body."

A noise sounded behind Clay, and he spun, reaching for his gun. Something white waddled out from behind the couch in the corner. A bird. A big white bird with pink feathers around a black beak.

He looked at Toni. "I saw a cage in the back bedroom."

"Hello there," Toni said to the bird.

"Hello," the bird replied.

"Did you hear that?" Clay shook his head. "It talks."

"It's a cockatoo," Toni said. "A type of parrot, so that makes sense."

"We should close the door. Don't want it getting out."

Toni backed up and pushed the door closed with her foot.

She walked closer to the bird. It ruffled its feathers and backed up. She squatted close to him.

"It's okay," she said, her tone soothing. "You must be afraid."

"Good bye, good bye, good bye," he said.

"Are you talking about Fritz?"

"Fritz. Fritz. Bird loves Fritz."

"Is your name Bird?"

"Bird. Bird."

"You're a good boy."

"Good boy, Bird."

Toni looked up at Clay. "I suppose he might usually have free run of the house, but we should try to put him in his cage so he doesn't get out when deputies arrive."

"Just a second, and I'll help." Clay finished taking pictures.

A tray table sat next to the recliner, a beer can in a cozy, and a large ashtray filled with butts sitting on the scratched top. A ratty couch was on the far side of the room and that was it. No pictures on the wall. No knickknacks. Nothing. Just dust bunnies.

He stepped to the ashtray, poked through the contents, and took a few pictures. "Pack on the table says he smoked Marlboros, but we have a few hand-rolled butts in here."

"Too bad we can't take one for DNA, and I'm not comfortable swabbing a butt as they're difficult to do and the water we'd use could change the composition."

"It's times like these that I wish I was still in law enforcement. Not finding the dead body part, but these butts could be from our killer." He picked one up and sniffed. "Not pot."

"Jason might be a smoker and the butts are from him, if he ever visited his dad. If Trent hasn't had Jason's Facebook page taken down, I'll search the photos, and maybe we can determine if these butts are from him."

"Sounds like a good plan."

"Let's get this guy in a room." She held out her arm to Bird, who sat bobbing his head. He hopped closer and jumped on her arm. She frowned.

"What's wrong?"

"His beak has blood on it." She slowly stood.

"Is he hurt?"

She looked him over. "Not that I can see."

"Maybe he pecked someone."

"The killer?" Hope raised her tone.

"Could be." Clay stared at the blood and took a moment to think. "I have swabs in my car. We could collect the tiniest of samples for Sierra and Emory to process."

"I'm okay with that. As long as it really is a small sample so there's plenty left for the forensics staff."

"You take this guy into the bedroom, and I'll grab the swabs." He waited for her to head down the hallway with the bird before bolting out the door.

This could be the lead they needed to get ahead in their investigation. *If* Rader was connected to Hibbard. A big if right now.

Clay grabbed a few swabs and tiny tubes of distilled water, put it all in his pocket, and rushed back inside. The bird's squawks led Clay to the back bedroom.

He knocked on the closed door. "Okay to come in."

"Yes," Toni replied. "But move slowly."

He opened the door a few inches at a time, slid in, and closed the door behind him. The large octagonal metal cage he'd glimpsed earlier sat in the corner of the room. The food and water dishes were empty. Probably the only reason blood remained on Bird's beak.

"There's blood on his talons too," Toni said.

Bird ruffled his feathers. "Stupid bird. Stupid bird."

"Obviously Rader wasn't real kind to Bird." Clay opened the swab container and wetted it with a drop of water, then handed it to Toni. "I think you have the best shot at not upsetting him."

She slowly pressed the tip of the swab against his beak, and it came away red.

"Perfect." Clay took the swab and put it back in the plastic tube.

They repeated the process with his talons, and Clay zipped his jacket pocket to keep the samples safe. "Can you get him into his cage?"

"Only one way to know." She eased forward.

"Hungry." Bird bobbed on her arm.

She slowly reached her arm out, and the bird hopped onto the perch in the cage. She moved at the speed of a snail and got the door closed and secured.

"For a while there I had visions of a bird permanently secured to my arm." She chuckled.

He smiled with her for a moment, nearly getting lost in her eyes, but it was hard to forget the reason they were in this house. "We should work our way through the house to look for other evidence, then get Trent out here so someone can feed Bird."

"Poor guy. Too bad food and water could contaminate his beak or I would give him some now."

"Bird hungry," he squawked from the cage. "Bird hungry."

Feeling bad for Bird, Clay headed to the kitchen, Toni following. He used his cell to take a wide photo of the old pea-green cupboards, ancient appliances, and an empty eat-in area. "The lack of furniture is odd when he'd lived here for so long."

"Maybe he was getting rid of things."

A frying pan on the stove held shriveled burgers and moldy buns sat on a plate.

Clay turned to Toni. "Looks like his dinner was interrupted."

"Think he planned to eat both the burgers or was he expecting company?"

"He's not a big guy, but maybe he could eat two burgers."

She opened the refrigerator. "Condiments and a twelve-pack with three cans missing."

Clay looked through the cupboards but found nothing odd. "Let's keep going."

He went back down the hallway to the first bedroom holding a double bed with a worn lavender comforter. He focused his camera on the bed, thinking the comforter was an unusual color for a guy. Maybe it belonged to the missing wife. He opened the closet while Toni pawed through dresser drawers.

"Nothing here," he said.

"Drawers either."

They went down the hall to the second bedroom, this one with a twin-size bed covered with a baseball comforter, and framed baseball posters hung on the walls.

"Maybe Jason's old room," Clay said.

She crossed to the dresser and opened the top drawer. "Whoa. Look."

Clay looked inside to find the drawer brimming with stacks of twenty-dollar bills. "Wow. Whoever killed Rader obviously wasn't looking for money."

She opened the remaining drawers to find them stuffed with cash too.

Clay let out a low whistle. "How much do you think's there?"

She flipped through the bills and looked up. "All total, I'd say sixty grand or more. Why was Rader living in this dump like this when he could afford something much nicer?"

"Based on this bedroom and the fact that Rader's still using the old comforter, maybe it was sentimental reasons. Or..." Clay didn't want to continue, but it had to be said. "Maybe he can't sell the place because the missing wife is still here."

Toni's eyebrow went up. "You mean buried out back or something?"

"Yeah."

"We need to mention that to Trent when we talk to him, but I want to take a look outside before we give him a call." Toni stepped down the hall ahead of Clay.

In the living room, the concentrated smell hit him hard again, and he hurried past the body. Outside, he sucked in fresh air on the way to the tall stockade fence. He opened the rusty side gate to reveal an expansive property with evergreen trees planted in neat rows, tall weeds and grass growing between them.

"Let's check out the garage." Toni slogged through the weeds to a ramshackle garage. She lifted the wide door. The rusty metal groaned on the hinges as the sagging door rolled up. She shone her phone's flashlight inside, revealing stacks of cardboard boxes and worn garden tools.

She set her phone on a pile of boxes and opened the flaps on a box on the next pile. "Miscellaneous household items."

Clay glanced inside to see a mixer with only one beater and stained pans. "Looks like junk. Wonder why he's keeping it?"

"If the house says anything, he's not a packrat or hoarder." She set the box aside and opened the next one.

Stained linens and torn towels. She moved on to the final box and found broken small appliances. She removed a chipped toaster. Jewelry tumbled out.

"Look at this." She held out several of the cheap costume pieces.

"Maybe belonged to his wife."

"The items seem too juvenile." She set down the jewelry and picked up a stack of rusted cake pans. A silver brush, comb, and mirror set rested inside.

"This could be the wife's, I suppose," she said, looking puzzled.

"Otherwise, why would he have it?" Clay reached past her to grab a Sugar Smacks box with a silver frame peeking out of the corner. "I remember when they changed the name to Honey Smacks in the eighties, so this box has to be at least that old."

He drew out a framed photo, brown with age. She took a look and stumbled back.

Clay looked at the photo, his heart rate kicking up. "This is the same picture as the one in your father's boxes."

She gave a wooden nod, and her eyes were tight with unease.

"Who is this?" he asked gently.

"Me and my mom." The words came out on a whisper. "My dad always kept this picture on his desk."

"It looks like your father *is* connected to human trafficking." He locked eyes with Toni. "And we now need to figure out how."

Toni could hardly breathe. She rushed out of the garage. The world spun around her, and she planted her hands on her knees to gulp in the fresh air. Her dad was connected to Fritz Rader. A man who'd likely trafficked young girls. There had to be a connection between Hibbard, and Rader too, and was the reason he showed up at the raid where he died.

"Hey." Clay came up behind her and rested a hand on her back. "We'll figure this out, and when we do, I'm sure your dad will be in the clear. He was likely investigating Rader, and Rader somehow got a hold of the photo."

"But why?" She stared at Clay without really seeing him, her mind a mass of questions. "What good would it do Rader to have my picture?"

Clay's eyes narrowed. "I don't know, but we'll figure it

out. Together."

Would they? Would they really, or was Clay being his usual positive self? Did he really believe his words?

Did it matter? Not really. She wouldn't stop investigating until she had an answer.

She stood up straight, hoping the posture would bring back her confidence like her dad had always taught her. But as she peered into the garage, she was so far from confident it wasn't funny.

She looked at Clay, his eyes filled with compassion. Made her want to cry, but she swallowed away the tears. "I'm glad you're here. I would hate to have discovered this on my own."

He raised a hand as if he planned to touch her, but let it fall. "I'm guessing this is more stressful than finding the body."

Yeah, but she wouldn't cry. Not even if she was off duty. She blinked the tears away and considered their next move. "I can't bear to leave the picture in his things. I don't want to have the detective see it and connect Dad to this."

Clay didn't answer right away, just looked at her as if he regretted what he was about to say. "You know we can't take it, right?"

She did, but her heart screamed not to leave something so personal behind. It would become a piece of evidence, likely to be trotted out in court and put on display. But it wasn't as if she had a choice. Rader and Hibbard had to pay for their crimes, and that meant putting everything back where they'd found it.

"Let's go through the other boxes," she said. "And take pictures of everything."

Clay nodded. "You take the pictures. I'll do the boxes."

"I need to look at everything too. An item might mean something to me that you'd miss." She squeezed his arm.

"But thank you for trying to protect me from anything else we might find."

He rested his hand over hers. "It hurts to see you suffer like this, especially when I can't do a thing about it."

"I'm sorry you have to deal with my personal baggage."

He took her hand in his, his big warm fingers wrapping around hers. "I don't mind. I just want to help."

Tears pricked her eyes for real this time. He was being so kind, she wanted to sink into his arms. He would hold her. No doubt. Give her a chance to collect herself, but allowing that would send the wrong message. She withdrew her hand and went back into the garage. Still, she was desperately craving Clay's strong arms around her, offering comfort. Something she missed after losing her dad.

Sure, she hadn't visited him very often, but a hug from him had made things better. But she wouldn't blur the professional line they'd set. Especially not with proof that her dad was involved in the investigation. It might turn out to be an innocent involvement, but he was connected all the same.

She reached into the box for the photo, jewelry, and brush set and arranged them on a nearby workbench.

"What do you think these items mean?" Clay asked from behind her.

He was close enough that his breath tickled her neck and too close for her fragile state. He could simply put out his arms, she'd turn and be in them.

*Focus.* She dug her phone from her pocket. "Everything is personal. Maybe they're souvenirs from trafficked girls."

"I was thinking the same thing. Except for the picture." The deep timbre of his voice settled around her like a comforting blanket, like the hug she was craving.

She snapped several photos and checked her phone to be sure she'd clearly captured every item. Once done, she shoved her phone in her pocket and started to put things back in the boxes. Clay helped, grabbing the photo, which she appreciated. They returned the boxes they'd reviewed to their proper places and moved to the next stack.

Clay opened the top one and set aside tattered clothing. His focus remained on the box, and he let out a low whistle as he lifted out a stack of pictures. He fanned out the pile, revealing close up shots of young girls, mostly teens, of all ethnicities, shapes, and sizes.

Terror flooding from their eyes was the one thing they had in common. Pain. Sharp. Horrific.

Toni's stomach roiled. Unable to speak, she clamped a hand over her mouth and watched as Clay counted the photos. Some were aged and yellowed. Some were dated in the eighties. Some early nineties. Others didn't have a date stamped on them but looked more current.

Clay kept counting. The numbers grew quickly. *Ten. Twenty-one. Thirty. Forty-eight.*

Each snap of a photo onto the box tightened her stomach, and she had a hard time breathing again. She gulped the musty air, and waited for the final number.

"Fifty-five." Clay shook his head, his eyes blazing with anger.

She steadied herself with a hand on the workbench. "This is horrible. So horrible."

Clay clenched his jaw. "As much as I hate to do it, I'll lay them out and take photos." He moved past her to the workbench. "Then we can have Erik search the internet for matches. I wouldn't be surprised if the results come back as missing or runaways."

Toni nodded but had no idea what to say. Had her father known about these girls and didn't stop it? Worse yet, was he part of it? No. He couldn't be. She didn't believe he would do such a thing. But other people might.

With six of the pictures lying on the scarred and gouged wood, Clay took the first photo. The flash lit up the room and seemed to show her the light.

The best way to help these girls wasn't to get nauseated or lose her breath. Helping them meant identifying them and finding justice for whatever horrific actions were taken against them. No matter who was involved. Finding her dad's killer or finding out what he was involved in was secondary. These lost souls looking at her in horror were top priority now.

"I'll keep going through the box." With renewed purpose, she dug into the items and found female clothing, small-sized, most of it slinky and sexy. She felt dirty just touching the garments, but she would tough it out and take pictures just like Clay was doing.

"Finding anything of interest?" he asked, not looking back.

"Suggestive clothing."

"We need to—"

"Take pictures. Yeah. I got it." She arranged the clothing on nearby boxes and got out her phone, revulsion swirling in her stomach. The photos might not lead them anywhere, but hopefully Trent's forensic team could locate DNA from the clothing to help find the girls.

Toni reached the bottom of the pile.

"No. Just no." She backed away from the box.

Clay hurried over to her. "What is it?"

She pointed in the box. He looked inside, his forehead furrowed.

He looked up, opened and closed his mouth a few times as if he didn't know what to say. Finally he looked her in the eye. "How can this creep have the clothes you're wearing in that picture with your mother?"

# 9

Clay squeezed his fingers on the steering wheel, working hard to eliminate his frustration. He would do just about anything to remove the shock and pain Toni was feeling. But all he'd been able to do was gently lead her to their vehicle and encourage her to get into the passenger seat and close the door while he'd returned everything to the boxes and called Trent.

As expected, Trent wasn't happy that they'd gone into the house and garage, even if they'd worn gloves and booties to protect the scene. He'd sent the closest deputies to the house to take over. Now, as he arrived, lights twirling on the top of his vehicle, his angry expression was evident even through the windshield.

"Wait here," Clay told Toni and got out. He prepared himself for a confrontation with the sheriff and searched for a way to pacify him.

Trent crossed the few feet separating them. He held his elbows wide from his body, his chest thrust out. His nostrils flared. He reminded Clay of a bull ready to attack. Clay would have to do some fast dodging.

"Don't go anywhere," he snapped. "I'll have a look at the scene, and then we'll talk."

"We'll be here." Clay waited for Trent to go inside before sliding behind the wheel.

Toni looked at him. "Trent looks mad."

"As expected."

She dabbed a tissue at her eyes.

She'd been crying. Clay wasn't surprised, but it hurt to see. He hated when any woman was in distress, but seeing Toni, usually so strong, distressed enough to cry? That was an extra punch to the gut. But this wasn't about him at all. It was about her and the personal connection to this creep that had to be shredding her insides.

She angled to face him, mascara smeared below her eyes. "Do we have to tell Trent about the picture and my outfit?"

"Those items won't mean anything without an explanation, and it could be the information he needs to find Rader's killer."

"Still..." Her words fell off with a choking sob.

"Aw, Toni. Don't cry." He took her hand and held it tightly. He wanted to do more. To get out, pull her from the vehicle, and give her a proper hug. But that would be too much for a crime scene with law enforcement present. "It'll be all right. I promise."

"How can you promise?" She pulled her hand free and retrieved a fresh tissue from her purse. "I hate crying like a helpless victim."

"You're far from helpless, but you *are* a victim. And it has to be horrible to see a man we think was trafficking girls in possession of something so personal."

"That's the thing, though." She patted her eyes. "I don't even remember the clothes. Not at all."

"How old were you?"

"My dad said I was nine, so I feel like I should remember."

"You wouldn't remember every outfit, right?"

"No, but my mom is dressed up, so it seems like a special day. Shouldn't I remember something like that? Especially since it was just before she died."

"Did you ever ask about the occasion?"

She nodded. "Dad said he wasn't sure. Mom dodged the question too. I thought it was odd, but after Mom died, it didn't matter anymore. I just enjoyed seeing my mom smiling in the picture."

She opened the visor mirror and used the tissue to remove wayward mascara. "Sadness had often made my mom frown when she didn't think anyone was looking. Not that she was unhappy all the time. She wasn't. But I think something bad must've happened before I was born. After she died, I asked my dad about it. He said she'd had a rough childhood, and they didn't like to talk about it."

She sighed. "I accepted that, as I accepted the way my dad always had to be doing something and keep me busy too. The way he expected perfection from me, but with them both gone, I wish I'd pushed for a better answer."

"After your dad died, did any of your mother's things shed light on her past?"

She shook her head and closed the mirror. "He only kept a few pieces of her jewelry. He gave it to me when I turned twenty-one."

"Do you have any relatives you can ask about the picture? Or anyone who could give you more insight into your parents?"

"My paternal grandpa is still alive, but my dad wasn't very close to him, so I doubt he knows anything. And my mom was an only child. Dad had a sister who never married, and she died about ten years ago. And my grandparents on my mom's side are both gone. Lung cancer. Both of them. Died before I was born."

"Might be worth giving your grandpa a call."

"I can do that."

"What about a family history? Any information on the older generations?"

"Not much." She lifted the visor back into place and shifted to look at him.

"Where did your parents grow up?"

"Dad was born and raised in Portland and lived there until he joined the DEA. Then he and my mom moved to Virginia, where I was raised. My mom was born somewhere on this coast. Not sure where though. She always changed the subject when it came up."

Odd that she knew so little about her family, but he didn't have much information on the older generations in his family either. "Ever considered looking into a genealogy website?"

She twisted her hands together. "I figure there's a good reason Mom wouldn't talk about her past, and I want to remember her and Dad as I knew them, not learn some family secret I can't ever unlearn. Like today. Finding out Dad might be connected to Rader and Hibbard."

Clay was about to say she could work through whatever she learned, but she didn't have the support of a family like he did to help her. "I once thought my family was an open book, but not too long ago, we learned that my dad isn't Sierra's biological father. My mom was pregnant when he met and married her. It was a big shock. To everyone. Sierra freaked out at first, but then she realized it didn't matter in her relationship with Dad. He'd always been her father. Nothing changed that. I've never respected Sierra more."

Toni looked like she might comment, but Trent stepped out of the house, taking their attention.

"It's show time." Clay said. "You up to talking with him?"

She firmed her shoulders. "I will be by the time I reach him."

Clay wanted to give her hand a squeeze. He didn't, just slid out of the car.

Toni joined him near the hood, and they waited as Trent strode toward them. He lifted his phone to his ear to answer. Clay heard him address the person on the call as Sam Griffin and he asked her to process the forensics here.

Trent paused for a moment, then nodded. "See you then."

He shoved his phone into his pocket and headed straight for them, his expression tight. He eyed them both for a minute. "It's Rader all right. Looks like he was strangled, but I'm sure you figured that out when you took a look through the place, and you found the money in the drawers."

"We had to confirm he'd died before calling it in," Clay said, but didn't acknowledge searching the dresser.

"With that smell?" Trent rolled his eyes. "You knew the minute you opened that door that he was gone."

"Did I hear you call Sam Griffin to do the forensics?" Clay hoped a change of subject might calm Trent down.

"Yes," Trent said. "Before you ask, I won't be sharing the results, and Sam's a professional, so don't bother asking her."

"But—"

"But nothing." He raised his shoulders. "This is an official investigation. I can only share what we reveal to the public."

"You wouldn't even know he was dead if we hadn't come out here."

"He would've been discovered eventually. And probably by someone who would've run from the body and not searched the place."

"Look at our visit here as positive," Clay said. "We captured the cockatoo and put it in the cage. You'll find blood on its beak and talons. Blood I suspect is from Rader's killer."

Trent chewed on the side of his cheek. "Thanks for corralling the bird and saving that evidence."

"See, we're not all bad." Clay grinned.

Trent didn't crack a smile.

"Bird needs water and food," Toni said.

"I'll have someone see to it after we collect the sample." Trent rested his hands on his hips. "I know the bird wasn't the only thing you touched."

"Speaking of that." Toni quickly told him about the boxes in the garage but left out her clothing and picture. "I assume you'll be running the photos against the database for missing girls, but I have no idea what the other items mean."

She took a long breath and shared about the personal items. "I've never heard of this man before today. I have no idea how my father knew him or why there's a picture of me or why the outfit I was wearing is in one of the boxes."

Trent's eyes flashed wide for a moment before he controlled his surprise. "I'm sure you'll dig into the connection. You might be able to locate information about your past that I don't have access to. I would appreciate updates."

"Information exchange goes both ways," Clay said.

"I've already told you I can't share." Trent tightened his hands on his hips. "But I'll keep you updated on anything I learn before we release it to the public."

"Fair enough," Clay said and meant it. "What do you know about Rader?"

Trent raised an eyebrow and didn't speak for a moment, then shifted his stance. "It's common knowledge that his wife took off in '95. After that, he headed into a downward spiral. The year after she left him, he was arrested for public drunkenness and lewd behavior. It was way before my time. Blake's too. He was just a kid then, but he keeps in touch with Sheriff Ziegler, so Blake might have at least a passing knowledge of what happened."

"From what Loraine said, it sounds like people thought he'd killed his wife," Clay said.

Trent frowned. "Loraine likes to gossip, but as far as I know, the wife just got tired of living in a small town and took off."

"We were wondering if maybe she was buried in the back yard," Toni said.

Trent's frown deepened.

This was where Clay could help and maybe gain some information along the way too. "Dr. Dunbar, the anthropologist at the Veritas Center, has a drone program that locates graves without digging. If you want to bring her in to scan this property, I'd be glad to foot the bill."

Trent tilted his head, his gaze roaming the property. "She'd report only to me?"

Clay nodded. "And she won't say a word to us, if that's what you want."

Trent's eyebrow lifted. "Then why are you doing this?"

"We're hoping it will lead to the girls in the photographs."

Trent gave a firm nod. "Get her out here, but make sure she's clear on who she reports to."

Clay wished he could be privy to her findings, but he had to respect Kelsey's position. Still, maybe he could accompany her back here and glean some info by simply being present.

"If there's nothing else, we should get going," Clay said.

"I'll call if I need anything else." He eyed Clay. "Just be sure you take my call."

"Will do." Clay and Toni got back in the vehicle, and he called Kelsey.

"I can't share my findings at the school," she said by way of answer.

"I know. I have another job for you." He explained. "Could you do that today?"

"I'm already back at the lab and would have to clear my whole day for travel back there." She let out a long breath.

"What if I could get someone from Gage's team to fly you here?"

"That would help."

Clay started thinking about the costs he was incurring. It was one thing to hitch a ride on the helicopter, but Gage would need to charge for a special trip. Still, finding these girls trumped everything. And besides, Clay could send Bird's blood sample on the chopper to Veritas.

"I'll give Gage a call and let you know." He disconnected and dialed Gage.

As it turned out, Coop was headed to Portland late in the afternoon, and Clay would only have to pay for Kelsey to be flown back home when the job was done. He texted her the information, and she responded immediately.

*Works for me.*

*I'll pick you up at Gage's compound*, he replied. *It will be late by the time you finish so you can stay with us if you want.*

He quickly texted Sierra to ask if her assistant could pick up the blood sample from the helipad and gave her the time. Before he could put his phone down she replied with a yes.

He set his phone in a cup holder and turned to Toni to update her. "We have a few hours before Kelsey arrives. How do you want to proceed?"

"I say we do an internet search on both Jason and Fritz Rader. See what we turn up. I especially want to see if I can find Jason's Facebook page, and I should call my grandpa."

"We can do that at my parents' place." He cranked the engine. "On the way, we can drop off the blood sample for Coop to take to Portland. And I want to find out which house Jason lured his victims to and visit the place."

"He's recently been arrested so it could still be sealed off."

Clay shifted into gear. "Not if the owner put pressure on Trent to return it to their control."

"But then they likely had it cleaned."

He wouldn't lose hope. "There's still bound to be forensic evidence there. We'll just need to look harder—and maybe get Sierra out here too."

Toni stared out the floor-to-ceiling windows in the Byrd's large ranch style house. The living room overlooked a path leading through grasses and flowers to a wooden stairway down to the beach. The wind whipped through the dried grasses and peppered sand into the window.

"This is a great location," she said to Clay when he joined her.

A fond smile spread across his face. "My grandparents grew up nearby and built this place. We spent so many summers out here with them. It was awesome. When they got older and moved into a smaller house, they passed it down to my dad. Otherwise we could never have afforded such a place."

His smile widened, and his love for his family was so evident in his expression, touching her deeply. What would it be like to really know your grandparents? To have such a big family instead of being alone in the world?

She felt a pity-party ramping up. *Stop it. Stop comparing. You live a blessed life.*

"As it is," he continued, "Mom and Dad rent it out part of the year just to pay the taxes and upkeep. But it's vacant a lot of the time in the offseason."

"I've never really gone to the beach much, but I like it best in the winter. To sit inside and watch the storms roll in. And when it lets up to take long walks in the fog and mist. One of my dreams is to go horseback riding on the beach, but I've never made the time to do it."

"A woman after my own heart." He chuckled. "Not the horse part, but I like the beach in stormy weather too. Especially when I'm struggling with something big. Helps seeing such an amazing part of God's creation to put things in perspective."

She faced him. "Does that happen often? The big struggles, I mean."

"Recently, a whole lot more than I'd like."

She didn't respond, just waited him out, hoping he'd tell her more.

"A good example is my dad's transplant," he said. "That's when Sierra found out he isn't her biological father. And your dad died about the same time."

She was still touched by his caring. "His death really bothered you, didn't it? I mean, more than the usual grief we face when someone is killed on the job."

"Of course." His face was deeply lined with concern, and her heart fluttered over the intensity of his gaze. "He's your dad. How could I not be impacted?"

"You're making it sound like there's something between us." She couldn't believe she'd just said that when she wanted to ignore anything personal between them.

"Isn't there?" He stepped closer and cupped her cheek, those long fingers gentle, yet firm.

She expected his touch would be thrilling, but she struggled to breathe. "We're attracted to each other."

His fingertips flirted with her hairline, and she waited a moment for them to plunge into her hair and draw her closer. They didn't, though. Instead, he stilled them. "I think it's more than that, don't you?"

*Yeah. Way more.* But she wouldn't admit it. Not now. Not with all they had to do. Even if his touch was like a match, kindling every emotion. She didn't want to disappoint him. She also didn't want to encourage him.

She gently removed his hand and held it for a moment, making it more difficult to say no to his touch. "I can't do this with you. When Dad was shot..."

She had to pause to breathe. She let go of his hand. "I was admiring the way you looked all suited up for the raid. And in that moment—that briefest of seconds when I took my eyes off the op—Dad stepped up to the house. I was too late to call out to him, and he was gunned down."

The memory of her father dropping to the ground. Blood oozing from his chest. Unable to go to him due to gunfire. Watching him bleed out before her eyes.

She shuddered, and Clay inched closer, his expression warm and comforting.

"It's my fault he's dead," she said, firming her resolution to keep Clay at arm's length. "If I'd been paying attention to my job, it would never have happened. And I won't risk anyone's life in this investigation because of a romantic attraction."

He looked at her long and hard, then gave a slight shake of his head. "You couldn't have stopped the bullet that killed your dad. Not even if you hadn't been distracted. It all played out too fast. None of us could've done anything. Unless we went back in time and changed the op. As leader, I had choices. We could've gone a few ways, and I chose the plan. So if anyone's to blame, it's me."

"What? No. Not at all." She grabbed his hand again. "I don't blame you or anyone else."

"Then why blame yourself? Because I guarantee each officer on scene that day went home and played the raid over and over again. Might still be playing it and trying to figure out how they could've stopped the shooting. And each person will have their own version of how they could've done something different to change the outcome."

"But they weren't negligent. I was."

"Negligent is a pretty harsh word."

"I deserve harsh words." She paced away from him and turned her back. She couldn't look at him or she might actually believe him and forgive herself. A forgiveness she didn't deserve.

His footfalls sounded on the tile floor as he came up behind her. He laid a hand on her shoulder. She wanted to lean back and rest against his strong body. To bask in the warmth. Draw strength from him, but touching him again would only take her to the wrong place. So she remained still. Didn't speak.

"Have you talked to God about this?" he asked quietly.

"Talk is probably a tame word for what I've done."

"Yelled at Him?"

"At times, yeah. Even blamed Him. He could've changed the outcome that day."

Clay didn't speak for a long time, so she turned to look at him. His eyes were narrowed, and he ran a hand through his hair, leaving little tufts sticking up. She wanted to smooth them down. She shoved her hands into her pockets and waited him out.

"I had to go to counseling once when I had to shoot a guy in the line of duty," he finally said. "Turned out I was repressing my feelings. And once I started to deal with the incident, I wanted to blame someone. Anyone. The counselor told me that I was simply redirecting my anger so I could learn to accept the fact that I'd killed a man."

Now, she wanted to take his hand, this time to comfort him, but she resisted the urge. "And what did the counselor say about the anger? Surely, that wasn't helping."

"It wasn't, and she said it was useless. It didn't actually do anything. It sure didn't help me get better or find a way to avoid it happening again in the future. She was a Christian counselor, and she said blaming God ultimately shows we believe that God is in our debt. That He has to do everything we ask of Him. It should be the other way around. Blaming God—that's not faith."

"Fine words, but..."

"Yeah, I felt the same way at the time. Then my pastor suggested that we should use the phrase, 'God, make me,' not 'God give me.' So I turned around my thinking. Decided to look at the death to see how it would make me a better person. I came up with all kinds of ways I could use it for good. That's when I was able to deal with the guilt."

She looked at him then. Really looked deep into his eyes. She saw the suffering this death caused, but she also saw hope. The determination to make life better because of the experience. He was an amazing man. A truly fine Christian. Someone she could strive to emulate and learn from while they were together.

She smiled at him. "Thank you for sharing."

"I wish I could say I put this kind of thinking into practice all the time, but honestly, I fail a lot. Like with your dad's death. Took me some time to deal with the guilt. But if you can get your mind right, it works great."

"I'll think about it for sure. But I doubt it'll change my mind about a relationship with a co-worker. I know I'm not technically on the job, but this isn't about technicalities. I want to keep things professional."

The brightness in his eyes suddenly washed away. "Sounds like you've made up your mind."

"Nothing is certain." She'd learned the hard way that life was lived minute by minute. But one thing she did know for certain. She wouldn't let herself become distracted like she had with her father and risk the life of this very fine man.

# 10

Clay sat next to Toni at the big dining room table where his family had gathered for so many years. They each had their laptops open in front of them. She'd already confirmed Jason's Facebook page had been taken down, killing that lead right off the bat. They continued their search for information on Jason and Rader, but Clay's disappointment in Toni's rejection was taking his attention. Big time.

Not that there was any point in thinking about his pain. He couldn't change her mind. Only she could do that. Besides, he was still smarting from the way the last woman he'd gotten involved with had betrayed him with another man. Yeah, sure, he hadn't been madly in love with Grace or anything, but betrayal by anyone still stung. Toni didn't seem like she would have a straying eye like Grace had, but Toni could give in to her growing feelings for him only to realize she couldn't be in a relationship and break things off. That was betrayal at its deepest sense, as there would be no other party he could get angry with or try to blame.

Sure, he'd just said he shouldn't be angry. Shouldn't blame. But the other thing his counselor had said was that he had to go through these natural stages, and he couldn't hurry the process. When the time was right, most people recognized when to move on. And the other thing he knew—he could talk about moving on. Talk about not feeling disappointed, not letting hurt get to him, but God also gave people feelings. Sometimes they took over until you could process, and no matter what you knew in your brain, your heart didn't go along with it.

He heard a key slide into the front door lock, and he spun, going for his sidearm.

Toni looked at her watch. "Probably your brothers, right?"

"You can never be too careful."

She rested her hand on her gun, but the minute the door opened and his brothers' voices traveled into the room—they were calling dibs on the bedrooms—she lifted it back to her computer.

Drake entered first, his face hidden behind three boxes. "Where do you want these?"

"In the corner." Clay said. "It'll be easier to review the files here."

"Good thing Mom isn't here. She wouldn't be thrilled to have boxes all over the dining room." He dropped them with a thud, and Clay's other brothers trailed in behind him and unloaded another stack.

Erik was last, holding four boxes. "Out of my way. I can't see a thing."

"Because you were the doofus who had to carry the most boxes." Drake rolled his eyes.

Pong cautiously entered the room and looked to Erik for direction.

"Hi, Pong." Toni looked at the dog with longing. She really did want a dog. Whoever she married, if she ever did, would have to love dogs. "Can I pet him again?"

"Sure." Erik looked at Pong. "You can go."

He trotted across the room and sat at her feet.

She leaned in to pet him. "You are the best mannered guy I have ever met."

"Hey," Clay protested. "You just haven't spent enough time with me yet."

"That's right, bro, your manners are so well hidden it'll take her a lifetime to find them." Drake grabbed Clay by the elbow. "C'mon. There's more where these came from, and you're not getting away without carrying your share."

Clay groaned, but he didn't mean it. He was messing with Drake as his brother had been messing with him.

"I'll help." Toni started to rise.

"Nah." Drake waved a hand. "We got this. You keep the pooch happy while we go."

"You're sure?"

"Yep." He smiled at her, a rare occurrence for sure, telling Clay his brother liked her. Not in a romantic way. At least Clay hoped not that way, or Clay was the one who'd have to call dibs.

Outside, Erik caught his attention. "I've been doing some searching on the drive over. Want a report on what I found?"

"We can hold an update meeting right after you guys get settled."

"This needs to be in private."

"I guess Toni and I can meet—"

"It's Toni I don't want in the room."

"What?" Clay asked. "You do a background check on her?"

"I'll explain when we talk."

Clay glared at his youngest brother. "I didn't ask you to look into her."

"Yeah." He stuck out his chin in the defiant look that usually preceded a fight. "But you didn't stop looking *at* her so I figured I better look *into* her." Erik said nothing else, just grabbed two boxes and marched away.

Clay stared after him. Clay was half proud of his little brother's initiative and half mad.

"He did the right thing," Drake said on his way past with boxes.

"And you know it," Brendan added.

Aiden shook his head. "Hard being the one in charge, isn't it?"

Clay grabbed the last three boxes and took them inside. After he set them on the piles, he looked at Toni. "I need to talk to Erik a minute. Be right back."

He spun and grabbed Erik by the arm as he moved past him.

"We've still got groceries to unload," Erik said.

"The others can handle it." Clay gave his brother a push down the hallway.

"Come, Pong," he called over his shoulder.

"Must be serious if you think you're gonna need your dog for protection." Clay laughed, but it was forced. He wasn't sure he wanted to hear what Erik had dug up.

Erik marched down the hall to the furthest bedroom, which happened to be the master. His silence put a pang of worry in Clay's heart. He hoped Erik was being dramatic.

Clay thought they were far enough away from Toni that she wouldn't hear them and entered the room their mom had redecorated when they were kids. The nautical theme included blue walls, a blue-and-white comforter that looked like rolling waves, and a porthole mirror on the wall.

Erik dropped onto the bed, patted the space beside him, and the dog hopped up.

"Mom won't like that Pong was on her bed." Clay closed the door.

"She doesn't have to know."

"You're gonna pick off the dog hairs one by one, are you?"

"Oh, right." Erik motioned for Pong to get down. He slunk down to Erik's feet but didn't look happy about it.

"So out with the big secret," Clay said, ignoring the dog's sad eyes.

"Not a secret really. I just thought you'd want to know before I said anything in front of Toni. Her father had some trouble in 1990."

"What kind of trouble?"

"He made a bad decision as an agent, and it almost cost him his job. He got into a shootout in Virginia, where he was assigned at the time. Guy he shot was Andrew Martin, and he died."

"An agent involved shooting." Clay understood the toll that took. "It's traumatic but it happens. So where's the problem?"

"Her dad was related by marriage to Martin. He was the brother of his wife's mother."

"Oh, man. That changes things." Clay clamped a hand on the back of his neck to rub away the tension that had been building all day. "Her grandmother's maiden name was Martin, so maybe Long didn't know about the connection."

"Nah, he admitted to knowing before he went to interview the guy."

Clay whistled, and Pong gave him a sharp look.

"Easy, boy," Erik said, his tone assertive yet soothing.

"Even working an investigation involving a relative is frowned on. Killing one had to get him in serious trouble."

"Like I said. He almost got fired."

"How'd you find this?"

"An old news article on the web told me Long was DEA, so I called Devon, and he did some digging." Devon Dunbar was a DEA agent and Kelsey's husband. "He said the DEA kept her dad on because he spoke several difficult languages, and they needed guys with that skill."

"I wonder if Toni knows about this."

Erik's eyebrow went up, and he looked so much like Sierra that Clay found it uncanny. "Toni hasn't mentioned it, then?"

Clay's gut twisted. It wasn't like she'd lied to him, but not mentioning something so important was unsettling. If indeed she knew about it.

"I asked the guys to give you some time with her alone but didn't tell them what was going on."

"Hey, thanks, man," Clay said. "I'll talk to her and let the others know at our update meeting."

Clay started for the door but turned back. "And thanks for taking the initiative to do the background check."

"Welcome." Erik slid forward, and Pong perked up. "FYI, Drake called Malone, and she didn't have anything helpful, but she'll talk to a few of her sources and call if she learns anything. You should also know Drake started reviewing your Safe Harbor files on the drive to see if he could pinpoint something you missed."

At that, a flash of irritation bit into Clay, but he let it go in favor of making progress on the investigation. "It's good to get a fresh pair of eyes on things. Oh, and I almost forgot. Can you run financials for Fritz Rader? We found a ton of cash at his place, but the place was a dump."

"Will do."

As Clay walked down the hall, he considered how he would bring up the topic of Toni's father and tell her what Erik had discovered. Would be touchy for sure. No matter what he said, his brother had done a background check on her, and that would sting. Sure, Clay didn't direct Erik to run the check, but Clay should have, as protocol in their agency would demand such a thing.

He passed the second bedroom, where his other brothers were hanging out. They looked at him as he walked past, but said nothing. He found Toni alone at the table, her laptop still open, the light reflecting on her skin. She looked up, her face pale, her eyes tight.

"What is it?" He hurried over to her. "What's wrong?"

"I...I...this." She stabbed a finger at the screen.

He stepped behind her, and caught a look at the ancestry site. "You looked up your parents?"

"I talked to my grandpa. He seemed evasive, so I thought it would help, but I..." She tapped a pink square holding a darker pink female silhouette. A caption next to it said, *Lisa Long, sister.*

"I have a sister." Toni's words held immeasurable distress. "How could my family have kept this from me?"

Toni had suffered tremendous heartache in life with losing so many family members, but discovering she had a sister—a sister who, according to the records in front of Toni, was still alive—tore a hole deeper in her heart than she could ever have imagined. And filled her brain with questions.

Were the records right and her sister really was alive? What did she look like? Did she resemble Toni? Did Lisa know about her? She would be how old now?

Toni glanced at the screen and tried to calculate her age, but her head was spinning, and she couldn't make sense of anything.

Clay scooted a chair next to her and took her hand. "These sites can make mistakes."

"I figured as much." She resisted shuddering over the

discovery and clicked on another tab. "Here's the birth certificate listing my parents."

He looked at the screen then stared at her as if he couldn't think of a thing to say. She understood his reaction. Completely. She could almost see the crazy thoughts pinging around in his head. The discovery had generated crazy ones in hers too.

"What do you think happened to her?" he asked.

*Happened? Right. Something had to have happened or she would've been in the family.* "I can't even imagine. The records say she's still alive, but maybe she died and her death certificate got mixed up or something."

"Could be." Clay placed his other hand over hers. "We should do an internet search. See what we can find out about her."

"Lisa Long is probably a very common name."

"Erik has programs designed to find missing people. With your permission I'll ask him to start on it right away."

"Sure. Yes. Of course." Was she about to find a long-lost sister? A hint of excitement rose up and mixed with her unease.

Clay started to rise, but dropped back down. "There's something else. Now's the worst time ever to ask about this, but I have to."

She'd thought her stomach was already in the tightest knot it could form, but his tone made it clench even more. She took a breath and let it out slowly. "Go ahead."

"Erik was doing some research on the way here. He found out in the early nineties that your dad killed a guy in a shootout on an op gone wrong. Guy's name was Andrew Martin. He's your grandmother's brother."

She gasped and pulled back. She couldn't get out a single question, but her mind was brimming with them to the point that it felt like it might explode.

"I take it you hadn't heard that either," Clay said.

She shook her head, starting slowly then letting it frantically swing to try to push all the horrible thoughts out of her brain.

Clay took her hands and held them tightly. "I'm sorry this is so upsetting for you."

"Upsetting?" She ground out the word through gritted teeth. "Did I even know my parents? And why all the family secrets? Why, oh, why didn't they tell me about Lisa? And where is she?" The questions streamed out now, and she couldn't stop them.

"Shh," Clay said. "Take a deep breath."

He locked gazes with her and drew in a long breath of air then let it out. He repeated it. Over and over. She joined him and finally caught his rhythm. Slowly feeling her mind calm. Her heart rate slowed. But what was she supposed to do now? "It feels like my whole life is a lie."

"No," he said firmly. "No matter what your parents did or didn't tell you, you're this strong, amazing woman. Nothing has changed that. And I'll be right here to help you get through this." He squeezed her hands.

She'd forgotten he was even holding them.

"Families keep secrets all the time," he continued. "Like my mom and dad not telling Sierra about her biological dad."

It helped to be reminded of his parents. They seemed like good people, but they'd withheld information from their children for years. So she nodded but she didn't put any force behind it as a single nod was all she could manage.

His eyes brightened. "Think of this as any other problem in your life. How would you go about solving it?"

*Okay, yeah.* She could distance herself. Shove away all the pain and hurt and step back to look at it logically. Like she'd been doing since her dad was killed. She hadn't even properly grieved him. At least she hadn't reached the stage of acceptance. She'd accepted the fact that he'd died, but not that he'd died for no reason. Not that his killer hadn't yet been brought to justice.

"I'd learn as much as I could about the subject and make a game plan," she said, answering Clay's question and trying to move those painful elements to the back of her brain.

"So we'll do exactly that, first by asking Erik to look for Lisa. He's trained for this sort of thing. Then we'll get everyone together and review the information we have and where we go from here."

He let go of her hands and stood but remained looking at her.

"Thank you." She came to her feet and took both of his hands, wishing she had a right to hold them and not feel guilty. But learning about her past made the likelihood of getting romantically involved with him even less likely.

She couldn't be anyone's girlfriend, wife, mother, or any of the logical stages to follow in her life, not until she found her dad's killer and figured out what had happened to her sister.

# 11

Clay was thankful for his family. At least most of the time. But after Toni's shocks, he appreciated his brothers seated on the large sectional in the living room even more. As he was thankful for Toni. He didn't know if it was seeing her vulnerability or just admitting to himself that he cared for her, but he needed to make sure she didn't walk away when this investigation was over.

She sat in his mother's favorite chair, a swivel rocker his mom had bought to curl up in and read whatever best-selling novel she could get her hands on at the library. Until now, this space had only held fond memories for Clay, but Toni's pain was his pain, and he could hardly look at her without marching across the room to sweep her into his arms.

And hold her. Just hold her until her pain receded.

Erik looked up from his computer. Pong, sitting at his feet, lifted his head too. "I have information." He turned his focus to Toni. "Sorry. It's about Lisa, and it's not good news. I'll hook my computer to the TV and you can see it there."

Pong whimpered and sat up as if he knew something

bad was about to go down. He was likely picking up on the tension in Erik's announcement.

"How about just cutting to the chase and giving us the details," Drake said.

"I think it's better if you read it." His computer desktop image was mirrored on the screen, revealing a large photo of Pong. "This story I found is from 1987, long before the internet, but this newspaper scanned their files into their archive." He clicked on his internet browser, and an article opened with the title, *Virginia Girl Goes Missing on Lost Creek Vacation*.

Toni gasped. "My sister?"

Clay tore his eyes from her face to read the article. Lisa disappeared from her grandparents' home in a beach town not far from where they sat right now. Only twelve years old, she'd traveled with Andrew Martin from Virginia to Oregon to stay with her grandparents."

"I wonder why my mom and dad didn't bring her here," Toni muttered.

"The article doesn't say that. But it does say on the third night of her visit she'd gone to bed, and in the morning, her grandparents found the bedroom empty, the window open, and no sign of forced entry.

The story contained a photo of Lisa, one of the grandparents, and one of Toni's parents too.

Toni knelt on the floor by the TV and touched Lisa's face on the screen. "She looks like me when I was younger, doesn't she? Like the picture Dad had in his office of me and Mom."

"Yes," Clay said.

Toni moved her long slender fingers to her grandparents' faces. "I've never even seen a picture of them. They died before I was born."

"And look at my mom and dad," she said. "They're so young, but the pain in their eyes is excruciating."

"Maybe they never told you about Lisa because they blamed your grandparents and didn't want you to know that."

"Maybe." Her word was whispery soft, as if imagining how they'd made the decision to withhold something so very big from her. Or maybe she was wondering what life might've been like if her sister hadn't disappeared.

"You should know," Erik said as he continued to type. "Your grandparents are still alive."

"They what?" She fired him a shocked look. "My parents lied about that too. Do you have an address for them?"

"Not yet, but I found additional articles," Erik said. "They say Lisa was never found. The sheriff's office uncovered very few leads and feared she'd gone out to the beach and drowned. But your parents never had her legally declared dead."

Another gasp from Toni, and Clay wanted to slug his brother for being so matter-of-fact when she was so distraught. But then, there probably wasn't a better way to give her such horrible news.

She looked at Erik, the pain in her eyes mirroring her parents anguish on the screen. "I want to read all the articles. Can you print them for me?"

"After I finish looking up your grandparents and set up our portable printer."

"Thank you." She turned back to the TV. Touched the faces again—one by one as if memorizing them. Clay couldn't stand by any longer and do nothing to help her. He dropped down next to her. "Is there anything I can do?"

"Just be here with me," she said, her voice barely a whisper. "That's all you can do."

"Your grandparents still live in the same house as when Lisa disappeared," Erik announced.

Toni grabbed Clay's arm. "We have to go there. To see them. Question them."

He took her hands and made strong eye contact to break through her sudden elation. "We'll go. For sure. But it would be better if we got a complete picture of this abduction before meeting them."

"But I want to see them."

"I know you do, and I want that for you. I really do." He squeezed her hands. "But I have to think of this from an investigative standpoint too. It wouldn't be good to go over there just yet. You're too emotional to see that now, so I need you to trust me and trust that I have your best interest at heart."

Trust? Clay wanted Toni to trust him. But could she trust anyone with something so important? She'd learned over the years that trusting people involved a measure of risk. Just like trusting God did. She'd trusted her parents, and look where that had gotten her. And God? He knew about Lisa. Knew Toni didn't have a clue, and so many years had passed.

*Why didn't you let me find out sooner? Why?*

Everyone was watching her, so she slipped back into the chair, her emotions on the biggest rollercoaster ride of her life. She had no idea what to feel. First shock. Then grief. Then hope and joy. She wasn't alone in this world. She had grandparents. Two people who were her blood relatives. Maybe there were more. The family tree at the ancestry site could tell her. She needed to finish it. But not now. Not with so many sets of eyes looking at her and so much up in the air. Tonight. She'd do it tonight. And she'd follow Clay's suggestion for now, but if anything happened to show her that she'd been wrong to trust him, she would go see her grandparents.

At the moment, she needed to stow her feelings. Remember she was an agent working an investigation with these men, not a woman following her family tree. She was on the hunt for a vicious man who not only trafficked young women but tried to kill her and Clay. Finding him. Finding the girls. That had to be her priority.

She swallowed a few times and balled her hands into fists, then looked up. As expected, the guys were still watching. She gave them the best smile she could muster. "So where do we go from here?"

Clay had stood, and he seemed relieved that she hadn't tried to race out the door. He grabbed a marker from the tray of a portable whiteboard. "This investigation is getting complicated, and we need to organize the leads."

He turned to the board and divided it into four sections. On the top right side he wrote: *High School*. Under that, he added *fire, beds, body, bedpost/Hibbard*.

He turned to look at Toni. "Since everyone knows about the school, why don't you update them on what we learned about Jason and Fritz Rader while I add all the items to the board."

"I hate to ask this." Drake scratched his neck in a moment of uncertainty she found odd for his straightforward personality. "But could the body at the school be Lisa?"

Toni gasped.

"I know that's tough to hear, especially on top of everything else you've been through," Drake said. "But I thought the question needed to be asked."

"Without access to the reports, there's no way we can answer that," Clay said. "We might be able to collect Lisa's DNA from her grandparents' to have it processed at Veritas. Or we can simply collect yours, as you're sisters. This will let Kelsey compare it to the remains. Trent might allow Kelsey to tell us if it's Lisa or not."

"Yes," Toni said emphatically. "Let's do that."

"Unless anyone else has something to say." Clay eyed Drake, who shrugged. "Toni will update you on the Raders."

Toni launched into the details of what they'd learned but watched as Clay wrote *Fritz Rader* as a heading on the top right and listed below, *picture of Toni* and *outfit*, *girls' pictures*, *female items/clothing*, and *Bird blood sample*.

As she spoke, she made sure to cover each point. "We took pictures of everything we found, including the photos of the girls, some going back to the eighties."

Clay looked at Erik. "I'll put them on our server so you can search the internet for matches."

Erik nodded. "I'll start with the database for the National Center for Missing and Exploited Children. However, older records might not be there or anywhere on the internet, for that matter. We might need to ask Trent to give us a list from his database."

"I'm sure he'll be doing his own search," Clay said. "Give me a list of girls you find, and I'll compare notes with him."

"I'll get started the minute we're done here. I'll also check in with Nick to see if he has any suggestions for doing a thorough search for the girls."

"Good thinking." Clay released an appreciative sigh.

Toni liked seeing the look of respect flash between the brothers. These guys really were an amazing team, and she was thankful they were helping her find her dad's killer, and now digging into what happened to Lisa too.

On the bottom right of the board, Clay wrote *Toni's*

*grandparents and parents*. And finally on the left, he added *Hibbard Investigation Files*.

"Did I get everything?" His gaze traveled from person to person, pausing on Drake.

"We have the pictures Sierra took at the school," Drake said.

"Right." Clay marked it down.

"And I noticed twine in the photos of the woman in the wall." Drake continued to look at Clay. "Looks white, though it's yellowed some. In reviewing your old case files, I saw twine was recovered when a woman was found murdered at one of Hibbard's places."

"Her name was Heidi," Toni said, the pain from losing the girl still in Toni's heart. "When we found her, she had a plastic bag around her head, twine holding it in place. Her wrists were bound with twine too, and the rest of her body was wrapped in green trash bags and more twine. Forensics said the twine was common poly sisal often used for commercial packaging and shipping, so it didn't lead anywhere. The other evidence didn't, either, and we were never able to connect Hibbard to her murder."

Drake shifted to look at her. "Common or not, the twine could match the evidence found with the skeletal remains at the school and be a link between them."

Clay wrote *twine* on the board. "I'll ask Sierra to act as a go-between for the forensics techs who worked Heidi's murder investigation and the techs working the high school to compare the samples."

"And you wanted to find and visit the beach house Jason Rader rented," Toni said.

"Erik," Clay said, "can you find the address of the property where he was arrested?"

"Should be able to." Erik started typing. "FYI, I ran the

financials for Fritz Rader. Nothing odd other than he didn't have much money. Was living off social security."

Toni wished she had a team at her disposal who jumped at the drop of a hat like these guys did. Sure, the Bureau provided incredible resources, but she often had to wait her turn to access them. "We need to go see Sheriff Ziegler about Lisa's investigation, and we can also ask him about the disappearance of Rader's wife."

"Blake should be able to arrange an appointment with the guy." Clay added it on the board and dug out his phone from one of the deep cargo pockets on his leg. "Let's call him right now to get the ball rolling."

The call connected after two rings.

"Blake Jenkins." Blake's confident tone came over the speaker.

"It's Clay," he said. "I've got you on speaker. All the guys and Toni Long are here."

"I hear you're still in my old stomping grounds," Blake said.

"That's why I'm calling." Clay succinctly brought Blake up to speed on the investigation and told him about Toni's connection to Lisa.

"Wow, Toni! I had no idea you linked to that investigation. I mean, I knew your last name was Long, but I never made the connection."

He sounded nearly as shocked as Toni had been. "I had no idea either until just now."

"Sheriff Ziegler talks about the investigation from time to time. It was his first case as a detective, and it doesn't sit well with him that he didn't solve it."

"He have a theory?" Clay asked.

"He really didn't have any solid leads. No forensics at all, and the investigation went cold almost immediately. They'd found one of Lisa's shoes near the ocean. With no sign of forced entry, they eventually concluded that she'd gone out there at night and was swept away in an undercurrent."

"And did you buy his theory?" Drake asked.

"I never had enough info to weigh in. I know Ziegler would've run a solid investigation. Still, he was new to the detective job, and there could be something there that can be reworked."

"I was hoping to pick Ziegler's brain about it," Clay said. "Could you arrange a visit for us like you did with Trent?"

"Ziegler's turned into kind of a hermit and doesn't see just anyone," Blake said. "Best if I come with you."

Clay frowned. "Do you have the time?"

"I'll make the time."

"If you can leave now, Kelsey's soon heading this way on Gage's chopper."

"I'll check in with Emory and let you know."

"You can stay with us if you want," Clay offered. "Kelsey will be staying here."

"Appreciate it. I'll let you know right away."

"I'll also want to talk about when Fritz Rader's wife took off when you get here. We found him dead today." Clay shared their story.

"I remember her leaving. Was the first year I was on the force. It was never reported as a missing persons case, but Ziegler might know more."

"Okay, if you can't make it, we can discuss it on the phone." Clay ended the call and stowed his phone.

"Got the address for Jason's beach house rental." Erik shared the location, and a map appeared on the TV. "Not more than fifteen miles away."

Clay dug out his phone and dialed Trent's office. "Hi, Lorraine. It's Clay Byrd."

He listened. "Oh, man, I was hoping Trent would be in

and could tell me if he released the beach house where Jason was arrested or if it was still sealed."

A satisfied smile lit Clay's face. "Oh, good. Good. Thanks. I won't have to bother Trent then. Have a good day." He lowered his phone. "Scene was just released. We need Sierra here so she can process the place."

He made the call and explained to Sierra about the scene and the helicopter that afternoon, then arranged for her to coordinate the twine forensics between the two teams. He smiled and lowered his phone. "Sierra's coming and will handle the twine comparison if we get buy-in from the other teams."

His phone dinged in his hand, and he looked at it. "Blake's a go too."

"We'll have a full house," Brendan said.

"Not any more people than when the whole family is here." Erik touched his index finger to his nose. "Not it. I'm not sleeping with any of you in Mom and Dad's bedroom."

Toni watched in amusement as they all tried to beat each other to touch their noses and claim "not it." Drake was lightning fast, Brendan next. Clay flashed his finger to his nose, but Aiden took his time.

"No way I'm listening to you snore," Clay said. "I'll take the couch."

"Was my plan all along." A smug smile crossed Aiden's face.

Clay groaned. "Just for that, I should change my mind." He glanced at his watch. "Erik, get started on those photos. If you have downtime while waiting for things to process, keep digging for info on Lisa and her grandparents."

"Understood," Erik said.

Clay shifted to face Aiden. "Call the owner of the beach house Jason rented. Offer to pay them whatever it takes to keep them from cleaning the place and reserve it for us. The rest of us can divvy up the items on the board and work on it until I run to Gage's place to pick everyone up."

Toni didn't even bother asking to go with Clay. She needed some time alone to regroup before everyone got here. She wasn't used to a big, boisterous family like his. Add more people when she was already stressed, and she might lose the sanity she was barely hanging onto.

# 12

Several hours later, Clay drove through the security gate at Blackwell Tactical and pulled up to Gage's house. Clay slid out and walked through the foggy night to the brightly lit ranch house. He knocked on a vibrant yellow door and stood back. A young boy with fiery red hair cracked it open.

"Come in," he said and fled back into the house.

"David." Hannah's voice sounded from the room on the right. "That's not the proper way to welcome a guest."

David slunk back to the door. "Sorry. We're playing *Mario*."

"Hey, I get it. I was young once and loved *Mario* when I was your age."

He stared open-mouthed at Clay. "They had *Mario* back then? That musta been a long time ago."

"David!" Shaking her head, Hannah came into the entry, an adorable little girl with the same hair color toddling after her.

Clay laughed.

"What, Mom?" David protested as he turned back to the family room. "He doesn't care. See. He's laughing."

Hannah swung the girl onto her hip and eyed Clay. "Don't encourage him."

"Sorry, but it doesn't seem like that long ago when my mom was in your place." Clay smiled.

Sierra joined them. "What are you saying? With five brothers, I can tell you our mom still does it."

"True that." Clay grinned.

Sierra rolled her eyes. "Just don't sound so proud of it."

"You better get used to it, Sis. You're having a boy, after all, and the male genes are strong in the Byrd family. The little guy's bound to take after his uncles."

"I'm choosing to think he'll take after his father."

Hannah laughed. "I love hearing the two of you spar. I hope our kids are the same way when they get older."

"It's my turn." David snapped the controller from a girl with dark hair who was about his age.

"But I wouldn't mind it if they stopped now." Hannah shook her head. "Blake and Gage are in his office down the hall. Please, excuse me while I referee."

Clay passed the family room filled with toys, and Kelsey sat on the sofa looking tired. She, like the rest of the Veritas staff, worked long hours, even though she was expecting. Plus, she had such a tough job. She was isolated in the basement without windows and only had bones and her assistants to keep her company. Before meeting her, he'd thought she'd be kind of a loner, but she was outgoing and fun to be around.

In the small office, he found Gage sitting behind a large desk, Blake leaning back in a leather chair facing him.

"Clay, join us." Gage gestured at the second leather chair. "We were talking about Toni learning she had a sister."

Blake sat forward. "I talked to Sheriff Ziegler. He'll be glad to see us tomorrow." Blake shook his head. "Last case I talked to him about was related to Emory, who also discovered she had a sister, Cait. They're twins. Separated at birth and adopted out to different families."

"And how did that turn out?" Clay took a seat on the buttery soft leather.

"Good. She also discovered she has a grandmother. They're all quite close now. We come down to visit often. I used to take Ziegler out for lunch a couple times a month when I lived here. We go out while Emory catches up with her sister. His health's been failing. He doesn't talk about it, but I get the idea he doesn't have much time left. He let the job consume his life and doesn't have family."

"I've seen that happen too much on the job," Clay said.

Blake gave a solemn nod. "Anyway, we'll talk to him tomorrow. Provided I bring his favorite apple fritters."

"Small price to pay."

"And speaking of paying a price," Clay said. "Drake is making dinner for us so we should get going."

"Before you go." Gage's serious tone wiped away Clay's good mood. "When Blake told me about Toni, I had Eryn do a little digging for you."

"She's their computer expert," Blake said. "Nick's the only person I know as capable as Eryn."

Clay should be irritated with Gage. He had no business asking anyone to dig around, but if it meant finding Hibbard, Clay would accept the help. "And what did she turn up that has you looking so serious?"

"It's about Toni's granduncle. Andrew Martin."

"If you're going to tell me her dad killed him, we already know that."

"News to me," Blake said. "When did this happen and where?"

"Nineteen-ninety," Clay said. "In Arlington, Virginia, where Long was stationed with the DEA."

"Ziegler must not know about that," Blake said. "At least, he never mentioned it."

"Probably didn't make the news out here," Clay said. "But we can ask Ziegler about it."

Gage tapped a packet of stapled papers on his desktop. "Have you seen Martin's rap sheet?"

"No," Clay said. "But it wouldn't surprise me if he had one."

"He does." Gage slid the report across the desk to Clay. "Was arrested for having sex with an underage girl. And when I say underage, I mean ten."

Blake muttered something under his breath and leaned forward. "This is news to me too. Where did it happen?"

"Virginia."

"Did Martin move out there with Long and his wife?" Blake asked.

"Not sure on the details. Eryn's still digging."

Clay curled his fingers into tight balls. "Was Martin convicted?"

"No. He got off on a technicality. But the day the verdict came in was the day Toni's dad shot him."

Clay looked at Blake. "Maybe he thought Martin abducted Lisa."

Blake's eyes narrowed. "Seems like it."

Clay didn't like where this was heading, but he needed facts. "Any way you can get us the investigation file for his arrest?"

"Since it's such an old investigation, I might have some luck there," Blake said. "I'll start on it first thing in the morning."

Clay picked up the report and stood, his gut clenching. Toni had barely recovered from her shock of finding a sister and living grandparents, and then learning her dad had killed her mom's uncle. Now Clay had to tell her that her uncle was a pedophile. This might be the very thing that would bring her to her knees.

~

Toni kept busy while Clay was gone by working on her ancestry page. She'd searched for and added Andrew Martin and her grandparents, but their addition didn't reveal any other living relatives. With nothing else to add, she'd made a cup of tea and sat at the kitchen counter watching Drake prepare dinner.

The other guys had turned on college football in the living room, and the Oregon Ducks were leading, putting them all in a good mood. Toni was enjoying her talk with Drake, even if she shared his attention with the TV. She was learning he was the devil's advocate of the family, pointing out all the possible downsides. Sometimes he came across as rude, but he also had this extremely intense look as if he was trying to work things out to his satisfaction. He clearly was a deep thinker, and his love for his brothers was obvious too.

He looked up from the cutting board where he was slicing tomatoes for the burgers he'd placed on the grill. "Must be freaky finding out you have a sister."

She picked at the wheat cracker she'd taken from the tray of cheese and crackers before his brothers consumed the rest. "Especially not knowing if she's alive."

"Yeah, that's rough," he said as if he had experience with something similar. "I was a deputy for the Marshal Service—fugitive apprehension, not WITSEC—but I still saw families in crisis. Some of them had lived a life of crime and deserved the situation they found themselves in. Others were just in the wrong place at the wrong time."

He poked the tip of the knife into the cutting board and

stared over her shoulder. "When I worked the WITSEC rotation in training there was this one family I tried to help. I'll never forget them."

"What happened?" she asked, totally captivated now.

He didn't speak for the longest time, the pain of the event racing through his expression.

"The mother witnessed a gang shooting," he finally said, his tone radiating apprehension. "Decided to testify. She had three kids under five. The dad refused to go into protection and wouldn't let her take the kids. She begged him. He refused. We talked to him several times. He said if she just kept quiet, everything would be okay. But she had to follow her beliefs and testify. After doing the right thing, she had to decide between staying with her family and her life. She said she could never leave her children. She had to know they were okay. She chose her family."

He took a long breath and let it out, his wide chest heaving with the exertion. "Not even a week passed before we were called out to their apartment. All five of them had been gunned down."

"Oh, Drake, that must've been horrible."

"The mom and kids were believers, so I knew they were in a better place. She sort of got what she wanted. No uncertainty. No wondering if her kids were fine. She knew where they were." He looked at Toni. "So I get what you're going through. The wondering, that is, and I'm praying for you. We all are."

"Thank you." She squeezed his hand.

He blushed as red as the tomatoes on the cutting board and shrugged it off to start slicing again as if he hadn't just shared a painful memory.

The door opened, and Toni heard laughter.

Still, she reached for her gun as she swiveled. Sierra and

Kelsey—Toni assumed based on the state of her pregnancy—and then Blake entered in front of Clay.

"We'll put the bags in the bedroom," Clay said, looking upset about something, and he and Blake headed down the hall with the luggage.

Sierra and Kelsey came over, and Sierra introduced them.

"Congratulations on the baby." Toni smiled.

"Thank you." Kelsey rested her hands on her belly and looked at Drake. "And this kid is ready for dinner. Something smells wonderful."

"That would be my mom's famous mac and cheese. She sent along two big casserole dishes." Drake grabbed an empty platter from the counter. "I'll get the burgers from the grill, and we can eat."

"A man after my own heart." Kelsey slid onto a stool. "If it wasn't already taken, that is."

"Does anyone mind if I set the table?" Toni asked to do something to settle her nerves.

"Mind?" Sierra gaped at her for a moment. "I know I'm speaking for the big lugs sitting like couch potatoes in front of the TV, but we'd be thrilled. Plates are in the right top cabinets. Glasses left. You can put the plates on the counter by the burger fixings."

Toni busied herself with the dishes while Sierra and Kelsey talked about an investigation they were working together. They didn't give any details, but Toni still caught that it was a particularly brutal murder case.

Clay joined them, his expression serious and leaning toward angry. "Way to go. Make the guest do all the work."

"She asked to do it," Erik called out.

"I did." Toni grabbed silverware from the drawer. "But if it will make you feel better, you can set these out."

He looked conflicted about remaining irritated with his

siblings, but he took the utensils from her hands, their fingers touching and their eyes locking for a long moment.

"So-o-o-o," Sierra said and swiveled on the stool. "Are you dating anyone, Toni?"

"Um..." She wasn't sure if she wanted to reply.

"You don't have to answer." Clay fired his sister a testy look. "Sierra's just trying to meddle."

"In her defense," Aiden said. "She comes by it naturally."

"Yeah, she's a mini-Mom." Erik laughed, and the others joined in.

"Not a bad thing to be." Clay hugged Sierra's shoulders, but his troubled expression didn't go away. "If you like being pushy."

She swatted at him, and he dodged her hand.

Blake came down the hall, and Drake entered with the burgers. The savory smell filled the house, and the guys were on their feet in a flash.

Drake set the burgers down and held up his hand. "Give our guests a chance to get their burgers first."

"I'm not shy." Kelsey went to wash her hands at the sink then grabbed a bun and slapped it on a plate.

Brendan helped Sierra to her feet.

"I should say thanks," she said, "but I know you're only getting me moving so you can get to your food faster."

He grinned at her, and Toni saw the resemblance to Clay, though Clay's mouth was turned down in a frown.

Drake set two casserole dishes brimming with golden cheese on trivets, and Toni's mouth watered. Mac and cheese was her favorite comfort food, and she needed a whole lot of comforting at the moment. Not only from the food, but she found herself wanting to step across the space and slide into Clay's arms. Her nervousness had somehow evaporated, and she had an odd feeling of belonging here.

Maybe it was because everyone was joking around and making things lighthearted. Like good friends gathering for dinner. Not a group of people on the hunt for a murderer or missing girls.

Erik moved closer to the counter. "I didn't know Mom sent mac and cheese."

"You better go next, Toni," Clay said. "Or there won't be any food left."

Drake added a large bowl of steamed broccoli to the counter. That combined with the casserole urged her to move. She washed up, fixed her plate, and sat across from Blake, Sierra, and Kelsey. Clay somehow managed to beat his brothers to the food and set his plate next to Toni's. He grabbed a pitcher of water and started pouring for everyone.

The brothers might joke around, but their mother clearly taught them proper manners. Whether they chose to use them was another matter. She smiled up at Clay, but he either didn't see it or he didn't want to see it. He seemed to be looking for things to fuel his bad mood.

When everyone was seated, Sierra offered a prayer, and they dug into the food.

"Yum," Kelsey said. "The baby and I both agree this is the best macaroni and cheese ever."

"I can get you the recipe if you want," Sierra said.

"Sure. Reed will love to make it for me." Kelsey laughed then looked at Clay as she held up another fork filled with the gooey cheesy mac. "So what time do we start tomorrow?"

"I'd like to get going as soon as it's light." Clay settled in his chair. "We can drop you off. Drake will stay with you."

Kelsey stopped chewing and swallowed. "You think I need a chaperone?"

Clay frowned at his empty fork, gleaming in the light from the chandelier above. "After finding two bodies in as many days, I think anything's possible, and we should take care."

"Besides," Drake said as he took a seat at the head of the table. "You'll be glad for my exceptional company."

Sierra rolled her eyes. "Kelsey will be far too focused on her work to know you're there."

"Even more of a reason for him to be there." Clay attacked his broccoli as if he were mad at it too.

Toni had turned to ask what was going on with him when Blake asked, "What do you want me to do while you're searching the beach house?"

"Would be good if you met with Trent. Maybe find out what's happening in the investigation."

Blake picked up his thick burger dripping with ketchup. "I'll be glad to stop by his office, but don't count on me getting any info from him."

"Maybe Lorraine is a better bet, and she'll share something."

Blake sighed. "She's the best assistant I ever had, but she was always the weakest link in our information chain. She'd never share anything with the press or the public, but if she likes you, she might give out more information than she should."

"Well, then." Clay looked at Blake. "Does she like you?"

Blake laughed and bit into his burger.

"Actually, I was serious," Clay said, burger in hand. "You can be kind of tough. Didn't know what she thought of you."

Blake swallowed his bite. "We got along fine. I'll be glad to ask what she knows, but I won't pump her for any info she's not comfortable sharing."

"Fair enough," Clay admitted reluctantly. "So Sierra, tell me you were able to talk to the techs about the twine."

"How about asking nicely instead of demanding?"

"Sorry. Were you able to talk to them?"

She nodded. "They'll try to get permission to send the samples to our lab for comparison."

"The FBI might not approve," Clay said, sounding down and raising Toni's concerns even more. Something was going on with him, and he wasn't telling her or anyone else what it was.

He looked at Toni. "Do you think it would help if you were to give someone a call at your office?"

"I'll try." She doubted it would help, but she didn't want to add to Clay's obvious frustrations.

Clay nodded, but he picked at his macaroni and cheese. She'd never seen him pick at his food in all the time she'd known him.

"What's with you, bro?" Drake asked. "You're rarely this cranky. Something happen?"

"Let's just finish eating and get to work on reviewing those old records." Clay bit into his burger and chewed as if he were eating a tough piece of steak.

So she wasn't the only one noticing something was off. Others besides Drake probably noticed too, but he was the only one blunt enough to mention it.

Everyone turned their attention to their meal, and the mood put a dark cloud over the table. Even a plate of gooey chocolate chip cookies from their mother didn't improve things. When they'd finished clearing the table and everyone had disbursed, she took Clay aside.

She met his gaze, and when he wanted to look away, she held on. "What aren't you telling me?"

Without a word, he reached for her hand and led her down the hallway to the bedroom at the end, where he closed the door behind them. He picked up a report lying on the bed. "I don't want to have to tell you this, but Gage's IT person uncovered something."

He handed her an arrest record, and she saw her granduncle's name at the top of the page. She skimmed the information, her focus landing on the words *sexual assault of a minor*. Her breath whooshed out, and her knees weakened. She dropped onto the bed.

Thoughts rolled through her brain like the surf crashing on the beach outside, and the food she'd just consumed threatened to come up. The room seemed airless. She gasped for breath. Struggled.

She tossed down the report and jerked open the patio door leading to the big deck that ran the length of the house. A soft mist was falling, and she lifted her face to let the moisture cool her skin.

"Come on, honey," Clay said from behind her. "It's cold out here, and you'll get wet."

"I can't breathe in there."

"You've had more than your share of shocks today, but things will start to look up tomorrow. We're sure to find some leads and move forward."

"But that won't change the personal things, will it." She spun on him. "After seeing my granduncle's arrest record, I have to wonder if he took my sister and..." She shook her head hard, and her damp hair clung to her face.

Clay gently brushed it aside. "We don't know what happened."

"But it seems likely, right, and that's why you were in such a bad mood during dinner?"

He looked her in the eye, and she waited for him to deny it. For him to say her grandmother's brother didn't hurt Lisa, but he didn't.

"I'm sorry, honey." Clay took hold of her shoulders and not even his endearing use of the word *honey* for the second time eased her pain. "I'm hoping it's not true, but from a law enforcement perspective, it seems very likely."

She couldn't hold back her tears. She wanted to run

away to hide and lick her wounds. She tried to move, but Clay had a firm hold of her shoulders, riveting her in place. That was just her excuse, though. She could certainly break free if she really wanted to.

"I'm sorry I made you cry," he said softly, releasing her shoulders. "I didn't want to have to tell you."

She waited for him to offer a hug, but he stood looking at her, a question in his eyes. Was he asking permission? Certainly something she could see one of the well-mannered Byrd brothers doing. But she didn't want well-mannered right now. She wanted to know someone cared.

She stepped forward and lifted her arms around his neck.

He circled his arms around her waist and held her with such tenderness. Her tears intensified. She would probably be sorry tomorrow. Embarrassed even, but at this moment she needed his touch, and she would take it for as long as he would hold her.

Tomorrow when everything ugly she'd learned was exposed to the light of day, she would once again become the strong agent her father had prepared her all her life to be, even if his actions were part of the very reason she was struggling so hard right now.

# 13

Toni stood with Clay in the doorway of the beach house, the morning sun climbing higher in glorious shades of orange and yellow over the sparkling ocean. She'd caught Clay sneaking looks at her as they'd eaten an early breakfast. He'd made omelets and toast for everyone before getting ready to leave for Jason's rental house.

And she could feel Clay looking at her now. He was probably trying to find out how she was doing after the shocking news yesterday. The answer was *not good*—so she forced a smile and pretended to enjoy the sunrise.

The roar of an SUV's engine shifted her attention to Drake, who was behind the wheel of one of the team vehicles parked in the driveway with Kelsey and Sierra in the back seat. Aiden sat behind the wheel of the other SUV, and Blake climbed into the passenger seat, Brendan the back seat. Erik stood halfway from the house to Drake's vehicle and gave a sharp nod.

Clay pinned his focus to her. "I don't think our suspect knows where you are staying, but stay by my side all the time. When we reach Erik, he'll take the other side. No stopping for any reason. Straight into the vehicle."

Clay was probably overdoing her security today. After all, he'd let her go out on the deck alone last night, but she was too emotionally worn out to question it. He stepped out, took a long look around, then reached for her elbow, drawing her into the crisp morning sunlight.

He closed the door behind them, and they hurried past Erik to the open back door of the SUV. Kelsey and Sierra had been waiting, and Toni felt guilty for her special treatment when she didn't think it was necessary.

Sierra looked at Toni. "You're in violent crimes, right?"

She nodded as she clicked her seatbelt in place.

"So you and Hunter work together."

"We do," she said, wondering where this was going.

"He's married to Maya, one of our partners," Sierra said. "Great guy."

"He really is a great guy," Toni said. "It was a good day when our supervisor decided we needed someone with cyber experience on violent crimes and moved Hunter."

"Violent crimes has got to be a tough area to work," Kelsey said. "I could never do it. Especially with the human trafficking and crimes against children."

"I didn't really choose it," Toni replied. "It chose me."

"How so?" Sierra asked.

"When I learned about the different investigative areas at the academy, I felt like victims of violent crime and their families needed me most of all. Plus, since I'm single, I can work the hours needed."

"Don't all agents work crazy hours?" Sierra asked. "I mean, that's what Reed tells me."

"Most do, but in some areas, like white-collar crimes, they often work a more regular schedule. But with violent crimes you can't just go home at the end of a typical work day. Lives are on the line in the cases we investigate. Means I need to work as long as it takes to make sure people are okay."

"Reed was in white-collar crimes when I met him," Sierra said. "I need to get him to switch back." Sierra laughed.

Clay looked over the seat. "You do, and he'll see how many hours you work."

"Oh, right. Don't want that." She shifted to look at Toni. "The job must wreak havoc with your social life."

"What social life?" Toni laughed, but she had to force it. "It's not like I have any plans to get involved with a guy in the near future, so I really don't mind."

"And the emotional toll?" Kelsey asked.

*Yeah, that.* "Some days are hard. Really hard. But when you put one of the perpetrators away and rescue people in difficult situations, it's all worth it."

"Is human trafficking really that prevalent in the United States?" Kelsey asked.

Toni gave a sad nod. "More than two hundred thousand children are bought and sold online in a year in our country alone."

"Wow, how sad." Kelsey frowned.

"ICE arrests nearly a thousand people a year involved in trafficking humans for sex," Clay added.

Kelsey shuddered. "I had no idea."

Toni had to work hard not to shudder with her. Working these investigations brought all kinds of emotional struggles to the people dedicated to end human trafficking. They even had to go through an annual psych evaluation to keep working in the area.

"Well, I say God bless you for doing the job," Kelsey said emphatically. "Some days I think my job is hard, but I could never find people in conditions you must see them in. Especially kids."

Toni could only imagine the things Kelsey must've been called in to do, and Toni could never be a forensic anthropologist. Proved people gravitated to the careers that best suited them in law enforcement.

Kelsey rested her hands on her pregnant belly. "I wish Devon worked a less demanding job. DEA agents face some pretty ruthless people."

Sierra shook her head. "After seeing what my mom went through with dad, I swore I would never marry someone in law enforcement, and here I am married to an FBI agent."

Toni leaned forward. "My mom had the same struggle. I wonder how she would've coped if she'd lived to see me become an agent too."

"I don't think I could handle a child being in law enforcement or the military." Kelsey cupped her hands protectively on her stomach. "This little girl will grow up to be a princess and that's all." She chuckled softly and looked at Sierra. "And your mom had all five boys in law enforcement at one time. She's a saint for sure."

Sierra nodded. "She struggled with it but never once tried to talk them out of it."

They all fell silent for the rest of the drive, and Toni assumed they were thinking about the cost of their jobs, not just to the law enforcement officer but their families. It was a heavy price, one Toni was willing to pay.

Drake turned into Fritz Rader's driveway so they could drop Kelsey off, and the tires crunched over rough gravel. Toni reached for her door handle.

Clay looked over the seat at her. "Do you mind staying here? I'll get Kelsey started, and Drake will stay with her for protection."

"No problem," she said, as she wanted to review her granduncle's arrest file obtained by Blake that morning.

As the others got out, she opened the folder, hoping to

see that her granduncle hadn't actually victimized a defenseless young girl.

~

Clay finished clearing the rental house and exited the building into a sharp wind. The place sat at the edge of the rustic beach, a large sand dune and tall swaying grasses hiding the property from nearby houses. Must be how Jason got away with johns coming and going at all hours of the day.

Clay nodded at Erik, who'd been standing watch with Pong while Clay cleared the house. They'd left Drake with Kelsey, and Aiden and Blake had gone to visit Trent, but Brendan was high up on a dune on overwatch. If anyone so much as approached the property, Brendan would report it on their comms unit.

Clay opened Toni's door. "Place is clear. Straight inside and stay there, okay?"

He expected Toni to argue, but she nodded.

"Can you please stay in the garage until I can shoot the interior wide shots?" Sierra asked as she opened her door. "Then you can go in, and Erik and Pong can search the place."

"Sure." Toni marched into the garage. She'd been far too compliant this morning. He liked her easy agreement, and yet, he hated it because he knew she was being so agreeable because she was still reeling from yesterday's news.

Sierra got out of the SUV and met Clay at the tailgate. "She's a trained agent and knows not to linger outside." Sierra grabbed her field kit, a near match to their dad's giant tackle box. "And you're setting a bad example."

"How's that?" He took the box from her.

She grabbed a bin labeled lights. "You were a target at the school too. You shouldn't be standing here helping me."

"Brendan's on the dune on overwatch."

Sierra lifted her eyebrows. "So what you're saying is, Brendan would let Toni get hurt but not you."

"No, I..." If Clay's hand was free, he would run it through his hair, maybe tear it out. "Okay, fine. You're right. And I hate it when you are."

"I know." She grinned. "You might want to tell Toni you're sorry."

"Yeah, I might." He followed Sierra into the house, noticing her gait had changed from her pregnancy. He started to mention it, but saying she was waddling was the *very* last thing he should say. Not even in jest. Not even if the comment moved her mind away from his concern for Toni.

After Clay had picked Sierra and Kelsey up at Gage's place, he'd listened to them compare pregnancy woes. He'd started to say something, but Blake slashed a hand across his throat to stop him. Later, he'd told Clay, "a woman may complain about getting fat, waddling, and many other things I wish I didn't know, but you are never to acknowledge them unless directed to do so by her. Ever."

Clay had laughed, but Blake had been deadly serious, and now Clay appreciated the advice.

At the front door, Sierra turned to him. "Where do you want me to start?"

"In the bedrooms with the bunk beds. It's the most likely place to find something related to the trafficking."

"Will do." She got her camera from her kit, and her phone chimed. She hung the camera strap around her neck and looked at her screen. "Text is from Chad. Whatever Toni said to Hunter must've worked because Chad said the twine samples are on the way."

Sierra's assistant was good, but... "You trust Chad to do the comparison?"

"He's a top-notch assistant. But do I wish I was there to compare the samples myself? Yes."

"Maybe things will go smoothly here, and you'll be back in time."

"You did not just say that, did you? Talk about asking for trouble." She shook her head, but he could tell she was kidding. "You can hang with Toni in the garage while I take the scene photos."

He went back to the garage. Now that he had Toni alone, it was time for him to apologize for being pushy about her safety. She was intently studying the file from Martin's investigation, but he wanted to get the apology in before talking to her about the report.

"I'm still coming on too strong," he said.

She looked up. "Yeah, you are."

"I know you're a capable agent. I really do. It's just..." He moved closer. "I guess I don't think of you as an agent anymore. At least it's not my first thought."

She arched an eyebrow. "What do you think of?"

"You're the woman who has captured my attention, and I want to get to know you better."

"But I—"

"Don't think of me that way."

"That's not what I was going to say."

"Then what?"

"I don't want to get involved."

"But you'd think of me as a guy you'd like to get involved with *if* you wanted to get involved?"

"Absolutely." Her conviction made his hope surge even in the face of her rejection.

"I don't think I've ever been rejected so kindly." He grinned to lighten the mood.

"I can do it differently if it would help remove that hopeful expression." Her eyes narrowed. "Because, honestly, even if I already didn't want to get involved, all this family drama would make me lean in that direction. I've got to work through everything first. I don't even know who I am anymore."

He'd already told her what her family had done was no reflection on her, but he wouldn't repeat it again. He knew she had to learn to embrace it.

He nodded at the report. "Finding anything useful?"

"Not useful, but I can sure see the case for charging Andrew." She frowned. "He was guilty. The evidence makes me sure, but the detective didn't get Andrew a lawyer when he requested, just kept questioning him, so Andrew went free." She shook her head. "I'm sure if my parents knew this about Andrew, they would never have let him live with them in Virginia. They would've protected Lisa and not let her travel across country with the man."

"It makes him a strong suspect in Lisa's disappearance."

"The beach visit would be the perfect place to approach her. Much easier to do than while he was living under my parents' roof. Plus, he probably figured even if they considered him for it, my grandparents would support him."

"You'll want to see this," Sierra called out from the house.

"You think she found something this quickly?" Toni tucked the folder under her arm.

"She *is* one of the best." Clay held out his hand. "After you."

They entered the house through a kitchen with stained Formica countertops, the small galley-size room smelling like garlic. They went down the hall and found Sierra squatting by the bottom bunk Clay had seen earlier.

"What did you find?" he asked.

She pointed a gloved finger at the side of the mattress.

He bent down. "I don't see it."

"I didn't at first, either. But you know how I like to shoot my way in and out of a crime scene so I don't miss anything. Well, on the way out, I focused on the bed and found this." She stuck her finger in a narrow hole on the side of the mattress.

"So there's a hole," he said, not overly impressed.

"This isn't from wear and tear. It was sliced open." She stood and unfurled her hand to reveal a folded slip of paper. "And this was inside."

He put on gloves and unfolded the paper to reveal the initials RSL written in red lipstick.

Toni stared at the paper. "What do you think this means?"

A cat-that-ate-the-canary smile crawled across Sierra's face. "It means this scene is connected to the high school."

Clay's sister was talented, but this conclusion seemed farfetched. "How can you possibly know that?"

"Give me a second, and I'll show you." Sierra dug a memory card from her kit and inserted it in her camera. She started scrolling through pictures, stopped on one of them, and held out the camera.

The picture held a shot of a drawer in the workbench in the janitor's closet, another small piece of paper boasting the same initials tucked in the corner.

Clay shot Toni a look. "RSL. Must be one of the trafficked girls."

"And she's telling us she was in these places." Excitement rang through Toni's tone. "Which is why we were sent to the closet."

"And just as important," Clay said. "She connected Jason Rader *and* Rich Hibbard."

# 14

"I need you inside, Erik, but not Pong yet," Clay said into the mic on his comms unit as he marched into the living room, where he could pace and think.

"On my way," Erik replied, the sound of Pong's whine coming from the background.

Toni entered the room and stood watching him, but he couldn't quit moving. This was a big lead. Big enough to break this investigation wide open. *If* they could identify RSL.

Erik stepped into the room, and Sierra joined them from the bedroom.

"I need that list of missing girls you're working on," Clay said. "And I need it yesterday."

He told him about the initials.

Erik tilted his head. "The information is public knowledge, but gathering it will take more time. Trent could get us a list a whole lot faster."

"I'll get Blake to request one." Clay dug out his phone and dialed Blake.

Thankfully he answered his phone even though he was meeting with Trent.

"We have a lead." Clay told Blake about the initials and the photos from Rader's place. "Trent knows about the photos but not the initials as we just found them. Can you get a list from him of every missing girl in the area since the eighties without telling him about this latest lead?"

"The database won't hold old records."

"Then get what he has."

"Let me ask." Blake sounded hesitant.

Why, Clay had no idea. He started pacing again across the dirty tile as he waited for an answer. His feet stuck in places, and he didn't even want to think about what might be on these floors.

Aiden joined them, a puzzled look on his face.

"Someone fill Aiden in," Clay said and resumed his strides. He heard Toni update his brother.

"Trent wants to know why you need the information," Blake said.

Clay halted his movements. He didn't want to share their lead. "If you tell him, he'll take back this scene."

"And well he should."

Not the answer Clay wanted to hear, but it was the right one. "Fine. Tell him. But only after he agrees to provide the list."

Clay shoved his free hand into his hair. They were being stymied by law enforcement at every turn, and he was getting tired of doing the right thing and sharing his leads with them. Sure, it hadn't been so long ago when he was on the other side of the fence, and he should want to help Trent, but he wanted to find Hibbard and make him pay more than anything.

Blake let out a long breath. "Trent's on his way over with your list, and he'll take over the beach house again."

"At least convince him to let Sierra continue the forensics. She's the best. If he doubts it, remind him that she found this lead and his team missed it."

"Will do." Blake ended the call.

Clay shoved his phone into his pocket.

"Well?" Toni asked.

"Trent will bring us a list of missing girls for as far back as their computerized records go, but he's going to take over the house again."

Toni frowned. "Then we need to get searching fast."

Clay looked at his brothers. "You heard her. We have about ten minutes to tear this place apart."

Sitting in the back seat of Clay's SUV, Toni was itching to get going to Ziegler's, so she was glad that the moment Blake slid into the passenger seat, Clay drove off. Even if Clay insisted on stopping to check in with Kelsey on the way. Erik had headed back to the family beach house to keep working on the photos and try to match them to the list Trent provided. Aiden and Brendan were staying with Sierra. Trent forbid them from going inside, but Clay insisted she have family members nearby in case she needed support.

Toni loved seeing the strong connections in the Byrd family even as hers had crumbled around her. The only solid family connections she'd had was with her parents, another thing in her life being called into question. So it wasn't surprising she craved any kind of human connection. Even another hug from Clay.

She had to watch her emotions. She could be confusing her feelings for him for thankfulness. Plus, it wasn't unusual for law enforcement officers to grow close on an investigation, but once the case was closed, they went their separate ways. More often than not, the bond was short-lived.

If she gave in to her feelings for Clay, would they split up after the investigation ended? She'd had a thing for him for over a year, so that could speak to something more long-term. Or not. She just didn't know this any more than she knew who she was.

Blake leaned over the seat. "You should know, there wasn't anyone on the list with the initials RSL."

Toni nodded, but her heart was heavy. She'd foolishly hoped the last initial could have stood for Long, even if it made no sense. Her sister would be in her early forties, far too old to be trafficked. Assuming she was still alive.

Clay glanced at Blake. "Do you think Ziegler has any info about trafficking in the area?"

"Not likely. He was retired before we had any issues in the county. And even then, it was mostly enforced labor, not sex trafficking."

"When did that change?"

"Three years or so before I retired. Was one of the reasons I called it quits. When something so ugly makes it to small-town America, you know things have changed. Wasn't hard to give the job up to be with Emory." Blake's dreamy smile spoke to his love for his wife.

A bolt of jealousy stabbed Toni. Surprising? Not really. She didn't want to go through life alone. She just didn't know if she was the marrying kind. With her mom dying when she was ten and her grandparents never in her life, she didn't have a good frame of reference for what made a strong marriage. She remembered her parents arguing frequently. Now she had to wonder if Lisa was the reason.

Toni had seen similar tragedies tear marriages apart. Often one spouse blamed the other. But who do you blame when a child disappears from their grandparents' house? Clearly her dad believed she'd been taken and had been doing everything he could to find her. But did Toni's mom think Lisa had drowned? Since Toni's father killed her grandumcle, she had to think he'd believed Andrew was involved. That was the only thing that made sense.

Clay glanced at Blake. "Tell us what you know about Rader's wife."

Blake took a long breath. "Her name's Ursula. She's a Russian immigrant. Rader once farmed his land for Christmas trees, and Ursula had married a Hispanic guy who traveled as a migrant worker. She traveled with him, and they came to work tree farms in the area in October to harvest trees for shipping out of state."

Blake shifted in his seat. "The husband was knifed in a bar fight and died. She was terrified of being on her own, and Rader took a liking to her. Asked her to stay on, and he married her within a month. She was a real looker, and there were rumors of her messing around behind Rader's back. But then they had Jason, and she settled down for a while. When the kid got older, she started up with other men again."

"You think she ran off with one of these men?" Clay asked.

Blake shrugged. "Since she was never reported missing, an investigation wasn't opened, but I know Ziegler made casual queries. From what others told him, she liked to go bar hopping in other towns and pick up random men. Many of the men were married, so they didn't volunteer a lot of information."

"What about twine?" Toni asked. "Anything unusual around that?"

"You can find twine on most farms, but like I said, they didn't investigate so I doubt they looked for it. And of course, they had no idea of what Rader was into."

They fell silent for a moment and Toni looked at Blake.

"Any chance we can get ahold of the file for Lisa's abduction?"

He glanced back at her. "It's possible Ziegler made copies of his unsolved cases. I thought about doing the same thing. Figured I might have some free time to work them. But then I decided if I had any free time, it would be spent with Emory. No more living for the job only. Leads to a very lonely life."

At the finality in his tone, she settled back. He was not so subtly telling them both to consider how they were letting work consume their lives. She got that, but she not only had her father's death to investigate, but her missing sister and a long list of girls counting on her. Now wasn't the time to back off. It was the time to do more. Much more.

Clay swung the vehicle onto Rader's gravel drive and killed the engine.

She reached for her handle, but Clay had already gotten out and was opening her door. "You've got me, Drake, and Blake here, but keep your head on a swivel, okay?"

"Sure." She walked beside him toward the backyard.

Blake fell into formation on her other side as if he were part of their team. A law enforcement officer might retire, but the cautious outlook remained. Always vigilant. Always carrying. Always protective.

They stepped through the tall grass and weeds toward Drake, who stood at the corner of the house. He'd already spotted them and nodded an acknowledgment.

"What's happening?" Clay moved past his brother and cupped a hand over his eyes against the sun to survey the property stretching out ahead of them.

"Looks like Kelsey's gotten six hits," Drake said.

Toni stared at him. "Six? You're kidding, right?"

"No. She's been flying the drone since we got here and pounded in six markers."

Toni scanned the area, counting the markers, all but one grouped in a far corner of the property. The sticks made her think of crosses in a cemetery. Was one of these markers resting over Lisa? Her sister? Killed at a young age and buried here like trash. Thrown away with five other girls. Or maybe with Rader's wife.

"Wonder how it works." Toni watched Kelsey pilot the drone over a marker-free area, trying to focus on anything but the possibilities of who was buried there.

"I asked Kelsey, and she was more than happy to tell me." Drake chuckled. "She said the thing uses infrared imaging to detect bodies both above and below ground. She said even if a body has been moved, the technology can find where a corpse was once buried and removed for up to two years afterward."

Clay spun. "Seriously?"

"Yeah, apparently the drone doubles her chance of finding a body." Drake changed his focus to Kelsey. "Then she got all technical, and I don't remember the details, but you can ask her."

"I will." Clay frowned and stood waiting.

Kelsey turned and marched toward them, and Toni didn't like the grim set to her expression.

"Six bodies?" Clay asked when she reached them.

"You know I can't say." She set her drone in a container and picked up a metal water bottle to chug the liquid.

"How about telling us exactly how the drone works," Toni said. "Drake couldn't remember the details beyond the infrared."

"His eyes did seem to glaze over while I was talking." She glanced at him and chuckled.

"Hey, yours would too if I started discussing my favorite subject."

"Which is?" She set down her water.

"Weapons and ballistics."

"Ah, yes. You're right. I would zone out." She laughed but quickly sobered and faced Clay. "About the drone technology. Decaying bodies release carbon and nitrogen into the soil. The soil then reflects less light. When a person is first buried, they release a flood of chemicals that kill plants around them. As the chemicals disperse into the soil around the body, it changes and becomes a fertilizer that reflects a ton of light. The drone's near infrared imaging can detect those light reflections."

"And just like that you know a body's buried where the light reflects," Toni stated.

"I *suspect* there's a body." She put her hand on a yellow-and-black machine that looked much like a lawn mower with a video screen mounted on the handle. "But in areas where it's feasible, I use ground penetrating radar to confirm."

"Why don't you start with that?" Clay asked.

"Quicker to use the drone, as it can go places this machine can't."

"And after you confirm?" Toni asked.

"I notify law enforcement, and with their permission, begin digging. Now if you'll excuse me, I have work to do." She pushed her machine across the dusty soil to the first flag.

"So without saying anything, she told us she suspects she has six bodies here," Toni said, her last meal churning in her stomach at the thought.

"Other than Rader's wife, who do you think it is?" Blake asked.

"Some of the girls he trafficked," Toni said. "Maybe their johns got too rough. Or they could even have gotten sick. Not like he could have taken them to see a doctor. He'd have to get rid of the bodies. Burying them on private property reduces the odds of them being found."

Clay worked the muscle in his jaw. "Could also tell us why Rader didn't move when he had that cash sitting around."

Drake pointed at the house. "Or even remodel the place. A worker might stumble on the first grave, which is pretty close to the house."

"*If* it is a grave," Blake said. "We don't know that for sure."

"And won't until Kelsey calls Trent," Toni said.

"*If* she found bodies and calls Trent," Drake added.

Clay looked at his brother. "We're heading out to talk to Sheriff Ziegler. I want you on the horn to me the minute Trent shows up here."

"Not sure it'll do you any good," Drake said.

"Sure it will. If he comes here when he already has so much on his plate, it tells me there's at least one body."

"Yeah." Drake raised his eyebrows. "But it doesn't tell you who and if there are more."

# 15

Clay and Toni followed Blake up the dirt path to a worn red door in a single-story house. The place had once been white but had grayed. Tall pines towered over the house, and shrubs and ferns filled in the space below.

The door was opened by a frail man around five-ten with slicked back silvery-blond hair. He wore ratty jeans and a red flannel shirt and had a gun on his hip.

"Hey, old man." Blake's fond tone told of his affection for the retired sheriff. "You doing okay?"

"I'm still above ground." He looked past Blake at Clay then Toni. "Your wife know you're keeping company with such a fine looking woman?"

Toni laughed and held out her hand. "I'm Agent Toni Long with the FBI."

"Good looking and a Fed." His gaze filled with respect as he shook her hand.

He shifted his focus to Clay. "And you're a traitor like Blake. Turning your back on law enforcement."

Clay had no idea what to say, so he offered his hand. "Clay Byrd."

For a fragile-looking guy, Ziegler had a strong grip. "I was just joking."

"Honestly, I wasn't sure. You still have the caught-you-red-handed sheriff expression down pat." Clay chuckled.

Ziegler laughed, and it was deep and hearty. He looked at Blake. "Now tell me what you need, boy."

Blake shook his head, and Clay had to believe it was because Ziegler called him boy. "Like I said on the phone, we want to talk to you about Lisa Long."

He shot a look at Toni. "Any relation?"

"Apparently, my sister, but I just found out about her yesterday."

Zeigler's bushy eyebrows drew together into a large gray caterpillar. "Guess we're even then. I never heard about you."

Blake held out a bag. "Your apple fritters."

Zeigler snatched it up and stepped back. "Coffee's on. Help yourself on the way past."

He scurried through a neat but small kitchen, grabbing a plate as he moved, and Blake went straight for the coffee pot. He took down three cups and filled them. "He gets a little cranky when you refuse his coffee. Lorraine taught him how to make it, so it's usually pretty good, but you can just hold it if you don't want it."

Cups filled, Blake led them down a short hall to a small living room with very little furniture.

Ziegler had dropped into a big leather recliner and had already placed the fritters on the plate. "Go ahead. Have a seat on the couch. Paid enough for it, so it should get some use. And help yourself to the fritters, but leave me one."

Clay waited for Toni to sit and perched on the arm next to her.

Blake leaned against the wall. "Mind telling us about when Lisa went missing?"

"Bad day, that was." Ziegler frowned then took a long slurp of his coffee. "Just got promoted to detective, and the call comes in right as I hit the office. Little Lisa was gone. Vanished, her—" He looked at Toni. "—*your* grandparents said they last saw her when she went to bed around nine. She was staying with them for the week, and this was day three. She flew from Virginia to Portland with your granduncle, Andrew Martin, and then your grandparents picked them up at the airport."

"Did Andrew always live in Virginia?" Clay asked.

"Nope. Lived right here, but when your parents moved to Virginia, he said he needed a fresh start. They let him stay with them while he got his feet under him in a new city. I got the feeling he was running from something, but I have no idea what as it never involved us."

"So you didn't know he was arrested in Virginia for having sex with a ten-year-old," Clay stated bluntly, earning a sharp look from Blake. "Got off on a technicality."

Ziegler snapped his chair forward and sloshed his coffee. "'Course I didn't know that, or he woulda been my top suspect for Lisa's disappearance. This changes everything. Gonna give Trent a call and have him get Martin back here for an interview."

"He's deceased," Blake said. "Killed in 1990 in a shootout with Toni's dad."

Ziegler looked at Toni. "Then let's get your dad on the phone. He can tell us why the heck he killed the guy."

"My dad died on an op a year ago," Toni said.

Zeigler rubbed his forehead and blinked a few times. "He woulda been too old to still be an agent, so what was he doing on an op?"

"It was my op, not his. He had no business being there, and I have no idea why he was." She explained about Hibbard.

He set down his cup. "Your mother, then. We can call her."

"Died when I was ten."

Ziegler rested his head back on his chair and closed his eyes as if too tired to go on.

"You okay, old man?" Blake asked.

"Just thinking about everything you sprung on me." He lifted his head and pinned his gaze to Toni. "You think your dad knew something about Martin? Knew he took Lisa and got his revenge?"

She shrugged. "My parents never told me about Lisa, so if Dad did know anything, he couldn't very well tell me."

"So say Martin was into sex with children," Ziegler said. "Then you've got this Hibbard guy who's trafficking all ages of girls. Maybe he has something to do with Lisa too."

"It's a possibility, but he would've been pretty young back then," Clay said. "But let's go back to Martin when Lisa disappeared. You didn't consider him a suspect at all?"

Ziegler's light blue eyes narrowed. "Sure, in the way you *always* consider male family members when something like this happens. But I didn't have any evidence pointing to him or a reason to believe it was him. I can tell a faker a mile away. Just ask Blake here."

"He really can," Blake said. "I never got away with anything."

Ziegler gave a gruff snort. "This guy wasn't faking. He was genuinely upset. Said he never had kids of his own and considered her his granddaughter."

Blake's turn to snort. "Doubtful with what we now know about him."

"If we'd only known it back then. Gotta figure your grandparents knew about Martin's proclivities. I found him to be sincere, but there seemed to be something off about them. Like they weren't telling me everything. Still, I could tell they wanted Lisa back, and I didn't think they were hiding anything that would help find her. But now..." He shook his head. "Now I wonder if I should've pressed harder."

"Hindsight always makes us question," Blake said. "You did the best job you could've at the time."

"Yeah, I guess." He twisted gnarled fingers together.

"What did he and my grandparents think happened to Lisa?" Toni's tone was tight.

"They said she was a well-behaved kid. Would never sneak out at night. And she didn't know anyone, so she wouldn't have left to meet another kid. They thought someone broke in and took her."

He paused to take a quick sip of his coffee. "But there was no sign of a forced intrusion, and her window was unlocked. No strange fingerprints on any of the windows or doors. No footprints on the ground outside any window or doors. And no evidence of forced abduction. If someone took her, she didn't cry out or struggle."

"Could've been drugged." Toni's anguished tone cut right through him.

"We toyed with that idea, but again, no evidence."

"And no one heard anything?" Clay asked.

Ziegler shook his head, sending the loose skin on his neck wobbling. "Your grandparents went to bed around ten, Martin closer to midnight. Your grandma got up at seven and went to check on Lisa. She was gone. She alerted your grandad and Martin. They looked for her near the house, and when they couldn't find her, they called us."

He leaned back in his chair again. "Our best hope in the early days were sex offenders in the area, but their alibis all checked out. Lost Creek being a tourist town coulda meant it was someone passing through, but that was a dead end too. Especially because of the no break-in thing."

"And I'm right in saying there were no issues with human trafficking back then," Blake said.

"Nah. Not around these parts. We were a pretty sleepy little town and a very rural county. Things have changed so much I hardly know the place anymore."

"Can we switch to Rader and his wife?" Clay explained why he asked. "Blake shared what he knew, but I'd like to hear your take."

"You know Rader didn't even report her leaving. Neither did their kid. Well not a kid. Jason was sixteen and already had a juvie record by that time. Wife was carousing with all kinds of men, and the parents let Jason run wild."

"We've connected him to our main suspect, a guy named Rich Hibbard," Toni said.

"You gotta be kidding me." Ziegler swung his head in wide arcs.

"Do you remember twine factoring in Lisa's investigation or Ursula taking off?" Toni asked.

"Twine?" Ziegler tapped his chin with a crooked index finger. "Not that I recall."

Blake looked at his old mentor. "I'm assuming you have a copy of Lisa's case files."

"You know I do." Ziegler grimaced. "Figured once I retired I could solve my open cases, but I haven't made any progress."

"Mind if we take them with us for a bit?" Blake asked.

"'Course I mind, but I'll let you have them anyway."

"We'll return them in the same condition we got them in," Toni said, her tone filled with respect.

"I believe you will, young lady." Ziegler rocked his chair a few times to propel him to his feet. He stared at Blake. "C'mon, boy, you can help."

Rolling his eyes, Blake pushed away from the wall and followed the older man out of the room.

"He's a character," Toni said.

"Seemed like he was on the ball for Lisa's investigation."

"Yeah."

Clay felt bad about his next question, but he had to voice it. "What did you think about his comment about your grandparents maybe withholding information from him?"

"I didn't like it, of course. But it will give me something to look for when I talk to them." She crossed her arms. "It's time to go see them."

"Yeah." He wished he didn't have to agree. "We can drop Blake and the files back at my parents' place. Then we'll go meet your grandparents."

Toni straightened her blouse and tugged on the collar as she slid out of the SUV into a break in the misty rain and the warmth of the sun. When they'd dropped Blake off at the beach house, she'd freshened up, changed clothes, and studied herself in the mirror for far too long. Wondering all the time what her grandparents would think of her. Would they be happy to see her? Sad because she reminded them of Lisa? Or even worse—would they refuse to see her because of the estrangement with her parents?

"Hey," Clay said as he came up beside her. "It'll be okay. They'll love you and be glad to meet you."

She took her focus from the worn but neat bungalow abutting the beach. "You can't know that."

"I can. After all, I'm glad I met you, and you're very easy to fall in love with."

How could she possibly respond? She couldn't. She straightened her blouse again and marched up the walkway. Her heels clicked in sharp staccatos on the concrete, mixing with the gulls' cries from the beach.

She knocked on the door painted a crisp white and stood back. She fidgeted with her hands, not knowing where to put them, and Clay took one in his. Her skin was clammy, but he didn't say a word, just held tight, and his firm resoluteness bled into her skin and warmed her heart.

The door opened, and she jerked free.

A tall man appeared. He had a long face and bushy gray brows beneath a partially bald scalp with bright white hair sticking out.

"Help you?" His voice was warm and crisp at the same time.

She was suddenly transported back to her childhood when she'd imagined all of her grandparents were alive. He sounded exactly like the daydreams of the grandpa she never knew. But he looked different. Much different than she'd imagined.

"Walt, who's at the door?" The woman, Toni's grandmother, she assumed, joined them. Toni drank in the sight of her. She had iron-gray hair cut in a cap around her face holding as many wrinkles as a cotton shirt left to dry in a ball. Her eyes were big and blue just like Toni's mother's.

Toni gasped.

"Say, what's this all about?" her grandmother asked. "Who are...oh." She paled and took a step back. "Your badge. On your belt. You're the law. Is this about...have you finally..." She grabbed onto her husband's arm.

"Is Lisa dead?" he asked matter-of-factly. His gaze flicked to Clay as if he was in charge.

"No...no," Toni got out. "We're not here to tell you she's been found."

Her grandmother let a breath out and sagged against Toni's grandfather, clutching his crisply pressed blue-and-white gingham shirt.

"Then why are you here?" Toni's grandfather asked.

"I'm Toni." She didn't explain, just let the words hang there to see if her parents had told them she existed.

"Oh my stars." Her grandmother stared at Toni. "Yes, yes, I can see Edie in your face."

They stared at each other, none of them knowing what to do. Toni felt like she was there under false pretenses and needed to introduce Clay. "I'm an FBI agent, and this is my associate Clay Byrd. We were working on an investigation, and I just learned about Lisa."

Her grandfather tilted his head. "They didn't tell you?"

"No." Her voice broke on the single word. "I didn't even know I had a sister until yesterday."

"Would you mind answering some questions for us?" Clay asked.

Her grandmother stepped back. "Come in. Please come in."

Toni crossed the threshold and caught the smell of arthritis cream mixed with something fried.

"May I give you a hug?" her grandmother asked.

Toni nodded, but she wasn't sure she wanted to hug this woman she didn't know. Sure, they were blood relatives, but she still felt like a complete stranger to Toni. *A stranger with your mother's eyes,* she reminded herself.

Her grandmother gathered her into her strong arms, her body solid and lean. She wore a feminine green blouse and khaki pants that matched her grandfather's pants. Toni held herself back a bit but inhaled her grandmother's flowery scent. Maybe roses or gardenias. Way too sweet of a scent for Toni or her mother, who'd never worn perfume.

But if this was the only time Toni saw her grandmother, she would always have this smell to remember the meeting. She pushed back.

"Come with me." Her grandmother took Toni's hand, her skin papery soft, and led her down a short hall to a living room that was straight from the eighties. The walls were paneled, and the room had a dark, dank feel instead of the lightness in the Byrd's house. A burgundy modular sofa with plush fabric took up a corner of the room and a large brown recliner that looked as if it was on its last legs was next to it. There was also a blue-and-mauve club chair, and an octagonal dark wood table nearby, plus an oversize matching coffee table with a glass top in front of the sofa.

"Please have a seat." Her grandmother released her hand. "Can I get you anything to drink? I could brew some coffee or tea. Water?"

"No, but thank you for asking." Toni perched on the end of the sofa.

"I'm good." Clay came to rest on the arm next to her. He'd gone into his protective mode and was giving her grandparents a wary look as they sat on the easy chair and recliner.

"I can't believe you're here," her grandmother said. "We'd heard you were born, but that was all."

"Who did you hear it from?" Clay asked before Toni could.

Her grandfather kicked back his recliner. "Gert's brother, Andrew. Right before he died. He was living out in the D.C. area with your parents."

"How'd he die?" she asked as if she didn't know.

"He was murdered. Drive-by targeting someone else was what the police told us." He took a breath. "How're your mom and dad doing?"

Toni didn't miss the sudden change in topic. "I'm sorry to say, both my parents have passed away."

Toni's grandmother clamped her hand over her mouth.

Toni hated shocking them like this, but she had no choice. "Mom died when I was ten from a fall off her horse. He was spooked by a rattlesnake."

"She always did love horses, so maybe that was a good way to go." Her grandfather's eyes were watery with tears, and he swiped a big hand at them. "And your dad?"

"Shot in an op just last year."

"I'm real sorry to hear that." He planted his hands on the arms of the chair.

It was then she noticed that he had long, narrow fingers like hers, though his knuckles were gnarled.

She wanted to take her time and absorb her grandparents' essence. To sit and look at them both and find other similarities between them, but she had a purpose in coming here, and she wouldn't forget the girls who were depending on her. "Would you tell us what happened when Lisa went missing?"

Her grandmother stiffened. "Is the FBI agent wanting to know, or is my granddaughter asking?"

"Both," Toni admitted. "I can't separate the two, but I've been an agent longer than I've known you were alive, so probably more agent than anything."

"They told you we were dead?" her grandfather asked. "Your parents, I mean."

She nodded.

He sucked in a sharp breath and gripped the arms of his chair.

Toni didn't like seeing him upset. It wasn't in a close or personal way, but more like an agent observing suffering people. Would she ever feel anything for this man? He seemed okay, but then she didn't know anything about him and needed to stay on track so she could learn something. She focused on his face, the wrinkles telling of his years of living, so many of them with the sorrow of losing a granddaughter and being estranged from a daughter.

"Can you tell me why my parents didn't want me to know about you?" She hated that the suspicion in her tone tightened her grandfather's expression, but her parents were good people and had to have had a good reason to lie to her. At least she'd thought they were good. Now she didn't know.

"Answer's as simple as can be." Her grandmother captured Toni's attention as she crossed her arms. "They blamed us for Lisa's disappearance."

"Were you responsible?" Clay asked.

Toni gasped and looked up at him, but his gaze was razoring between her grandparents like a bullet seeking a target.

"In as much as she was in our care at the time, yes." Her grandfather crossed his long arms and glared at Clay. "But in every other way, no."

"She just vanished!" her grandmother cried out as she sat forward. "We said good-night, and she was gone in the morning."

"What was she wearing when she disappeared?" Toni asked.

Both of her grandparents shook their heads. "She was wearing Rainbow Brite pajamas, but those pjs were on the bed. So she must've changed at some point, but I didn't know what she'd brought with her. And even your mother couldn't come up with what was missing from Lisa's suitcase."

Clay shook his head. "Do you think she left voluntarily?"

"She wouldn't do that," her grandmother said forcefully. "She'd only been here three days. She didn't know anyone, and no one knew her."

"No one," her grandfather echoed.

"Just me, Walt, and Andrew."

"And you don't think Andrew had anything to do with her disappearance?" Clay asked.

"Of course not. Why would we think that?"

"Because of his near conviction for sex with a minor."

Her grandmother waved a hand. "He was innocent and cleared. He volunteered for a church youth group, and a girl got it in her mind that he'd assaulted her at camp. But they never proved he did it."

"They didn't prove he didn't, either," Clay said. "He was released on a technicality, not because he didn't do it."

Her grandmother glared at Clay. "I know my brother. He wouldn't have done such a thing."

Ah, now Toni was seeing the hesitancy and unease that had Ziegler questioning if there was more to the story than they were letting on.

"What about Andrew's friends?" Clay asked. "He grew up here. Did he see anyone while he was home?"

"He was kind of a loner," her grandfather said, not really answering the question.

"But did he see anyone while he was here?" Toni asked.

"Maybe," her grandmother said. "Was a long time ago."

"Maybe or he did?" Toni pressed.

Her grandmother's chin lifted, and Toni almost sucked in a breath at the similarity to her mother. An older version, but her mother nonetheless. And she was stubborn like her mother. Like Toni too.

"Did he see someone while he was here?" Toni asked again.

"Yes, all right," her grandmother snapped.

"Now, Gert," her grandfather said.

"I'm so tired of holding onto this. It's time to let it out." She knitted her fingers together in her lap. "Andrew was an elder in our church before he moved to Virginia, and he mentored our church youth leader, Nolan Wilshire. Nolan came over for a few minutes the night before Lisa went missing. He met Lisa while he was here."

"Why didn't you want the police to know that?" Toni asked.

"Because Nolan didn't do anything wrong." Her grandfather glared at her. "He was a good Christian man. The sheriff was so eager for a lead he would've hounded him."

"If he had nothing to hide, he would've faired okay," Clay said.

"He was going through a nasty divorce." Her grandmother reached for a glass of water and took a long drink. "His wife cheated on him, but she claimed it was Nolan doing the cheating, and he was faced with losing custody of his kids. Any suspicions cast his way would've made sure he *did* lose custody, and he had nothing to do with Lisa, so why ruin his life?"

"And did he? Lose custody, I mean?" Toni asked.

"Sadly, yes. His ex lied so very convincingly."

"So you could've told the sheriff about Nolan then," Toni said.

"No. No." Her grandfather pointed his long chin at her. "Would've made us look like liars and call into question everything else we told him. And what would the point be? Nothing. 'Cause we told him everything else. Honest."

When someone felt a need to add the word *honest* to the end of their statement, they were most likely hiding something else, but the stubborn tilt to her grandfather's head declared he had said all that he planned to say about that point.

"Might Nolan, Andrew, or either of you have mentioned Lisa's visit to someone else?"

"I mighta told my golf buddies," her grandfather said. "Not sure if I did or didn't."

"I know I didn't say anything," her grandmother said. "The trip was a quick thing. The DEA wanted to send your dad to Chicago, and your parents needed to decide if they wanted to move before telling Lisa. That was why they sent her out here. To give them time. If we'd had a Sunday before she arrived, I woulda told everyone at church because I was so excited to have her stay with us. But they called on a Monday, and she was here by Wednesday. No time to tell others with getting a room ready for her."

"But Nolan might have?"

"No. I asked him. He swore on his Bible that he didn't say a word."

Swearing on a Bible meant nothing. People lied and used every method to cover it up, but clearly her grandfather didn't think so.

"Did you ever hear the name of the woman he supposedly had the affair with?" Clay asked.

Her grandparents both shook their heads.

"And does he still live here?" Toni asked.

"No." Her grandmother looked so sad. "Poor man went a little crazy when he lost his children. Threatened his wife. She got a restraining order. He was so dejected he took off."

"To where?"

"He went to live at his grandfather's old farmhouse in Douglas County," her grandfather said. "He wanted to be on his own. Find some seclusion and live off the land, and I don't blame him. We wanted to do the same thing back then. You have no idea what we went through."

Clay eyed her grandfather. "Nothing compared to what Lisa went through."

"Well, yeah, of course. That goes without saying." Her grandfather pointed his chin at Clay. "You sound like you don't believe us. That we did something to get our sweet little Lisa taken. We didn't. We loved that child. Love her now, too. What I wouldn't give to see her walk in the door. We'd throw a party for her."

"We need her DNA," Clay said. "Might you have anything of hers, like a hairbrush?"

"We kept her suitcase and everything in it." Her grandmother looked at Toni. "Your parents stayed in a hotel in town for six months or so looking for Lisa. When they went back home, they left Lisa's things behind. I was surprised they didn't want them, but maybe the memories were too much for them." She stood, rising slowly, her hand on her back. "I'll get her brush."

She hurried out of the room as if a marauding army had arrived and not her granddaughter asking a few questions.

Clay looked at her grandfather. "You wouldn't happen to have a church directory from that time, would you?"

"Probably, but why?"

"I'd like to see who Nolan might've talked to. To see if he lied to you and knows something about Lisa's disappearance."

"I hate to dredge all this up again, but if you can find Lisa, it's well worth the pain of getting your sister back." He peered at Toni.

She didn't think her sister was coming back, but she didn't say so. She wanted to hope for Lisa too, but statistics said children who weren't found in the first twenty-four hours were rarely found alive. With those dire stats, what hope was there for Lisa after being missing for more than thirty years?

# 16

Toni looked around the family room while Clay talked to Erik about looking for Nolan Wilshire. The Byrd's beach house was now familiar and comfortable to her and felt like a sanctuary. Like the house was surrounding her with protective arms and helping her come to grips with everything.

She'd been desperate for family since her dad died. Now that she knew about the others, she honestly had no clue what she was feeling. Or even if she was feeling anything for them. She probably should. But they were strangers to her, and they may have withheld valuable information on Lisa's abduction. Toni couldn't move forward until they were cleared of any involvement.

Tears wetted her eyes, and the very last thing she wanted was to cry. She was an agent, for goodness' sakes. She'd been shot at before and didn't start boo-hooing. At least not in front of anyone. She could hold back the emotions today too. After all, she'd been containing them in front of the team for days now. She could manage it until she was alone.

She went to her boxes sitting near the dining table. She

started pawing through the top one holding her dad's work items and picked up the picture with her mother.

She'd been gone for over twenty years, but at times, to Toni, it felt as if she'd lost her mom just yesterday. She'd missed so many years of being with her mother, so many important moments. Her first date. Prom. Homecoming. Graduation from high school, college, and the Academy.

These special milestones weren't the only difficult days. She missed her mother's comforting arms. Their conversations. Sharing triumphs and hurts. Oh, how Toni missed her. She still remembered the day it really hit her that her mother was gone. It happened a month after the funeral. Toni had a craving for her mom's chocolate chip cookies—crisp and extra sweet.

Without her dad knowing it, Toni grabbed her mother's recipe box, mixed up a batch, and baked the first pan. But they didn't turn out crispy. They weren't like her mother's at all. At first she'd thought it was because she was just a kid and shouldn't have been baking. Her mind flashed to thinking, *I'll just ask Mom*.

Then it hit her. She couldn't ask her mom. Not ever again.

She'd dropped to the floor in the kitchen and sobbed. Her dad had found her there. He tried to comfort her, but Toni only wanted her mother's special touch. Then and right now. Toni needed her mother.

Tears flooded her eyes, and she made sure Clay couldn't see her face from the family room. The front door opened, and his brothers came barreling inside. A tornado of testosterone.

She swiped a hand over her eyes and swallowed hard.

Clay left everyone in the family room and joined her.

They looked at each other for a long moment, and something unspoken passed between them. Another thing she couldn't put a name to, but the feeling cheered her.

He nodded at the frame she was still clutching. "You looking for something in that photo?"

"Some comfort, I guess," she admitted. "The meeting with my grandparents has left me a mess."

He stepped closer while his brothers settled onto the big living room sectional and clicked on the television. Erik released Pong from his crate and took him outside.

"Me too, but I'll deny ever having said it." Clay smiled at her, a soft, intimate smile only for her.

He really was a special guy, and she wanted to get lost in his eyes. Maybe seek comfort in his arms again, but not in front of his brothers. She turned her attention back to the photo and tapped it. "I'm still wondering how Rader got this outfit."

"May I?" Clay held out his hand.

"I just don't get it." She handed over the frame. "What's his connection to me?"

Clay flipped the picture then looked up. "You said your dad kept this on his desk."

"He did."

Clay ran his fingers over the brown paper glued to the frame in a neat seal. "There's no stand affixed to the back like most desktop picture frames include."

She dug in the box and pulled out a Lucite easel. "He used this."

"Wouldn't it have been easier to get a frame with a built-in stand?"

"I suppose. Do you think it's important?"

"What if the paper is covering something up?"

Was it? She'd never considered the idea. Not once in the countless times she'd looked at the picture when she'd visited her dad's office. But she'd been too focused on drinking in the sight of her mother. Of trying to remember this day. Remember the feeling of joy. Of love. Not of sadness over her loss.

"Mind if I take the paper off?" Clay asked.

"Go ahead," she said, doubting they would find anything.

Erik returned with Pong and settled on the sofa as Clay dug a small knife from his pocket and flipped out the blade. He sliced around the back, set the knife on the table, and lifted the paper.

He revealed a brass key taped on the back of the photo. She gaped at the shiny key sparkling in the overhead light.

"Oh my gosh!" She ripped the key free and studied it. "There's a bank's name engraved on it."

Clay looked at her, excitement burning in his eyes. "It's likely for a safe deposit box."

"Not for his regular bank. I closed those accounts. And there weren't any statements or correspondence for this bank in his things. Not at home or at work."

Clay locked onto her gaze. "Sounds like he didn't want anyone to know about this."

"Another secret."

"Which means it's something we really need to see. Hopefully your dad left money in this account to keep paying the rental fees. Otherwise, the bank could've disposed of the contents."

"My dad was very thorough. He probably paid rent on it for a year or two. If the items are important, that is. Which they must be." She felt the heaviness of the key in her palm. "I need to overnight this to Vance. I'm sure he'll check it out for us." She got out her phone to call her father's former boss.

Clay started to set down the photo but stopped and

stared at it as if the picture might jump out of the frame and bite him like the rattler they'd encountered.

Her stomach started churning. "What is it?"

"Something's written on the back, but prepare yourself." He held it out. "It's a shocker."

# 17

Clay reached out to catch Toni as she dropped to the stool, her face as pale as the white countertop in the attached kitchen. He didn't think she could survive another family secret, but she was working hard to do so. Breathing deeply and exhaling, obviously trying to cope.

She traced her finger over the crisp handwriting on the photo back. Clay checked the words again to be sure he'd read them right. *Lisa and Edie.*

"He lied to me again." Toni shook her head. "All these years I've been trying to place this day in my memory, and it's not my memory at all. It's Lisa and Mom."

Toni tossed the photo on the counter and turned her back on it. "Finding a copy of this picture and the clothes in Rader's garage makes more sense now."

"You're thinking Rader took Lisa."

She flashed him a look. "Aren't you?"

"Yes, but we can only prove that Rader knew about her and the other girls and perhaps took souvenirs from them."

"Then we need to find that proof." She made strong eye contact. "Do you think Lisa is buried in his backyard?"

"First, we don't officially know if Kelsey found graves. Second, we have no indication Lisa died."

A knock sounded on the door, and Clay spun, his hand on his weapon. He looked at his brothers. "Anyone expecting a visitor?"

He received head shakes in response, and Pong's head came up, his posture hyperalert. Clay went to the door, drawing his gun on the way. He looked out the peephole.

"It's Trent." Clay holstered his sidearm and opened the door.

"Heard you went to meet the Longs." Trent pressed his lips together.

Clay had done nothing wrong but he felt a need to raise his shoulders. "We did."

Trent rubbed the back of his neck. "Let's talk about it."

Clay didn't want Toni to have to relive the conversation, but he didn't want to alienate Trent either, so Clay stepped back, and Trent strode past him. Clay introduced him to his brothers, and they shared a look of mutual respect that one law enforcement officer automatically had for the other. No judgment for leaving law enforcement. Just respect.

"Can I get you some coffee or water?" Clay asked.

Trent rubbed a hand over a tired face. "I'd kill for a cup of coffee."

Clay led him into the kitchen and looked at Toni. "Want a cup?"

She shook her head, still seeming like she was barely hanging in there.

Trent took a seat at the counter, three stools away from Toni. "You look like meeting them has left you shaken up."

Toni bit her lip and looked at Clay, probably trying to decide if she should mention the key and the picture. He gave her a quick nod.

"I am, but it's more than that now." She slid the picture over to Trent. "The photo we thought was me and my mom is actually Lisa and Mom."

Trent took a long look at the back of the picture. "You didn't ever suspect that?"

"Sure, all my life I wondered if my parents were hiding siblings from me. I used to check the closets, just in case."

Her sarcastic tone was so unusual that Clay turned to check on her.

"Sorry." She clutched her hands together on the countertop. "I'm at the end of my rope."

"This is big." Trent tapped the picture. "Ties Rader to Lisa's disappearance."

"Yeah," was all Toni said.

The single-serve cup of coffee started dripping, and Clay rested against the counter. "While we were there, we got Lisa's hairbrush. Emory will process it for DNA. And I'm hoping you'll give Kelsey permission to tell us if it matches the remains found at the school."

Trent sucked in a sharp breath. "My department should've taken that into evidence."

Clay might be cooperating but he wasn't going to be blamed for doing something wrong when he didn't. "You don't have an active investigation open on Lisa, so I figured it was okay for us to handle."

Trent continued to stare at him.

Clay pushed off the counter and planted his feet. "She's Toni's sister, and she's missing for Pete's sake. Toni has every right to find out what happened to her."

Trent let out a breath and looked at Toni. "Sorry. Yeah, you do have the right. And I don't have an open investigation."

"Can Kelsey tell us if there's a match?" Toni asked, looking like a lost little girl instead of a strong FBI agent.

Trent shook his head, and Clay wanted to deck the guy.

"But I can." Trent gave her a tight smile. "The remains are from a young girl, and they haven't been in the wall long enough for it to be Lisa. We think we have an identity but we're waiting on DNA to confirm."

Clay smiled at Toni. "Good news, right?"

She nodded and let out a hissing breath, looking like she was deflating as her shoulders sank and she clutched her arms around her stomach.

The urge to hold her nearly had Clay crossing over to her, but the coffee finished, so he handed the mug to Trent. "Cream or sugar?"

"Black's good." Trent blew on the liquid and took a sip.

Clay started another cup brewing for himself. "What can you tell us about the graves at Rader's place?"

Trent took a long sip of his mug. "Who said Dr. Dunbar found graves?"

"I stopped by to check on her. She had six markers and she was looking for bodies, so I put two and two together."

Trent sighed.

"Look," Clay said. "We're sharing information with you. You can at least confirm the graves exist."

"Okay, fine. Six graves were located on Rader's property."

"Has Kelsey begun to dig yet?" Clay asked.

Trent nodded. "And you should know, I banished your brother to the front of the property so don't expect him to report any findings to you. I assigned a deputy to assist Kelsey."

"Will you let us know if Lisa's DNA is recovered?" Toni asked.

Trent nodded.

"How are you coming along with matching the photos from Rader's garage?" Clay asked not only because he wanted to know, but for Toni's sake, he wanted to move them away from discussing Lisa.

Trent set down his cup and rubbed his eyes. "I've got murder investigations for the high school and Rader. Not to mention Jason Rader's beach house investigation. And my IT guy is stretched to the max. He's just now starting a search on the photos. What about you?"

"Got an algorithm scraping the internet," Erik called out from the family room, Pong's alert expression matching Erik's tone. "Should have something by end of day."

"Good." Trent took another sip of his coffee and stood. "Keep me updated on what you find."

"You do the same." Clay walked Trent to the door and stopped in the family room on the way back to look at his brothers. "Please tell me someone has located Nolan Wilshire."

"I have," Brendan said. "But you won't like what I found."

After a planning meeting with the team, Toni was back in the SUV with Clay, heading down a country road toward Nolan Wilshire's secluded property. Brendan had discovered the guy had drawn a gun on the last law enforcement officer who'd visited him, and she was feeling way too vulnerable to handle a guy aiming a gun at her. The loss of her mother and father told her life was fleeting. Add to it the loss of a sister she'd never even met and probably never would. And then there was Clay. She now knew she didn't want to lose him from her life too. But was she ready to commit to more than a passing interest?

*Am I?*

Irritated at the turn of her thoughts, she got out the church directory from her grandfather and started flipping through the pages, looking for anything to help with their questioning of Wilshire. The directory held names, addresses, and family photos. She paused at her grandparents' picture and sucked in a deep breath.

"What is it?" Clay asked.

She tapped the photo. "My grandmother looks like my mom in the picture with Lisa."

Clay nodded but didn't say anything as he came to a stop at a red light.

She moved on. Turning past the names in alphabetical order and coming to a stop again when she saw a familiar name in the R section. "The Raders were members."

She held out the photo of a much younger looking Fritz Rader with Jason and Ursula.

Clay glanced at it and got the car moving again. "She really was a striking woman."

"Probably why Rader didn't want her to leave him. Maybe Wilshire will know more about them." She continued on through the directory.

The GPS voice announced their last turn ahead, and Clay clicked on his blinker. He slowed and made the turn onto an even narrower road, then looked at Toni for a long moment. "You've been awful quiet."

"Thinking." She left it at that. She wasn't about to tell him her thoughts about him were racing across her forehead like a billboard in Times Square, and looked away before she said something she might regret.

He focused on the road again and sped up. "I know our risk assessment said the risks with this guy are low, even if he drew down on a deputy, but I want you to be careful."

"Will do," she said, her mind still on the directory,

wondering if someone listed in the pages might know what happened to Lisa.

"Remember, our doors are armor-plated, so please stand behind yours until we have his buy-in."

She locked gazes for a moment. "I can do this, Clay. Just trust me."

He opened his mouth as if to respond but pressed his lips tight and looked back at the road. He pulled into Wilshire's driveway and passed the posted *No Trespassing* sign. He continued to a tiny clearing in a property surrounded by tall pines and holding a minuscule house.

He shifted into park, and she got out of the SUV. He slid out on his side, but her attention went to a man stepping onto the porch, rifle in hand. His head was shaved, his beard scraggly, and his face wrinkled. Baggy jeans hung on his slight frame, and he'd paired them with a green undershirt, and an open plaid shirt with the sleeves cut off. She spotted a large tattoo on his left forearm but couldn't make it out.

"Get going now," he shouted. "This is private property. Whatever you're selling I don't want it."

She remained behind the door. "I'm not selling anything."

"Don't care. Don't want you here."

"My name is Toni Long. My father was murdered a year ago, and I'm trying to find his killer."

"And you think I had something to do with that? Don't even know him."

"No, no." She started to wave a hand, but realized he might think she was going for her gun and stopped.

He nodded at Clay. "And who's this guy?"

"My friend, Clay Byrd. He's helping me find my father's killer."

"Again. What does this have to do with me?"

"While investigating my father's death, I learned I have a

sister. Lisa. She went missing from my grandparents' house when she was twelve. Do you remember her?"

"Of course I do," he said, but his tone had softened. "Everyone in town knew about that. Your grandparents attended my church. We prayed for Lisa and them for months."

"My grandparents mentioned that you visited before Lisa went missing."

His gun jerked back up. "So they finally told someone. Suppose you'll be thinking I had something to do with it."

"No," she said in her most believable tone. "I just want to ask you a few questions. Mind if we come in?"

His eyes narrowed for a moment, deepening his many wrinkles, then he stepped back from the door. "I'll give you five minutes. I'm not putting my gun away, so don't think you can pull one over on me."

"Thank you." Toni stepped around her open door.

"Hands up where I can see them," he demanded.

She lifted her arms and started up the dirt driveway and into the small clearing. His bare feet were planted on the porch, his eyes pinned on her. How had a former youth leader changed to this suspicious man standing before them? Was he even a believer anymore?

Maybe he knew who abducted Lisa. Maybe someone he trusted. That could account for his change. She would ask, but that would put him on the defensive right off the bat.

She reached the rickety steps, and he backed off even more. She smiled at him, but he kept glowering at them as they climbed the creaking wooden stairs. Inside the dark cabin where an overhead light struggled to illuminate the single room that contained the kitchen and small dining area, she caught a fishy smell and spotted a large bass half cleaned on the kitchen counter.

She strolled across the pine floors to the worn plaid

couch by a stone fireplace spitting out oppressive heat. No wonder the guy wore the sleeveless shirt and no shoes. She removed her jacket, as did Clay. He didn't sit but leaned against the wall nearby. Thankfully, she had on a blazer to cover her gun, and Clay's was hidden under his overshirt.

Wilshire stopped nearby, his rifle pointed their way. "Ask your questions."

Toni smoothed her hands over her jacket. "Why did you visit my grandparents when Lisa was visiting?"

"Not that it's any of your business, but I was going through a divorce. Got me down, and your grandparents were great supporters, so I went to talk to them. Was surprised to see Andrew there, but he was great too."

"And while you were there, you met Lisa?" Toni asked.

He nodded, but his gaze remained wary.

She smiled to try to relax him. "Tell me what she was like."

"Cute kid. Funny. Seemed real happy. And seemed to have a strong love for the Lord. I remember thinking it would be great if all my youth were like her." His expression softened for a moment.

"So you were taken with her," Clay stated.

Wilshire jerked the rifle in Clay's direction. "Not in the creepy, dirty way your tone is suggesting. And that's exactly why the Longs didn't tell the police about my visit. I was fighting for shared custody of my children, and that would've put an end to it."

"Why the fight?" Toni tried to sound casual about the question.

"My wife claims I was having an affair and was an unfit father."

"Were you?"

He didn't answer right away. "She thought I was sleeping

with a woman named Carla Meadows. But I wasn't. She chaperoned one of our youth sleepovers, and one of the kids took a few pictures of us together. Like in one, we were sitting by the campfire. Just the two of us. Close together. I was holding her hands because I was praying with her. It was totally innocent. At least on my part. But here's the thing. I later learned she was into me, and she said we were having an affair. She lied because she figured if I left my wife, we could be together."

"Did she know what her claims were doing to your custody situation?" Clay asked.

"Yeah, but she thought her kids would be enough for me."

"I'm so sorry that happened to you," Toni said sincerely. "Sometimes our courts don't get it right."

"Sometimes? Ha! Way too often." He gritted his teeth. "I couldn't take all the hypocrisy and self-serving nature of the world anymore, so I moved out here. Been alone ever since."

"Did you ever get to see your kids?" Clay asked.

"Once a month until they turned eighteen. Once a month! I saw kids in my youth group more than that, so what good did that do? They're all grown now, and they don't know me, and I don't know them. I keep in touch through email, but they never invite me to their family events and always find an excuse not to accept any of my invitations."

The anguish in his tone broke Toni's heart. If he was telling the truth and he'd been cheated out of his children's childhood, he'd lost such a precious gift. She felt the same way about Lisa, and she'd never even met her sister. She couldn't comprehend Wilshire's pain.

"I'm sorry," she said, trying to convey her sympathy in her expression.

"Sorry doesn't do me any good."

"Tell us about the Rader family," Clay said.

Wilshire didn't answer right away. "Not sure who they are."

"Their son Jason was in your youth group."

He shook his head. "Don't remember them."

"Fritz and Ursula Rader," Clay clarified. "Ursula left Fritz and Jason."

"Sorry. Doesn't ring a bell." He looked at a clock over the fireplace. "Your time is almost up."

"Did you tell anyone about Lisa?" Toni asked before they were thrown out.

His eyes flashed an emotion Toni couldn't pinpoint, but it didn't look good. "Not that I remember."

"Are you sure?" Clay asked. "Because very few people knew Lisa was staying with her grandparents, and if you told someone, they could be responsible for taking her."

Wilshire firmed his stance. "Doesn't matter. Not really. Anyone I might've told wouldn't have abducted a child. I know that for certain."

"We don't always know people as well as we think," Toni said. "They keep secrets and lie. Like Carla did."

"You're heading down a dead-end path. Like I said. I don't remember telling anyone." He jerked his rifle up. "Time's up, and you need to go."

Toni didn't want to leave before pushing him more on this question, but with his rifle pointed in her direction, she had no choice but to comply.

She started for the door, and Wilshire backed up to let her pass. Once outside and on solid ground, she turned. Wilshire stood in the doorway, his rifle still raised.

"Thank you, Mr. Wilshire. I appreciate your time. Might I leave a business card in case you think of anything to help?"

"Don't bother. I won't think about this again."

Disappointed at his attitude, she headed for the car. Once the doors were closed, she turned to Clay. "Do you believe his story?"

"He's hiding something. He knows something about the Raders and maybe more."

# 18

Clay ended his call to Trent and grabbed his laptop from the beach house bedroom. He and Toni had decided on the drive back that they would share their latest information with Trent. Hopefully if Trent brought Toni's grandparents and Wilshire in for questioning, the unease of being called into the sheriff's office would encourage them to reveal whatever they were withholding.

Clay headed down the hallway and met Aiden and Sierra as they entered. Sierra's chin was smudged with dirt, and her eyes were droopy.

"This one needs a nap," Aiden said.

"I can keep going." Sierra stifled a yawn. "The car ride made me a little sleepy, is all."

"Kelsey's napping," Clay told his sister, hoping she would feel better about resting.

"With her due date fast approaching, she needs to rest." She gave Aiden a pointed look. "But *I'm* fine."

He held up his hands. "Don't bite my head off."

"I'm not...okay, fine. I did snap at you. I just don't want you guys to look at me like I'm an invalid."

"Not doing that," Aiden said. "Just concerned for my big sister."

She snorted. "You all never think of me as older. You treat me like a kid."

"Only because we love you." Clay circled an arm around her shoulders. "And to prove I'm not giving you special consideration, how about fixing me a cup of hot chocolate?"

She laughed and slipped from under his arm. "I'll get cleaned up for dinner. Who's making it anyway?"

"Erik," Clay said.

"Guess that means tacos."

"Yep," Clay said. "And if we're still here tomorrow night, Brendan has KP duty."

"I don't want this investigation to drag out, but I'd be happy for one of his omelets." She gave a tired smile and headed down the hallway.

Clay looked at Aiden. "Did you pick up on anything at the beach house?"

Aiden shook his head. "Trent's deputy made sure I stayed at my vehicle."

Clay felt like punching the wall, but he continued into the family room instead. The sun had set long ago, and blackness stared back at him from the big picture windows overlooking the beach. The cold feel deepened Clay's frustration, and he lowered the blinds. Someone had started a fire and a pleasant aroma of browning taco meat mixed with wood smoke filled the air. If life were normal it would be an idyllic time to sit down, kick up his feet, and take a break, but they weren't there to relax. They could always come back later for that.

Except for Toni.

Clay turned to where she sat near the fire, her cheeks rosy from the heat. She was staring at her computer, the white light highlighting the frown on her face. Maybe she was thinking about their talk with Wilshire. Clay sure had been. For the entire drive home. Both their law enforcement sixth senses told them the guy had been lying or withholding information, and Clay hoped to find out what.

He took his laptop along with the list of missing girls and the photos for the girls found at Rader's house and went to the dining table where he could spread out. Maybe these girls would connect to Wilshire's youth group.

Clay looked at Erik, who was shredding cheese in the kitchen. "Your algorithm finish on the girls yet?"

"For ten of them. Emailed the report to you. And I matched their info to the pictures from Rader's house."

Clay found the report on his computer and sent it to the printer. "Give me a summary."

Erik stilled the block of cheese midair. "The pictures I matched are for missing or runaway girls. I had five more possible matches. As I predicted, the older photos returned nothing."

"So a potential fifteen of the fifty-five girls are identified," Toni said, joining them with the report from the printer.

Erik nodded. "We can't rule out the ones without a match. We'll need to manually review them."

"Then we best get to it." Clay took the report from Toni.

"Dinner's in thirty minutes." Erik resumed shredding. "You'll have to clear the table."

"No worries." Clay opened his laptop.

Toni sat next to him. He suspected she was still wondering if Wilshire had told someone about Lisa. After all, Clay couldn't let that thought go. Nor could he quit wondering if Lisa was one of the bodies Kelsey had unearthed today. Not that she'd said she'd done any digging, but she'd returned to the cabin far dirtier than Sierra.

Since Trent told them there were six bodies found at Rader's place, Kelsey's disheveled state could only mean one thing. She'd begun excavating and would probably have recovered DNA. With the evidence likely on its way to the lab and Trent's promise to inform Toni of the results, in twenty-four hours or so, she would know if her sister was buried on Rader's property.

~

Dinner so far had been a somber meal. The brothers weren't their usual joking selves, and the mood change worried Toni. Did they think Lisa was dead? She was beginning to think so. And Blake and Kelsey seemed to take a clue from the atmosphere and quietly ate their meals.

"I'm finished with the beach house," Sierra announced as if she couldn't stand the quiet. "So I'll be heading home in the morning."

Kelsey set down her taco. "Would it be too much if I asked you to stay and take photos for me?"

"I have to move a few things around on my calendar, but I should be able to arrange it. Means I can keep these guys in line." Sierra laughed, but the others kept eating, raising Toni's concern even more.

"You need Sierra's help tomorrow only or for longer?" Clay asked.

Kelsey shifted her attention to Clay. "We'll take things one day at a time."

"Nice way to sidestep the fact that you likely unearthed more than one body today," Drake said.

Kelsey wrinkled her nose then looked at Sierra. "Of course, anything you learn on-site will be confidential."

Sierra frowned. "I've never had to keep so many secrets from my brothers. At least not since high school."

Aiden arched a brow. "You kept things from us?"

She forked a bite of the tangy Spanish rice and giggled like a young girl.

"We might know more than you think," Drake said wryly. "We all read your diaries."

"You what?" Sierra's fork clattered to her plate. "Those were private."

"Then you shouldn't have forgotten your box in the treehouse. We had some fun with them."

She ran her gaze over her brothers. "You didn't?"

"Sorry," Brendan said. "But they were too hard to resist."

Sierra crossed her arms. "I am *so* mad at you."

"If it helps, we swore each other to secrecy," Clay said. "Didn't tell Mom and Dad or anyone else. At least I didn't."

The rest of the brothers quickly assured her of the same.

Blake shook his head. "You guys have stepped in it now."

"That's all in the past, and we can leave it there." Clay knuckled Sierra's arm.

"I'm still mad, so don't touch me." Sierra's words said one thing but her arms had relaxed, and she leaned closer to Clay, her mouth starting to quirk up at the corners.

Toni wasn't surprised to see the inconsistency between her words and body language. Years of interviewing suspects told Toni people could usually manage to withhold their thoughts, but they couldn't control their body's responses. Like Wilshire. When she'd asked about telling anyone about Lisa. He'd said one thing, but the flash in his eyes gave him away, and she needed to know what he was hiding.

The moment she'd returned from his place, she'd started an internet search on him. She'd found the legal recording of his divorce but zero details on the proceedings and nothing about the custody disposition. Those records were likely sealed to protect the children. Meant she couldn't see if he ever tried to contest the custody decision or if there was any hint of his wife lying.

Clay's gaze remained on Sierra. "So does this mean that after dinner you won't help us review files?"

Sierra pushed her empty plate away. "What are you reviewing?"

"Sheriff Ziegler's old case files, the church directory from Toni's grandparents, and the photos found at Rader's house."

Sierra's expression softened. "I'll help. For these poor girls."

"I can help too," Kelsey said.

"Count me in as well," Blake said.

"Then let's have dessert and get to work." Erik stood. "Whose turn to clear the table?"

Toni hopped up. "I can do it."

"I'll help," Clay offered.

"Was my turn, but I'll just have to sit here and suffer." Brendan grinned as he leaned back and put his hands behind his head.

"You can have my turn tomorrow instead," Aiden offered.

Brendan laughed and socked his brother in the arm.

If Toni and Clay never got together, she wondered if this family would adopt her. She liked their joking and the love permeating everything they did. And their Christian values. She had to admit that her faith had suffered after her dad died—the last person she truly knew on this earth. Sure, her grandpa was alive, but they weren't close. But now she had a set of grandparents to get to know. If she wanted to. And Lisa? Could she be alive?

"You're deep in thought." Clay passed her with a stack of plates.

"Thinking about when this investigation is over. If my

grandparents are cleared of any wrongdoing, I don't know if I'll want to get to know them."

"Not that I have ever experienced this, but why wouldn't you?"

She set down the serving platter. "I guess they remind me of my parents, and if Lisa is dead, of that too. I don't know if I can take it."

"Maybe as time passes it'll be easier."

She started dropping silverware into the dishwasher basket. "They've got to be in their eighties. Seems like I don't have the luxury of letting time pass."

"They both appeared pretty healthy, though."

"Yeah, they did, didn't they?" She thought about them as she grabbed the tortilla chip bowls from the table. She finally had a chance to ask some health questions. From the way her parents died, she couldn't determine anything about her potential longevity. Seeing her grandparents' fitness at their age gave her hope she might live a long life too.

Erik passed her with a platter of giant cookies. "Mom's monster cookies. Oatmeal, peanut butter, peanuts, M&Ms, and chocolate chips, in case anyone needs allergy information."

Sierra grabbed the first one. "I'm eating for two."

"Guess since I'm the oldest I should get the next one." Blake snatched a cookie before anyone could argue.

"We are *not* doing the age thing." Erik took the next cookie and passed the plate to Brendan. "I've been last all my life, and I have to take small victories where I can get them."

Kelsey took a cookie and sank her teeth into it. "Seriously, I want your parents to adopt me."

The others laughed, but this was too close to Toni's

recent thoughts for her to join them. She returned to the table and helped polish off the plate of gooey cookies. Everyone settled into the family room, and she and Clay cleared the final dishes and loaded the dishwasher.

"Thanks for dinner," she said to Erik when he came in with Pong's empty water bowl.

He rinsed the bowl and looked at her. "You won't thank me if you're still here when it's my time to cook again. You'll get the same meal."

"Hey, who gets tired of tacos?" She grinned.

"I appreciate your attitude." He filled the bowl. "You would be such a welcome addition to our family."

He passed Clay and gave him a pointed look.

"I'm working on it," Clay said.

"And here I thought you were the family charmer." Erik laughed and put the bowl down for Pong, who started noisily lapping up the water.

"Ignore Erik." Clay grabbed his work things and spread them out on the table again.

She wanted to ignore the comment. To focus on her work instead. But her thoughts were filled with this wonderful family, and her heart had softened toward Clay. Getting together with him now seemed like it could be a great thing, but her reasons weren't clear. Was she opening up to him because he and his family seemed easy when everything with her family was so complicated? Or did she truly care for him and want to get to know him better?

She started to sigh but quietly let out her breath so she wouldn't draw Clay's attention. She switched her focus to reviewing the background of one of the girls Erik had identified in Rader's pictures.

An hour later, Clay leaned back and stretched his arms overhead. "You find anything?"

She shook her head. "I've looked at five girls, and none of them seem to have a connection. And they're not linked to Lisa, Wilshire, Rader, or Hibbard."

"Yeah, I'm striking out too." Clay pushed his computer away. "We need to find something actionable soon."

"You want actionable?" Sierra called out from the sofa. "I've got something that could blow this thing wide open."

Clay jumped from his chair and eyed Sierra as he charged toward her. "What is it?"

She smiled. "Emory got a match for the DNA on Rader's bird."

"Who is it?" Toni rushed into the family room.

"Guy's name is Sheldon Sharkey."

"For real?" Clay peered at Sierra. "That's the guy's real name? Sounds made up."

"It's what was in CODIS, so yeah, it's real," Sierra said.

Clay knew she didn't bother to explain the acronym for the FBI's Combined DNA Index System as everyone in the room would know what it stood for. "Erik, can you—"

"Find some info on him," Erik replied, his fingers flying over his keyboard. "Give me a minute or two."

Clay didn't want to wait even that long, but he had no choice. He started pacing, passing Toni several times as she stared at Erik from behind the sofa.

"It's his legal name, all right," Erik called out.

"We could be looking at a killer here and need to proceed cautiously," Clay said.

"Guy could've just visited Rader and the bird attacked him," Drake said.

"But why?" Toni asked. "Bird was totally friendly with

us. I don't think he would attack unless provoked or unless Rader was in danger."

Clay crossed his arms. "So like I said, we need to be cautious."

"Do you know where Sharkey lives?" Toni's excited tone held the same enthusiasm burning in Clay's gut.

"Got his address." Erik grabbed his phone. "Let me try to get a contact at PPB to ping Sharkey's phone and see if he's home."

"Do that," Clay said, but Erik was already typing the text. "While we wait, put up a map of Sharkey's address on the TV."

Erik completed his text and everyone pinned their focus on the TV. The map populated the screen.

Erik pointed his cursor at a large parcel of land. "He's a Christmas tree farmer."

Clay looked at Blake. "Didn't you say Rader used to grow Christmas trees?"

Blake nodded. "Maybe they knew each other."

"Or not," Sierra said. "When Mom homeschooled us she had a module on Oregon farming and—"

"I sorta remember that," Drake said. "But don't tell Mom I forgot the details."

Sierra wrinkled her nose. "She told us there were over seven hundred tree growers in Oregon back then. I remember because I love Christmas."

"So our guys might not have known each other," Brendan said.

"Still, look at the map." Blake went to the TV and tapped two locations. "Sharkey's farm is within thirty miles of Rader's place. They could've connected in a tree growers association."

"Could be," Clay said. "But it doesn't mean they were working together to traffic people."

"True that," Erik said. "I'm still searching for more info on Sharkey."

"The guy could draw down on us." Clay moved to the TV and tapped the image of the old farmhouse on the map. "And we need a plan to take him."

His brothers sounding nearly as excited as Clay, threw out ideas and discussed different approaches for the next thirty minutes. Blake had been totally quiet as had Toni, who looked like she was trying to process.

"We need to get Sharkey to come outside where we can manage the situation," Drake said. "I doubt he'll open his door for one of us guys."

Toni pointed at the TV screen. "There's a gas pump at the back of his property. I can pretend I ran out of gas and ask him to help."

"Should work," Brendan said.

Clay's gut screamed to outright refuse, but her idea was sound. Didn't mean he wouldn't voice his concern. "I don't like it. He could open fire through the door."

Erik looked up. "No reports of Sharkey attacking anyone."

Toni lifted her shoulders. "I'll wear a vest."

Erik's phone dinged, and he grinned. "Sharkey's home."

Clay forced himself to accept putting Toni in danger. "We'll go with Toni's plan."

"You really need to let Trent and his deputies handle this," Blake said. "Looks like Sharkey killed Rader, and they'll want to bring the guy in for questioning."

"They can." Clay eyed Blake. "We'll call them right after we talk to Sharkey."

Blake frowned. "You'll do whatever you want, but I'm going on record as not being on board with this decision."

"I respect your opinion." Clay locked gazes with Blake.

"If you feel compelled to call Trent, I hope you'll at least give us a head start."

Blake didn't respond for a long moment. "All I can say is when you get to Sharkey's place, don't mess with any evidence, and whatever you do, don't hurt the guy."

# 19

Toni crept down the gravel driveway behind Clay, the pebbles underfoot crunching no matter how carefully she walked. His brothers followed. They'd brought Pong to search the house after they'd detained Sharkey but had left the dog in his crate in the SUV. He was so well trained he wouldn't bark at anything and wouldn't alert Sharkey.

Toni glanced through her night vision goggles at the tall maple trees swaying in the wind. Everything was tinged green by her NVGs. Though the night helped them approach unseen, she wished they were approaching this suspected murderer's house in the daylight instead of the dark. Sure, the moon and starlight provided ambient light to help their NVGs function properly, but nothing beat daylight to get eyes on a suspect.

The house lights shone ahead like a beacon of hope in the foggy night, but hope didn't live in that house. A criminal did. Perhaps a murderer. And she would soon be walking up to the door and trying to lure him out. Erik had discovered Sharkey was once an active duty Marine, but when he separated, he traveled around for some time before buying this farm, where he lived alone except for harvest time. Then he hired migrants just like Rader did, and they were in business at the same time. Blake was probably right about Sharkey knowing Rader. Maybe they shared migrants or met while organizing the workforce. Either way, they had a connection.

Clay held his hand up, and everyone stopped. He turned and lifted his NVGs. The others followed suit.

"Surprisingly, Sharkey doesn't have any security cameras." Clay's volume was quieter than normal. "He's in the front room. His face matches the DL picture we have of him. I'll go to the door with Toni, and the rest of you have the house perimeter as planned. Any other questions or comments, speak now."

No one said a word.

"Okay, then we're holding here while you move into position."

The guys set off, sticking to a nearby tree line on the way, barely visible in the darkness. Clay dropped his NVGs to his eyes and faced the area where his brothers had disappeared. She followed suit with her goggles but watched the house instead. Thankfully, the Byrd's had top of the line equipment. Their NVGs were equipped with FLIR—forward-looking infrared—technology allowing them to safely switch from nighttime to light and not hurt their eyes if they had to rush the house.

She saw Sharkey get up, scratch his belly, and turn to go into the other room. He was tall and fit for his age. His face was narrow, his cheeks high, his hair in a ponytail, and he matched the driver's license photo they'd seen.

"Suspect's moving," she said into the comms unit. "Heading to the rear of the house."

"Heads up, Brendan," Clay said. "That's you."

"Got him," Brendan said. "Looks like he's going to the can."

"Perfect time for everyone to get in position. Toni and I are advancing." Clay looked at her and she nodded her readiness.

They crept forward, drizzle starting to fall and dampen her face. Clay held his assault rifle and took sure steps down the drive. He arrived at the crumbling walkway and signaled a halt at the bottom of the steps leading to a small covered stoop.

"Report," Clay whispered into his mic.

His brothers all confirmed they were in place.

"Then we're knocking." Clay climbed the steps to pound loudly on the door.

They both stepped to the side where Sharkey couldn't see them through his peephole. She would try getting him to open up with just hearing her voice first. She removed her NVGs and set them on the floor in case Sharkey demanded to see her. She tapped her foot silently while counting down the time.

She'd hit two-hundred when footsteps sounded by the door. "Who's there?"

"I'm sorry to bother you," Toni said. "But I ran out of gas. This being a farm, I hoped you'd have a pump on your property."

He flipped on the outside light. "Show your face."

She set down her rifle, blinked a few times to adjust to the light and stepped in front of the door, feeling vulnerable without the gun.

"Please," she said as pathetically as she could. "I really need help. I'm late for a class at the community college, or I'd call for help."

"Fine," he said, not sounding happy about it. "Got a pump by the barn. I'll be right out."

She stepped to the side.

"I'll take cover to get the jump on him," Clay whispered

as he picked up her things. He hopped off the stoop and disappeared in evergreen shrubs by the house.

The door creaked open, and Sharkey poked his head out, his gaze sharp and intense.

“Thanks bunches.” She smiled.

He grumbled something but stepped out wearing a glowing headlamp. She noted the gun at his hip and prayed he wouldn’t draw it. If he did, Brendan—a former sniper who’d taken a stance in a nearby tree—might be forced to shoot, and that would cause all kinds of problems for him. And someone would be dead, because if Brendan fired, it would be a deadly bullet.

“Follow me.” Sharkey set off with quick and powerful steps for a man his age.

She heard Clay moving behind her, but only because she was listening for him. She doubted Sharkey heard a thing. She fell back to signal her intention to move up next to Sharkey to distract him, allowing Clay to get the drop on him.

She caught back up to Sharkey and pretended to look around. “Do you sell U-cut trees here?”

“Nope. We ship everything we grow out of state.”

“Too bad. It would be fun to cut them.”

“Don’t want people all up in my property. Besides, there’re plenty of places to do that.”

Clay reached Sharkey and jabbed him in the back with his handgun. “Don’t move.”

Sharkey went for his gun, but Clay was faster and removed it with his free hand. “On the ground now. Face down. Nice and slow.”

Sharkey gave Toni a sharp glare as he lowered himself down.

“Hands behind your back,” Clay demanded.

Sharkey complied with Clay’s request. “Who are you?”

Clay gave the guy a snide grin. "We're the people who are going to prove that you murdered Fritz Rader."

~

Clay and Toni searched the living areas and kitchen finding nothing. Now they were going through the bedrooms, where people often hid valuables and things they didn't want found, and Clay hoped to score a lead.

But Sharkey's sparse bedroom had few hiding places. It held a double bed with a worn wood headboard, a matching nightstand, and a four-drawer dresser.

"I'll take the dresser," he said to Toni.

"I got the nightstand and closet." She went to the nightstand and pulled out the single drawer.

He opened the top drawer to find underwear and socks rolled into tight little bundles. He took his time in all the drawers, careful to look for anything small like a flash drive. He heard Toni move to the walk-in closet. In the bottom drawer, he plowed through sweaters and found a large manila envelope with Hibbard's name written on the front.

Clay carefully opened the envelope and withdrew several photos. The top one was of Toni's dad lying in a pool of blood in the parking lot where he was murdered. Whoever took the shot must've used a telephoto lens, but then the bullet that killed Toni's dad had been fired at a long distance too. Clay hated to show the photo to her, but she had a right to know this guy not only likely killed Rader, but maybe her father too.

"Toni," he called out. "You need to see this."

She came into the room, and he displayed the photo.

She gasped and looked up at Clay. "He could've killed Dad."

"Seems very possible, and based on these other pictures,

he could've killed these other people too." Clay flipped to a photo of Rader lying on the floor in his home. The next one of a teenage girl and then two of other men.

She tapped the last picture. "Olin Kraus. Hibbard's second in command."

"Yeah," Clay said. "Maybe Sharkey was the one who murdered Kraus. Then he took over as number two."

"But why would he have these pictures in his house much less label the envelope with Hibbard's name? The pictures don't prove Sharkey or Hibbard killed these people, but it does make Sharkey look suspicious. Why keep them?"

"Blackmail, maybe."

"You think he was using them to blackmail Hibbard. That Hibbard is the killer, and he shot my dad."

"Could be. We just don't have enough to know for sure. But Hibbard always kept his hands clean, so if I had to guess, I'd say Sharkey did the killing."

"Yeah, you're right."

They needed additional information to figure this out. "We should wrap things up here and call Trent to take Sharkey in. You done with the closet?"

"Almost."

"I'll take pictures of these while you finish up."

She nodded and started to turn.

He took her gloved hand, wishing it were bare to give them a more personal skin-on-skin touch. "I'm sorry you had to see that."

She looked at their hands. "At least this one was taken from a long distance. I saw far worse pictures in the investigative files."

"Still, it's got to hurt."

She drew in a deep breath. "What hurts is knowing that smug jerk out there could've killed my dad and others and helped traffic helpless girls. We have to make sure he goes away for a long time."

"Agreed." Clay's mind raced. "Time to bring Pong in to search the place."

"Let me finish the closet first." She hurried back there, but her shoulders were drooping. She'd been through so very much. Yet she got up each day with a positive attitude and did her job. Right now the urge for revenge was likely fueling her. How would she do if they actually proved this guy killed her dad and the creep was convicted?

What would motivate her then? If Clay didn't find a way to break through her defenses, he wouldn't be there to provide any needed help. He desperately wanted to be there for her. Not just for the horrible situation she was going through now, but for little everyday things.

*Face it. You're in love with her.*

A lot of good that did either of them. He couldn't sway her mind about getting involved. Only she could change it.

*Help me to get through to her. Help her to want a relationship. If not with me, with someone else. She doesn't deserve to be alone.*

*No.* She couldn't be with another guy. She belonged with him, didn't she?

He couldn't think about that now. Not when he had a job to do. He snapped the photos then slid the pictures into the envelope and put them back in the drawer. He pressed his mic to talk. "Erik, we need Pong in here to search for electronics."

"Roger that." His tone was beyond excited. Probably because he'd struck out at the beach house, and Erik loved showing off Pong's skills.

Toni returned. "Nothing in there."

"Let's wait for Erik up front." Clay led the way to the door and spotted Erik jogging up the drive with Pong running next to him. They both looked excited, but as a handler, Erik would tone the excitement down the minute they stepped into the house.

Clay and Toni moved back to give the dog room. Erik crossed the threshold, and Pong stopped to sit and peer up at him.

"How does this work?" Toni asked.

"Pong's trained to detect TPPO and HPK," Erik said. "TPPO's short for triphenylphosphine oxide. It's used to coat memory chips in electronic devices to keep them from overheating. HPK—hydroxycyclohexyl phenyl ketone—is used in removable media, such as CDs, DVDs, Blu-Rays, and even floppy disks."

"I've seen other sniffer dogs alert, but how does Pong do it?" Toni asked.

"He sits, and I ask him to show me. He points to the exact location, and I reward him with food." Erik smiled. "He's really something to see."

"Let's get to it, then," Clay said, losing patience.

"Seek." Erik ran his hand along the sofa.

Nose down, Pong hopped up and sniffed the cushions before jumping back to the floor. He poked his snout underneath. Erik continued forward, leading the dog through the rest of the room.

Erik shook his head. "Nothing here."

They stepped down the hallway. Through each bedroom. The bathroom. No success.

Clay's hope evaporated. "Only room left is the kitchen."

Erik took Pong into the dingy space. The dog lunged toward a twelve-pack of water bottles sitting in the plastic wrap on the floor. Sharkey had ripped open the plastic, and several bottles were missing. Pong sat by the water and looked up at Erik.

"Show me," Erik said.

Pong pointed his snout at the bottles. Erik squatted and started pulling out the bottles and looking at them. When he got to the fourth one, Pong jabbed his nose at it.

Eyes narrowed, Erik looked at the bottle. "It's just water, boy."

Pong shoved his nose hard at it.

"Let me take a look." Clay grabbed the bottle and tipped it over, studying it. "Ah-ha. Sharkey's smarter than we thought."

Clay pulled the upper half of the bottle free from the bottom.

"Two bottles sandwiched together?" Toni stepped closer.

"Top part is sealed and holds liquid so it looks like an average bottle of water. But these are hidden behind the label." Clay dumped out four micro SD cards into his hand, each one about the size of a pinkie nail.

"Memory cards from cell phones." Erik bent down to give Pong a treat. "You did it, boy. You found it."

Clay could barely contain his excitement over the find, but he still had work to do before they could call Trent. "We need Pong to finish the room and the outbuildings. Then I need you to copy whatever's on these cards."

Erik faced Pong. "Seek."

He led him through the rest of the room, but Pong didn't light on anything else. They searched the other buildings with the same results, so they headed for the SUV. Rain spit from the sky, but Clay didn't care if he got wet. They'd made good progress and adrenaline left him pumped.

He paused to glance at Sharkey, still face down with Clay's brothers standing over him. Good. The guy deserved it. And now they had the evidence they needed to help put him away. Unless Hibbard sent someone else, Toni was safe. Clay would be too. Not that he'd ever really worried about his own skin.

Erik put Pong in his crate in the back of the SUV and took his laptop to the passenger seat. Clay gave Erik the cards, and he slid one into an adapter before inserting it into a slot on his computer. His gaze was riveted to the screen glowing white in the darkness.

Clay wanted to nudge his brother. Urge him to move faster, but Erik was working as fast as he could, so Clay waited patiently next to Toni.

Erik looked up and let out a low whistle. "Pay dirt."

"What is it?" Toni cried out. "What do you have?"

Erik shook his head in disgust and looked at Toni. "Hibbard. In videos with young girls in compromising positions."

Toni's face paled, and Clay stepped closer to her, his protective instincts kicking in. "How many videos?"

"Way too many to count."

"Ballpark number," Clay demanded.

Erik squinted at the screen. "This folder alone has twenty. There are eighteen folders."

Clay gritted his teeth. "Hibbard will go away for a long time for this."

Toni's mouth tightened. "*If* we can find him."

"We will." Clay lifted his shoulders into a hard line, trying to transmit his confidence that the team could find Hibbard when the task force had struck out so many times.

And if they found the guy and arrested him, he and Toni would both be safe. Then the only questions left, the big questions, were where were the missing girls and Lisa, and after all this time, was she still alive?

# 20

Trent had kept everyone at Sharkey's place for most of the night. The sun would rise in a few hours, and Clay yawned as he stepped into the beach house behind Toni, his brothers bringing up the rear. All he wanted right now was a hot shower and a giant cup of coffee.

His feet came to a stop. "You smell that?"

Toni looked back at him. "Someone's baking."

"Mom," the brothers said in unison.

"What's your mother doing here?" Toni asked. "Besides baking."

Clay shook his head. "Guess there's only one way to find out."

They entered the living area, and Clay spotted his dad seated on the couch watching a cable news show.

"You're finally home." Clay's mom stepped into the entryway and smiled at them as they started ripping the Velcro straps on their vests. "I can tell by your attire you were out playing cops and robbers just like when you were little boys."

"We're grown men, Mom," Clay said. "When will you start treating us that way?"

She linked arms with him. "Maybe when you stop letting me take care of you so often."

"We don't—"

"Don't even bother." Aiden came over and kissed their mother's cheek. "No point in denying it. We let her cook for us all the time and do even more."

"What he said." Drake planted a quick kiss on her cheek too, and the remaining brothers followed suit as they passed by to go to their rooms and stow their gear.

Clay looked at his mother. "What are you doing here? I mean, I'm always happy to see you, but you should've let me know you were coming. Maybe I could've saved you the trip."

"There was no stopping her," his dad said from the couch.

"Oh, you." His mom waved a hand at his back. "I'm here because I knew the kitchen would be a mess."

"It's not, is it?" Toni removed her vest and tugged the tails of her shirt down. "I've been trying to keep it clean."

His mother smiled. "I could tell someone besides the boys was taking care of things."

Clay rolled his eyes. "There you go again with the boys comment."

"I'm embarrassing you in front of your young lady."

Clay groaned. "She's not my young lady. She's an FBI agent and part of the team."

She looked at Toni. "I know that, and I'm so in awe of you. Let's sit down and have a long discussion about what that involves over a cup of coffee, if you're up to it."

"Sure," Toni said and sounded truly willing and not like she was putting up with his mom, earning Toni huge brownie points in his book.

"We have to stow our gear and do some research," Clay said, trying not to sound irritated.

A timer buzzed from the kitchen.

"Perfect timing. The cinnamon rolls are done. I'll brew a fresh pot of coffee to go with it and serve you all."

"None for me." Toni patted her stomach. "I already had one of your wonderful monster cookies after dinner."

His mother stared at Toni. "That was last night. We're starting a whole new day here."

"Mom's cinnamon rolls are out of this world," Clay said.

Toni tilted her head. "Maybe a small one."

Clay eyed his mother. "Now, why else are you here?"

"I heard about everything that's been happening, and I thought you all could use some good home cooking instead of takeout."

"Drake and Erik have cooked."

"So burgers and tacos then?"

"Yes."

"You need something far more nutritious. I'll make your favorite kale and quinoa salad and homemade bread. But first breakfast. It won't be for a few hours, but what do you want?"

"Aren't cinnamon rolls breakfast?" Toni asked.

"Just a middle of the night snack for these guys." His mom grinned.

"Whatever you want to make is great."

She looked at Toni. "Do you have a favorite breakfast?"

Toni seemed like she didn't want to answer but nodded. "My dad used to make chocolate chip pancakes for me on special occasions. I haven't had those in eons."

"Then chocolate chip pancakes it is."

"I don't want you to have to go to the store for anything."

"Don't worry," his dad said. "I'll be going if there's anything she forgot, but based on the amount of food I loaded in the car, she's got one of everything already."

She laughed and stepped over to plant a kiss on his head.

"Now would be the time to escape," Clay said to Toni.

They shared a laugh as they walked to their rooms to offload their gear. He'd expected to find Brendan and Drake in his room, but he was surprised Aiden was sitting on one of the four bunks, his belongings next to him. "I see Mom or Dad moved you out of the master."

"Must be our inimitable mother." Aiden chuckled. "She already has the bedding stripped and washing."

Clay shoved his vest into his gear bag. "She really is the best mom ever, but there are times you don't need to have your mom around. I hope she doesn't pull this with paying clients."

"She won't." Drake kicked off his boots.

"How can you be so sure?"

"She's here because of Toni." Drake moved toward the door.

Clay looked at his brother. "What?"

Drake rolled his eyes. "For such a smart guy, you can be so dense at times."

"What do you mean?"

"This thing you have for Toni. It's been obvious since day one. Mom wouldn't have missed it."

Clay opened his mouth to deny it but couldn't. He wasn't the best at hiding his feelings. "So what?"

"So Mom's here to make sure you don't blow it." Brendan leaned back on a lower bunk. "She may have one grandchild on the way and Karlie soon to officially be hers, but she wants more."

"Trust me, I know." Aiden shook his head. "She bugged me all the time until Harper and I set a date for the wedding."

"Well, then she'll be disappointed in me." Clay dug

clean clothes out of his tote bag for the shower he hoped to take after scarfing down numerous cinnamon rolls. "Not that it's anyone's business, but Toni's not in a good place to start a relationship right now."

"I'm sure you can change that." Drake slid off the bed. "I don't know about you guys, but I plan to be first in line for whatever Mom made."

He headed out the door and the others followed, each of them retrieving their computers, as did Clay. He brought up the rear so he could think about how to get his parents to leave without offending them. Once his mom had her mind set on something, it was nearly impossible to change it. Nearly, but not totally. Clay just had to think of the right thing to say about Toni, and maybe his mom would go home.

He looked at the doors to see if Kelsey or Blake were awake and spotted light shining under Blake's door. Clay knocked.

"Come in," Blake called out.

Clay found Blake seated on one of the bottom bunks, his iPad on his lap.

"You might've heard my mom and dad arrive," Clay said. "She's made her famous cinnamon rolls for a snack. Thought I'd see if you want to join us."

Blake's expression waffled for a moment. "Sounds good, but I gained a few pounds with Emory during her pregnancy and still haven't lost them."

"I heard that can be a problem."

"I just need to work out more, but once you have a kid, time for yourself pretty much disappears. Not complaining. Just stating a fact." He closed his iPad case. "So how'd Trent react to the delayed call for Sharkey's place?"

"As well as you'd expect."

Blake grinned. "He was beyond mad then."

"Yep." Clay laughed. "Not that it was a laughing matter at the time. He threatened to haul me in for obstructing an investigation."

"He won't," Blake said. "When I was sheriff, I often tangled with Gage and his operators. Trent has, too, so he's used to it. When he calms down, he'll be thankful the guy's off the streets."

"That and Pong sniffed out several micro SD cards Trent's team would've missed."

"And I'm sure you got a look at them before Trent arrived."

"Videos of Hibbard in bed with young girls."

Blake shook his head. "That'll help nail the guy, but man, having to watch them will be awful. I saw my share of videos like that on the job."

Clay had too, and he wasn't looking forward to it. "Any way you can find out if Sharkey rolled over on Hibbard?"

"Doubtful."

"It's also doubtful that he *did* roll over, but it would be good to know if Trent is looking for Hibbard too."

Blake glanced at his watch. "I'll give him a call during office hours and see what I can find out, but no promises."

"Thanks." Clay patted his belly. "Time to fatten up."

"Eat some for me, too."

Laughing, Clay closed the door and started down the hall.

Instead of his mother butting out, he found her seated with Toni at the table, munching on the cinnamon rolls and talking about Toni's job exactly like she'd promised. And by promised, he meant threatened.

"We need to get to work now, Mom," Clay said, trying his very best to keep his irritation at bay.

Surprisingly, she got right up. "I'll grab the pot and fill mugs, then join your dad."

Right. Sit in the family room within hearing distance so she didn't miss a thing.

"I uploaded the videos to our server," Erik said.

Clay set his machine on the table, grabbed a plate, and loaded it with two gooey rolls. "Let's go ahead and eat before looking at the files."

"Agreed." Aiden chomped off a large bite of the cinnamon roll, and Clay followed suit.

"How are they?" Clay's mom poured him a cup of coffee.

"Perfect as usual," Clay said between bites.

She smiled, her face soft with the love that made him forget his frustration.

Toni swallowed her bite and picked up her mug. "Your rolls are really good, Mrs. Byrd."

"Surely I told you to call me Peggy, but if I didn't, please do." His mother ran a hand over her hair. "I'm getting a bit scatterbrained with age."

"Just a bit?" Their dad laughed.

She smiled and shook her head. "Okay, maybe more than a bit."

She started to pour coffee for Erik but he put his hand over his cup. "I'm still wired from the op and Pong's searches."

Drake jabbed a finger at Erik's plate. "But I see you're not worried about the sugar making you hyper, considering you're on your third roll. Not that I'm counting or anything."

"Just trying to keep up with you, bro." Erik grinned and took another bite.

His mom set down the pot and stopped behind Clay and kissed his head. "Must be some hard stuff you're planning to view if you're waiting for me to leave the room."

She grabbed a small plate of rolls and went into the family room. He wasn't sorry to see her go. Here he was, a former ICE agent, and his mother was kissing his head in front of a co-worker. Okay, fine more than a co-worker.

Toni leaned over to him. "I like how your mom cares for you all. My mom was like that too. I'd like to think if she'd lived that she would've been the same way."

Toni's sadness got to him, and he took her hand and held it on the table, not caring what anyone thought. But of course his mother picked that moment to come back to the kitchen for something.

"Um-hm," she said and smiled broadly.

He wouldn't touch that with the proverbial ten-foot pole. "Toni, why don't you start with the most current folder, and I'll take the next one in line. We might recognize something from our investigation."

Clay put in his earbuds, made sure his screen was down so his mom couldn't see, and opened the first video. He paused the file to take a screenshot of the girl's face for their records and then named it with the date and time it had been recorded and told the others to do the same thing. Then he continued through the video looking for leads on location. The bed had the same decorative post, so he took a screenshot of that too and moved on. Once finished, he followed the same procedure for the other files. They had only a few more to go when the girl in the video, her eyes scrunched closed, tears on her cheeks, looked familiar.

He turned his computer to face Toni. "Look at this."

"It's Heidi," Toni said.

She didn't need to identify her as they both knew she was the girl who ratted out Hibbard and he'd had her killed. Problem was, they hadn't been able to prove it.

Toni looked up. "If we'd had this when we tried to prosecute Hibbard for her death, he would've been behind bars, and we wouldn't have tried to arrest Kraus that day. Maybe my dad would still be alive."

"But seems like your dad was looking for Lisa, and he wouldn't have stopped just because we arrested Hibbard. Plus, I think Kraus would've kept the business going."

"True," she said, a faraway look on her face.

"If Hibbard was serving time, you would never have found out about Lisa and your grandparents."

She sat back. "I wonder if my dad would ever have told me about them."

"Doesn't seem likely, right?"

"Right." Her voice broke, and her eyes were dull with pain.

Clay took her hand again.

She stared at their hands as if contemplating something big, then looked up. "Can I talk to you in private for a minute?"

"Sure." He nodded at the deck. "How about outside? I could use some fresh air after this."

"Sure."

"I'll grab our jackets." He went to the hallway, where they'd hung their coats on pewter whale tail hooks, wondering what she might tell him as he put his on.

Would she ask him to stop touching her? Tell him to back off? Leave her alone?

He didn't know how he'd react if she did. Or maybe this was just about the investigation.

He held out her coat, and she shrugged into it. He started to reach for her hair stuck inside the collar, but if she planned to tell him to back off, he didn't want to compound things. Plus, his mother was watching them, and he didn't want such a personal touch to get her hopes up.

He opened the door for Toni, and she stepped out. The rain had cleared, and a million stars filled the sky as the rolling ocean waves lapped the shore. The moon shone bright, but soon would give way to the morning sun, and the air temperature was chilly, but otherwise he couldn't ask for a more romantic setting. When had he gone to wanting romance with her in the middle of a horrific investigation?

She went to the railing and leaned on the weathered wood. He joined her but faced the house to be sure the blinds were all closed and they had the privacy he desired.

He turned to face Toni and rested his elbow on the deck rail, acting casual when his insides were quivering. "What did you want to talk about?"

She looked at him and held his gaze. "I wanted to make sure you knew how thankful I am for your care and concern. For everything you're doing to help me."

"I hear a *but* coming."

"Not a *but,* really. More of a *What are we doing?* I mean, you've made no secret of the fact that you're interested in more than a working relationship with me. Not only telling me, but you've held my hand several times tonight."

*Here it comes.* "Does that bother you?"

"Bother me? No. But it makes me wonder if we're confusing support with other feelings. We could be caught up in one of those relationships that can happen when two law enforcement officers work an investigation together. Those relationships often fall apart when they return to the real world."

"Does this thing between us feel temporary to you?"

"I could be confused, especially with all the stuff going on in my life."

He came to his full height and turned her to face him. "I know what I'm feeling isn't comfort. Isn't temporary."

"How can you be sure?" She sounded breathless.

"First, because I'm in awe at how amazing you are. Strong. Independent. Someone who stands up to me."

"I didn't think you liked that."

"I don't really, but I respect the fact that you're comfortable enough in yourself to stick up for what you believe in."

"Good to know. I'll be sure to keep doing that." She gave him a coy smile.

His heart warmed. "But it's not just that. When we're not together, I think about you and want to be with you. When we *are* together, I feel a sense of completeness that I've been missing. I've had these feelings for you all along. They haven't faded one bit.

"And right now," he plunged ahead. "You look so beautiful in the moonlight, and I want to kiss you."

She let out a soft breath that fanned over his face, but didn't speak.

He took her silence to mean she was considering the kiss. "Can I?"

She glanced at the house. "Your family."

"Not even my mom would peek through closed blinds. My dad wouldn't let her." He smiled and cupped the side of her cheek, touched by the softness of her skin. "Unless you say no, I'm going to—"

She plunged her hands into his hair and pulled his head down. Their lips met. He was stunned for a moment but quickly circled his arms around her slender waist and drew her tight against his body. He gave in, and surrender had never felt so good.

Toni lost herself in the kiss. In the warmth of Clay's lips in the cold air. In the feel of his hair, coarse yet soft. His toned body against hers. He was all guy most of the time, and yet, he was tender and kind. Caring and compassionate. And he could be all hers if she wanted.

But did she want? She had no idea, but at least she was

considering it now. And until she knew the answer to her questions, should she be kissing him and encouraging him?

Breathless, she leaned back, suddenly feeling shy. This wasn't her first kiss by any means, but she hadn't dated much and had never felt this deeply about any other guy.

"That was wonderful." His smile was intimate and dazzling at the same time.

Her heart tumbled, rolling over and over, falling, and she had to rest her hands on his shoulders not to cup the back of his head and initiate another kiss.

"I feel like I might've misled you," she said. "I'm not ready for anything more."

"I know." His smile remained. "But was it great for you too?"

"Yes," she admitted, but at his joyful expression, she extricated herself from his hold and took a few steps back before her determination melted. "I don't want to do that again until I'm sure of my feelings."

"Don't want to or won't?"

"Won't." She had to shove her hands into her pockets to keep from touching him. "It's not fair to you."

He looked at her long and hard. "And if I say it's fair?"

"You can't though, can you? And be truthful."

His smile evaporated. "No."

"So let's agree to keep things professional until the investigation is over, and then we can revisit this."

He started to reach out for her but let his arms drop. "Obviously it's not what I want to hear, but sure. I can do professional. At least I hope I can. If I mess up, tell me."

"Thank you. Your positive response just confirms what a great guy you are." She smiled at him.

"I'm disappointed, but you didn't completely shut me down, so I have hope." He gestured at the door. "We should get back to work before the way you look in the moonlight destroys my resolve."

She'd gotten what she wanted—time to figure things out. So then why did she drag her feet as she headed back inside?

Clay took her coat to the hooks, and she watched him as she took a seat. When he started in her direction, she jerked her focus to her computer, but as he sat next to her, all she could think about were those hands on her. That body next to hers. Those lips kissing hers.

She touched her lips and felt the warmth. Could almost feel him kissing her again.

Frustrated, she got up and almost ran to the kitchen to get a glass of water. She drained it in seconds.

Drake joined her to refill his glass. "Having a hard time, huh?"

"What?" Did he know what had transpired between her and Clay? Could he? Did she look like she'd just been kissed?

"Your feelings for Clay," he said, his tone low as if he wanted to keep this between them, for which she was grateful.

She should've known the family would notice the tension when she came back inside with Clay.

The heat of a blush crept up her face. "We're just two professionals working together."

"You may be, but Clay's been obvious about his feelings for you from day one." Drake shoved his glass under the refrigerator dispenser and ice clinked down into his glass.

She glanced at Clay to find him watching her and Drake. He didn't look away when she caught his eye.

"He's a terrific guy," Drake said. "One of the best. I might razz him a lot, but he's great. All my brothers are. Mom and Dad made sure of that." He gave her a playful smile and put his glass under the water dispenser. "Oh, and God might've had something to do with it too."

She smiled at Drake and realized how much she'd missed in life by being an only child. No, not an only. Just an only for the first thirty years.

"Uh-oh." Drake pulled his glass free. "What did I say to put that look on your face?"

She'd thought his big family would overwhelm her, but they were so open and caring, and she was starting to feel a part of the family. "I was thinking about how great it was to have siblings."

"And your only sister is missing."

"Yeah."

"I might be known for being blunt, but I didn't mean to be insensitive. It's gotta be rough for you right now."

"It is."

"Then let's get back to work. And remember. Clay's a great guy." He grinned. "Almost as wonderful as me."

She smiled back as she knew he was hoping for when he made the joke. "You, Drake Byrd, *are* a great guy and quite a catch too."

His mouth dropped open, as she'd hoped, and on that note, she spun and marched over to her computer. Somehow her talk with Drake put things with Clay in perspective for her, and she could now settle down and do her job. Be sure her father's killer was prosecuted and find her sister. Then, she would seriously consider her conversation with Clay, and maybe, just maybe, she would become part of this very special family in the future.

# 21

Sierra yawned as she drank her tea across the dining table from Clay at six a.m. His parents were still sitting on the couch, and everyone else was vying for a shower. Thankfully, Clay had gotten in the guy's bathroom first.

Sierra's phone dinged.

"Who's texting this early?" Clay asked. "Let me guess. Reed."

"Nah, I talked to Reed while you were in the shower. It's Chad."

"Anything interesting?"

"He got the twine samples from both agencies. They're a match." A victorious smile lit her face.

"That's great." Clay considered grabbing another of his mother's cinnamon rolls sitting in a container within reach. "Anything that sets it apart from the average twine out there?"

"It's a common polypropylene sisal tying twine, but here's the thing." She paused and a self-satisfied grin crossed her face. "It's made locally and specifically manufactured to be used in machines to bind Christmas trees for bulk shipping."

"Christmas trees?" Clay's excitement piqued. "Then I wonder if Trent's people recovered any twine at Sharkey's place. Or even Raders."

"I wish we had access to all the evidence," she said. "Would make things so much easier."

His sentiments exactly. "You're taking pictures for Kelsey today, right?"

She lifted a hand. "Don't even ask me to tell you what I see."

"I wasn't planning to," he said, but maybe she knew him better than he knew himself. Maybe he *was* going to ask. He was desperate for official information, that was for sure.

Frustrated, he planted his hands on the table. "The only thing left to do is review more videos, but they're not telling us anything. It would be great if we could interview the families of the missing girls we identified, but I won't do that."

Sierra set her mug down. "Why not?"

"They need to hear about their missing daughters from law enforcement. Not us. And I don't have much else to go on. I had Erik and Nick both hunt for any connections to Hibbard. Both struck out."

"Sounds rough."

"You want to hear rough." He snapped forward. "Let me tell you about the countless videos we watched. Defenseless young girls violated by a monster. Hibbard in all of them. And he's still free to keep doing it. This is now just as much about stopping the abuse than anything. I have to stop it. Don't you see? Just have to." Exhausted from his tirade, he leaned back.

Sierra squeezed his hand. "I'll pray for the girls and all of you. I'm sorry you're going through this. Those videos must've been horrible to watch."

"It was worse for Toni, but of course she was adamant

about reviewing her share. The whole time she had to be imagining what happened to Lisa. I wanted to protect her, but she's an equal partner in this investigation, and I need to respect that."

"I get it. Reed still keeps trying to shield me from the bad things I see, but it's the profession we've chosen, and you both have to let us do our jobs."

"But I don't have to like it."

Sierra's mouth dropped open. "You're in love with her."

"Am I?" he asked, but he knew the answer.

"Sure seems like it." Sierra sounded a little bit too eager. "She's a wonderful person, and I'd love to have her in the family."

"You're getting a little ahead of yourself there."

"You know me."

"Yeah, mini-Mom." He laughed and it felt good to let a bit of his frustration and angst go. And good to have a talk with Sierra. Since she got married they didn't get together as often as they used to, and he missed her. Not that he would admit that to her.

Footsteps pounded down the hallway. Blake, dressed in his usual work attire of black tactical pants and coach's shirt embroidered with the Veritas Center's logo, stepped into the room. He bid Clay's parents a good morning on the way past.

"Mom made coffee," Clay said. "Mugs are above the pot, but I gotta warn you. It'll be strong."

"The stronger the better. Amelia might not be here, but I still woke up like it was her middle of the night feeding." He shook his head and made his way to the counter.

Sierra poured more hot water into her mug. "So that's what I have to look forward to."

"For a while anyway." Blake turned with a stoneware mug, steam rising from it.

Clay told him about the twine. "Means we've tied Rader and possibly Sharkey together in another way."

"Tied?" He groaned. "Pretty bad pun for this time of the morning."

"His puns are usually bad, no matter the time of day." Sierra laughed.

"Guilty, but in this case I'm so tired, I didn't even know I said it."

Blake took a sip of his coffee. "You still want me to talk to Trent this morning."

"Actually, I'd like to meet with him again. Compare some notes. Maybe he'll reciprocate if we share more of what we know."

Blake's eyebrow went up. "If I were still sheriff, I wouldn't, but then he's not me."

"Why wouldn't you?" Clay challenged.

"Fear of details getting out to the public and compromising the investigation."

"Here's the thing, though." Clay leaned forward. "He's got to be dealing with far more than he can handle. He either takes our help or he'll have to call in the state police or FBI."

Blake leaned back against the counter. "He doesn't have to do either of those things."

"But he has so much on his plate. The body at the high school. Rader's murder. Likely six or more bodies found on Rader's property. And now, he has Sharkey in custody and pictures of murdered individuals and videos of Hibbard with underage girls. Tons of them. How does Trent handle all that himself with limited resources?"

"I agree he needs help." Blake crossed his feet at the ankles. "Just pointing out he doesn't have to call in help. It's up to him."

Clay was starting to get frustrated with Blake. "And what would you do if you were in this situation?"

Blake tapped his finger on his mug and stared at it for a few seconds before looking up. "You know me. I'm a control freak and would like to keep things in house if I knew we could do the job well. So maybe I'd look for people I could trust to deputize and bring onto my force."

"You wouldn't call in another agency?" Clay clarified.

"Not if I had qualified people I could tap. Too much red tape and jockeying for control. Wastes time. But if I had someone I could trust to run point on each of these areas, that's what I'd do."

"Like who?"

"Me for one. Trent could use me." Blake's eyes brightened. "In fact, I might go ahead and suggest it. Even go so far as to volunteer."

"Then who else?"

"Gee, I wonder. If I only knew someone who was a former law enforcement officer." Blake grinned.

"That settles it." Clay stood. "Get your things. We're going to see Trent."

Toni sat at the dining table feeling odd being at the Byrd's beach house without Clay. She'd laid down for a quick nap before her shower but was so exhausted that she actually slept through her alarm and didn't hear others stirring. By the time she got up, Clay and Blake had gone to meet with Trent. Clay had left a cryptic note saying that he had high hopes for the meeting and would be back soon to tell her about it.

Peggy set a plate of pancakes on the table. Drake

grabbed the platter, but instead of taking any, he handed it to Toni. "Take them while you can."

She smiled her thanks and forked two of the perfectly browned discs dotted with dark chocolate.

"Since when did you become such a gentleman?" Brendan asked his brother.

"What, me?" Drake asked, sounding offended. "My mama taught me right."

"She didn't teach you to be such a smart aleck, though." Peggy playfully cuffed him on the head and set the warm maple syrup in front of Toni.

Toni smiled with them as they continued to joke while cutting and consuming pancakes faster than she could've imagined possible. She'd been in a foul mood for having missed the meeting with Trent, but her crankiness was disappearing with the food.

"See," Drake said. "We're all vultures."

She laughed, but the door opened and she spun to see Blake and Clay step in. Clay's eyes were bright with excitement.

Peggy turned from the griddle. "Just in time for pancakes."

Both guys went to the kitchen to wash their hands then settled at the table.

"So tell us already," Toni said. "What happened with Trent?"

Clay reached into his pocket and held up a deputy's badge. "Blake has one too."

Drake's eyes narrowed. "You stole badges to make it easier to get info?"

Clay rolled his eyes. "Trent deputized us."

Toni gaped at Clay. "What in the world?"

"Was all Blake's idea." Clay forked a bite of pancakes and chewed contentedly.

Everyone looked at Blake. "With all Trent has on his plate, he needed help. I suggested he could deputize people with law enforcement experience to help. Then I might've volunteered." He grinned.

Clay swallowed and took a long sip of coffee. "The rest of you guys are included in the plan. After breakfast, you'll be sworn in, and we'll meet with Blake to review leads for each investigation."

"You said guys," Toni said, trying to sound calm when her emotions were flaring. "Did you mean just your brothers?"

Clay looked at her, a hint of unease tightening his expression. "Sorry. Yeah. You're already sworn by another agency."

"Yeah, I figured." She tightened her hands into fists under the table and gritted her teeth. She needed time to think before she snapped at him in front of his whole family. "So this means I'll be cut out of the investigation while you all not only investigate but have inside information."

Clay swallowed again. "It was the only way to get access to the things we need to move forward."

"Ah, man." Drake shook his head. "Not a wise move, bro."

"I thought it was a genius idea." Clay challenged his brother with a glare.

Drake gave Toni a pointed look. She was trying hard, but she wasn't hiding her frustration. Clay was too excited by this new direction to see how making such a decision without talking to her would hurt. She wished Drake hadn't caught on and wasn't giving her a sympathetic look. His kindness brought tears to her eyes, totally unacceptable for an FBI agent. Especially in front of this group.

"Excuse me." She hurried to the bedroom, firmly closed the door, and paced off her frustration.

A knock rattled the door. Had to be Clay, but she couldn't talk to him right now. Not until she thought about what had just transpired.

"Toni, please." He sounded desperate. "Let me explain."

"Not now." She turned her back to the door as if that would help.

"Please," he said again,

His pain-filled plea got to her, and she almost opened the door. *No*. He'd hurt her. She remained in place until she heard his footsteps retreat down the hallway. The few bites of pancakes she'd eaten churned in her stomach. She didn't know how long she stood there, but another knock sounded on the door, this one less insistent. Less demanding. Probably his mother. That would be even worse than talking to Clay. She was warm and wonderful and might be able to convince Toni that her son was sorry for his actions.

"Toni, it's Drake."

*Drake?*

"Can I talk to you?"

*Unexpected.* Should she let him in? She didn't think he'd plead Clay's case. If she'd learned anything about Drake, she'd learned that he knew his mind, and he understood that Clay had messed up. Plus, it would be good to have someone to talk to. Maybe it would also keep their mother at bay for now.

Toni opened the door and went to sit on the lower bunk.

Drake stepped a few feet inside the room and left the door ajar. "I wanted to check on you."

"I'm fine. Mad, but needing to make a plan."

"What kind of plan?"

"For starters, I can't stay here."

He didn't speak for a long moment. "That bad, huh?"

"I don't even want to look at him."

"Ouch."

"He brought it on himself."

"If it helps at all, he tried to get Trent to call your office and ask for you to work a joint task force with them. Trent refused. Said if he did that he might as well call in the Bureau to start with."

She liked hearing that, but it didn't change the fact that she was out in the cold on an investigation involving her father and missing sister. Not to mention countless girls that she felt personally responsible for finding.

"And Clay said after watching the videos he had to do something," Drake continued. "He couldn't stand thinking about the girls Hibbard was holding in such deplorable conditions."

Her heart softened another notch, and some of her anger vanished with it.

Drake shifted his feet. "Seems like that might've helped."

"Yeah, a little, but I'm still leaving. For professional reasons I can't stay here and have you all stop talking whenever I'm near, or worse, ask me to leave the room so you can talk. It could impede the investigation, and I wouldn't want to stand in the way of finding the girls. And I also need to keep working things on my own. Find these girls and Lisa. And my dad's killer."

"Yeah...yeah. I get that." His eyes narrowed. "Where will you go?"

"Hotel, or maybe my grandparents."

"Want one of us to go with you? I mean, not Clay obviously."

"I'll be okay."

Drake frowned. "Sharkey's behind bars, but Hibbard isn't. He could still come after you."

"I'll be careful."

He took a step closer and locked gazes. "Then take pity on me. On my family. We won't sleep at night knowing you're alone. Let me come with you. I know I resemble Clay, but I promise to do my best not to look at all like him." He made a funny face.

She laughed and felt instantly lighter. Maybe it would be good to have Drake with her. They could work this investigation together.

She stood and held out her hand. "Okay, you have a deal as long as we never talk about Clay."

He shook hands, a cute grin on his face. "Clay who?"

# 22

In the entryway, Clay glared at Drake. "What do you mean you're going with Toni?"

"I need to make sure Hibbard doesn't get to her, and instead of glaring at me, I'd think you'd be thanking me."

Clay curled his fingers. "You got a thing for her?"

"No way, man." Anger darkened Drake's eyes. "She's your girl. Just doing a brother a solid, and I happen to respect her too."

"She's not my girl."

"That's your problem, not mine." Drake shifted his duffel bag over his shoulder. "I'll make sure she's safe. I promise."

"He's doing the right thing," his mother said from the family room, where the rest of his brothers were waiting to leave for Trent's office.

She was the last person Clay wanted to hear from right now. In fact, he only wanted to hear from one person. Toni. And she refused to talk to him. His fault. He knew it. He'd put the investigation before her. Put these girls before her. Law enforcement officers often did that. He'd seen his dad do it enough. It was the sacrifice they made to help others in these demanding careers.

But Clay could've been smarter about his decision. Instead of running off to Trent, Clay could've talked to Toni first. Explained his reasons. And if he had talked to her first, he knew she would've understood because she had a heart for others too. She wanted to save these girls as much as he did. He should've woken her up. That would've been the smart thing to do.

He scrubbed a hand over his face and watched as Drake joined the other brothers. Thankfully, Sierra and Kelsey had gone with one of Trent's deputies to Rader's house, so they hadn't seen the mess he'd made of things. And Blake had gobbled down his pancakes and gone to the bedroom to rearrange his schedule so he could play deputy. Clay figured the guy knew when to get out of the room.

The irony of it all was that Clay was the one with a trust issue from his last relationship, and he'd been the one to violate Toni's trust, while she'd been straightforward and honest with him. Not wanting to lead him on when she wasn't ready for more. And yet, here he was falling in love with her, and she didn't even want to look at him.

"Maybe now would be a good time for prayer," his mother suggested. "Prayer might be the very way to get Toni to soften her heart toward you."

He didn't feel much like praying, even *if* it could help, but he joined the family. She offered a genuine prayer. *Right.* This was why his mother was so special. In time of crisis, she held the family together with faith. Like the stitching when she'd mended their clothes, she patched their issues with faith-filled pleas. She'd always said prayer wasn't just about asking God to help, but it was putting into words the unwavering belief that He *would* help. Maybe not as we wanted, but help would be forthcoming.

Blake came into the room. "We should get going. Trent's waiting for us, and it's not the best start to keep him waiting."

"Let me say good-bye to Toni."

"Sure you want to do that, bro?" Drake asked.

"She doesn't want to hear from me. I get it. But I left this house once today without saying good-bye. Big mistake. I won't make the same one again." He took a long, cleansing breath as he headed down the hallway.

He knocked on the door gently. "Toni, it's Clay. I know you don't want to talk to me, but I wanted to tell you I'm heading over to Trent's office. If you need me for anything, call. Stay safe, okay? I care about you more than you know."

He waited by the door, hoping for a response.

"Good bye," she said, and the finality of her tone left him wishing she hadn't spoken after all.

Back in the family room, he tossed his keys to Drake. "You'll need transportation."

Drake held them out. "Dad said I could use his car."

"The armored vehicle is safer for Toni. And thanks. You're right. I will feel better if you're with her." Clay looked at his other brothers, his gut so tight he might hurl. "The rest of you ready to roll?"

They got to their feet, and without a word, followed Blake to the other SUV. Aiden unlocked the doors, and Clay climbed in the back with Erik and Brendan while Blake sat in front.

Normally Clay would fight for shotgun, but seating position seemed so irrelevant now. He would just have to pin his focus on finding those missing girls and Lisa and making sure Sharkey paid for killing Toni's father. Then maybe she could at least stand to be in the same room with him. He could hope anyway.

~

Toni had taken her time packing her bag, waiting to hear the sound of the front door closing and the SUV taking off before creeping out of the bedroom she shared with Kelsey and Sierra. She was sad to leave them. Leave the whole family. But she had to get away to a place where there weren't so many people who would advocate for Clay and cloud her mind and to allow them to talk freely.

She set down her suitcase at the door, plastered a smile on her face, and stepped into the family room. Peggy and Russ sat together, each reading a book, but Drake was missing. Maybe he was packing too.

She hated to steal him away from his family, and she really didn't think she would need his protection. After all, no one had tried to kill her since the high school fire. But if it helped him and his family worry less, she would accept his help.

Peggy came to her feet. "Oh, sweetie, I'm so sorry you feel like you need to leave."

"It's okay, really."

"No, it's not. You're our guest, and we treated you badly."

"You were wonderful."

Drake came down the hall and joined them.

"Clay is sick over what he did," Peggy went on. "But I won't try to defend him to you. That's his job." She eyed her son. "And only *his* job."

"I got this, Mom. Don't worry so much."

"Mothers are made to worry."

Drake's dark eyebrow went up in a perfect arch. "What about you always telling us to trust God?"

"Trusting Him doesn't mean that one of you won't go and do something to create a problem."

Case in point, Clay's recent decision, Toni thought and waited for Drake to say it, but he didn't.

She looked at him. "I booked two rooms at the Rugged Point Inn, and they'll let us check in now."

"Great. After you."

"Wait," Peggy said, and Toni expected a plea to stay, but she hurried to the kitchen and came out carrying a few containers. "I packed some goodies and snacks for the two of you."

Toni took the containers and smiled at Peggy. "That was very kind of you."

Peggy stepped closer and lowered her voice. "I want you to enjoy them, but it's for your self-preservation too. Drake gets a bit ugly when he's really hungry."

"I can hear you, Mom." Drake grinned.

"Well, you do."

"I do at that." He kissed his mother's cheek. "Thanks for the snacks, and I'll check in routinely."

"Which means don't keep bugging him with texts and phone calls, Peg," Russ said, his tone joking.

Peggy grabbed Toni in a hug. "I hope we see you again."

Toni didn't think it was likely, even *if* she'd been invited to Sunday dinner, she would never join them now. So she kept her mouth shut and tried not to cry over Peggy's kindness and the way she reminded Toni of her mother.

Drake picked up Toni's bag.

"We'll come back for my boxes of records." She hurried out the door with the containers still smooshed against her chest from the hug.

Drake inserted his key in the passenger door and unlocked all the doors. "I'm surprised you don't have electronic locks on this fancy vehicle."

"We did but found out they were hackable. So we replaced them with old-fashioned keys."

She set the containers on the floor and turned back while he put their bags in the back. She went inside to move two of her file boxes to the door and took one last look around the dining room to be sure she had everything and that she was only leaving Ziegler's and Clay's files.

"That it?" Drake asked from the door.

She nodded and glanced at Peggy. "Thanks again."

Toni rushed out and into the vehicle. Drake got behind the wheel.

She looked at him, her smile for Peggy still frozen on her face. "Do you know where the hotel is located?"

"Yes, ma'am." He mimicked tipping a hat. "I'll take you right to the front door, but I hope you aren't expecting anything special."

"The exterior pictures looked nice online." She clicked her seatbelt into place.

"I think they were taken before I was born." He laughed and pulled onto the main road. "Do you think it's too early for one of Mom's monster cookies?"

"For me, yes, but I can get one for you."

"Let's stop for some coffee to go with it, and I'll have it while we plan our next move."

"I didn't ask if you're willing to help me work the investigation without your brothers."

"Sure. I won't go against them in anything, but we can do a lot without that happening."

"You really do have an amazing family." She remembered thinking about being adopted by them and chuckled.

He glanced at her. "What's so funny?"

"At dinner one night I thought I wanted your mom and dad to adopt me." Her good mood vanished. "Losing my dad so suddenly when he was the only consistent person I had in my life was a big deal. I'm working through it, but I guess I was jealous."

"Trust me, we have our issues too."

"I know. But the love and faith you all share is something I would like to be a part of someday."

"Too bad the guy who shall not be named blew it."

"Actually, I don't know if anything would've continued after the investigation ended anyway."

"Why's that?"

"Too complicated." She looked out the window at the beach under spitting rain and heavy fog. "The weather reflects my mood."

"Better change quick because the fog is predicted to burn off. We're supposed to have a sunny day."

Change her mood. No. She didn't want to. She wanted to be mad.

*That's not what God has taught you. Forgive.*

She ignored her own voice and pointed out the window. "Is that the hotel?"

"Yep."

The three story rectangle was painted a calming beige with small balconies on the top floor. The building sat near the beach with rolling waves, and a portico covered the wide entrance.

Drake pulled under the overhang and killed the engine.

"I'll grab our keys and be right back." She waited for him to argue about going alone like Clay would do in this situation, but Drake didn't utter a word. She climbed out, and surprisingly, she missed having Clay at her side.

Which was ridiculous. She was mad at him. Or more correct, hurt by him.

She stepped into the lobby, and an older woman with frosted short hair and a wrinkled face smiled from behind the desk. "Welcome."

Her nametag read Joy Graber.

"Toni Long," she said. "I reserved two adjoining rooms." She got out her credit card, and Joy looked over her shoulder to the front doors, likely focusing on Drake, and frowned.

Did she think something funny was going on?

Toni couldn't have gossip starting in this small town. She got out her FBI credentials and laid them on the counter too. "In case you need additional ID."

"Oh...oh. FBI." Joy's eyes flashed open. "Wow. Are you investigating something?"

"We are," she said and left it at that.

Joy's head bobbed one time, and she started entering Toni's credit card number into her computer. "You let me know if there's anything I can do to help."

Toni hadn't planned to pick this woman's brain, but she might have information on Lisa's disappearance. "Have you lived in town for long?"

"Me and my Earl have owned the hotel since the mid-seventies."

"Then you might remember the disappearance of Lisa Long from her grandparents' house."

"Oh sure, she...wait." Her mouth dropped open. "Long. Are you related?"

Toni didn't answer.

"None of my business then." Joy waved her hand. "It was the talk of the town. Her parents stayed right here for nearly six months looking for the poor little thing. She came to visit and disappeared. Sheriff Raintree decided she'd washed out to sea, but Earl and I don't believe it."

*Interesting.* "What do you think happened?"

Joy leaned closer. "I think a vagrant was involved. Told Sheriff Raintree as much, but never even saw the guy's name mentioned as a suspect. So I got back to Raintree. He said he ruled that man out, but I don't see how. He was kind of a creepy guy. Former military. Living on the beach back then. Not sure what happened to him."

"What was his name?"

"Sheldon Sharkey. Ain't that just a name?"

Toni did her best not to react. "I appreciate the information."

"Maybe you can do something with it. God knows that the old sheriff would rather sit in his office than do his job. An outsider, he was. Came in as a highfalutin deputy from the big city and made pals with the mayor. Got himself elected by promising all kinds of good things. Didn't do anything he promised."

"Tell me about Lisa's parents," Toni said, feeling weird talking about her parents like this.

"Interesting couple. The mom was moody. Sad most of the time, as you can expect. He was a doer. Didn't sit still for a minute. Spent every second looking for Lisa."

"Didn't the mom help?" Toni asked.

"Sure, yeah, but she was really depressed. I think the doc had her on tranquilizers, and she couldn't cope like the dad. He was a DEA agent and had the skills to conduct a search. Left his wife to fend for herself most of the time in the early days. But he finally convinced her to accompany him, and she gradually pulled herself together."

Toni couldn't imagine her parents going through such a difficult time, but Joy had described her parents as Toni had known them, only with less intense emotions. She finally understood so much about them. Maybe her dad had been so hard on her because she wasn't Lisa. Or maybe he wanted to make sure she was tough enough to withstand anything, even learning that he'd hidden her sister from her or being kidnapped like he'd feared had happened to Lisa.

Joy slid metal keys and a small map across the counter.

"This time of year we aren't as full, so I gave you our best rooms. They're on the third floor with a balcony."

"Thanks so much." Feeling emotional and vulnerable, Toni tucked her card and ID into her purse and grabbed the keys.

"Elevator's over there." Joy pointed over Toni's shoulder, but Toni had already seen the elevator when she took in the eighties lobby décor. Bad décor or not, the hotel was clean, and that was all Toni cared about.

She exited the building and slid into the SUV.

Drake smiled. "All set?"

She nodded. "But turn the SUV around. We're heading back to your parents' place to look at Ziegler's old files before Blake and your brothers get back there."

# 23

Clay tapped his foot under the conference room table as Trent wrote the suspects' names on the board. But Clay couldn't concentrate. Not with the way he let Toni down. Everything tasted sour in his mouth. He was desperate to know what she was doing—if she was okay. Sure, Drake would do his best to keep her safe, but safety could depend on more than just one person having her back. Because Hibbard was still on the loose, and he—along with any number of men he assigned—could be out to kill her.

*Please keep her safe.*

Trent finished printing Sheldon Sharkey, Rich Hibbard, Jason Rader, and Fritz Rader in sharp red letters, then grabbed a black marker and added Naomi Dawson under Fritz Rader's name.

Trent tapped on her name. "The girl Kelsey identified from the high school. Her photo was also found at Rader's place."

"How did Kelsey find the girl's ID?" Clay asked.

Trent faced the group. "After Kelsey dated the bones, we searched that timeframe for missing girls and narrowed it down to two girls. DNA officially confirmed the identity."

"Do we have any information on her?" Aiden asked.

"She's a runaway from Portland," Trent said. "I talked to her parents last night. A typical scenario. Naomi was troubled and acting out after her parents' divorce. She wanted to live with her dad and fought with her mother. Mom said no. Girl took off three years ago."

"Can we see her picture?" Brendan asked.

Trent unclipped a photo from his folder and handed it to Brendan. He studied it carefully, then shaking his head, he passed it on to Erik, who took a quick look and gave it to Clay.

"She's definitely one of the girls in Rader's pictures," Clay said. "I remember the scar by her eye."

"So now we know Rader had a connection to this girl." Trent jotted Jason's name with a question mark on the board. "I need to push Jason harder to see what he knows."

"I keep thinking about Rader's wife," Aiden said. "Maybe she found out what Rader was up to and split before she got in trouble with the law."

"If so, wouldn't she have taken Jason with her instead of leaving him with a horrible father?" Trent asked.

"The kid couldn't have been involved then, could he?" Clay asked. "He was only sixteen."

"He does have a juvenile record for misdemeanors, so he was often on the wrong side of the law," Trent said. "But he was never even on the radar for trafficking."

Clay looked at Trent. "When you arrested Jason, did you look for the mother?"

He shook his head. "Didn't seem relevant."

"Not sure it's relevant even now," Blake said. "Unless she's one of the bodies buried out back."

"She's not." Trent wrote *Six deceased girls* under Rader's name. "None of them fit Ursula's build, and none have borne children. Kelsey said she would provide specifics for each girl by the end of the day. Age, height, hair color, et cetera, and hopefully an approximate time of death."

"How does she do that?" Clay asked. "The time of death, I mean."

"She'll have to give you all the details, but she said she factors in the temperature and the humidity over the years to make her determination. And she said another element she uses is animal bites on the bones. Like bites from squirrels and rats."

"Rat bites?" Erik shuddered.

"Yeah, apparently rats like greasy bones and tend to chew on the ends to gain access to the marrow. Squirrels prefer drier and more brittle bones. She said the squirrels use the bone's calcium to ensure strong litters. To get dry bones, they would have to be fully exposed to the elements at some point."

Clay didn't want to think about these young girls and scavengers. "Hopefully we can match the DNA to the list of missing girls you provided us."

Trent nodded. "Kelsey took samples yesterday, and one of Gage's guys flew it to Veritas to deliver to your wife." Trent looked at Blake. "Emory said she'd get back to me later today. But here's the problem. We don't have DNA for the girls who've been missing the longest, except for Lisa. So if it's one of them, we'll have to find a different method to make an ID."

"And I'm assuming cause of death will take some time to obtain," Blake said.

Trent nodded. "Kelsey has to transport the bones to her lab. She'll review them and get the info to me as soon as possible, but she said that could take weeks."

Trent turned back to the board and wrote the word *photo* under Sharkey's name. "Naomi is also in the photos we found at Sheldon Sharkey's house."

Clay didn't add that he and his brothers had already looked at those photos. "So that brings us up to date on the murder at the high school and the girls presumed murdered at Rader's house, but where do you stand on the beach house?"

Trent wrote *beach house* and the initials *RSL* under Jason Rader's name. "Your sister lifted prints from the note and sent them to Veritas for her assistant to handle. No match in the databases. No additional evidence. Though Sierra did lift other prints and DNA, and they've also been transported to Veritas."

"Did she locate any twine at the scene?" Clay asked. "Or did Kelsey find twine in the backyard graves at Rader's place?"

"Twine?" Trent's dark eyebrows went up. "No, but Kelsey's not done recovering the bodies. Why?"

Clay explained how the twine connected Heidi and Naomi Dawson with Rader and Sharkey's Christmas tree operations.

"One of those details no one shared with me." Trent shook his head and added *twine* under Sharkey's and Rader's names and put Heidi's name under Hibbard's listing. "What else have you been holding back?"

Clay told Trent about the unique carving on the bedposts that matched the bed in their prior investigation. "So Hibbard is very much a suspect in all of this."

Trent jotted it down under Hibbard's name. "The videos we found on the SD cards from Sharkey's house also indicate Hibbard's involvement."

"Have you made any progress in locating him?" Erik asked.

"I had the Portland police check out his last known address. Place was vacant. Looked like no one had been there in a long time."

"Guessing they went to the Hillsboro address on Baseline," Clay said. "He moved out of there over a year ago."

"I've put out a statewide alert," Trent said. "If he shows his face, we'll find him."

"Mind if I suggest some of his prior hangouts for PPB to look into?" Clay hoped officers could check out the locations and ask a few questions.

"Already did that." Erik leaned back, a smug smile on his face. "I've had one of my contacts at PPB scope them out the last few days. No sign of Hibbard."

Clay looked at his youngest brother. "You didn't tell me that."

"Didn't figure it mattered if they didn't find anything. Besides, we all think Hibbard's moved on to this area."

"And yet, there hasn't been any sightings of him or any sign of his business dealings." Trent set down the marker.

"What about doing a public appeal?" Brendan asked.

Trent planted his hands on his hips. "Could send him even further to ground."

Brendan crossed his arms. "Or someone might've seen him and come forward."

Looking confident, Trent glanced around the table. "Who's in favor of the public appeal?"

Everyone raised their hands, and Clay watched Trent to see how he handled being outvoted by his deputies.

He gave a sharp nod. "I'll schedule a press conference today and get his name and picture out there."

"I would've agreed with you if we hadn't been looking for the guy for years," Clay said. "I think it'll take someone rolling over on him to catch him."

Trent nodded again. "That's settled. Let's talk about Sharkey. I've interviewed him, but he continues to say no comment. It looks like it'll take a deal to get anything from him. I don't think the DA wants to offer a deal to a guy who possesses photos that seem to point to his guilt in multiple murders. Not to mention that he's in possession of child pornography and the bird had Sharkey's DNA on it."

"Gives Sharkey a solid connection to Rader and puts him at the murder scene," Clay said. "Plus, Sharkey has the strength to strangle Rader. We just need to prove motive, and we got Sharkey on this one."

"Agreed," Trent said.

"And we haven't even mentioned Lisa Long's disappearance. Her clothes found in Rader's garage connects him there too."

Trent ran a hand through his hair. "I've been considering reopening the Long investigation but there's not enough manpower."

"We've already reviewed Ziegler's records," Blake said. "Looks like he did a thorough job. Only oddity was that Sheriff Raintree was very active in the investigation. From what I've heard about him, that was unusual. Could be an issue to look into or it was a matter of a child going missing and he couldn't sit back and do nothing."

"Did Ziegler say anything about that?" Trent asked.

"No, but he never badmouthed Raintree no matter what others said. It was a high-profile case and an election year. Could explain Raintree's behavior."

"Could indeed." Trent shared an insider's look with Blake.

Clay couldn't imagine what went into getting elected and reelected as sheriff. Never made any sense to Clay that the sheriff's position was often an elected position. He'd seen men and women elected who knew very little about policing.

"Okay." Trent clapped his hands. "That's it. Let's make assignments and get to work catching a killer and trafficker of humans."

~

Toni felt Peggy watching her, but she kept on digging through the records, not commenting on anything to Drake to keep Peggy from overhearing. When Toni had turned the last page of the three-ring binder, she sat back to wait for Drake to catch up.

Unless she'd missed something in the four large binders, Sharkey hadn't been mentioned in Ziegler's files. Notes did say Raintree canvassed the hotel area as part of the initial assessment, but he claimed not to have learned anything. No mention of Joy at all.

Drake closed the book.

"We should get going," she said before he could speak.

He didn't question her but stacked the books on top of Clay's investigation files and headed for the door.

"Bye again," he said to his parents.

"Thanks for the coffee," Toni added.

In the SUV, she turned to Drake. "You see anything about Sharkey in the books?"

"Nada." Drake cranked the engine. "I say we go to the local newspaper office to review archives. We might even be able to search for mention of Sharkey or a homeless issue. Something like that."

"Sounds good. And if we don't find anything, we can talk to Joy again. I'm sure she'll be glad to provide more information." Toni got out her phone. "I'll find the newspaper office's address."

"No need. It's on Main Street. At least it is if it hasn't moved since I was a kid."

She swiveled to face him. "Sounds like you guys spent a lot of time here."

"We each had a week alone with our grandparents every summer plus two weeks all together. We did chores for

Grandma and Gramps, and they gave us an allowance. We'd save it up and ride bikes into town to buy saltwater taffy and souvenir junk. You should've seen our parents roll their eyes at it when we got home."

He smiled and his eyes lit with warmth as if he had fond memories. "My favorite was a grabber with a shark's head. I can't tell you all the things I picked up with that thing. Or how many times I got socked from grabbing my brothers with it."

He laughed, but she couldn't. If she'd been allowed to see her grandparents, would she have had a similar experience? She might've even met the Byrd brothers. Been lifelong friends and not someone who had no idea what her future might be with this family.

She could always forgive Clay. He hadn't meant to hurt her. She knew that. But the hurt was still too fresh to consider anything with him. She had to find out if it was in his nature to act like this again. If something important came up that he wanted and she was in the way, would he cut her out?

"Main Street." Drake turned onto a typical beach tourist road. Colorful restaurants, souvenir stores, a combo sweet and ice cream shop, and an arcade. She could easily imagine the Byrd siblings exploring the town.

"The paper's just ahead." Drake pulled into a parking space in front of a two-story building with a covered patio.

Inside, she could still smell the ink from days gone by, and a giant printing press with rubber letters took up the back wall. She doubted they'd printed the paper this way in eons, but it was fun to see.

An older gentleman with snowy white hair who was likely pushing eighty got up from behind a desk and came to lean on a scarred counter. "Help you?"

"We were hoping to look at your archives for the late eighties," Toni said.

"Anything particular you're looking for?"

"Lisa Long's disappearance."

He frowned. "Why would you want to see that? Was a sad thing for Walt and Gert Long. They barely survived it."

Toni took a breath. "Lisa is my sister."

"Never knew she had a sister."

"It's complicated," Toni said. "We were hoping to read about the investigation."

"Boxes are off-site in a storage facility. I own the paper and covered the incident. I can tell you whatever you need to know."

She wondered if he would remember much, but it seemed like this was their best bet. "Did Sheriff Raintree get involved in the investigation?"

"He did. We didn't see him much except at ribbon cuttings and official meetings. I was shocked when he took over the investigation."

"Did he talk about suspects?" Drake asked.

"Weren't any. He maintained from day one that the poor little girl wandered off and got swept up in the current. Nothing seemed to change his mind."

"Do you think he was covering something up?" Toni asked.

His bushy eyebrow arched. "Like what?"

"I don't know." She played it down, hoping he would respond. "Just asking."

"I think the only thing he was covering was his butt. It was an election year, and he hadn't done a thing he promised. He didn't want people to think it wasn't safe here so it was easier to say she drowned."

Toni nodded as he confirmed Joy's story. "You ever hear of anyone with the last name Sharkey?"

"Connected to this investigation?"

"Or to anything in town, really," she said.

"Hmm." He tapped his chin. "I have, but I just can't place it."

"Sheldon Sharkey," she clarified.

"No. No. That's not it."

*Then what?* she wanted to scream and push him to remember.

"It'll come to me, but never know when. Still, I'll think on it. Give me your phone number, and I'll let you know."

She jotted her cell on the back of her business card with a pen from the counter and passed it to him.

"FBI?" His interest perked up. "This an official investigation?"

Toni shook her head. "Just looking into my sister's disappearance."

He looked at Drake. "You FBI too?"

"A friend."

"When that name comes to me, I'll give you a call." He tapped the card on the counter.

"Can you think of anything else that might've seemed off or odd about the investigation or Lisa's disappearance?" Drake asked.

"Not really, other than those things don't happen in our little town. Sure, they might these days, but not back then. Was a gentler, kinder time."

She glanced at Drake to see if he had any questions but his eyes had taken on a faraway look. Maybe he was remembering his youth spent here.

"Okay, thank you." She started to leave.

"Starts with an S. Yes, I'm pretty sure it's an S," the owner said.

"But not Sheldon."

"No, not Sheldon."

She headed for the door. On the sidewalk, she looked at Drake. "What do you make of that?"

"I think we should get back to the hotel and start looking for a Sharkey who's related to Sheldon with a name that starts with S."

# 24

The room had a kitchenette and balcony, but Toni cringed at the worn comforter with a wavy beach pattern. She set her bag on the luggage rack and unlocked the adjoining door for Drake before sitting on the bed to dial the front desk.

Joy answered on the third ring.

"It's Toni Long," she said. "I wondered if you knew of another Sharkey in the area."

"Might've been, but Sheldon didn't say much."

"You talked to him?"

"Found him sleeping near our pool. I fed him breakfast and politely asked him to move on. That's when I learned his name. He was on some elite military team that saw conflict at that time. He said he came here because the beach erased the memories from his service. Was the only place he could sleep, and he didn't have the money to stay anywhere."

She paused to draw in a deep breath. "I asked if he had family around, and he shook his head sadly then got up and left. I saw him around the beach after that, but never at our hotel again. I took him food sometimes. I didn't like to encourage vagrancy, but the guy seemed down on his luck. 'Course I never went near him at night. He was a trained killer, after all. I'll ask Earl if he knows another Sharkey and give you a call if he does."

"Thanks, Joy." Toni hung up and heard voices in the other room.

"You have adjoining rooms?" Clay's voice rose. "What's the point of that?"

"So we can work the investigation together, and I can make sure Toni's safe," Drake said. "Why are you here?"

"To update you on the things Trent authorized me to share. He doesn't have any leads on Hibbard's location, so he's issuing a public appeal today. This could put Hibbard on the move or make him take defensive actions. Means Toni could be in danger and you need to be extra vigilant on her safety."

"Good to know," Drake said.

"Also, they identified the body at the school," Clay said. "It's Naomi Dawson, a runaway from Portland. Trent will make this public today too. What he won't say is that she's in the pictures we found at Rader's house and the photos from Sharkey's place."

Toni jotted down the information and noted the additional connections between Rader, Sharkey, and Hibbard.

"Thanks for the update," Drake said.

"You two finding anything out?" Clay asked.

"Not much," Drake said. "But we've got a few leads that I really need to move on so..."

"I get it. Move on." Clay sounded disappointed. "Tell Toni I'm thinking about her."

"Sure."

She heard footsteps then Drake's door opened and closed. Drake came to the connecting door, his computer under his arm. "I suppose you heard all of that."

She nodded.

"Clay's really down."

"Yeah, sounded like it. I've forgiven him, but I'm not ready to talk to him. The hurt is still lingering, and it'll take some time to go away."

"I get that." Drake dropped onto one of the chairs by a small dining table.

"On his news, I have to believe Rader, Hibbard, and Sharkey were all in cahoots until Sharkey killed Rader. Maybe he killed Hibbard too, and that's why there's no sign of him."

"Could be, but why's his name on the envelope, and why isn't there a picture of him dead?"

"For that matter, why the photos at all?" she asked. "Blackmail? Or maybe Sharkey worked as Hibbard's hitman, and the pictures were proof he'd done his job."

Drake frowned. "Naomi died a couple of years ago. Why still have her picture?"

"Maybe he takes pictures instead of souvenirs from a crime scene."

"Could be."

"I called Joy. She doesn't know another Sharkey. She'll ask her husband."

"Let's do some digging and see what we can find." Drake opened his computer.

"If we could get Sharkey's basic info, I could use one of the ancestry sites to look him up like I did when I found Lisa. It would give us his relatives right away."

"Then let's find that info."

She retrieved her laptop and sat across from Drake. They worked until lunchtime, when they ordered burgers and fries sent from room service.

Joy easily balanced the large tray as she entered the room. She set the plates on the table next to their computers. “I asked Earl about another Sharkey. He said Sheldon was the only one he’d ever heard of. I did think of one other thing, though.”

“What’s that?” Toni lifted the metal lid from her plate and inhaled the savory scent overpowering the room’s air freshener.

Joy set a tall bottle of ketchup on the table. “I saw Sharkey talking to a woman one day. She had her back to me, but they were arguing.”

Toni looked up. “Can you describe her?”

“Slender. Tall. She wore a floppy hat hiding everything else, but her clothing was expensive. Designer stuff. They only talked for five minutes or so, but I saw her storm off down the beach.”

“Where did she go?” Drake asked.

“To a Mercedes idling at a boat ramp. It was black and shiny, but I didn’t catch the plates.”

“Was this before or after Lisa went missing?” Drake asked.

“Before. Earlier in the week.”

Toni grabbed the ketchup bottle. “How much earlier?”

“Maybe the day before. Could’ve been two.”

“Did you tell Raintree that?” Toni asked.

“Told him, but he didn’t seem interested.” Joy held out the bill.

Toni signed it. “Thanks again for all the information.”

Joy left the room, and Toni took a huge bite of her burger.

“Good burger.” Drake set his on his plate and swiped a fry through ketchup.

“I learned over the years that burgers are usually safe hotel food. Pretty hard to screw one up.”

“You travel a lot?”

“Some. For the job, and my dad was usually too busy to

come here so I visited him." Now that she knew about Lisa, Toni realized it could've been too painful for him to come to Oregon.

Drake gestured at his laptop. "Did you find anything?"

She shook her head. "The guy isn't on the internet at all."

"Maybe we should pay Ziegler a visit."

She'd been thinking the same thing. "Blake said Ziegler doesn't like surprise visitors."

"Yeah, but you can charm him into talking to us, can't you?" He popped another fry into his mouth.

"You aren't really asking me to exploit the fact that I'm a woman?"

"Not politically correct these days, but come on. Look at me. No way I'm charming a retired sheriff." He grinned.

She might not like fighting with Clay, but she was enjoying getting to know his brother. "Fine. I'll try. But I have to warn you. I'm not very good at charming people."

"Then play on his sympathies for your family."

"That would just be wrong."

Drake sat up, and his jaw clenched. "I might not like the way Clay handled getting everyone deputized, but one thing I agree with him on. We have to do whatever we need to do to save these girls."

Her appetite vanished, and she set down her burger.

Her cell chimed. Good. Just what she needed. A distraction. She grabbed it from the table. "Text is from my dad's old boss. He got the key we sent. He's headed to the bank now. He'll report back on what he finds."

Drake smothered another fry in ketchup. "You must be excited to finally find out what's in the box."

"Excited. Apprehensive." She picked up her soda and took a long drink. "Maybe more apprehensive after the recent surprises."

Drake polished off his burger and wiped his mouth. “Can’t even imagine, but you seem to be holding up pretty well.”

“My ability to compartmentalize, I guess. I learned it at work.”

“Yeah, we all learn that skill in law enforcement or burn out. I don’t honestly know how the officers without any faith make it.”

She covered her plate and closed her laptop.

Drake picked up his glass. “Looks like you’re itching to go.”

“That obvious, huh?”

“Then let’s get after it.” He chugged his drink and grabbed a handful of fries. “Just don’t get into any trouble and need rescuing until I finish these fries. They’re too good to have to pitch so I can go for my gun.”

She laughed with him, grateful for his company. Without him, she would be sulking over Clay instead of laughing. Drake chowed down on his fries on the ride down the elevator and dusted his salty hands on his cargo pants.

He leaned out the door to take a look before pushing it all the way open and standing back. He might’ve joked about his fries, but like the other Byrds, safety came first for him. They crossed the lot to the vehicle, and thirty-five minutes later, they were pulling into Ziegler’s driveway.

“Let me get out first so he recognizes one of us,” she said. By the time she slid out, Ziegler was pushing open the screen door.

“Agent Long.” His tone was a cross between annoyance and surprise.

“Sorry to come by unannounced, but I had a few more questions about my sister’s disappearance.”

He tipped his head at the vehicle. “Who’s with you?”

“Drake Byrd.”

"Thought you were sweet on the other one. Clay. Why the brother?"

"I never said I was—"

"Save it." He held up a hand. "I wasn't in law enforcement for a lifetime to miss seeing the looks between the two of you the other day."

"Clay's working with Trent, so Drake and I have partnered up," she replied without divulging personal stuff.

Ziegler stood back. "Come on in, but he can stay in the car."

She glanced at Drake. He nodded his willingness to stay put, and she followed Ziegler inside.

He took a seat in the same recliner but didn't insist she have coffee this time. "Now, what can I do for you?"

"Did you know a Sheldon Sharkey?" She sat on the couch.

He narrowed his eyes. "Name rings a bell, but I'm not sure why."

"He was a homeless guy living on the beach when Lisa disappeared."

"News to me."

"So Sheriff Raintree didn't bring him to your attention regarding Lisa's disappearance?"

"No, I..." He went totally still. "Sharkey. I know why it rings a bell."

"Why?" She sat forward.

"Sheila Sharkey."

The name they were looking for, but...

"Who is she?" Toni held her breath as she waited for the answer.

"Raintree's ex-wife."

~

The call came in on the county radio issued by Trent, and Clay floored the gas on the vehicle borrowed from Gage. Hibbard had been seen entering a local bar where a patrol deputy had stopped to question the bartender. When the deputy spotted Hibbard, the deputy backed off and called it in.

Clay was the closest of the brothers to the bar, and Blake and Trent rode together and were just down the road. Clay intended to be the first one to arrive. He wouldn't race in, though. No matter how much he wanted to. He'd wait for backup. No way would he risk Hibbard squirting out the back door and escaping. He and Toni had waited far too long to bring this creep in to let the guy skate.

*Toni.* Man, he wished she was here by his side. They should be arresting this guy together.

The bar came into view just ahead. Covered in weathered rough-sawn cedar siding, it had a blue neon sign. The door stood open and small windows lined the wall facing the road. Clay slowed. Wouldn't do to slide into the lot on two wheels and draw attention.

He parked on the side of the building without windows and got out. The outside smelled like a cross between stale fish and beer. Not exactly appetizing. Blake and Trent pulled into the lot in Trent's unmarked car and parked next to Clay. The sun was dropping below the horizon behind them, leaving the area covered with a reddish glow.

"I'm going in after the guy," Clay said before anyone could speak.

"I'll be glad to take the back," Blake said.

Clay gave him a thankful look.

Trent frowned. "I'm first in, and I'll do the talking."

Clay widened his stance. "The second he sees your uniform, he's either gonna take a stand or skate."

"Clay's got a point," Blake said. "Might be better if Clay

goes in alone and brings him out before we have a shoot-out or a hostage situation on our hands."

Trent ground his teeth.

"Hey," Blake said. "I get it. You're in charge. You want to take the guy down. But sometimes you gotta stand back and let your people do the job when it's the best option."

"I know that." Trent glared at Blake. "But this guy isn't really one of my people."

"Still, we gotta do the right thing," Blake said. "Protect life at all costs."

Trent shook his head. "I figured after being sheriff for a couple of years, I was done with lectures from you."

"I'm never going away." Blake grinned.

Trent laughed and looked at Clay. "You go in first."

"Does Hibbard know you?" Blake asked.

"Never seen me in person, but yeah, he might know of me from the task force."

"You'll need a cap to hide your face." Trent looked around and walked over to a nearby truck with a window open. He grabbed a Seattle Seahawk's cap from the dash and handed it to Clay.

"Never thought I'd see the day a sheriff steals in broad daylight." Clay grinned and settled the cap on his head.

Trent rolled his eyes. "You need help, you call out. You hear me. Don't try to be a hero."

"I got it." Clay checked his gun and tugged his jacket closed to hide the bulge.

He offered a quick prayer, counted down from ten to calm himself, and stepped in. Neon lighting from a wall of video games lit up the dark space. Old wood tables and chairs filled the middle with three couples drinking beer and eating appetizers. The bartender was at one of the tables serving drinks. Two pool tables sat on the other side of the room with beer lights hanging over them. Two young guys were playing.

Clay spotted Hibbard right away. Would be hard to miss. Not only because he was a big guy, but he was the only person sitting at the bar. He wore jeans and a black windbreaker and sat close to the emergency exit.

Clay's years in ICE had trained him to take this guy in without a fuss, so he started across the room, skirting the bartender to avoid him calling out a greeting and alerting Hibbard.

Clay reached Hibbard and caught a whiff of strong body odor. He drew his weapon and put it in Hibbard's fleshy back. "You're under arrest, scumbag. Don't move."

"There must be a mistake." His low voice rumbled through the space.

"No mistake, Hibbard. We're arresting you for so many charges, I can't name them all here. Hands behind your back."

He dropped his feet to the floor.

"Go ahead. Take off." Clay made sure he sounded cool. "The place is surrounded. You won't get far, and you catching a bullet would make my day."

He reacted as Clay had hoped, putting his arms behind his body.

Clay snapped on cuffs then tugged Hibbard to his feet and marched him to the door. This had been too easy. Way too easy. Anticlimactic, even. Clay almost wished the jerk had run. Would've given Clay a chance to tackle him to the sticky bar floor and press his face in the stale beer.

But more than anything, Clay wished Toni were here. He'd shortchanged her from something else she'd wanted to do for so very long, further putting a divide between them when all he wanted was to get closer to her.

# 25

A text from Clay came in just as Toni and Drake had called it quits for the day. They'd been looking for additional information on Sheila Sharkey but struck out. Drake was headed back to his room for the night.

She read the text aloud.

*"Hibbard in custody. Confirmed Sharkey killed your dad and looks like Hibbard's providing details. No info on Lisa yet."*

Drake met her gaze. "Just like that, we know who killed your dad. And with Sharkey and Hibbard both behind bars, you're no longer in danger."

"Right. I'm safe."

He eyed her. "So why the frown?"

"I wanted to be at Hibbard's arrest."

"Ah, right. Yeah." He shifted his laptop under his arm. "I would've wanted that too."

"But you know what?" She forced a smile. "It doesn't matter. He's behind bars."

"True that." Drake smiled. "Any news on the girls?"

"Let me ask." She thumbed a response to Clay. *What about the girls?*

*Hibbard's clammed up on that. Trent and Blake are working on him.*

"Nothing yet." She texted Clay to keep her updated.

*I will and I'm so very sorry about earlier. I hope we can talk soon.*

*Maybe tomorrow.*

He sent back a smiley emoji, which for some silly reason made her miss him more. She locked her phone and looked up at Drake. "I feel like I should celebrate, but all I want to do is go to sleep and wake up to hear everything's been resolved."

Drake nodded. "Maybe we'll know by morning if Lisa's been found too."

"Yeah, maybe," Toni said, but she was dreading that bit of news. She couldn't imagine it would be good. "It's probably time for me to face facts. If she was abducted in the eighties, the odds of her being alive are close to zero."

"But there's a chance."

She smiled up at Drake, this one sincere. "Thanks for being here to cheer me up. Since no one's out to get me anymore, you can go back to the beach house."

"And miss a chance to sleep the night without snoring keeping me awake." He grinned. "No way."

"Then we'll meet for breakfast as planned at eight."

"I'll text Clay to keep me updated too so you don't have to. 'Night."

"Good night. And thanks again, Drake."

"My pleasure." He strode to his room, the confidence in his walk like his brothers. Like Clay.

*No, don't think about him.*

She closed and locked the door behind Drake and forced Clay out of her mind. She quickly took a shower and dropped into the bed after setting an alarm for seven. She fell asleep right away, dreaming of Lisa running on the beach, calling out for help, but no matter how fast Toni ran, Lisa remained out of reach.

A piercing alarm brought Toni awake, and she sat up. She blinked a few times to get her bearings and smelled smoke. The fire alarm. That was what woke her. And she didn't think it was a false alarm.

She grabbed her phone, slid into some shoes, then fixed her gun at her waist. Tossing a jacket on, she opened the door to Drake's room just as he was releasing his side.

He met her gaze, his eyes concerned. "Seems real enough."

She nodded, fear starting to rise in the pit of her stomach. "Let's go."

He led her to his door and ran his fingers around it. "Not hot. Should be safe to exit."

He opened the door, and smoke poured in. He tugged his shirt over his mouth. "Follow me."

She put her arm over her mouth and plunged into the smoky hallway. They hurried toward the stairway at the end of the floor. An elderly woman with a cane trudged out of her room. Drake held the stairwell door open for her. Lungs starting to protest, Toni stood back to let the woman go first. They moved slowly down the steps behind her, the smoke growing and making it difficult to see. The woman stumbled.

Drake grabbed her arm to right her. "Let me help you, ma'am."

She looked up at him. "Bless you, young man."

He guided her down to the second floor landing just as the door flew open.

"Help!" A frantic woman's high-pitched voice cut through the smoke. "My daughter. I can't get her out."

Drake glanced at Toni. "I'll go."

"I'll come with you."

"Help this woman down. I'll be fine."

Toni didn't want to leave Drake behind, but the older woman was coughing hard and had stopped moving. She needed guidance, or she wouldn't make it out.

Toni pulled her shirt up over her nose and took the woman's arm. "Here we go. Nice and slow."

"Bless—" A coughing fit took her words.

Toni waited for the spasm to stop, and they inched down the stairs. The smoke deepened in color and grew thicker. A wave of panic hit Toni, but she swallowed it down and kept the woman moving through the exit and into cleaner outside air.

Toni gulped the fresh air, but the woman launched into a gut-wrenching coughing fit.

Joy rushed over to them. "Mrs. Draper. I'm so sorry. Please. Come with me. I called the fire department. They should be here soon."

Joy flashed Toni a thankful look. "You should move back from the building."

Toni waited until Joy got Mrs. Draper settled on a bench in a wide parking strip. Toni backed to the rear of the parking lot as Joy directed but kept her eyes trained on the exit.

What was taking Drake so long?

She started counting, reaching five minutes, but he didn't come out. She closed her eyes in prayer, begging for Drake's and the little girl's safety.

Maybe he needed help, and she should head back inside.

She'd decided to do just that when a gun jabbed her in the ribs and her gun was jerked from the holster. She flashed her eyes open and tried to turn, but a hand clamped on her shoulder, stopping her.

"You're not going anywhere," the gruff female voice said. "Except with me."

~

Clay curled his fingers into fists. He could barely stomach watching Blake and Trent grill Hibbard through a one-way window. Clay wanted to be in that room. Be across the table from Hibbard. Sure, fine, Clay should be thankful to see the interview at all, but Clay wanted more. Wanted to sit across the table and force the man to confess to his many crimes. He wanted Toni there too. By his side.

Why waste time wishing for those things? Neither of them would come to fruition. He'd have to settle for the observer role.

Blake slapped the photos found in Rader's garage on the table, one at a time until all fifty-five had been laid out.

Clay watched Hibbard relax against the chair, smug and confident. All Clay could see when he looked at the guy was the man in the videos violating young women. A disgusting sight.

"Fifty-five counts of abduction, kidnapping, and statutory rape of these girls," Trent said. "And if that's not enough to put you away for the rest of your life, we have these."

Blake slid the photos found in Sharkey's place. "Five counts of first-degree murder should do it."

"I didn't do any of this." Hibbard shoved the photos across the table. "I had nothing to do with any of it."

"Then why did we find these pictures with your name on the envelope in Sheldon Sharkey's home?" Blake asked.

"You'd have to ask him."

"Don't worry, we will," Trent said. "And when he cuts a deal and rolls on you—and he will—you'll be looking at very serious time."

Hibbard puffed out his chest. "He's not the kind of guy to snitch."

"We'll keep at him until he talks," Trent said. "You can be sure of that."

Hibbard sputtered.

"And of course we have all the souvenirs and clothing Rader took from the girls. Your DNA is bound to be on it."

Hibbard shrugged, but his eyes were darkening with a hint of unease.

Trent woke up the screen of a tablet computer. He started a video of Hibbard with a young girl and turned the screen toward Hibbard. His fleshy face paled.

Trent paused the video. "It's obvious you're the star of this and seventy-six other videos. So we can add seventy-six counts of rape and start adding more as forensic evidence comes in."

Hibbard crossed his arms and sunk down on his chair. "They weren't all minors."

Clay's mouth fell open. The guy had all but admitted his role. Maybe he figured there was no way for him to get out of the charges.

"We'll see once we ID all of them." Blake sat back, looking relaxed as if he didn't have a care in the world. "And then we'll begin on the abduction, kidnapping, and murder charges."

"I told you I didn't do those things." The color returned to Hibbard's face, leaving it blotchy red.

"But you know about them," Trent said. "And that makes you an accessory."

Hibbard's gaze traveled around the room at a frantic rate as if looking for a way out of the charges.

"Tell us who's responsible," Trent said. "And we'll make sure the district attorney hears about your cooperation."

Hibbard ran a hand over a little patch of hair remaining

on his otherwise bald head. "Fine. It was her. Ursula. Ursula Rader."

*Ursula? Seriously?*

Clay couldn't look away from Hibbard on the far side of the glass, but Trent and Blake remained passive as good interviewers would do.

"Tell us about her," Trent said.

"She's something else." Hibbard shook his head. "Her mother was a prostitute. Ursula vowed to do better in life and never prostituted herself, but she wasn't above putting other women in that position. She started when she was married to a migrant worker. Conned female workers into having sex with the bosses for money. Built a good stable of girls. But then found out she could make more money with younger girls, but she'd need to quit traveling. She had her husband killed and hooked up with Fritz Rader."

"Was he into the business, too?" Blake asked.

Hibbard shook his head, his fleshy jowls swinging. "But he found out a few years after their kid was born. He said she needed to quit, but she refused. Rader was obsessed with her, so he turned his back, but he also stored away souvenirs she'd taken to ensure she stayed with him. On the surface they were a perfectly normal, church going family. But when the kid got older and joined the youth group, she took a liking to the leader, and they had an affair."

*So that was what Wilshire was hiding.* Clay blinked to try to make sense of the news. "Why didn't she just kill Rader? I mean, she'd already killed once."

"Don't know."

"Did the youth leader know about the girls?" Blake asked.

"Nah, but he did put her on to one of them."

"Who?" Blake asked, but Clay already knew the name he would mention.

"The girl who went missing from her grandparents' place."

"Lisa Long," Trent clarified, and Hibbard nodded. "And where is Lisa now?"

Hibbard shrugged, but a knowing look crossed his face.

"Come on, now," Trent said. "You expect me to believe you don't know the answer to that?"

"Don't care what you believe. I don't know."

"So why did Ursula walk out on her son?" Blake asked, changing the topic, but Clay knew Blake would come back to Ursula's location.

"Rader threatened to out her to the police if she tried to take him."

"But wouldn't he implicate himself if he did?"

"Yeah, sure, but he said he'd rather go to prison than let Ursula take the kid." Hibbard got a smug grin on his face. "But she didn't let it go. She secretly met with Jason. Problem was, he found out what she was doing. He wasn't disgusted or anything. He wanted a cut. Just eighteen years old, and she let him work with her. Then he gets arrested." Hibbard shook his head. "Rader has a fit. Says he's got cancer and has only a few months to live, so he's going to rat her out to the cops. So she had him killed too."

"Why didn't she take the things in the garage that implicated her?" Blake asked.

"You'll have to ask her. All I know is she had him snuffed out before he could squeal, and she hired a high-priced lawyer for her kid."

Trent rested his hands on the table and stared at them for a moment. He was going to change direction. Clay could feel it from Trent's body language. Blake must have too, as he leaned back and looked like he was giving the floor to Trent.

"She the one who's been trying to kill Agent Long and Clay Byrd?" Trent asked.

"Her boyfriend, yeah. Not her."

"Boyfriend?"

"Sharkey. They been shacking up for years."

So Sharkey had been trying to kill them. Clay curled his fingers. Thankfully he was in jail right now as this creep would be soon, and Toni was no longer in danger.

"Why did she want to kill them?" Trent asked.

"Another thing you're gonna have to ask her."

"Don't worry, I will when we bring her in."

Hibbard scoffed. "Like you'll find her."

"We will." Trent sounded so confident, but locating Ursula would be a challenge. "Because you're going to tell us exactly where she is."

# 26

Toni drove the compact car while the woman rode in the backseat and held her gun to Toni's neck. She wanted to slam on the brakes and force the woman forward, but she couldn't. Not without taking the risk of getting her head blown off.

She glanced in the rearview mirror, trying to get a good look at the woman's face. Impossible. A big floppy hat hid it in shadows. Toni had gotten a look at the woman's wrinkled hand with age spots, suggesting she was older.

"Why won't you tell me who you are?" Toni tried again.

"There's plenty of time for that. Just keep your focus on the road."

They wound along the Rogue River, the area mostly forested with very few residences or businesses.

"Where are we going?" Toni asked.

"If I have to tell you to shut up one more time, I'll shut you up right on the spot." She jabbed the cold steel of her gun into Toni's neck. "Permanently."

Toni doubted she'd actually fire right now as the car would crash, but Toni wouldn't put it past this woman to hold a grudge and end her life the moment they stopped.

Toni needed to quit wasting time on identifying the woman and figure out how to escape. But how? The woman had tossed Toni's phone out the window as they'd driven off the hotel's property. She doubted anyone had seen them leave. They were too busy looking at the burning hotel.

And even if they did, this was a rental car. No way this woman used her real name for the rental agreement, keeping her identity a secret.

"Make a right at the next corner," she said.

Toni memorized the woman's voice. Just in case Toni got away, and this woman was arrested, Toni could pick her out in a voice lineup.

She sounded a bit manly. Deep and gravelly. Hoarse sounding. And she had a hint of an accent. Just a hint. Russian maybe. *Russian.* Someone in the investigation was of Russian descent.

*Wait. No. Couldn't be.*

~

Clay's phone rang. He didn't want to be disturbed, not when Hibbard was about to tell them where to find Ursula, but it was Drake. "What's up?"

"You talk to Toni?"

"I thought she was with you." Clay held his breath.

"There's a fire at the hotel."

"A fire." Clay's heart dropped. "Toni. Is she—?"

"We were separated during the evacuation. When I got outside, she was driving off in a car with a woman in the backseat. She had a gun to Toni's head."

*Gun? No.*

"A woman? Who?" Clay asked though he knew Drake wouldn't have an answer for him.

"Don't know, but I got the plates," Drake said. "Erik's

having someone at PPB run them, and he's also pinging Toni's phone."

Clay gripped the edge of the table. *Ursula.* Had to be her. The woman who had no regard for life. The woman who'd sold out her fellow females. The woman who had people killed. Could she have taken Toni?

*Dear God, no. Please, no.*

Clay shared what they'd learned from Hibbard.

"Wow. Just wow." Drake's voice was unusually high. "Never figured she'd be behind this. I mean a female pimping out other females. That's really low."

"It tells us what kind of woman she is." One who could easily kill Toni if she was the one holding her captive. "Hibbard says she's the one behind trying to kill Toni and me, but she had Sharkey do her dirty work for her. Maybe with him behind bars, she had to take over."

"There are security cameras on this side of the building, but to review the footage, I'll have to wait for the fire department's okay to enter the building."

"Get in there as fast as you can."

"Hang on," Drake said. "My phone's signaling a text."

Clay's gut churned as he waited for Drake to come back on the line. He couldn't stand still, so he started pacing. Planning. Figuring out how to find Toni, but he hadn't a clue where Ursula would have taken her.

*Please let Hibbard give up Ursula's location.*

If, in fact, it even was Ursula who had Toni. Might not be her.

An icy chill settled over Clay, and he struggled to breathe.

"She's driving a rental car," Drake said. "Sharkey rented it three days ago." He shared the vehicle's make, model, and license plate.

Clay wrote down the info, his hands shaking so badly his

writing was barely legible. "I'll have Trent put out an alert, and Hibbard could always give up Ursula's address. Hopefully that's where she's headed with Toni. If not, I have no idea how we'll find them."

"Not with her phone. Erik said it pinged at this location. I'll look for it and let you know what I find. Erik also texted me Ursula's photo so I can ask around to see if anyone saw her."

"Keep me updated." Clay disconnected and saw Trent and Blake leave the interview room.

Clay raced to the door. "Trent, a word. Now!"

Trent spun. "You want in on bringing Ursula in? Fine. Follow me."

"No." Clay grabbed Trent's shoulder. "Toni's been abducted. Looks like it's Ursula in a car rented by Sharkey." Clay handed the paper with the vehicle's details to Trent and shared Drake's call. "We need an alert put out on the car."

"I'll do it from my vehicle." Trent spun. "Let's move."

"We need a plan," Clay called after him.

"We'll make one on the way." Trent marched down the hallway.

Blake followed. "Hibbard told us where to find Ursula. She's moving the girls tonight. We have to stop her."

"Yes, of course." Clay's mind spun. "But what if she's not taking Toni there? What if she's taking Toni somewhere else?"

"Then we'll need your brothers' help." Trent pushed open the exit door and faced Clay. "We're going to search for the girls. Either come with us or wait for your brothers to show up with another lead. Your choice."

~

Toni followed the narrow drive among tall trees lining the way, certain now that Ursula was her kidnapper, which meant she had to be involved in trafficking the girls. Toni didn't know how or why, as there'd been no hint of this woman's involvement in the operation, but why else would she take Toni? Hopefully Toni would have an answer to that soon.

The driveway opened into a large clearing with three buildings—a house, a large metal barn-like structure, and an actual wood barn that looked fairly new. Light shone from under the door of the wooden structure.

A semi-truck was backed up to the barn, and a stocky man stood at a door with a rifle—not big barn doors, but a regular-size entrance door. He wore a ball cap, a heavy jacket, and jeans. A solid shank of metal, chains, and a padlock held the main door closed. Much like the lock at the school. A prison.

"Park by the last building," Ursula said.

Toni drove slowly to get the lay of the land and plan an escape route. Underbrush encroached on the buildings as if no one had tended to this property in quite some time. With the recent wildfires in Oregon, it should all be cut back for a firebreak. If a wildfire burned nearby, the whole place would go up in flames. But maybe this was a temporary home for Ursula. A home for what? Trafficked girls?

Toni reached the door, shifted into park, and tried to get a better look at the man.

Ursula jabbed her gun into Toni's side. "Get out."

Toni killed the engine and grabbed the keys.

"Leave them," Ursula demanded.

Toni did as she was told and got out. A fog was settling over the property and left her feeling wet and cold. She took long breaths to fortify herself for what she would find behind the guarded door. If this was where Ursula kept the girls she trafficked, Toni would have to find a way to save them too.

Ursula shoved her gun into Toni's back. "Inside the barn. Go."

Toni took her time, giving the guy who opened the door for them a *don't mess with me* look. He replied with a snide grin.

She fisted her hands and considered all the ways she would make him and Ursula pay. Not physically with her own arms, but with the long arm of the law. She'd get them on kidnapping, assault and battery, sex trafficking... She'd probably think of a few more charges before the night was over. When these two were behind bars, they'd never see the light of day again.

Light spilled out, and she stepped into the building. The front was partitioned off. There was a small door with a steel bar, chain, and padlock. Another guard stood at this door, this guy sturdy and rugged-looking too. She turned her attention to the space. Folding chairs and end tables holding pornographic magazines sat by the chairs. If not for the magazines, the guard, and the massive lock on the inner door, it could be any business.

She smelled recently sawn wood. Everything looked new, as if this operation had just opened. Maybe they'd moved here after the high school.

"Through the door," Ursula said.

The guard opened it, but Toni didn't move and Ursula shoved her inside a long hallway. "Come with us, Tanner."

Toni took a good look at the new area as she walked, vaguely aware of Ursula's and Tanner's footsteps behind her. Each side of the hallway had four doors. One was open, and Toni looked in to see the dreaded bunk beds, but this time, they weren't empty. Two girls per bed sat up and looked at Toni, despair dulling each pair of eyes.

Toni's heart crumpled for them. How could they go on each day?

Toni wanted to swipe an arm at Ursula and try to get away to free these girls. But even if Toni managed to escape, Tanner or the guard at the front would stop them.

"All the way to the back," Ursula directed.

Toni gave the girls a look that she hoped said *I'm on your side and I'll be back for you* before she marched down the hallway to the end. The door was secured by the same kind of heavy lock. The guard got it open and stepped back to give Toni access.

A space the width of the building was set up as a one-room apartment with a tiny kitchen, living area, and two beds. Two children slept in one of the beds, a woman in the other.

Ursula flipped on the light.

The woman rolled. She brushed her dark hair from her face to reveal eyes wild with fear as she got to her feet.

Toni came to a sudden stop, and her mouth dropped open. She was looking at herself only with aged skin, wrinkles, and worry lines around her eyes. Maybe ten to fifteen years older.

"Lisa?" Toni asked. "Is that you?"

Choice? What kind of choice had Trent given Clay? He didn't know where Ursula was taking Toni. He knew nothing about the woman other than that she'd been married to Rader. He couldn't predict how she would act. Would she want to oversee the movement of the girls or steer clear of it?

Perhaps she would normally stay away, but with Hibbard and Sharkey in jail, she had no choice. Just what

Clay had counted on when he'd jumped into the back seat of Trent's cruiser after grabbing his vest and assault rifle from his borrowed SUV.

Clay's phone dinged. He looked at the satellite view Erik sent of the address Trent was racing toward.

Clay read the message. "Place belongs to the RRH Corp. Erik dug into the corporate documents. RRH stands for Richey Rich Hibbard."

"He didn't mention this place," Blake said.

"Looks like he's trying to hide behind his company." Another text came in, and Clay read it. "Hibbard has six properties under this company name. He isn't mentioned in any of the corporate filings, but Erik dug deep and found the ownership information."

"No wonder you couldn't find Hibbard," Blake said. "He had all these hidden places to retreat to."

"Erik also sent the satellite image for our target location. Three buildings, a house, and two barns. One looks temporary. Lots of brush overgrowth. Place doesn't look like it's been cared for."

"What are our options to breach the perimeter?" Trent asked.

"One entrance. Mile long drive. Surrounded by wooded land. We should be able to approach on foot from the highway. There's foot access about a half mile beyond the drive and then a mile hike to the place." Clay would hand the phone to Blake to view for a second opinion, but the metal mesh meant to keep a prisoner at bay was in Clay's way. "I can text the image to you, Blake, if you want to confirm my suggestion."

"Sure thing," Blake said.

Clay forwarded the satellite image and sat back to think about their approach. "The trafficked girls—if we're right on the large number—would have to be housed in one of the two barns. They could be escorted to the house when a john comes around. Or maybe they have rooms in the barn too."

"Either way, it's likely we'll find them in one of the barns." Trent pointed out the front window. "Driveway's just ahead."

Clay watched the road as Trent's headlights cut through thick fog trying to smother the dark roadside.

"Satellite is just as you described it, Clay," Blake said. "I concur with your plan."

"Okay, I'll park ahead, and we'll go in on foot," Trent said. "We need to be prepared for armed guards."

"Fog should help us," Clay said, imagining what was at the end of the driveway and praying that Toni was there.

Because if not, he'd tossed the dice and made a fatal choice.

# 27

"Yeah, I'm, Lisa." The woman eyed Toni. "Who are you?"

"Your sister."

"Surprise." Ursula's sarcastic tone grated on Toni. "Isn't it nice that the two of you could meet before you leave this earth?"

Lisa snapped her gaze to Ursula. "Richey won't let you do anything to harm me."

"The fool's gone and got himself arrested. With everything he's done, he won't be coming back, and I have no use for you. But Rachel's another matter. Take her, Tanner."

The guard stepped in, jerked the girl from the bed, but left the boy behind. She looked to be ten or eleven and resembled pictures Toni had seen of herself at that age.

"Mom," the girl cried out.

Lisa charged forward, and Ursula pointed her gun at Lisa. "One more step and Henry won't have a mother."

Lisa looked at the bed where a boy who seemed to be about five lay unmoving. She shifted her focus to the guard dragging the girl in fuzzy footie pajamas out the door. She was sobbing and calling out to Lisa. Over and over. Her voice was strained and pitiful.

Toni ached to go to her. To the girl who had to be Toni's niece.

*Please don't let them take her. Don't let them hurt her. Help me to free everyone.*

Ursula backed to the door. "I'll give you some time to get acquainted."

"Wait," Toni said. "Why bring me here? Why didn't you just kill me?"

"You don't have a clue, do you?"

"Clue about what?"

"Zack Wilshire. The fifteen-year-old boy you put into juvie for bank robbery not more than six months ago. He was innocent. Got shanked in juvie. Died. He was my son."

Toni had to work hard not to gasp. She remembered the boy. He'd been part of a group of boys who terrorized a local bank clerk and nearly left her for dead.

But she'd said his last name was Wilshire. Could he be Nolan Wilshire's child? A child no one mentioned until now. Toni had to know. "Nolan Wilshire's child?"

"You know about him, do you?" A self-satisfied smile crossed Ursula's lips. "We were lovers once, but he couldn't handle losing his other children. Didn't even complain when I left when Zach was a baby. I don't think to this day he thinks of him as his son. And now he's gone. So I'll take your niece as payment. But don't worry. I'll let her live. She'll service my clients for years. Then, who knows. I might let her go." Ursula laughed and backed out of the room, her gaze wild and unfocused.

Toni suspected she was half mad and half evil. There would be no reasoning with her. She stepped out, and she heard the bar slide into place, and the chain jingling.

Lisa ran to the door and jerked on it. Pushed frantically. It didn't budge.

"I have to get to Rachel." Lisa shot a look around the

room. There was only one exit and no window. A sob wrenched from her throat, and she fell to her knees on the hard ground. "Oh, God, no. Not Rachel. Please."

Toni put her hand on Lisa's shoulder to comfort her.

Lisa jerked back, her gaze that of a captive animal afraid for her life. "Don't touch me."

Toni raised her hands and backed off. She needed to get Lisa talking. Maybe then Toni could figure a way out of there. "I can't believe you're alive after all these years."

"I always hoped Dad would find me. He was DEA, after all. But he must've given up. Thought I was dead." She lifted her chin. "Maybe when you were born. He had a replacement. He didn't need me anymore."

"No, don't say that. He never gave up. He died a year ago still trying to find you."

"Richey showed me his picture in the paper in a story about him being killed, but he wouldn't let me read the details. And he never told me I had a sister." She ran her gaze over Toni. "If you're telling the truth. This could be one of Ursula's mean jokes. She likes to punish me because Richey took me out of the rooms and made me exclusively his."

So Hibbard had taken a liking to Lisa. Likely fathered these children. As much as Toni was grossed out by the thought, it was better than years forced to abide the touch of hundreds of men.

None of that mattered anymore. The only important thing was escaping with the girls. "I don't see a way out of here."

"There isn't one. They make sure of that. No windows. No daylight unless we're chained and cuffed and paraded outside for fresh air so we don't look so pale." She shuddered and wrapped her arms around her waist. "And now they've taken Rachel."

"What's her full name?"

"Rachel Sarah Long, though she has no birth certificate. She's eleven and Henry David is five. I had her and Henry in places not fit for animals." She ran a trembling hand over her hair.

"Rachel left her initials on a paper in the high school and at the beach house."

"She what?" Lisa's eyes got wide with fear. "If they'd caught her, they would've killed her." She jerked on the door handle again. "Maybe it's better than what they have planned for her. Oh, God, I have to get to her."

A hint of smoke snaked into the room. Toni had seen a large firepit in the yard.

"Do you smell that?" Toni asked, trying hard not to panic.

"The firepit," Lisa said.

Toni looked at the floor. Smoke seeped through the crack.

Toni pointed under the door. "Not with this much smoke. Ursula's set the building on fire."

Seemed like fire was Ursula's thing. She could very well have set the fire at the school and hotel.

Toni had to figure out how to get out alive. How to get a bunch of girls, her sister, and her nephew out before the smoke or flames overcame them all.

"Smoke," Clay said and shot a look around. Now was not the time for the stealth approach they'd planned. Now was the time for action.

He burst past Trent and Blake and barreled through the trees. Branches slapped at his body, but he didn't care. Toni could be in the barn. Or the house. The girls too. And it could be on fire.

If Ursula set this fire, she could also have set the one at the hotel and high school. Could be her choice method to kill.

He had to hurry. Move. He plowed ahead. Reached the clearing and stopped behind a large tree. The small car rented by Sharkey was parked by the house.

"Thank you, God," he whispered, but lost his voice when he saw fire crackling through the barn wall.

Toni could be in there. So could the girls. No sign of anyone, but a semi-truck sat out front of the barn, and a light shone from the house.

Were the girls in the barn? Toni?

"Rental car's here," he whispered to the others who'd come up behind him. "Means Toni's on the property somewhere. Light at the house. Likely Ursula. Maybe Toni."

Flames burst through the roof of the barn and high-pitched screams shrieked from inside.

"The girls," Clay said. "They're inside. We have to get them out."

"Someone needs to go to the house to stop Ursula from leaving," Trent said.

Clay had another choice to make and a split second to make it. Was Toni at the house or in the barn? Ursula obviously wanted Toni dead. So if the barn was on fire, Clay would find Toni there.

"I'll arrange for backup. Trent got out his phone. "But put them on standby. Don't want anyone rushing in and alerting Ursula to our presence."

"Good," Clay said. Out in this rural area deputies were few and far between and it would be good to have someone waiting if needed.

Trent looked at Clay before he made the call. "You and

Blake take the barn. I'll take the house. I'll keep my phone on vibrate, so you can update me."

Clay bolted for the front door. The screams intensified. Girls crying out for his help. His gut clenched over their distress. He grabbed the padlock and shook it, but the heavy-duty lock was bolt-cutter proof. "No way we're getting this off."

"Let's check the sides." Blake started off.

Clay passed him by as the smoke oozed out of the siding. He shone the beam from his phone's flashlight along the wall. At the ground. Searching. Hunting. Trying to find a way into the building.

He spotted an old chain-link fence. "I'll free a post. You find a place where we can wedge it into the building and pry off some of the boards to get in."

Clay grabbed the post and started working it free. He heard Blake moving by the wall. In the background, the girls cries grew hysterical. Clay offered a frantic prayer.

"Got a spot," Blake called out.

Clay shimmied the post free and charged toward the light Blake was focusing on a hole. Clay jammed the pole in and pried. He loosened a board and ripped it free but came up against drywall. He'd have to break through that too. He pried a few additional boards loose and rammed the pole through the wallboard. Once. Twice. Three times. Then he backed up and looked inside.

A small apartment. A woman huddling with a boy on the bed. A second woman by the door jamming the handle of a cast iron pan into the wall. She turned.

"Toni! Over here." He spit the words out between coughs. "I'll clear a place for you to get out."

She shook her head. "The girls are in there. I have to get them."

"I'm coming." He summoned every ounce of strength to

kick a hole large enough to slide into the smoky space. He looked at the woman cradling the boy, covering his mouth and nose with a blanket. "Go out the back."

She didn't move. Shock?

"Now, Lisa!" Toni yelled. "You'll be free."

*Lisa?* When she didn't move, Clay led her to the exit, and handed her and the boy off to Blake. When they were safe, Clay rushed to Toni.

"Stand back," he shouted and got a chest full of smoke.

She moved, a wracking cough taking her, and he jammed the pipe into the drywall as he'd done before. He made a large hole and lunged through. The smoke was thicker in this room, but he could make out empty beds.

"Hello," he yelled. No answer. "I'm Deputy Clay Byrd. I have an exit for you." He kept calling out as he went into the hallway.

He found the girls huddled by the bolted door. The sight of so many girls clinging together, abject terror in their eyes, tore at his heart. "Follow me. I'll get you out of here."

One girl stood and woodenly walked his way. The others followed, looking like zombies in a cheap horror film, except they were coughing and gasping for air. He'd expected them to flood toward him, but their reaction mimicked Lisa's fear of leaving or disobeying their captors.

"Come on, girls," Toni encouraged from the opening, her mouth covered by her shirt. "I'm Lisa's sister. I'm here to help."

They picked up speed and headed toward her. He urged them to move faster. Faster.

The flames burst through the front wall. The desire to bolt hit Clay hard, but he swallowed hard and remained in place until they all passed him. The heat curled against his back as he dove into the back room. He raced across the space and plunged outside.

"Where's Rachel?" In the darkness, Lisa picked her way among the girls, who were gulping in fresh air and coughing.

"My daughter, where is she?" She gripped Clay's jacket. "Ursula took her from me, and she's not here."

"She has to be at the house," Clay said, already planning to go after her. He looked at Toni. "You stay here with the girls."

"I'm coming with you." Toni's voice was raspy but firm.

"You don't have any protection or a weapon," he said, but wished he hadn't said a word.

Not when she cast him a tortured look. One that reminded him of when she'd learned he'd become a deputy. He wouldn't make the same mistake again. He pulled his backup gun from an ankle holster. By the time he gave it to Toni, Blake had shrugged out of his vest and handed it to her.

Since she wasn't deputized, Clay thought Blake might've objected, but he gave her a firm nod. She had to do this. He got that. So did Clay. Even if he didn't like it. Clay texted Trent to tell him they were coming.

He replied. *At rear of house. A woman and girl in front room. Guard at front and back. You take front. We'll go on my command.*

*Will let you know when we're in position.* Clay texted back.

He shoved his phone into his pocket and looked at Toni, whose trembling hands were fumbling with the straps on her vest.

He gently moved her hands and fixed the Velcro then looked her in the eye. "Deep breath. You got this."

She took the breath and gave a sharp nod. "I'm ready."

Clay eased along the edge of the metal barn and followed the tree line. They would have to dart across the drive, so he made his way deeper into the woods. He kept going until they could take the guard sitting in a rocker on the porch from behind.

Clay waited for Toni to come alongside him. Their approach would be dangerous. They could catch a bullet from the guard. Or from Ursula when they got inside. He would do his best to stop that from happening.

"You ready to charge when Trent gives the word?" he whispered.

She nodded.

"Before we do, I want you to know I'm falling for you and I'm sorry—"

She silenced his words with a kiss. Her lips were cold, and yet, he couldn't imagine not kissing her.

"All's forgiven," she said. "Let's get this done."

Elation worked hard to replace all other emotions, but Clay calmed his brain and texted Trent. *In position.*

*Then we're a go.*

He signaled for Toni, and they shot out of the woods, careful to move as silently as possible. He climbed onto the porch, the wood creaking.

A gunshot sounded from the rear of the house.

The guard spun, lifting his gun.

"Drop it!" Clay warned. "Don't end up dead like your buddy."

At least Clay hoped the guard had taken the bullet and not Trent.

The beefy man slowly lowered his rifle to the porch.

"Hands on the wall above your head," Toni snapped.

He turned and planted his hands on the rough siding. Clay moved slowly forward, keeping his gaze pinned on the man should he go for another gun. He didn't move.

"Cuffs are on my belt," Clay told Toni, not bothering to be quiet as the gunshot had alerted whoever was in the house to their presence.

She took them and jerked the guy's arms down to cuff him. She searched him and recovered a handgun from a waist holster.

Clay let out a slow, silent breath. They'd gotten this far unharmed.

"Sit," he commanded.

The guy dropped to the floor.

Toni looked Clay in the eye. "I'm going in for Ursula and my niece."

# 28

Toni moved past the guard. He was the one who'd taken Rachel. Toni had to fight the urge to kick him after the way he'd treated Rachel and the other girls, but she held her anger. He would go away for a long time, and that punishment would have to be good enough.

She glanced into the window, seeing Ursula on the couch in the front room with one arm around Rachel and a gun to the child's head.

Toni would have to negotiate with the crazed woman, but how? She wouldn't know until she started talking to her. Toni eased open the door. She didn't hear anyone moving inside, but assumed Trent had breached the back door. For all they knew, he'd been shot. Meant she needed to be prepared to face the other guard.

She turned the knob. Found it unlocked. She pushed the door in and darted away from the opening in case Ursula or the guard fired.

No bullet.

She waited a few seconds and took a quick look inside, stifling the cough trying to work its way out of her body. She spotted Ursula, still on a sofa with the gun pressed against

Rachel's head, before Toni jerked back. Poor Rachel was terrified.

"Come in, Agent Long," Ursula said. "But leave your gun in the hallway."

Toni didn't want to enter unarmed. It was a foolish move and one law enforcement officers were trained never to make.

"Do as I say." Ursula's irritated voice came from the room. "I'll let the child go if you do. You'll work far better as a hostage."

Toni wasn't falling for that. She didn't believe Ursula would let Rachel go under any circumstances. But Toni could never leave a child to fend for herself. She set her gun on the floor, going against everything she was trained to do, and stepped into the room with her hands raised.

"Now, that's a smart woman," Ursula said. "Isn't she smart, Rachel? She listened to me."

Toni took a quick look around the room. Searching for something. Anything she could use against Ursula. Nothing but a club chair, a wood coffee table, and an end table holding a yellow glass lamp. There was an arched opening behind the blue velvet couch, and she had to watch for someone to approach from that direction, but her gaze locked on poor Rachel, her hands clasped in her lap, her eyes wide and terror-filled.

"It's okay, Rachel." Toni cleared her throat to try to make her raspy voice sound more normal. "I'm here to free you."

Ursula scoffed. "Like you have any way to do that."

"I'll serve as your hostage," Toni said. "Let the girl go."

Ursula's red-lacquered lips slid into a slimy smile. "Did I say I would do that? I must've been mistaken. Take a seat in the chair, Agent Long."

"I'll stand." Toni needed to exert some control here.

"With the sheriff and his deputies outside, how exactly do you plan to get away?"

"You'll have them bring the car right up to the porch, leave it running, and the three of us will slide in and drive off."

"You don't really think they'll let you leave, do you?" A cough worked itself up Toni's throat, but she did her best to minimize it and not scare Rachel even more.

"Of course they will." Ursula tightened her hold on Rachel's shoulders. "Or this one will die."

Rachel whimpered.

"She's lying, Rachel," Toni said in her most soothing tone. "You aren't going to die, and I'll make sure you're reunited with your mother. Did you know she's my sister? That makes me your aunt. And we'll have the best time getting to know each other."

"Oh, do shut up," Ursula said. "Now, slowly open the window and call out to your fellow officer to get my car. Keys are inside."

"Always planning for a swift getaway, are you?" Toni asked, stalling while she figured a way out of this. "Only people who break the law need to do that."

"Please. After all these years, you can't insult me."

"You mean because you've been a criminal for so long?" Toni noticed movement behind the arch, but didn't let on and needed to stall. "I don't get it. Why start the fire to kill the girls?"

"I had no one left to manage them. I need to start over. This child would be my beginning again like I'd hoped with Lisa."

"Then, *you* took Lisa?" Toni tried not to sound surprised.

Ursula stroked Rachel's hair. "She was a beauty like this one. When Nolan told me about her, I knew I needed to have her. So I put Sharkey in charge. He was infatuated with me and did whatever I asked. Luckily, Lisa played right into our hands. Came out to look at the ocean, and he snatched her up. I took Sharkey on as my lover as a reward."

Through the arch, Toni saw Clay moving her way. He signaled for her to keep talking, and she had to work hard not to let on that he was creeping up behind Ursula.

"And you've had her all these years," Toni said.

"Not me. The fool Hibbard. He fell for her. He wanted her in his life and kept her pure, kept her with him until she was old enough to bear a child."

"So which one of you tried to kill Clay Byrd and me at the school?"

She frowned. "One of my stupid guards. He fell for one of the girls and wanted to take her out of the business. No way I could allow that. She convinced him to leave you notes to come to the school. Hoped you'd find her there. But I got wind of it, of course, and moved them. Can't pull anything over on me. The fire and snake were my little surprise for you."

Toni opened her mouth to say Ursula didn't know about the initials Rachel left behind, but Toni didn't want Ursula to get angry at Rachel, so she clamped her mouth closed.

"He was just like Hibbard, except I let Hibbard live because of his connections and what he could do to increase my business," Ursula continued. "They should both have known there's no room in this business for sentimentality. We don't need relationships."

"So that's how you could so callously leave Jason behind," Toni said, seeing Clay inch closer.

Ursula's face turned to an iron mask. "I didn't have a choice. Fritz forced my hand. But make no mistake. I saw the boy from the day after I left until you all arrested him. And I had Zach until you took him from me."

"And Jason is going to spend most of his life in prison, if

we have anything to say about it. You'll be right behind him, but you'll never be released."

Ursula sat forward, her chest rising and falling as her face contorted with anger, just the reaction Toni was hoping for as it took her mind off the fact that Toni wasn't listening to her command. Her hand with the gun lowered a fraction, and she launched into a tirade about how unfair law enforcement officers were and how Jason didn't deserve to be where he was and Zach shouldn't have died. She seemed not to remember she was holding Rachel anymore.

Toni gave Clay an almost imperceptible nod.

He took the last steps and grabbed Ursula's arm. He raised it to the ceiling and wrenched the gun from her hand then poked her gun in her back. "Don't move."

Toni dropped to her knees and held out her arms. "Come here, Rachel."

The child bolted across the room and flung herself into Toni's arms. Toni held her fast. "I got your notes. The ones with your initials. That was very brave of you."

"I wanted to leave. She was being mean, telling Daddy I had to go to work. I know what work means. I didn't want to."

Toni met Clay's gaze over Rachel's shoulder. "I promise she's going to prison, and you'll never have to worry about that kind of work ever again."

Clay stood outside the house, the area lit up with flames and the twirling lights of emergency vehicles. He watched as Trent's deputies put Ursula and her two goons into patrol cars. Thankfully, Trent hadn't been hit by the guard's bullet, and had secured both guards in a patrol car, and was directing the activity. A fire crew was fighting the fire that was quickly engulfing the structure, battling it back from the thick trees in the area and medics were checking out the girls.

Clay could hardly look at the girls without getting so angry he wanted to punch something. Punch it hard. But he kept glancing over there because Toni had insisted on staying with Lisa, Rachel, and Henry. He watched as her family was loaded in an ambulance. Toni stepped back.

"I'll meet you at the hospital." She gave a tentative wave.

The ambulance drove off, lights twirling but no siren blaring.

Toni hurried across the lot to Clay. "I need a ride to the hospital."

"I didn't want to bother you while you were with Lisa and her kids, so I already arranged it." He pointed at Drake. "I don't have a vehicle here so I called Drake, and he insisted on driving you."

"You have a very nice brother."

Clay forced a smile and started for the vehicle. He took a moment to appreciate his family, which he didn't do often enough, but he'd seen such loss and hardship today. The girls' families would be ecstatic to hear their daughters were safe, but the road to a normal life would be rocky for everyone.

Maybe even harder for Lisa after more than thirty years in captivity. Clay had heard stories about women who emerged years after being abducted and spending years as prisoners, but it seemed Lisa could hold the record for the length of time. Not a record anyone would want to claim.

Drake stood by the SUV, holding the rear door open for Toni. "Glad to hear about Lisa."

"Yeah. Good news. But what she endured?" Toni shook her head and started coughing. "I can't even imagine it."

Even at a distance, Clay could see the same anger

burning in Drake that was burning in him, but he also contained it. He handed over Toni's phone. "Found it at the hotel."

"Thanks." She slid into the vehicle.

"We're all praying for Lisa and her kids. For all of these girls." Drake looked over at the barn, and his gaze darkened even more. "But the good news is, Clay got here in time."

Drake gave Clay a knowing look, then closed the door and slid behind the wheel as if eager to get out of there. Clay didn't blame him. This was one of those nights that would stay with all of them for the rest of their lives. Clay only wished Toni had asked him to come with her so he could leave too.

As if she'd heard his thoughts, the car door opened, and she crooked her finger at him. "Come on. Lisa will be waiting for me."

He didn't have to be asked twice. He climbed in the back with her. She smelled like smoke and had dark patches of soot on her face, but she'd never looked more beautiful to him.

She shifted her gaze to him. "I didn't have a chance to thank you."

Ah, so that's why she wanted him to come with her. She'd likely forgotten all about her hasty kiss. A heat-of-the-moment kind of thing.

"No thanks needed. Just glad I chose the right thing." He explained about the choice Trent had given him.

"Sounds logical." She smiled at him, a generous glowing one that lit a very tired face. He wished Drake weren't there and she was in his arms so he could show her what her smile did to him. But it was probably for the better. She didn't need relationship drama on top of everything else that had happened tonight.

Drake turned onto the highway. "Seems like you two made up."

"Pretty hard to be mad over something so petty when you see what we saw tonight." Toni glanced at Clay. "And to face death? Puts everything into perspective."

Clay cringed. She could have died. If they hadn't gotten her out of the barn, she would have. She'd resisted medical attention, but Clay would insist she be checked for smoke inhalation at the hospital. He wouldn't risk losing her to the fire's aftereffects.

Toni stared at the door to the ER exam room. She'd been examined by a doctor and pronounced physically fit, as had Lisa and her children. For that, Toni was thankful. But emotionally fit? No. Any little sound had Lisa and the kids jumping and looking over their shoulders, fear lodged in their eyes.

Toni had never felt such anger in her life. She wanted to march down to the jail, wrap her hands around Hibbard's and Ursula's necks, and squeeze until their last breath left them. She hadn't even been this angry after her dad had been gunned down. He was an adult. He'd known he was putting himself in danger. He'd understood the consequences of his actions and had chosen the risks. But Lisa and her children? No. They'd done nothing to deserve their captivity and the life they'd been forced to endure.

Toni's phone rang. Good. She needed a diversion.

Vance Danby's name showed on her screen. He'd left her three messages while she'd been away from her phone. She swallowed her anger and answered as cheerfully as possible. "Sorry I didn't call you back. I was in a situation here."

"No worries," he said. "The key fit a safe deposit box, as

we thought. I sent the items to you but also wanted to let you know what to expect."

She pulled her focus from the ER door and turned her full attention to the call. "What was in the box?"

"Five journals. In them, he details his search for Lisa. Even explains why he was at the op when he was killed."

"Did he say he knew my task force would be there?"

"No. Just that he was looking for a man named Sheldon Sharkey. Said this Sharkey fellow was working with the person who took Lisa."

"What about killing Andrew Martin? Did Dad mention that?"

"Yeah. Once Martin was arrested for sexual assault, your dad started to believe Martin was involved in taking Lisa. Your father tried to prove it, but he couldn't. His rage is obvious in his writing, and he said even if Martin wasn't guilty of taking Lisa, he was guilty of victimizing that young girl. Your dad couldn't abide Martin getting away with it."

So he'd murdered a man. A relative at that.

She shuddered, her mind racing with crazy thoughts.

Had she known her father at all?

No. Clearly not. The man she knew wouldn't commit murder. But then she couldn't comprehend a parent's turmoil after having a child abducted. To live year after year wondering. Waiting. Knowing if they were alive that they were in a horrible situation. Probably pleading with God. There would be anger. So much anger. Pain. Despair.

How had he gone on, day after day? Especially after her mother died. He talked to no one about it. He must've felt so very alone. If only he'd told Toni. She could've helped.

"Toni, you there?" Vance asked.

"Yeah, sorry." She shook her head to clear the pain, the thoughts. "Thanks for mailing the journals."

"No problem. And Toni. No matter what you're feeling

right now, know that your dad loved you very much. Talked about you all the time and about how proud he was of you."

"Thanks, Vance." She ended the call and pocketed her phone.

She had no time to think about that. The exam room door opened, and Lisa stepped out. Henry was hanging onto her, and Rachel was nearly glued to Lisa's other side. Fear lingered in their eyes. They'd never experienced life in the real world. Shock and anxiety would be with them for some time.

*Please help them. Please.*

"Ready to go?" Toni made sure she sounded cheerful.

Lisa gave a sharp nod.

"Clay is waiting outside." Toni got up from the bench. "He'll drive us to the hotel." She led the way through the busy ER to the exit. At the door, she spotted Clay in their vehicle idling at the curb. He'd dropped Drake off at his parents' beach house and returned for them.

Lisa faced Toni. "We should let Grandma and Grandpa know I was found. Would you be okay with stopping by their place for a few minutes?"

"Tonight?" Toni asked. "Are you sure you don't want to get some rest?"

"I think it's important to face the situation head on." Lisa lifted her chin, looking so like their father when he was resolute that it put an ache in Toni's heart. She opened the door before she started crying and made things worse for her sister and kids.

Clay jumped out and came around the back. "I stopped at a store and got a car seat for Henry. I also saw the new guidelines for kids Rachel's age suggesting they now ride in booster seats so got a booster seat for her. They're both top-rated, so they're good ones."

"You did?" Lisa gaped at him. "That was very kind. Thank you."

"Glad to do it," Clay said. "If you need help buckling them up, let me know. I read the manual while you were inside."

Lisa smiled at Clay, and Toni's heart burst with pride over Clay's consideration. He really was an amazing guy.

"We're going to stop at our grandparents' house," Toni said to Clay.

He cocked an eyebrow but didn't speak. Once everyone was settled, he got the SUV headed in the right direction.

Grandma and Grandpa. How foreign it felt to Toni to hear those words as related to her. She had no idea how she felt about them. Or how Lisa was feeling. If they'd told the police about Wilshire, would Lisa have been found years ago? Toni didn't think Wilshire would've been honest about his relationship with Ursula, but the police could've questioned others about Wilshire and potentially learned about Ursula. It was a long shot, but possible.

So, were her grandparents off the hook? No, but they deserved to know that Lisa was alive and not just from some phone call or a visit by a deputy.

She looked over the seat at Lisa, who was twisting her hands together. "You sure you want to stop there?"

Lisa gave a firm nod.

Clay drove in silence, and Toni listened to the conversation going on in the back seat.

"We never had seats like these," Rachel said.

"That's because your dad didn't know about them," Lisa answered calmly.

Toni looked back to see Lisa's mouth in a grim line.

"Do we really get to do what we want to do now?" Rachel asked. "No one is going to tell us to stop? Or take us away from you?"

Lisa stared at her daughter. "You'll still have to listen to me."

"Yeah," Rachel said. "But I mean other people."

Lisa clutched her hands together. "That's kind of a tricky question. There are some people you need to listen to and obey. Like the police."

"But Ursula said they're bad."

"Don't believe anything Ursula has told you. She's wrong, and she was trying to control you. No one can control you like she did." Lisa brushed Rachel's hair back from her forehead. "You'll get it as time goes on, and I'll be right there to help you."

"I can help too." Toni smiled at Rachel, but the child's expression was filled with distrust.

Toni's heart shredded even more. How could this happen to Lisa and these poor children? To all the people who were trafficked? Such a horrific crime. Just terrible. Now that it was so personal to Toni, she couldn't handle this pain every day. Couldn't keep working in this area.

Clay pulled into the driveway and parked near the house. A light shone through the living room window, and Toni glanced at Lisa. She looked frozen. Unable to move.

"Maybe I should go to the door," Toni said. "And have them come out here to talk to you."

Lisa gave a wooden nod.

"Be right back." As Toni opened her door, Clay squeezed her hand. She smiled at him, but her heart was so broken for Lisa and the kids that she had to force it.

She rushed up the sidewalk and rang the doorbell.

Her grandfather opened the door, his face haggard and tired. "Never expected to see you again."

"I'm sorry for leaving things the way I did." Toni searched for the right words. "I'm trying to figure this all out."

"I understand."

"Walt? Who is it?" Her grandmother stepped up behind her grandfather.

"Oh, Toni. Oh." A smile lit her face.

"I have someone in the car I want you to see."

"If this is about Nolan Wilshire," her grandfather said.

"I'll explain about him later, but first, come with me." She didn't wait to see if they followed but marched to the SUV and opened the back door.

Lisa slid out.

"Grandma and Grandpa," she said. "It's me. Lisa."

# 29

On Sunday afternoon, Toni sat in a hotel suite in a place just down the road from Joy's damaged hotel, listening to the waves curling up on the beach, and trying to forgive her grandparents. She'd attended a beach sunrise service under a cool but misty sky that morning with her grandparents, Lisa, and her children. Lisa had already forgiven them for holding information back on Nolan Wilshire, so why couldn't Toni? Maybe it was because Lisa had known her grandparents in her childhood and loved them.

She studied Lisa, who was calmly reviewing their father's journals. She'd been calm ever since she was reunited with Rachel. Not happy. Not sad. Just an even calm that felt a bit eerie. Maybe it was a coping mechanism Lisa had developed over the years. Toni wanted to ask, but she wouldn't put Lisa on the spot.

Thankfully, most of the girls they'd discovered at the barn had been reunited with their families, and a special FBI task force was working to identify the girls whose photos were found in Rader's garage. They were also working on the videos, and Toni couldn't be happier that she was still on leave and didn't have to view them again.

She wasn't sure what she would do once her leave ended other than to talk to her supervisor about moving to a different unit.

Lisa looked up. "Dad really didn't stop looking for me, did he?"

"No."

Her eyes creased, the first sign of real pain. "Why didn't they tell you about me?"

"I wondered the same thing, but I've come to believe they wanted to spare me the pain."

"That makes sense. If Rachel or Henry were in your place, I might've done the same thing." A soft smile played on her lips. "Thank you again. You and your friends saved Rachel in the nick of time. If she'd had to..." She shook her head. "I'm not going to think about that. No point in it. God brought you to us in time."

"Can I ask a question?" Toni asked.

A wary look Toni had seen on their mother's face so often landed on Lisa's. "I guess."

"How did you keep your faith through all of this?"

Lisa let out a slow breath. "It was the only thing they couldn't take from me or exploit. And, better yet, my continued belief in God made them mad." Lisa's gaze darkened. "When I was in horrible situations, I called up my favorite verse and repeated it over and over again."

"What's the verse?"

"'For I know the plans I have for you,' declares the LORD, 'plans to prosper you and not to harm you, plans to give you hope and a future.'" That calm that Lisa had been exhibiting returned. "I clung to the promise of hope and a future. And here I am with two beautiful children, my future wide open. No man to control us any more. Richey interacted very little with our children so they're used to not having him in their lives, and they'll be fine without him."

"I can't believe how strong you are. I hope as we get to know each other that my faith strengthens." Toni told her about her struggles. "But my challenges are nothing compared to what you experienced, and I have so much to be thankful for."

Lisa touched Toni's hand for the briefest of moments. "I see strength in you. Reminds me of Dad. He always wanted me to be strong. To be able to withstand the world he'd said was deteriorating by the day. He never told me that, of course. I was just a kid, but I heard him talking to Mom."

"He raised me the same way."

"I miss them."

"Me too," Toni said, tears coming to her eyes.

Lisa's eyes glistened too, and Toni wanted to hug her sister, but Lisa clearly didn't like to be touched. Toni would have to wait for Lisa to initiate physical contact.

A knock sounded on the door, and Lisa pulled back, her calm evaporating in a puff of air. "Who is it? Who could be here?"

"You'll have to get used to the fact that not everyone means to harm you," Toni said as she got up.

Lisa gnawed on her lip. "Who do you think it is?"

"Let me find out." Toni crossed the room, enjoying the sound of Henry and Rachel playing in the bedroom. Toni peered through the peephole. "It's Clay."

What was he doing here? She'd last seen him two days ago when he dropped them off after visiting her grandparents, and he hadn't tried to contact her at all. She appreciated the break. He'd given her the space she'd needed to realize without a doubt that she wanted him in her life. She'd been planning to go to Portland this week to tell him.

Now he was here. Had he come to tell her how he felt? To talk about a future?

She smoothed a hand over her hair and took a breath to

calm the butterflies in her stomach. She opened the door and drank in the sight of him. He wore his usual attire of tactical pants, a knit shirt, and boots. He looked tired, but when he smiled, the fatigue disappeared, and his face glowed with happiness.

Could his reaction be from seeing her? Because the same feelings filled her heart.

"I wasn't expecting you."

"I should've called, but I didn't know if you would see me, and I have something I want to talk to Lisa about."

He'd come to see Lisa. Not her. That stung. Big time. "I'm not sure if she's ready for a visitor, but I'll check."

"I'll only be a minute, and it's a good thing. I promise."

"Wait here." She left him at the door and found Lisa looking out the sliding glass doors to the ocean. "It's Clay. He wants to talk to you if you're up to it."

"Clay? I don't..." Her eyes clouded for a moment then cleared. "Yes. Sure. I owe him so much, and I haven't thanked him properly."

Toni went back to the door. "For only a minute, okay?"

He nodded, and Toni stepped back, feeling like her sister's guard. A prisoner for so long, Lisa needed to learn what it meant to be free. Toni would soon have to let her sister fend for herself or she might never fly as she should.

Lisa had moved to the sofa, and she smiled up at Clay as he approached, her hands tightly clasped on her lap. "Please. Have a seat."

He sat in a plump chair on the other side of a large coffee table. "I won't take up much of your time, but I wanted to make you an offer."

"Offer?"

"You know about the agency my brothers and I run, but you might not know we live in condos on the same property as our offices."

"Toni told me about it."

"I got to thinking that Toni's apartment would be too small for all of you, and you and the kids will need a place to live. We thought you might want to be in the city where you'd be close to therapists and..." His voice wavered, and he shrugged. "So I wanted to offer my condo to you for as long as you would like. I figured you'd feel safe there with all of our security, and you'd be close to doctors."

Lisa tilted her head. "But where would you live?"

"I'll bunk with one of my brothers."

"I couldn't put you out like that."

"No biggie. I mostly get along with them." He grinned, the cute one that sent Toni's heart into a tailspin.

Lisa firmed her shoulders. "I'll tell you what I told Toni and my grandparents. I'm not ready to live in a city yet. I have to first get used to being able to make my own decisions and not be afraid all the time. To do that, I can't depend on anyone else. But I also believe a smaller town will make this transition easier."

She looked at Toni and smiled. "Toni has graciously given me her inheritance from Dad, so I have money and time to decide what to do. Right now, I think I'll rent a beach house. Not here. The memories are too strong. But somewhere peaceful. And once I gain my confidence, I'll start branching out and exposing myself and the kids to new things. Then the counseling."

"Sounds like you have a solid plan," Clay said. "If you decide you might want to move to the Portland area, my offer will still stand." He stood.

Lisa did, too, and held out her hand. "Thank you, Clay. Without you, we might not be alive or together. I will forever be in your debt."

He shook her hand, and Lisa didn't cringe, giving Toni hope her sister could have a normal life someday.

"No thanks needed. I'm glad we could help." He released Lisa's hand and looked at Toni. "Thanks for letting me in."

"Sure, I..."

An awkward moment passed between them, and he turned to leave. Toni stood there, not knowing what to do as this wonderful man walked out of her life. The door closed behind him.

"For such a smart woman, you're acting kind of dumb," Lisa said. "He's an amazing man who's clearly in love with you. Go after him."

"He is, isn't he?" Toni didn't think this through like her father would've wanted her to do. Instead, she let her emotions rule and rushed to the door. In the hallway, Clay was about to step on the elevator.

"Clay, wait," she called out.

He let out a huge breath and strode back to her. When he stood in front of her, that smile, the intimate one he reserved just for her, spread across his face. "I didn't think you would come after me."

"Playing hard to get?" She grinned at him.

His smile widened. "I *am* quite the catch. Women are breaking doors down to get to me."

"I'm not surprised." She smiled. "You are a real charmer."

He stepped closer. "Charming enough to convince you to come have dinner with me and my family? They're all still in town, and the rest of the crazy crew are joining us. They'll be glad to see you, and if you come over, my mom will realize you've forgiven me, and she might quit giving me the stink eye."

He chuckled. "But seriously. I haven't had a chance to say how sorry I am about making decisions without you. But I am. Very. I should've consulted you first. Not only as the woman I love, but as a partner in the investigation."

She stepped back. "Love?" The single word came out a squeak.

"Oh, man." He plunged a hand into his hair, leaving it all messed up. "Me and my big mouth. I didn't want to say anything here. I wanted to tell you under a moonlit sky. Or maybe at sunset. If you'll come over early for dinner, that is. We usually eat at six, so four would be great. Or even earlier. Three or two. I mean, you could even come with me right now."

"Um, Clay." She smiled at him. "You might want to take a breath."

"Yeah, right. It's just...this is important to me."

"Me too."

"Then I'll see you at four?"

"I'll be there."

"Lisa and the kids are welcome to come too."

There he was, being so considerate again. "I'll ask, but don't be surprised if they're not up for it."

He clutched her hand tightly for a moment and turned to walk away.

"Wait," she said, her heart bursting with love.

He turned, a wary look on his face. "You're not changing your mind, are you?"

"No." She grabbed his hand. "I can't let you leave without this."

She slid her fingers into his messed up hair and drew his head down for a kiss. His eyes flashed wide before she pressed her lips against his, the touch electrifying. She lost herself in the moment. Forgetting the location. The dingy hallway. Thinking only about this amazing man. The man who loved her. He loved her. Wow!

He deepened the kiss. She reveled in it but soon forced herself to pull back and look into his eyes. She took a moment to catch her breath, enjoyed knowing she had the power to cause him to struggle for breath. She wanted to hold onto him forever. To keep kissing those full lips. To feel that heady feeling and never come up for air.

And she suddenly knew this was what love felt like. She'd never known a feeling quite like this before. She wanted to savor it. Which she would. All afternoon while clinging to the promise of seeing him again. But now, she needed to let him go so she could think about their future and know her mind and heart to clearly communicate with him tonight.

"This seems to be becoming a habit for me," she whispered. "Initiating a kiss, that is."

He gently touched the side of her cheek, and the contact fired off a rush of emotions. "A habit I hope will last a lifetime."

Clay opened the beach house door feeling like he was floating on a cloud. Literally above the ground so high he might not make it through the doorway. Toni had given him hope for a future together. If he didn't mess things up again. He would do his best not to.

"You're back," Aiden said from the sectional, where most everyone in the family was crammed in.

"Guess this means you didn't get locked in any closets along the way," Brendan joked.

Everyone laughed, and Clay knew he was never going to live down the incident at the janitor's closet, but he was in such a good mood, he laughed with them.

"Toni coming to dinner?" Drake asked.

He nodded, afraid to say yes in case speaking it aloud would make something happen to change her mind. His family responded with a cheer, and his mother jumped up to come to him.

"I'm so pleased, son." She smiled at him and clutched his hands. "Toni really is special, and you deserve someone special. Just don't—"

"Mess it up again," he said. "Yeah, I know. Trust me."

"Of course you do. Don't let what happened steal your confidence. You're a very caring and conscientious guy, and that was a fluke." She gave him the same smile she'd given whenever he'd gotten in trouble. He couldn't describe the look, but it was a cross between *I love you* and *You didn't make the best choice.*

"Thanks, Mom. I think I've got this."

"What about Lisa and her children?" his mom asked.

"I invited them, but I doubt they will be coming."

"You gonna do something special for Toni?" Drake asked.

Clay looked at his brother. "You're awful chummy with her."

"That a problem?" Drake asked.

"No. Just saying."

"She deserves to be treated right, so if you need my help with anything, let me know."

Their mother looked at Drake and smiled. Not the one Clay had gotten, but an *I'm proud of you* smile.

"Toni will be here at four," Clay said. "I have a few things to organize before that."

"We're all going antiquing this afternoon," his mother said.

"Say what?" Their dad swiveled to look at her. "Since when—?"

"Since Clay might need the place to himself at four. Everyone be ready to leave at three-thirty." She ran her gaze over the group, daring anyone to argue with her, but they wouldn't. Not on a Sunday, which somewhere along the way she'd declared her day to be in charge of the family. Truth was, she was in charge every day, she just didn't admit it.

"Go ahead, son," she said to Clay. "Make your special arrangements, but remember we eat at six when we'll all welcome Toni to the family."

Toni knocked on the beach house door and straightened her shirt. She'd brought a very limited amount of clothing with her from Portland. Mostly work clothes, but she'd tossed in one pair of jeans and dressy boots, which she'd paired with a pale green blouse and navy suit jacket. She hoped she fit in, but she might be a bit too dressy. She was almost glad that Lisa decided not to come, as Toni's attention would be split between them and the Byrd family and tonight she wanted to focus on only one person. Clay.

The door opened, and Drake stood there. "Glad to hear you and Clay made up."

She didn't know how to respond, so she smiled.

"He has something special planned for you, and I'm supposed to take you to him."

"But what about your family?" She looked around him to an empty house. "The dinner?"

"He'll bring you back in plenty of time. Trust me. Mom would never let a Sunday go by without family dinner." He grabbed a jacket from a hook by the door and stepped out to close the door and start down the walkway. "She owns Sundays. Totally. Well, next to God, but she's a great copilot." He grinned at Toni.

She laughed. "I like your mom. She's like the rest of you. She knows what she wants, and she goes after it."

"That she does." He started down a sandy path toward the stairway leading to the beach.

"What do you want, Drake?" She looked up at him. "What are you going after?"

"Actually, I'm pretty content with things as they are."

"No special someone for you?"

He shook his head. "I have so many places I want to visit and things I want to experience. Life is meant to be exciting and lived full throttle. No settling down. At least not at my age. Getting married would put a hitch in that. Shoot, even a girlfriend would crimp my style."

"You could find a woman who wants the same things."

"Yeah, sure. That could happen, I suppose. I'm just not looking for it."

She hadn't been looking for someone either, and then God had changed everything, but she wouldn't say any more. If Drake was meant to find someone special, God would arrange things.

They reached the steps where she spotted angry clouds darkening the sky, and the wind kicked up, buffeting her face. When they hit the beach, Drake headed for a large tent anchored in the sand.

The sand shifted underfoot, making it a challenge to keep up with Drake's long steps. A noise like a horse's whiny sounded from the tent. A horse in a tent? Not likely.

She rounded the front of the tent, and Clay sat at a small table set with appetizers, a bottle of sparkling grape juice, and tall crystal glasses filled with the juice. He was dressed in his usual attire, but it looked as if he'd spent time on his appearance after exiting the wind as every hair seemed to be in the right place.

Clay got up and looked at Drake. "Thanks for bringing Toni down here."

"Welcome." Drake looked at her. "See you at dinner."

She nodded, and he spun to leave, kicking up sand as he walked.

"Hi." Clay crossed over to her with a glass of the juice.

"Hi," she said back, feeling a bit awkward. "What's going on?"

"Since this is kind of our first date, I thought we should do something special."

She hadn't considered this a date, but he was right. It was a date. She took a sip of the sparkling juice and grabbed a cracker with cheese to busy her hands.

He looked out the opening. "I was hoping for clearer weather, but you know it's Oregon in winter. Typical fog and rain."

"But you like it that way." She held the cracker but couldn't take a bite as her mouth was too dry, so she set it down and sipped the juice instead.

"I do when I'm struggling with something big. But I'm not struggling with anything right now. My mind is clear. I know what I want." He lifted his chin and held her gaze.

"Me too. I've finally accepted the loss of my parents. Lisa helped with that. She's so strong and her faith unwavering."

Clay frowned. "I hope they're going to be all right. My family and I are praying for them."

"It'll take time and therapy, but I think they'll do okay." She set down her juice and took his hand. "It was very sweet of you to offer your place to them."

"I just wanted to help."

"Which tells me so much about you. You're a wonderful guy, and as I get to know you better, I know I'll discover so many more things to prove that."

His face colored, and he brushed a hand over it as if trying to erase his embarrassment. He put his drink on the table and drew her closer, looking like he was going to kiss her, but didn't. "You ready for your surprise?"

"This isn't it?"

"No." His expression morphed into uncertainty, and he led her out of the tent.

The mist had stopped, but it was still cold and foggy. A perfect day at the beach.

He rounded the corner of the tent, where a stocky man held the reins for two saddled horses.

"This is my friend, Davis," Clay said. "He owns stables nearby and agreed to let us take his horses for a ride on the beach."

She went to the closest horse, a black beauty, and caressed her neck while looking at Clay. "Do you know how to ride?"

Davis snorted.

"Hey," Clay said. "I've been on a horse a time or two."

"Uh-huh." Davis grinned. "And off a time or two."

Clay chuckled and looked at Toni. "It's possible I'll get thrown, but I still want to ride with you."

"Then let's get going." She climbed onto the horse's back and looked at Davis. "What's her name?"

"Charm." Davis rested his hand on the black and white horse's neck. "And this is Blue, the safest horse you can find. He won't spook or take off. Perfect for Clay."

Toni stroked Charm's neck and watched while Clay mounted his horse. Clay was tentative and looked nervous, but the horse stood rock solid. Clay obviously didn't ride, even had bad experiences, but he remembered what she'd said about wanting to ride on the beach, and he was doing this for her. Her heart was so full she didn't know if she could handle all the goodness.

They started off at a walk side-by-side, the salty spray from the ocean wetting her face. The urge to move, to race, hit her hard, and she kicked her horse into a trot. Clay kept pace.

"You ready to gallop?" she asked, her voice raised to be heard over the pounding surf at the horse's feet.

"I won't be ready for that for quite some time." He smiled. "You go ahead."

She didn't want to leave him behind, but galloping on the beach had always been one of her dreams. "You sure?"

He nodded. "I'm content with just seeing your happiness."

"You heard him, Charm. Let's go." She urged Charm forward, her hooves pounding as they raced along the water's edge, the wind on her body, the salty air tangy and sharp. This truly was a dream come true.

So why wasn't she feeling exhilarated? She only felt alone. Very alone.

She'd once have raced off by herself and thought nothing of it, but now she wanted Clay at her side. She didn't need him with her every second in the future, but doing things together when possible would hold more meaning.

She circled back. Racing forward. Watching him sitting on the horse, a broad smile on his face. She trotted up next to him and took his hand. "Thank you for this."

"You came back awfully fast."

"I want to share it with you. So how about we take a nice slow ride."

"I can do that."

She turned Charm around, and they rode in silence, the churning of the waves and thumping of the hooves the only sound.

Clay glanced at his watch. "We need to head back. Wouldn't want to be late for dinner."

"Right," she said, but a knot formed in her stomach. But why? She might've once been worried about such a big family but then she'd gotten to know most of them. Plus,

Clay had been nervous about riding a horse, and he'd braved his fear for her. She could do the same.

By the time they turned the horses over to Davis and got up to the house, the family was seated around the table, Pong lying on the floor at Erik's feet, his eyes begging for food. The house smelled like rosemary mixed with the savory scent of baked bread, and Toni's stomach grumbled.

"Quick," Peggy said, a platter with two large roasted chickens in her hands. "Wash up and join us."

They went to the sink and washed, Clay playfully splashing water at her. She laughed and they locked eyes. The intensity in his expression nearly took her breath. She would give most anything to be alone with him right now.

He kissed her forehead. A soft, gentle, love-filled kiss. She almost melted in a puddle of happiness.

"We want to eat, you know," Drake said. "You can play kissy-face later."

Embarrassed, Toni dried her hands and willed herself to turn and look at the family. They were all watching. The heat of a blush bloomed again.

Clay didn't seem bothered by their display and took her hand to lead her to the table. He introduced her to Harper, Jenna, and Karlie.

"I'm going to be a Byrd in twenty sleeps," Karlie announced.

"That's wonderful." Toni sat in the empty chair next to the little girl.

Karlie looked at Toni. "Nana said she hoped you'd be a Byrd too."

Toni glanced at Clay's mom, and Peggy smiled broadly. "We all hope that."

"Being a Byrd doesn't mean you can fly," Karlie said, very serious now. "I thought it did, but Daddy said it doesn't, right?" She looked up at Brendan.

Brendan nodded. "I guess this is a good time to tell everyone that Karlie asked if she could call me dad."

"He said yes." Karlie's eyes burned with love. "I love him."

"Right back atcha, little bit." Brendan brushed strands of hair from her face and kissed the top of her head.

No one spoke, the moment too special for words.

"We should pray," Peggy finally said, her voice choked up.

Everyone took hands, and Toni was acutely aware of the difference between little Karlie's tiny hand and Clay's beefy one. But no matter the size difference, they both spoke of a future filled with the love of this amazing family.

*Thank you, Father,* she offered, then listened to Peggy's eloquent prayer and added her own amen with the others at the end.

Plates and bowls of food were passed around the table, and Toni loaded her plate with chicken, onions, carrots, and potatoes.

Karlie held her hands over her plate. "Too much, Mommy. Nana made chocolate cake, and I haveta have room."

"You can eat this and still have a little piece of cake." Jenna gave her daughter a very serious look, but Toni could tell she wanted to smile instead like everyone else was doing.

"Not little. I want big." Karlie shoved a carrot into her mouth and chewed.

Toni's only experience was being around her niece and nephew that weekend, and they were skittish from their ordeal, so she didn't think it was a true picture of what children could be like. But if this darling little girl was any indication of how kids behaved, Toni might like to find out how she felt about them. She would surely need to know her stance before she ever got into a serious relationship with Clay.

The conversation turned to Harper's latest ski competition.

"I have to leave first thing in the morning," Harper said.

"But you just got here." Peggy narrowed her eyes then waved a hand. "No, don't listen to me. We're happy to have you for however long you can be here."

Harper and Aiden shared a look, and Toni could see Aiden felt the same way. As Harper talked about getting back for training and her next event, Toni admired the woman's dedication.

Toni glanced at Clay. She was still dedicated to a career in law enforcement, but she wanted time with him, too, and Lisa and the kids, the family she never really had. She understood the joy of family now, and she had to tell Clay about her change in priorities. Not now. Now she would just sit back and learn more about his family she might someday call her own.

After the cake had been devoured, Karlie asking for two pieces, Toni offered to help clean up.

"It's our night," Aiden said. "You'll come up in the rotation in two weeks."

Toni loved that he expected her to be at dinner in two weeks because she sure planned on it. And she needed to tell Clay how she felt. He'd admitted his love and she had to tell him she loved him too. She looked at him. "Can we talk in private?"

He looked around the room. "How about the deck?"

"Perfect." Even though Aiden told her not to help, she couldn't leave her dishes at the table and took them to the kitchen.

Clay raised an eyebrow but didn't say anything.

She grabbed her jacket and passed Pong, who was still looking longingly at the table.

"Despite Pong's sad look, he's fine," Erik said as he tossed a chew toy. "He has to earn treats or he won't do his job."

She nodded, but when she got the dog she'd always wanted, she figured she'd be spoiling it all the time. She joined Clay, who'd stepped into the clear night with a sharp wind. It would be warmer if the clouds and rain returned, but the sky was filled with sparkling stars and a big moon.

"You really didn't need to do that," Clay said. "Take your dishes in, I mean."

"It feels wrong to impose."

"You're not imposing. We'll take our turn and pay them back. Not that everything needs to be paid back in our family. We don't operate that way."

"I can see that."

He leaned against the railing. "What did you want to talk about?"

"I wanted to let you know I get it now."

"It?"

"When I watched your family, I saw how present they were. Listening. Responding. Making jokes. But now that I look back on when my parents were alive, I can see it was different at our house. There was a reserved tone. Likely due to Lisa. She'd been missing for years, and yet, she was there. Always there. Always in my parents' hearts and minds. And always making them hold back. They loved me. I know that. But at a distance, if that makes any sense."

He nodded. "Maybe they were too afraid to love deeply and get hurt again."

"I think you're right. I read in my dad's journal that I was a surprise and that the idea of having a second child had to grow on them. Dad struggled between raising me and finding Lisa. He said he knew I was safe and Lisa needed him more. She needed him to find her."

"Had to hurt to read that."

"It did, but he was right. She did need him more. And now I understand their struggles, and I can understand my upbringing. It makes me appreciate your family more. They're so open and caring. I like that. And I like you. I love you."

A wide smile slid across his face, and he took her hands. "You mean it?"

"I do. With all my heart." She smiled at him but suddenly felt shy.

"I've learned something the past few days with you," he said. "Something I never realized."

"What's that?" She inched closer to him.

"I might be a Byrd, but until I met you, I've been grounded. Now I want to soar with you." He held up a hand. "And before you say anything about my corny Byrd comment, you should know there will be a lifetime of them."

"I didn't think it was corny. It was sweet and true. I feel the same way, though I have to say I've never thought about a relationship in terms of a bird." She circled her arms around his neck. "But you are a special Byrd, and I would love to make a nest with you."

He tossed his head back and whooped.

"I've never heard a bird call quite like that." She laughed.

"That's because I'm a Byrd of a different feather." He grinned. "And I hope you'll take me under your wing for the rest of our lives."

## NIGHTHAWK SECURITY SERIES

Protecting others when unspeakable danger lurks.

Keep reading for more information on the additional books in the Nighthawk Security Series where the Cold Harbor and Truth Seekers teams work side-by-side with Nighthawk Security.

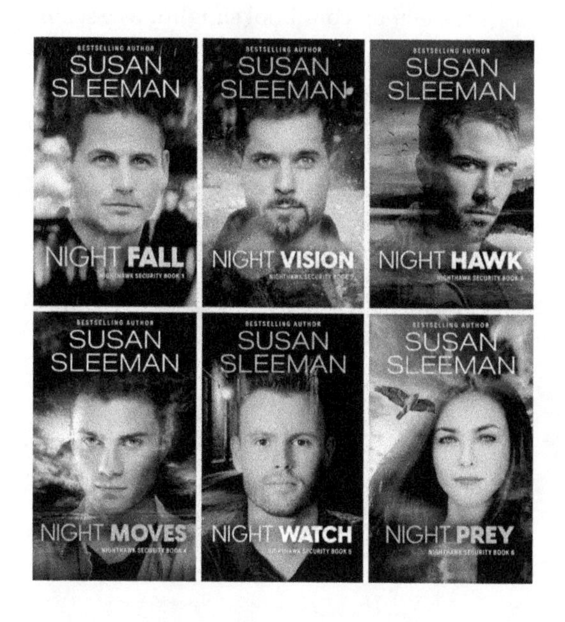


A woman plagued by a stalker. Children of a murderer. A woman whose mother died under suspicious circumstances.

All in danger. Lives on the line. Needing protection.

Enter the brothers of Nighthawk Security. The five Byrd brothers with years of former military and law enforcement experience coming together to offer protection and investigation services. Their goal—protecting others when unspeakable danger lurks.

Book 1 Night Fall – November, 2020
Book 2 – Night Vision – December, 2020
Book 3 - Night Hawk – January, 2021
Book 4 –Night Moves – July, 2021
Book 5 – Night Watch – August, 2021
Book 6 – Night Prey – October, 2021

For More Details Visit -
www.susansleeman.com/books/nighthawk-security/

## THE TRUTH SEEKERS

People are rarely who they seem

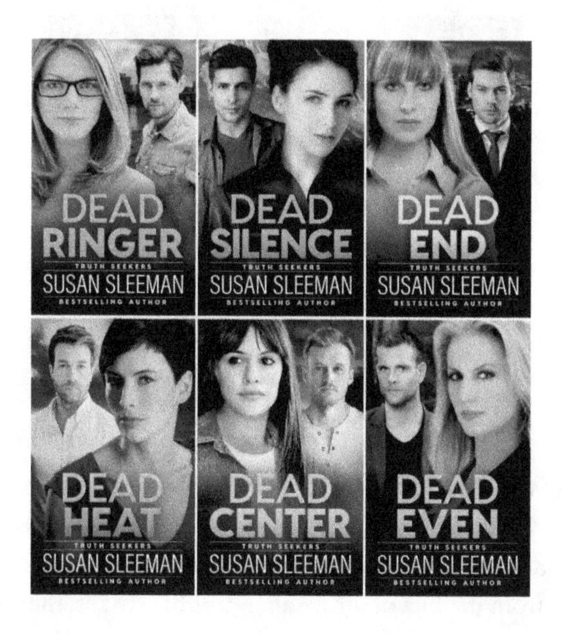


A twin who never knew her sister existed, a mother whose child is not her own, a woman whose father is anything but her father. All searching. All seeking. All needing help and hope.

Meet the unsung heroes of the Veritas Center. The Truth Seekers – a team, that includes experts in forensic anthropology, DNA, trace evidence, ballistics, cybercrimes, and toxicology. Committed to restoring hope and families by solving one mystery at a time, none of them are prepared for when the mystery comes calling close to home and threatens to destroy the only life they've known.

For More Details Visit -
www.susansleeman.com/books/truth-seekers/

**BOOKS IN THE COLD HARBOR SERIES**

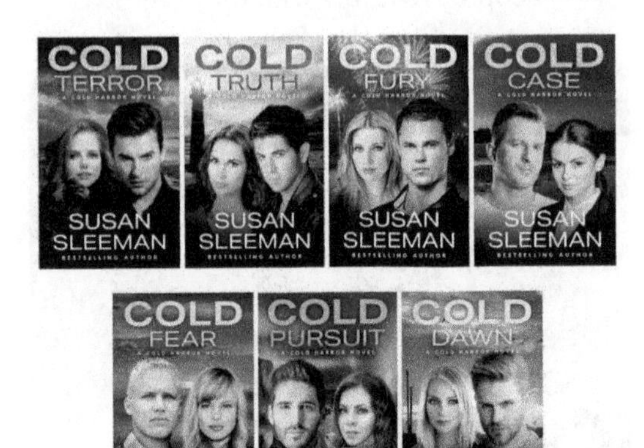


Blackwell Tactical – this law enforcement training facility and protection services agency is made up of former military and law enforcement heroes whose injuries keep them from the line of duty. When trouble strikes, there's no better team to have on your side, and they would give everything, even their lives, to protect innocents.

For More Details Visit -
www.susansleeman.com/books/cold-harbor/

## HOMELAND HEROES SERIES

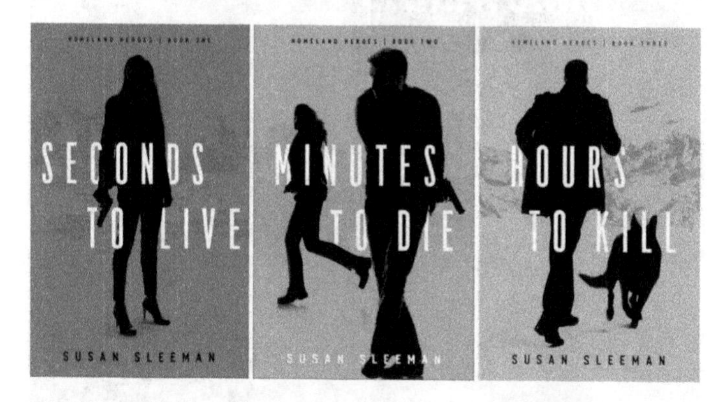


When the clock is ticking on criminal activity conducted on or facilitated by the Internet there is no better team to call other than the RED team, a division of the HSI—Homeland Security's Investigation Unit. RED team includes FBI and DHS Agents, and US Marshal's Service Deputies.

For More Details Visit -

www.susansleeman.com/books/homeland-heroes/

## WHITE KNIGHTS SERIES

Join the White Knights as they investigate stories plucked from today's news headlines. The FBI Critical Incident Response Team includes experts in crisis management, explosives, ballistics/weapons, negotiating/criminal profiling, cyber crimes, and forensics. All team members are former military and they stand ready to deploy within four hours, anytime and anywhere to mitigate the highest-priority threats facing our nation.

www.susansleeman.com/books/white-knights/

## ABOUT SUSAN

SUSAN SLEEMAN is a bestselling and award-winning author of more than 35 inspirational/Christian and clean read romantic suspense books. In addition to writing, Susan also hosts the website, TheSuspenseZone.com.

Susan currently lives in Oregon, but has had the pleasure of living in nine states. Her husband is a retired church music director and they have two beautiful daughters, a very special son-in-law, and an adorable grandson.

*For more information visit:*

www.susansleeman.com

CPSIA information can be obtained
at www.ICGtesting.com
Printed in the USA
LVHW042224070622
720747LV00001B/160

9 781949 009354